PRAISE FOR

A World of
THIEVES

"Blake writes with a command of the language and a deft ear for dialogue that few novelists possess. . . . *A World of Thieves* is classic Blake, mixing violence with passion, the hardnose with the sensitive. No one out there does this better."
—Tom Walker, book editor, *Denver Post*

"Blake is one of the more talented practitioners of tough-guy fiction. . . . *A World of Thieves* is a powerful book [with] compellingly drawn characters." —Tom Pilkington, *Dallas Morning News*

"In a splendid ode to hard-drinking Jazz Age desperadoes, James Carlos Blake jimmies open Cormac McCarthy's safe and runs off with the twanging strings McCarthy brings to the American sentence. . . . Blake remains a poet of the damned who writes like an angel." —*Kirkus Reviews*

"A hard-driving, entertaining novel full of outsized characters and as much humor as brutality." —*Publishers Weekly*

"Writing doesn't get much better than this. Unforced, honest. . . . A novel that delivers. Fabulous and unforgettable."
—*New York Review of Fiction*

"A deliciously visual story. . . . Blake seems to revel in biting off big chunks of American history and letting the blood dribble between his teeth." —*Austin Chronicle*

Maura Anne Wahl

About the Author

JAMES CARLOS BLAKE has written seven
books of fiction, including *In the Rogue Blood*
(winner of the Los Angeles Times Book
Prize), *Red Grass River* (winner of the
Chautauqua South Book Award), *Borderlands*
(winner of the Southwest Book Award), and
the critically acclaimed *Wildwood Boys*. He is
also the author of *The Pistoleer* and *The Friends
of Pancho Villa*. He resides in southeast Arizona.

A World of
THIEVES

A Novel

James Carlos Blake

Perennial

An Imprint of HarperCollinsPublishers

A hardcover edition of this book was published in 2002 by William Morrow, an imprint of HarperCollins Publishers.

HarperCollins books may be purchased for educational, business, or sales promotional use. For information please write: Special Markets Department, HarperCollins Publishers Inc., 10 East 53rd Street, New York, NY 10022.

First Perennial edition published 2003.

Designed by Renato Stanisic

The Library of Congress has catalogued the hardcover edition as follows:

Blake, James Carlos.
A world of thieves : a novel / James Carlos Blake.
p. cm.
ISBN 0-380-97750-8
1. Louisiana—Fiction.   2. Criminals—Fiction.   I. Title.
PS3552.L3483 W67 2001
813'.54—dc21   2001024566

ISBN 0-06-051247-4 (pbk.)

03 04 05 06 07 ❖/RRD 10 9 8 7 6 5 4 3 2 1

The jury, passing on the prisoner's life,
May in the sworn twelve have a thief or two
Guiltier than him they try.
—WILLIAM SHAKESPEARE, *MEASURE FOR MEASURE*

Howsoever a man's nature be bent,
be it even to thieving and violent mischief,
he must hold true to it
or be miserable in his soul.
—ANONYMOUS

Pike: I'd like to make one good score and back off.
Dutch: Back off to what?
—WALON GREEN AND SAM PECKINPAH, *THE WILD BUNCH*

All the trouble I ever was in was caused by getting caught.
—CORMAC MCCARTHY, *CHILD OF GOD*

I

A steeple bell rang the noon hour as Buck and Russell tugged their hatbrims low over their sunglasses and went into the bank. I watched from the car, the engine throbbing into the steering wheel under my hands. We'd nabbed the Packard in Baton Rouge and would abandon it down in Plaquemine, where we'd left Buck's Model A parked beside the police station. Buck said it was the safest place for it. "World's full of damned thieves," he'd said, grinning big. "A man can't be too careful." I said I'd always wondered if that meant a man could never be careful enough or that he couldn't be excessively careful. Buck looked at me like I was speaking Chinese. Russell said he only hoped the car didn't have a red light on the roof and "Police Department" painted on the sides by the time we came back for it.

Verte Rivage, Louisiana. A hot July day. The sky pale blue and streaked with thin clouds. Mockingbirds squalling in the oaks. Spanish moss tilting in a weak breeze carrying the smell of the bayou from the edge of town, the tang of fresh-cut grass. Cajun music fiddling faintly from a radio in a screen-door barbershop. The headline in the newspaper rack heralding William Varney's nomination for president by the Prohibition Party. More people on the sidewalks than you'd expect at dinnertime, but hardly any street traffic. According to Buck's informant the town had a sheriff and two deputies, one man for each shift, but we'd seen no sign of the day cop. The informant also said the bank was holding five thousand dollars in farmer's market receipts. We figured it for an easy score.

But as Buck and Russell never got tired of telling me, you never know. They hadn't been in the bank two minutes when the sudden howl of a siren made my heart jump and my gut clench like a fist. In the backview mirror I saw a sedan with a flashing red light come around the corner two blocks away. Behind it came another one with its light and siren going—and then another. I had the top-break .44 in my hand before I was aware I'd picked it up from the seat. I knew Buck and Russell could hear the sirens—the whole parish must've heard them. Cars kept turning onto the street and joining the row of red lights and adding to the caterwaul. I couldn't believe all the cops. I thought we were had. I put the Packard in gear, everything in me saying *Go!*

The rule was, if a job went to hell it was every man for himself. That's what they'd told me. But the way I saw it, as long as they hadn't gone down, the job hadn't gone to hell. Besides, I knew damn well they'd never in the world run out on each other or on me. So I stayed put—clutch to the floor, .44 in hand, eyes on the mirror—and watched the line of cars coming down the street.

That's when it struck me something wasn't right. They were coming too slowly, hardly faster than a jog. For all the flashing and wailing, they were in no hurry to get anywhere. And nobody looked alarmed. More people were out on the sidewalks now, most of them smiling and waving at the cops. The barber stepped out of his shop, spat a brown streak, grimaced at all the hoorah and went back inside.

Now the lead car came abreast of me and I saw four men inside, none in uniform except for the sameness of their white skimmers, all waving back at the folk. The side of the car said "Ascension Parish Sheriff"—though we were in the parish of West Baton Rouge. The next car was from St. John the Baptist. Whatever was going on had nothing to do with us, but still, it was unreal. Of all the possibilities you plan for in a heist, a slow parade of friendly smiling cops driving by with their lights going and sirens howling isn't one of them.

Buck and Russell didn't come out of the bank until the lead car went past it, which must've been when they realized the police weren't there for us. Then they were both at the door, still wearing the dark glasses. Buck had one hand in his coat pocket and the other holding his valise. His face fixed on me for a moment, then he walked off down the street as casually as a businessman going back to the office. Russell put his little fingers in his ears and screwed up his mouth to get a laugh from a couple of kids who had their ears covered against the screeching sirens. He smiled at them and tipped his hat to their mother and strolled off after Buck.

I watched as they went down the street and around the corner, then tucked the .44 in my waistband.

But I couldn't pull away from the curb while the parade was still passing. I cursed its slowness under my breath and kept an eye on the bank. There were only a few cars left to go. That's when a bald guy wearing a teller's visor peeked out the door and in the direction Buck and Russell had gone—then ran out into the street, flapping his arms and shouting something nobody could make out for the sirens. A car braked sharply to keep from hitting him, and the one behind it banged into its rear and shattered a taillight, and the two last cars behind them stopped short too. Now I was really blocked in.

The halted cars cut their sirens and their doors slung open and the cops came out, some looking pissed and some of them laughing. One grabbed the teller by the shirtfront, but the baldy was talking fast and pointing down the street. Then the cops were pulling pistols and running for the corner where Buck and Russell had vanished, yelling at the onlookers to get out of the way. Now the cars up ahead had stopped too, and more sirens were shutting down and more cops getting out and asking what was going on. Bystanders were hollering and gesturing at the bank.

Any second now somebody was going to take notice of the stranger in the Packard. I had to quit the car fast. The barbershop was twenty feet away—I'd go in for a haircut, a guy passing through, all big-eyed and curious about the to-do in the street. . . .

"Say, young fella, you happen to see—"

He'd come up on my blind side. Coatless and burly, brown vest with a badge, big cowboy hat over quick black eyes that spotted the .44 against my belly. He stepped back and yanked up a revolver. *"Freeze!"*

With that Colt muzzle not two feet from my face, I didn't even think to do anything else.

"What're you, boy, seventeen?"

"Eighteen, sir."

That was about all the truth I gave them. They'd sent my prints to Baton Rouge and New Orleans but they wouldn't get anything.

I said I was Lionel Buckman from St. Louis, where I'd been a bookkeeper for a shoe company till the place burned down. I'd come to Louisiana looking for work but hadn't had much luck finding a position that paid enough to hold me. Yes sir, I did have papers to prove who I was, but wouldn't you know some sorry pickpocket stole my wallet down in the French Quarter? The .44? Strictly for protection, should the need arise, knock wood. I was headed for Opelousas on a tip about a good job and stopped to get a bite. When I heard all those sirens I figured something awful serious was going on, so I grabbed the gun from under the seat in case I could help the police in some way. The car?—*stolen?* Sweet Baby Jesus, don't tell me. No wonder that fella gave me such a fine deal on it. Just yesterday in Baton Rouge. My rattletrap Model T and forty dollars. Said he was in bad need of the cash. It about broke me but was too good a bargain to pass up. Wrote me a bill of sale on a café napkin and promised to mail me the proper papers care of general delivery in Baton Rouge. Seemed a right enough fella so I trusted him. Lord only knows what I did with that napkin. *Damn* me for a careless fool.

Damn me for a lowdown liar, the cops said. Then tried smacking my partners' names out of me. But I kept my mouth shut and didn't cave.

The Southeast Louisiana Sheriffs' Convention is what it was. There were more than sixty lawmen in Verte Rivage that day, and we hit the bank just as they'd set out to the fairgrounds for a barbecue and decided to make a loud parade of it. Ten minutes later there wouldn't have been a cop in town. You'd think Buck's informant would've known about it and passed the word. It might've been of some benefit to our planning.

I was three days in the Verte Rivage jail while they searched for Buck and Russell. They'd stolen a truck outside of town but abandoned it with a ruined wheel ten miles away, near the edge of the swamp. The cops sent in trackers and dogs, but finally gave up the hunt.

"Most like your buddies drowned or the gators got them," a cop told me.

Maybe, I thought, and maybe not. Buck and Russell had grown up prowling the swamps and they weren't about to be killed by one. But the talk in the jailhouse was that they'd made off with ten thousand dollars, and everybody knew how some cops would shoot robbers they caught with holdup money and out of sight of witnesses. They'd dump the body in the swamp and report that the man got away. Easy loot and hardly any paperwork.

The embarrassment of having the town's only bank robbed right under their noses had put a lot of the conventioning cops in a vile temper. Lucky for me some of the older sheriffs thought the whole business was fairly amusing and they restrained the hotter ones from busting me up too bad. All the same I took a drubbing. But I used every trick I knew to protect my teeth and I didn't lose any. No bones broken. It could've been worse.

They booked me into the Baton Rouge jail a little before dark. While I was waiting for permission to telephone my lawyer, he showed up. He asked to see Lionel Buckman, and so I knew Buck and Russell were all right, since the only way he could've known the alias I'd be using was if they'd been in touch with him.

I was taken to the visiting room and got my first look at Edward Longstreet Charponne. Sharp Eddie. Buck and Russell had told me all about this criminal attorney they kept on retainer. He came from old Louisiana money but had always been a black sheep. After graduating from Tulane he set up offices in New Orleans and Baton Rouge and became immensely and notoriously successful at defending criminals of every stripe. His embarrassed family disowned him. The newspapers regularly reproached him for his choice of clientele and had called him as much a menace to decent society as the rogues he represented. Eddie in turn routinely accused the papers of an un-American disdain for every man's constitutional right to a fair day in court.

The simple truth of the matter, Buck told me, was that Sharp Eddie got a kick out of dealing with crooks.

"It's true," Russell said. "He's another one of them educated types who like to rub elbows with what is commonly called the underworld." They'd both given me a look and I couldn't help but grin back at them.

We sat on opposite sides of a long table partitioned lengthwise by a heavy wire screen. A guard stood over by the wall on my side of the partition. Sharp Eddie was short and heavyset but impeccably groomed and expensively tailored, his blond hair combed straight back and his goatee closely trimmed. A white Panama lay beside some papers laid neatly before him.

"I was alerted to your situation via long-distance telephone," he said in a low soft lilt I suspected was his normal tone rather than a deference to the guard's presence. He was of a class of men rarely obliged to raise their voice.

I asked in a whisper where they were. He said he hadn't asked and they hadn't volunteered the information. "Better for everyone that way," he said.

He glanced down at the papers. "The Verte Rivage report states that you had multiple facial lacerations and various other bruises at the time of your arrest. It speculates that perhaps you'd been in a motorcar accident immediately prior to the holdup."

His eyes roamed my battered and discolored face, my bloated ears, my dirty rumpled suit. I smiled and shrugged and both actions hurt.

"Yes, well," he said. "Hazards of the profession." This from a man I would've bet had never felt a punch.

He said I'd be arraigned in the morning and a trial date set, and five minutes after that he'd have me out on bond. The robbery charge was nothing but air, entirely and flimsily circumstantial. If the state didn't drop it before trial, he'd move to dismiss and ten-to-one the judge would grant.

"If not," he said, "I'll dismantle it in court in a minute."

The Packard might be more of a problem. I *could* have come by the car exactly as I'd said. Who could prove that I hadn't? My stupid story might strain the court's belief, yes, but most judges had heard stupidity in such quantity and size that few examples of it surprised them anymore. It could be argued—and he would so argue, he assured me—that however foolish I'd been, I was as much a victim of fraud as the Packard's owner was of theft.

"The court might go for it," Sharp Eddie said. "Even if it doesn't, you have no record of previous arrest, so there's a good chance of immediate probation. Worst possibility? Six months in the parish lockup and you'll be out in two."

He consulted a large gold wristwatch and stood up, gathering the papers and slipping them into a tooled leather briefcase.

"All things considered," he said, setting the Panama at an angle over one eye, "things could be exceedingly worse, as so many residents of this institution could tell you. See you in the morning, lad."

The tank was lit by a low-watt yellow bulb with a wire cover in the middle of the ceiling. The turnkey locked me in and went back down the hall to join the other cops in an adjacent room whose door stayed open and bright with light. There were eight bunks all in a row with stained smelly mattresses and I stretched out on the one against the rear wall.

Only two other guys were in there at first. The well-dressed drunk who'd smashed up his car got bailed out pretty soon after I arrived. The other one was a little fellow who didn't look to be more than a kid, although he was probably about my age. You could see he was a nancy—he might as well've worn a sign. One of his eyes was swollen purple. Most likely he'd come on to the wrong guy. My own face should've made him feel better about his. He hadn't said a word, but he kept staring at me like he wanted to talk, so I gave him a hard look and he quit the eyeballing and curled up on his bunk.

I'd been dozing when they brought in a pair of loud ones. They wore T-shirts that showed off their tattooed arms and I thought they might be merchant seamen. One of them was insisting they had only been playing a joke and hadn't been serious about strong-arming any-body.

"Yeah, sure, Horton," a cop said, "you're always innocent."

The jailer clanked the door shut and turned the lock. The Horton one stood at the bars and yelled down the hall after them about a man's right to make a phone call.

"We want a lawyer!" the other one said. He looked like an Indian. They finally quieted down to muttering between themselves.

I didn't know how long I'd been asleep when something woke me and I rolled over and saw the kid kneeling on the floor, the Indian behind him and twisting his arm up high on his back. The other guy had the kid by the hair and was trying to make him suck his dick.

The kid was whimpering like a dog and jerking his head away. The guy yanked harder on his hair and smacked him in the face and told him to shut up and *do* it.

The Indian looked out to the hallway, then said through his teeth, "Holler again I'll break your arm."

I told myself the fairy had it coming. Likely said something to them. Maybe they wanted some of his action and he suddenly got particular. Whatever it was, it wasn't my concern.

And then the Indian saw me watching and said, "Mind your fucken business."

That's what I should've done. Never stick your neck out for anybody but yourself and kin—even Daddy had always said that. But the beating I'd taken in Verte Rivage had put me in a mood. I was *aching* to punch somebody, I was right at the edge. The glare the Indian gave me, like he thought he was spooking me, pushed me over.

I stood up and the Horton one got that look they get when the thing doesn't go how they expect. He hustled his dick back in his pants and said, "Hey boy," and raised a finger at me in warning. I feinted left and clipped him with the right. It wasn't flush but it sent him sprawling.

The Indian tried to get me in a headlock but I wrenched free and hooked him hard in the kidney and he hollered and dropped to his knees. I gave him one in the neck and he fell on his side, gagging loud, and then puked on the concrete floor.

"What the *hell's* going on?" A cop was at the hallway door but couldn't see into the tank from there.

The kid was over by the wall, gawking at me. I felt like smacking him too, for being such a rabbit. I should've been watching the Horton guy—he came up from behind and locked a forearm around my throat. I heard the cops clamoring at the cell door as I got the footing I needed and lunged back hard and banged Horton against the bars, knocking him breathless and breaking his hold on me.

I held him against the bars with one hand and hammered him with the other, feeling his front teeth go, his nose. Somebody clubbed me from behind and I spun around and drilled him with a straight right and saw it was a cop as he went backpedaling into the wall and down on his ass.

Now the other cops were all over me and I knew better than try to make a fight of it. I hunkered down and covered up with my arms the best I could but still took a lot of thumps before the one in charge yelled, "All right, enough!"

I felt like I was wearing a ten-pound headache hat. The Indian was up on hands and knees now, dry heaving, his face gray. Horton was curled up on the floor with his hands over his broken mouth and nose. The sergeant gave him a kick in the ribs and said, "You never been nothing but trouble in this jailhouse, you shitbird."

"Shooo," a cop said, "lookit old C.J. That boy is *out*!"

He nodded at the cop I'd hit. He was sitting against the wall with his chin on his chest. One of them went over and shook his shoulder and said, "Come on, old son, get up and piss—the world's on fire!"

The C.J. guy slumped over, eyes half open. The other cop's mouth fell open and he knelt and put an ear to the C.J. guy's chest.

Then looked up and said, "Lordy, this boy's *dead.*"

Dead and the sole son of John Isley Bonham, a longtime deputy sheriff down in Terrebonne Parish and something of a legend all over the delta. I didn't know who he was until one of the cops referred to him as John Bones and I remembered having heard Buck and Russell mention the name one time in discussing the roughest cops they knew of. I heard plenty more about him, from jailers and jailbirds both, while I was waiting to go to trial.

They said he'd killed more men than any other cop in Louisiana. He'd claimed self-defense in every case but rumors persisted that some of the shootings had been point-blank executions. He'd been investigated a dozen times and suspended from duty a time or two but never found guilty of malfeasance or anything else. The local newspapers had long celebrated him as a lone wolf of justice whose fearsome reputation kept bootleggers and other criminals out of Terrebonne Parish. One robber he shot lived long enough to pull the trigger on a shotgun and remove most of Bonham's left hand, a maiming in the line of duty that made him even more of a public hero. For ten years now he'd worn a set of chrome pincers in place of the hand and they said just the sight of that thing put suspects in a sweat when he entered an interrogation room.

He had outlasted a string of high sheriffs and for a long time now he could've had the job for the asking but didn't want it. He wasn't one for politics or smiling for the cameras. It was common knowledge he wasn't well liked by his fellow cops—he was too stand-offish, too given to working without a partner. But they all said he was the most respected man among them, which I took to mean he was the most feared.

"He is that," Sharp Eddie said. "And he's got a lot of admirers that don't know the first thing about him except that he scares the *merde* out of crooks and that he's had some sad luck in his life. Lost his first wife nearly forty years ago when she drowned off Grand Isle on their honeymoon. Their *honeymoon*, son. That's the kind of thing that gets a man a lifetime of sympathy. He married again sixteen years later and they had a baby boy, but then twelve years ago wife number two hanged herself. Didn't leave a note, but everybody knew she had a nervous condition and it most likely got the best of her. The man did not marry again. And *now*, with that sixty-year-old stalwart of the law so near the end of a long and illustrious service to the state, his only begotten son is killed in a fight with a jailbird."

He paused to give me a cigarette, then lit it and one for himself. "It's hardly surprising," he said, "what with John Isley Bonham being such a tragic hero and all, that the state is charging his son's killer with murder in the first degree and the newspapers are cheering that decision."

Given the circumstances, I didn't see how in purple hell they thought they could nail me on murder in any degree. But Eddie said he knew of weaker cases that had sent men to the gallows.

"In most courtrooms across our grand republic, the facts of this case wouldn't support even second-degree charges," Eddie said. "But we're in Loosiana, my boy, and if the jury wants your ass it'll have it. I got my work cut out, son, believe me."

I said if he was trying to boost my spirits he was falling a little shy. He said he just didn't want me looking cocky in front of the jurymen.

The only word from Buck and Russell came with a packet of cash which arrived at Eddie's office. The envelope was postmarked Houma, and a note attached to the money said, "Buy it."

They were obviously keeping up with the news.

But Eddie said they ought to know there'd be no buying me out of it, not with the victim being son to a policeman—especially *this* policeman. He did buy me a nice suit to wear in the courtroom.

The state presented Charlton John Bonham—"C.J." to all who knew him—as a large-hearted young man cut down in the bloom of his life, as a prime candidate for such law enforcement greatness as his father had achieved. Witness after witness told of C.J.'s genial nature, of his deep devotion to a mother whose tragic loss came when he was but ten years old, of his avid desire since boyhood to be a policeman like his daddy, of his dedication to duty.

At our table Sharp Eddie gave me a look. More than one person in a position to know had admitted to him in private that C. J. Bonham was one of the worst bullies in the Baton Rouge Police Department. He'd been assigned to jail duty while the department investigated him for beating to death a fifteen-year-old boy he'd caught breaking into a warehouse. Even so, the only reason the killing was being investigated was that the boy was white and his father had died heroically in the war—and because his grieving mother had raised a stink in public. Some of the jail cops had told Sharp Eddie in detail how C.J. loved to use his club on prisoners, but of course none of them would testify to it. They said if he tried to make them repeat their stories on the stand they'd deny every word to John Bones personally and call Eddie a liar in court.

John Bones—the daddy wolf himself, the two-time widower and famous crook killer—sat in the front row of spectators. Tall and lean in a black suit and black string tie, his gray hair close-cropped, his gray mustache thick and drooping, his face stone-stiff and void of all expression. He held his planter's hat on his lap and covering the contraption on the end of his arm. I didn't catch him looking at me until midway through the first day's proceedings. His eyes were brightly black and fixed on me like a hawk's.

I gave him a look right back: Up yours, mister.

On the night it had happened, after they took the body away and charged me with the killing and transferred me to a regular cell, I'd lain in my bunk and waited to feel whatever I was going to feel about it. My pulse was still jumping and I was still trembling a little, but that wasn't unusual after a fight, in or out of the ring. I was sorry I'd killed him, which of course wasn't the same thing as being sorry he was dead, but how could I be sorry about that when I didn't know a thing about him except he was a jailhouse cop? Later on, when I found out the kind of cop he'd been, the fact that he was dead didn't bother me at all. On that night, however, all I had in mind was that I'd killed him, and I waited for guilt or regret or fear or whatever mix of feelings might descend on me. Over the next few hours I felt a twist of them all, but they passed fairly quickly. Except for anger. That's the one that stuck.

The look John Bones gave me in court brought that anger back in a rush. What did he expect—I'd take a knock on the head and not do anything about it because his son was a cop? Buck once said the main reason he hated cops was they were naturalborn bullies. They loved the action when the odds were all on their side, but let them get the worst of it and then listen to them cry.

The old man and I held stares for a long moment—and then he showed a trace of a smile and brought that chrome thing up from under the hat and gently stroked his mustache with it, letting me see it in all its wicked gleam like some kind of surgeon's tool. Then he slipped it back under the hat and turned away and didn't look at me again.

To hell with you too, I thought.

The prosecutor reminded the jurymen that C.J.'s life had been taken by a man already in jail on charges of bank robbery and car theft. And now that man had committed murder, the most horrid sort of theft there was—the theft of a human life. *And*, the prosecutor added, this awful theft didn't stop with C.J. The murder of that fine boy also robbed the father, John Isley Bonham—robbed him of his only son, robbed him of his lineage.

"And there he sits, gentlemen," the prosecutor said, pointing at me. "The man who committed all of this unspeakable thievery."

And so forth.

Sharp Eddie had wanted the fairy I'd defended to testify, and the kid agreed to it, but as soon as he'd served his ten days for solicitation of an unnatural sex act and was turned loose, he took off. Horton and the Indian disappeared too. So Eddie went to work without witnesses.

He looked the jurymen in the eye as he explained the woefully mistaken arrest in Verte Rivage that placed me, an innocent man, in the Baton Rouge jail on that fateful night. He described the frail and helpless boy who'd been there too and would have fallen victim to the sexual depravities of a pair of brutal inmates but for my intervention—an act of selfless bravery that almost cost me my own life. The blow young Bonham took was inadvertent, a random, instinctive punch in the midst of a melee. And while the mortal skull fracture he received on striking the wall was certainly tragic, it was no act of murder, but an act of God, a death by misadventure.

And so on.

A few of the jurors seemed receptive to Eddie's argument but most of them looked unmoved. They talked it over behind closed doors for about three hours before settling on one of the alternatives the judge gave them and convicting me of manslaughter.

Better than murder in any degree, yeah . . . but still. When I heard the verdict I felt like the world abruptly tilted way the hell over.

And when the judge sentenced me to thirty years at Angola, I felt like I was falling off.

The newspapers thought both jury and judge had gone too easy on me. John Bonham refused to comment on the verdict or any other aspect of the trial. Sharp Eddie said he'd appeal, of course—first the conviction, and if that went nowhere, the sentence. But I'd learned to read him fairly well by then, and I had a feeling he knew the thing was settled and done. Which meant the most I could hope for was parole in ten years.

Ten.

*L*ionel Loomis LaSalle—that's my name on the dotted line. I was still a child when Daddy apologized for it. Lionel Loomis was my mother's father, and Daddy'd had to agree to both names for their firstborn son before she would marry him. But he never did use it. He called me Sonny and that's what I went by. My mother called me Lionel until I refused to answer to it and she finally gave in and called me Sonny too. Except when she was vexed with me—then it was always Lionel.

I wouldn't have been too happy with Daddy's name, either—Marlon—though the name didn't seem to bother him any, maybe because he went by Lonnie. He was Buck's and Russell's elder brother by ten years. He'd grown up the same sort of wildhair kid they would become—always in trouble at school and getting in fights and doing petty thieving and such. At sixteen he was caught breaking into a warehouse by a night watchman who whaled on him with a club until Daddy took it away from him and whipped him bloody before the cops showed up. The judge gave him the choice of a year in jail or lying about his age and enlisting in the military. Three days later he was on his way to a naval training camp. He learned to box in the navy and made it to the semifinals of the fleet championships. He liked the sailor's life but not the navy with all its saluting and regulations and petty punishments. At the end of his hitch he returned to New Orleans and signed on as a merchant seaman.

He met my mother one chilly autumn morning in a French Market café. She was a librarian, a pretty but shy girl who'd grown up with stern warnings about sailors. But she was a romantic at heart and couldn't help being amused by this handsome mariner just returned from distant ports and so happily drunk at such a saintly hour. She gave him the chance he needed to impress her and four months later they got married and moved into an apartment on St. Philip. I was born on the next New Year's night.

Although Daddy was often gone to sea I never heard my mother complain of it. She'd known the life she was making when she married a sailorman. They were always happy when they were together. Some nights I'd lie awake listening to their husky whispers and low laughter from the bedroom down the hall. But she was a solitary woman of few friends, and when Daddy was away what she mostly did was read. She read to me too, every night from the time I was a baby until I was almost five and was reading for myself. All through my grammar school years she made sure I did my homework and would test me on it every night. She was forever correcting my grammar and pronunciations, and she'd despair to hear me lapse into the regional drawl and locutions. It was something I did now and then to fit in with the people I found myself among—though sometimes I did it for no reason except I liked how the accent felt in my mouth. When I pointed out that Daddy and Buck and Russell all spoke that way, she said that was all right because they couldn't help it, but I could.

"Whether we like it or not, people judge us by the way we speak," she said. "Why give the impression of being uneducated if you don't have to?"

"I ain't got no good answer to that, I don't reckon," I said.

"Lionel . . ."

When I finished the sixth grade, she persuaded Daddy that it was worth the cost to enroll me in a private school where I could get an education befitting my intelligence. He always deferred to her in matters of my education, and so the following year I found myself attending Gulliver Academy, overlooking Lake Ponchartrain.

Daddy had been teaching me to fight since I was old enough to make a fist, and I'd applied his lessons to the jerks in grammar school who'd made fun of my name before the teachers took to calling me Sonny. But it was at Gulliver that his tutoring served me best. The school's motto was *Mens sana in corpore sano* and varsity athletes were much admired, especially the boxers. My mother had been opposed to my joining the team but I told her I wasn't really boxing, I was engaged in the pugilistic arts—which got the smile from her I'd hoped it would. We made a bargain that I'd quit the squad if my grades slipped. They never did. The only promise she ever asked of me was to do well in my studies, a simple pledge to keep because schoolwork came so easily to me.

When I won the interscholastic welterweight championship at the end of my sophomore year, I was the youngest champ in the history of the school. Daddy's ship had come into port two days earlier, and Buck and Russell were with him in the arena that night.

My uncles were fraternal twins, only twelve years older than I. It was never any secret to me that they'd been breaking the law since boyhood. I'd heard all about the card and dice games they'd operated behind the school gym, knew all about the burglaries they'd been doing since the age of thirteen.

I was ten when they came back from the war. Buck brought me a bayonet he took off a Hun he'd killed. "Fourteen of the bastards for sure," he said. "No telling how many I potted in the dark."

He pulled up his shirt to show me the pinkly puckered scars where the bullet passed through that cost him a kidney. Russell was still using a cane then. He'd been an ace sniper until a machine gun knocked him out of a tree with one leg so shot up he almost hadn't been able to talk the surgeon out of amputation.

After hearing the first few of their war stories my mother excused herself from the room. They later begged her pardon and promised not to talk of such things in her company again, and they didn't. They usually kept to their best behavior around her, rarely using profanity in her presence and quickly apologizing when they slipped up. But I'd heard her talking to Daddy and knew she was as much bothered by their cavalier attitude toward the violence they'd seen as by the horror of their stories. She'd known them since they were wild boys in constant trouble with the law, and she was afraid they would revert to their old ways. Daddy didn't think so. He believed the war had changed them for the better, had made them realize it was time they became responsible men.

"They'll find themselves a right trade, you'll see," he said.

They'd come out of the army with enough money to see them through for a while and they told Daddy they wanted to take their time deciding what to do for a living. When they still didn't have jobs after two months and he offered to help them get seaman's papers or at least some kind of job on the docks, they said they didn't want to lie to him anymore and confessed that they were back at their old trades. Daddy couldn't understand why, after nearly being killed in France, they'd want to risk jail or even worse by going back to thieving and the gambling dens.

"Hell, Lonnie," Buck said, lowering his voice and glancing toward the bedroom to make sure my mother wasn't in earshot, "it's *because* we didn't get killed in France, man. I promised myself if I ever made it back to the world I'd never take another order or live another minute by somebody else's rules."

Russell nodded and said, "Amen, brother."

They made a joke of his concern over their gambling, saying it wasn't really gambling, not the way they did it. That made me laugh out loud, and Buck and Russell grinned at me. Daddy gave me a look like I'd said something he never heard before, then told them that the way they did it was even riskier than real gambling. Buck smiled wide and said, "You reckon?"

In truth Daddy knew how good they were at what they did. I'd heard him tell my mother he'd never seen a better cardsharp than Buck or anybody who could palm dice as slickly as Russell.

"How wonderful," she'd said. "With skills such as those, can notable achievement be far behind?" She had a sardonic side that rarely showed except when something scared her that she couldn't do anything about, like the felonious ventures of her brothers-in-law.

Over the next few years they gambled and grifted and now and then did a burglary. Daddy was afraid they might step up to armed robbery or already had but every time he asked them about it they assured him they hadn't. They said pulling holdups was risky enough even if you knew what you were doing—and if you didn't, it was sheer recklessness.

"There's an old saying," Buck said. "A hundred things can go wrong in a holdup, and if you can think of fifty you're a damn genius. Pretty lousy odds, man."

Daddy was glad to know that's how they saw it. Armed robbery was the fastest way he knew of to get put in prison or an early grave. "At least they're not doing holdups," he told my mother.

"Yes," she said. "That's something to boast about, to be sure."

As it was, they had their share of scrapes and sometimes carried the evidence of them—Buck with a black eye more than once, a few times with an ear puffed like a portion of cauliflower, once with his arm in a sling; Russell with a deep cut across his cheek, another time with his ribs too sore to permit him to cough, and then with his left hand swathed in a bandage until the day he and Buck came over while my mother was at the library and we saw that the gauze was off and he was missing two fingers.

"Jesus Christ, Russell," Daddy said. "What the hell happened?"

A dice game in Chalmette had turned unsociable when somebody accused him of cheating.

"That dickhead couldn't have spotted me palming if I'd been wearing fireman's gloves," Russell said. "His problem was he lacked the proper sporting spirit—sometimes you win, sometimes not."

What the fellow didn't lack was a razor, nor the inclination to use it. Russell fended with his left hand and *zup,* his little finger vanished. Then *zup,* the next finger at the second knuckle. At which point he yanked out his bulldog and shot the guy one time in the heart.

It was the most exciting thing I'd ever heard—but Daddy's face dropped. "Holy shit, man, you *killed* him?"

"What was I supposed to do, Lonnie?" Russell said. "Let him carve me up to the elbow?"

Buck said he'd been playing stud in the next room when the gunshot sounded—and the men at the table grabbed up their money and scattered like spooked birds. He pulled his piece and ran in the dice room and there was Russell wrapping his hand in a bandanna and nobody else in the room except the dead guy on the floor. They casually walked out and on down the street back to their car, and if anybody in the neighborhood heard the shot they must not've paid it much mind.

"Tough place, Chalmette," Buck said. "Anyway, this doc we know in Metairie did the stitch job. Does good work."

They told Daddy not to worry so much about it, they figured they were clear. Nobody knew their real names or where they were from or even that they knew each other. The police weren't likely to give much of a damn anyhow about some razor-toting grifter laid out in a gambling scrape.

"Goddam *razor*," Buck said. "That's no weapon for a white man."

"I wish I'd thought to scoop up my fingers," Russell said. "I'd've buried them decent. Some broompusher probably swept them out with the trash."

It's why the three of them were always so cautious in their conversation when my mother was around—they didn't want her getting an earful of any such story.

When she came home and saw Russell's hand she nearly wept. He told her he'd been working at a packinghouse and got careless with the saw, but I could tell she didn't believe that for a second.

All the same, they could usually make my mother smile with stories about their girlfriends or with some of their cleaner jokes or with their imitation of a robber being chased around the apartment by a Keystone Cop. The biggest grin they ever got out of her was when Buck said he was getting married.

It was all fairly sudden, he'd only known the woman a few weeks—Jena Ragnatela her name was—but he was as in love as a man could be. We didn't even meet her till the day they got hitched in the city hall and we had a small reception for them at our place.

Jena wasn't one to talk much, and when she did say something you had the feeling it wasn't what she was really thinking. She rarely smiled, and if she ever laughed I never heard it. My mother had wanted Buck to get married but I could see by her face that Jena wasn't what she'd had in mind. Still, it was easy to see why he'd gone for her—she was a knockout. Black-haired and green-eyed, lean-hipped, high-breasted, as easy in her moves as a cat. She always drew every eye in the room and you could tell she always knew it.

It was at Buck's wedding that we also met Charlie Hayes, Russell's latest girlfriend. Her real name was Charlotte but she didn't care for it. She was nineteen, only five years older than me, a copper redhead, slim and pretty. She liked to joke and cut up and she taught me to do the Charleston. Sometimes when we were slow-dancing I'd get such a stiffie I knew she could feel it. The first time it happened I tried to back away a little but she only smiled and pulled me tighter against her and whispered, "Don't fret about it, honey, it's perfectly natural." That's how she was. Every time it happened, she'd give me that same smile and hold me close, and I couldn't help smiling back at her, even though my ears were on fire and I felt like everybody in the room knew what was going on.

Russell himself had been shy about dancing ever since the limp he got from the war but Charlie got him over that and he pretty soon enjoyed dancing as much as anybody. He'd had a lot of girlfriends but she was the best of them and he knew it. She would still be his girl four years later when I started partnering with him and Buck. I asked him once if he planned on marrying her and he laughed and said hell no. Well, did he love her, I asked. He said he didn't know but didn't lose any sleep over it.

"Lots of people say they love each other and don't do nothing but cause each other heartache," he said. "Love's harder to figure than long division. All I know is we like being together without a lot of talk about love. That's fine with me."

Despite my mother's reservations about Jena it looked for a while like Buck's marriage had done as she'd hoped and turned him and Russell away from the criminal life. They bought a filling station across the river in Algiers and seemed to be doing all right at it. Daddy was as glad as my mother was, but I had my doubts about the new leaf they'd supposedly turned. Even back then I didn't believe that falling in love would change a man's nature.

And sure enough, it wasn't long before they admitted to Daddy that they were running a nightly poker game in the back room of the station and selling hooch for a local bootlegger.

"It ain't like we're really in the life anymore," Buck said. "I mean it's not but cards and a little moonshine, for Christ's sake."

Daddy smiled sadly and shook his head like it was no surprise to him. And like he didn't really believe that was all they were up to.

It wasn't. In addition to the gambling and the booze sales, they were doing burglaries again and had already pulled their first holdups—only small jobs so far, groceries and filling stations, a couple of cafés. They were learning the trade slowly and carefully, but they had ambitions. A fellow in Algiers named Bubber Vicente—who had a hand in everything from bootlegging to burglary to armed robbery—was setting up jobs for them and giving them pointers.

I knew all this because Buck and Russell told me. They were secretly giving me shooting lessons, and when it was only the three of us they talked pretty freely. They'd asked me at the start if I could keep my mouth shut and took me at my word when I swore I always would. When I'd asked them to teach me to shoot they said sure—as long as we kept it between the three of us, so as not to upset my mother or get an argument from Daddy.

That was fine by me. And so once or twice a week they took me out to the boonies and taught me all they knew about handling and shooting their pistols and shotguns.

The day I busted twelve bottles in a row at forty paces with the .44 top-break, Buck gave it to me for a present.

*E*very day began with a big bell clanging in the dark. I'd wake to the darkness and remember where I was and for a moment I'd feel like I was suffocating and my heart would bang against my ribs like some trapped thing. I'd have to fast remind myself that you never know—*you never know*—before I could breathe a little easier. It was like that for the first few seconds of every morning.

Then the ceiling lights would come on and the floorwalker did a headcount and told us to unass the bunks. The barrack windows were screenless and my ears were always swollen with mosquito bites. We jostled each other going in and out of the latrine, getting to the piss troughs, the shitters, the water faucets. The usual bunch playing grab-ass and cracking wise, the usual ones cussing at nothing in particular or muttering to themselves, the same ones of us rarely saying a word.

We'd form up in the darkness like rows of broken ghosts in our black-and-white stripes and trudge off to the mess shack for a break-fast that rarely changed—sweet potatoes and blackstrap, grits and coffee. Then out in formation again and off to the toolshed. The east-ern sky only now turning gray and the trees still black against it, the roosters crowing at the chicken house behind the captain's quarters, the air still wet and heavy with the smells of muck and overripe vege-tation. The toolshed trusty gave us whatever tools we needed for the day—cane knives, shovels, axes, hoes. Then the bosses took us away to trim or cut cane or hoe the fields or lay down shell on the camp roads or fell trees or clean out shit ditches, something.

We started before sunrise and went at it till dusk. I'd arrived in the hottest part of the summer, and we'd be dripping sweat before the sun even cleared the trees. By the end of my first few days I was as eaten up with sweat rash as every man in camp. Dinner came out to us in a truck—beans and rice and cornbread, now and then some greens, once in a while some pork. Supper back in camp was the noon left-overs.

During my first few weeks in Camp M, I would come in from the fields so tired I'd sometimes lie down to rest for a minute before strip-ping off my filthy skunk suit and going to the showers—and next thing I knew I'd wake up mudcaked and stinking, feeling like I couldn't breathe, my heart thrashing, the morning bell clanging in the dark.

Angola was set on an oldtime plantation of that name. It was a most serious prison with no need of stone walls. Some sixty miles north of Baton Rouge, it was bordered on three sides by a long mean-der of the Mighty Mississippi and on the fourth by the Tunica Hills—a lay of land naturally isolated and perfect for its purpose. It covered nearly twenty thousand acres of forest and swamp and marshland and fields of sugarcane.

We were housed in various and scattered camps, and as bad as it was in the white ones, everybody knew it was worse for the coloreds. I was put in Camp M, one of the smallest, with only about eighty men, and the most remote. It stood between a cypress swamp and a cane field. A narrow corduroy road ran through the swamp and out to the levee more than a mile away.

There were only three freemen on the place—the captain, his foreman and his clerk. The guards were convicts, most of them doing long stretches for some crime of hard violence. They wore khakis instead of stripes and carried .30-caliber carbines or twelve-gauge double-barrels with buckshot loads. Out in the field, they'd keep an eye on us from the shade of the trees and left it to the pushers to keep us working. Pushers wore khaki too, but they were unarmed. They moved along the line and made sure we never slacked off—"flogged the dog," as they called it. If a con gave a pusher any backsass, the pusher called for a gun boss to come deal with him. They were the most hated men in camp, the pushers, and they lived in the guard barrack for their own safety.

Besides the guard barrack, which had its own mess, there were three convict barracks, each one run by a floorwalker, a trusty who bunked in the barracks storeroom behind wire walls that let him keep watch on things. The captain lived in a big clapboard house with a screened front porch and a backyard vegetable garden and henhouse, and the foreman and clerk shared quarters in a sidehouse. There was a mess shack, a stable for the mules and where the camp's two trucks and two long flatwagons were kept, a tin-roofed laundry without walls, a toolshed, and a pen of large tracking hounds that went half crazy with snarling at anybody in stripes that came near them. There were three sweatboxes and a whipping log.

Camp M covered about ten acres. It was surrounded by a chain-link fence twelve feet high with rolls of barbed wire along the top. A guard tower stood at each corner, and the tower bulls had high-powered rifles.

❧

I never got a letter from Buck or Russell and I never wrote to them. They had told me the hacks opened every bit of convict mail, going out and coming in, no matter how much they might deny doing it. So never write to anybody you did business with on the outside, and never expect to hear from any of them. That was one of the rules they taught me in case I ever took a fall.

They'd also told me that if I ever found myself in the joint some hardcase was sure to try me soon and in front of everybody so they could see what I was made of. When the guy braces you, they said, get right to it without any talk. I hadn't been there two weeks when it happened. The lights had just come on one morning and I was sitting on my bunk when one of the camps' daddy hardcocks, a big redhead named Garrison, snatched up my shoes and dropped a raggedy pair in their place, saying he was making a trade and I could swap with the next newcock to come in.

He was ready for me and clubbed me on the face with a shoe as I came up off the bunk at him. I hooked him in the belly and over the eye and he went on his ass. He scrabbled up quick and swung wild and I hit him twice on the ear and he went down again. He was back up on one knee when I gave him one to the jaw with all my shoulder behind it and he hit the floor on his face, out cold.

I threw his shoes down the aisle and retrieved mine and put them on. I figured I was headed for the sweatbox for sure, but the floorwalker, a trusty named Gaylord, walked on by like he hadn't seen a thing and said for us to get outside and form up. I found out later that he had it in for Garrison and was glad to see him get cooled.

A couple of Garrison's pals brought him around and helped him up and out to formation. His ear looked like a bunch of red grapes. His jaw wasn't broken but over the next few days he'd have a devil of a time eating. I'd jammed a couple of knuckles on my hand but at least it wasn't broken. Most people have no idea how easily you can break your hand on somebody's head. It's why they invented boxing gloves.

As we went out to formation some of the cons were grinning at me. "Ain't this boy something," one said. "A regular Dempsey."

"Dempsey, hell," said another. "Tunney's more like it."

And from then on, Tunney's what they called me. None of the cons would try me again, not even Garrison, who would tell me I had a hell of punch and then let me be, like all the rest of them.

The pushers were a different story. They rode me hard from the very first day, cursing me, ordering me to work faster. I'd set my jaws tight and keep hacking at the cane and if I ever said anything it was only "Yeah boss, working faster." But as the days became weeks they pushed me harder still. Sometimes they'd hit me across the back and legs with a stripped cane stalk and it was all I could do to keep from going at them with my cane knife. I'd have to remind myself over and over of everything Buck and Russell taught me.

Still, word had it that the captain wanted the cop killer to earn a whipping and a day in a sweatbox, to get an early taste of what was in store for him if he tried getting tough in Camp M. Some of the cons told me he wouldn't let the pushers ease up on me till I was punished. It was no secret why I was there—every con's crime was common knowledge in the camp. They said I was lucky the gun bulls were convicts too, because they didn't have it in for cop killers like freeman guards did. A cop killer in a prison with freeman guards was real likely to get shot dead "while trying to escape."

I figured the sooner it happened the sooner the pushers would quit riding me, so the next time a pusher hit me with a stalk I snatched it out of his hand and cut it in two with a swipe of my cane knife and flung the stub in his face.

The cons around us laughed and one said, "Do that to his fucken neck, Tunney."

The pusher hollered, "Trouble here!" but the gun bosses had been watching the whole thing and were already on their way.

I spent the rest of the day in leg shackles, trying to dig a six-foot hole in the soft muck beside the bayou, a swarm of mosquitoes feeding on my face and neck. The hole naturally filled up with muddy water as fast as I shoveled it out, but that was the idea—it was a job that couldn't be done, no matter how long and hard you went at it. After a couple of hours, I hadn't managed to do much except dig a small pool of muck up to my shins.

One of the gun bulls came over and said, "How you like your new job, hardcase?"

"It's a Sisyphean ordeal," I said.

That took the smirk off his face. "You watch your fucken mouth, boy," he said.

When we got back to camp at dusk, the field boss made his report and the captain sentenced me to thirty lashes and a day in the box.

I had already witnessed a couple of whippings by then, so I knew what I was in for. If you were going in the sweatbox after the lashing, you stripped naked, but if you were getting nothing more than the whipping, you only dropped your pants. Either way, you knelt in front of the whipping log—a portion of oak trunk about three feet thick—and hugged yourself to it with one arm and held up your balls with your other hand in case the whip tip snapped up between your legs. The whipping guard would lay into you with a leather strap some three inches wide and four feet long and attached to a long wooden handle. With the proper wrist action, he could tear up your ass pretty well in twenty strokes, the usual number the captain called for.

The first guy I saw whipped got twenty, and he couldn't sit for a week after. The second guy I saw get it had it worse. Fifty strokes for punching a pusher. He passed out at forty and his legs slacked apart and he revived with a scream when the next stroke popped him in the nuts. Then he fainted again till it was over. He had to be carried to the sweatbox, his ripped ass dripping blood and his testicles looking like purple baseballs.

I'd learn later that only one guy was willing to bet I wouldn't squawk for the whole thirty lashes. He lost on number twenty-three. Once you cry out it's hard to keep from doing it the rest of the way, and I yelled again on the next stroke. But I managed to hold it to a grunt on the last six. I could feel my legs quivering with the effort of staying clamped together—and felt the piss run hot over the hand I held my balls with. I didn't know how hard I was biting my tongue until it was over and I tasted the blood.

Then it was into the box. Four feet square and solid oak. At the bottom of one wall was a small opening about a foot long and three fingers high. That was where they slid in your bread and water twice a day. The floor was dirt and packed with the waste of the countless men who'd been in there before me. The smell was something to choke on, and at first I thought I might suffocate, but after a while I wasn't even aware of it—there's probably nothing you can't get used to when you don't have any choice. I couldn't sit up because of my wounded ass, only lie curled up on my side. By law, a man could be boxed for up to three days at a time, and I'd heard of guys who went crazy, guys who died of the heat.

Buck said the way to beat the box was to form a red dot in your mind and concentrate on nothing but that. You'd go into a kind of trance and the time would be up before you knew it. He said it helped with pain too—you could put it all in the dot and contain it better. I tried it, and it took a while to get right, but I finally did. Sometimes I'd doze off, then snap awake and the pain would be there again, like a rat that snuck in while the room was dark, and I'd have to chase it back into the dot.

I heard things through the night—stirrings and splashings from the swamp, the rough coughs of gators in the bayou, the cries of weak things getting killed by stronger ones. I heard the camp rouse in the early morning. Heard footfalls and then the rasp of a tin plate pushed in through the slot. The shallow plate was filled with water and two slices of bread were soaking in it and I slurped down the whole soggy mess. The slot was showing gray dawnlight when I heard the cons go off to work. And I went back to the red dot.

The slot light was almost entirely faded when the cons returned to camp. I couldn't see the slot at all by the time the bolt shot back and the door swung open and a boss said to get out of there.

The rush of fresh air made my eyes water and burned my nose and throat, and I felt the barely scabbed wounds on my ass come open as I crawled out. The boss dropped my clothes in front of me and walked off through the shadows to the guard barrack. The other cons were already at supper in the mess shack.

My cramped muscles ached to the bone as I stood up, but it wasn't as bad as I expected, and I slowly got dressed. The worst part was pulling my pants up over my raw ass. But an amber half-moon was well up in the east and I couldn't remember the last time I'd taken such pleasure in looking at the sky, in simply breathing the night air. On some French Quarter evening, probably. A memory of Brenda Marie lying naked in moonlight of exactly this color caught me so completely off guard I felt like I'd been seized by the throat.

I chased the image out of my head and cursed myself for a careless fool who deserved another ass-whipping. Then limped off to the mess shack.

Never think about what your woman might be doing on the out-side—that was another Buck-and-Russell rule. Pretty soon you'd start imagining her with another guy and make yourself crazy. The guy who didn't have a woman when he took a fall was the lucky one. If you did have one, forget her, forget her completely. If you *had* to think of her, think of her as married to somebody you never met, as a mother of six kids and fifty pounds fatter than you last saw her. Think of her as dead if you had to. If she knew where you were and wrote you a letter, don't even open it before putting a match to it.

Brenda Marie didn't know where I was, so there was no chance I'd be tempted to read a letter from her, and when I saw how miserable so many of the cons would be for days after receiving a letter from a woman, I was glad none came for me. She wasn't the only girl I'd been spending time with in New Orleans but she was the smartest and best-looking, a rare combination for damn sure. I'd had a lot of swell nights in her Vieux Carré apartment. But I wasn't in love with her. The hardest thing about imagining her with another guy was in wanting to *be* the guy, and that was hard enough.

You never know—that was the chief rule and the one I held to the tightest. You never know what'll happen. I reminded myself of it every damn day. That one and the one about never believing the only way out was by the state's permission. Buck said anybody who passed up a chance to escape didn't deserve to be a free man. Russell only partly agreed. He thought a guy ought to escape whenever he could unless he had less than six months left to do. It wasn't worth the risk if he was so close to getting let out anyway.

Buck said he'd take any chance that came along, even if he only had a month left to do, a week, a goddam hour. He could get pretty extreme in his arguments in order to drive home a point.

But it wasn't just talk with them. When they were hardly more than kids they pulled down a one-year sentence in the St. Tammany Parish jail for burglarizing some rich guy's house in Covington. They weren't there three months before they cut a hole in the roof and escaped with two other guys. And there was the time Buck took a fall in Texas and got sent to a prison farm—and a few weeks later Russell and a partner delivered him out of there in broad daylight.

They had stories to tell, Buck and Russell.

The way the cons explained it, there was good news and bad news about escaping from Angola. The good news was that if you escaped and could make it out of Louisiana, the law wouldn't bother to go hunting after you—you'd be free as a damn bird as long as you stayed out of the Bayou State. The bad news was that you probably had a better chance of being elected governor than you did of busting out.

For one thing, it wasn't simply a matter of escaping from Camp M, which would be easy enough. You didn't even have to try to go over the camp fence—you only had to sneak off past the gun bulls when we were working out in the fields or in the woods. But then what? You'd still be on the prison ground, a mighty big and truly rough piece of property. The river flanked the prison on three sides and was way too wide to swim across and get to Mississippi. Even if you had a boat or some kind of raft, you couldn't make it halfway over without somebody spotting you and picking you off easy with a rifle. There was a ferry, yeah—and a squad of armed guards posted at the landing. You could try going out by the front fence, of course—which had guard towers and dogs and no cover to hide in. It was a pipe dream to think you could escape that way.

The one other thing you could try was running the levee.

It wasn't impossible to get around the guards at the south end of the prison by circling through the woods, and then all you had to do was make your way back to the levee and follow it for sixty miles or so down to Baton Rouge. You had other choices, of course. If you thought you were up to it, you could cut away from the levee and try crossing the swamps to the west. Chances were you'd drown in the quicksand or get bit by a viper or eaten up by the alligators or go crazy from the mosquitoes or poison yourself with bad water or break a leg or starve to death after getting so lost the Devil himself couldn't find you. Or you could run into some swamp rat who'd shoot you on sight so he could claim the state reward for fugitive convicts, dead or alive. They said not one convict who ever took off into the swamp was ever heard of again. But that didn't mean you couldn't try to be the first.

All things considered, you'd probably do better to stay on the levee, although they'd be coming right behind you with dogs and high-powered rifles. Plenty of cons had tried running the levee over the years and some were shot down from as far off as a half mile away, but most were caught by the dogs, and more than a few were killed by them. There was no outrunning the dogs. Only two men were known to have made the run all the way to freedom, both of them coloreds, and both had done it a long time ago.

Well, if it was so goddam hard to get out of Angola, I said, why did they even bother having tower guards at every camp like they did? Why did they even bother having fences around the camps?

"Why hell, boy," old Dupree said, "they don't want to *encourage* nobody."

One afternoon a convict slipped out of the cypress stand where we were axing timber and was gone a good ten minutes before a pusher noticed and harked the news to the gun bulls. The runner was a big old boy named Watkins, from Slidell. He'd been married less than a month when he and his wife were at a carnival one night and some galoot gave her a passing pat on the ass. Watkins didn't see it—he'd been trying to win her a prize by ringing the bell on one of those "Test Your Manly Strength" machines you hit with a mallet. If she'd kept her mouth shut nothing would've happened. But she had to pitch a fit, so naturally Watkins had to do something, and since he already had the mallet in his hands what he did was hit the guy with it. Broke his head open like a watermelon. Drew fifteen years. He'd been at Camp M only a few weeks when his pining for his wife got the better of him.

The bosses rounded us up in a hurry and took us back to camp and put us in the barracks so they could all go join the hunt. Out by the pen the dogs were yelping as they were put on a truck to be taken out to the fugitive's trail. By the captain's standing order, the floor-walkers couldn't hand out the musical instruments before sundown except on Sundays, but Gaylord didn't care what else we did while we were in lockdown, and so we played nickel-ante poker and read and napped and sat around bullshitting. Everybody wished guys would try to escape more often.

We knew when the dogs got turned loose by their sudden higher howling. For the next half hour the baying grew fainter as they chased after Watkins—and then it abruptly intensified.

"Sons of bitches run him to ground," Red Garrison said.

There was the flat crack of a distant rifle shot, and a moment later another, and then the dogs began to quiet down and then we didn't hear them anymore.

They brought him back draped over the hood of a truck. We stood at the windows and watched the captain come out of his house and pull Watkins' head up by the hair to have a look at his face. He said something to his foreman and went back into the house. The dogboy got the dogs back in their pen and a couple of the bosses untied the corpse and lugged it around to the back of the truck and laid it out on the bed and then drove him away. We heard they took him to the main hospital and from there notified his wife to come claim his body.

I saw what the dogs did to another con who tried to run. He wasn't even a half mile away when they caught up to him. The hunting party brought him back and dumped him in the middle of the camp yard so we could all have a good look. He was barely recognizable, a heap of bloody rags and flesh, his throat torn and parts of his face and hands ripped open to the bone. He didn't have any kin listed in the records, so the captain had him buried in the small cemetery on a rise by the back fence. None of the graves had markers except one with a small flat headstone that said "Rollie," who had been the captain's favorite dog.

I saw guys deliberately break their arm to go to the hospital and get off the work parties for a time. They'd position their forearm between two logs and let another guy bust it with the flathead of an ax. Some guys knew just how to hit the arm to fracture the top bone, but some did the job with a little too much enthusiasm and the poor bastard's arm looked like a battlefield wound. After the guy regained consciousness he'd go staggering off to show the misshapen arm to the bosses and tell them he'd broken it in a fall. They knew it was bullshit but what could they do? Some guys preferred to have a leg busted because it kept them off work longer. But as soon as a broken arm or a leg was sufficiently healed, sometimes even if it was still in a cast, the man was put back to work.

Some cons went for more lasting damage by cutting their heel-string, the Achilles tendon. They figured it was worth a permanent hobble to get out of hard work for good. It didn't always turn out that way. Sometimes they got sent back to the fields anyway, back to labor made all the harder for being crippled. That's the way it was for the weaklings of the world, in prison or out of it—when nobody else was making it hard for them, they were making it hard for themselves.

I saw a crazy guy named Verhoven brandish a cane knife in the face of a hardcock named Burnett and threaten to cut his head off for being an agent of Satan. Burnett knew Verhoven was a lunatic, we all did, but he stood there with his thumbs hooked in his belt loops and a cigarette in one hand and said, "You couldn't kill me if you tried all day."

The last word was hardly out of his mouth when the blade swiped through his neck. Burnett's head rolled off his shoulders as blood sprang up in a pair of bright red twirls and fell in a spray. The body stayed upright for a moment like it wasn't sure yet what happened, the shoulders blooming deep red, then toppled backwards, the thumbs still in the belt loops, the cigarette still smoking between two fingers. Burnett's head on the ground stared up at nothing and had lost most of its sneer.

They said when Verhoven went to the gallows six weeks later he was chatting happily with God right up to the minute the trap opened under him.

I saw a con get down on his belly to rinse out his bandanna in a bayou and a cottonmouth struck him over the eye. The man jumped up shrieking and started running, the snake snagged to his face by one fang and whipping every which way. A couple of cons wrestled him down and one severed the snake just under the head and flung the writhing body into the water, then pried the fangs out of the man's brow and pitched the head away too. By the time a truck carried him off, the convict's darkly swollen face looked like a spoiled melon. They said he was dead when they got to the hospital, that the doctor listed the cause of death as "excess of venom in the brain."

I saw these things and more through the summer and the fall and into the first cold days of a new year.

And every morning when I woke to the clanging bell in the dark, I'd remind myself once more: You never know.

*B*uck and Jena didn't quite make it to their first anniversary before she ran off. She left a note saying she'd had enough of being bored and for Buck not to hold his breath till she came back. He was half drunk and close to tears the night he came over and told us about it. It was storming hard and a gusting wind flung the rain against the shutters like handfuls of gravel. He said he knew she hadn't been happy staying at home all the time while he took care of business. He knew she thought he was having a high old time playing cards and dealing hooch while she was home with nothing but the radio for company. But he hadn't known things were so bad she'd leave.

My mother went over to sit beside him and put an arm around him. "It's for the best, Buckman," she said softly. "You'll see."

Later on I'd realize she knew better than the rest of us how much he loved that woman and what terrible things it could mean.

But because he was in love he could not let it lay. He had to try to find her. He made inquiries around the neighborhood, thinking that maybe she'd told somebody where she was meaning to go. What he learned from several of the nosier folk on the street was that she'd frequently had a visitor these past weeks. A man, yes, they told him—sorry to say, but yes. An insurance salesman named Wilkes who one day had called on several houses along the block until he got to the LaSalle place and then called on no others. He came back almost every evening. Drove a green Lincoln. Always parked it at the end of the street and then walked up to the house and knocked on the door and was let inside.

Buck went to some people who knew how to find out things and in about two weeks he had it all. Roman Wilkes worked for a life insurance company that had branches in Texas and Mississippi in addition to Louisiana. He had recently requested and been given a transfer to the Beaumont, Texas, office. Buck even had the man's home address.

We learned all this from him one evening when he and Russell had supper with me and my mother. Daddy was out to sea. Buck told it in a voice I hadn't heard from him before—sort of flat, like he was talking about somebody else's troubles, somebody he wasn't all that much concerned with. My mother said for him to please not do anything foolish, and he looked at her like the request was too strange to comprehend.

They disappeared for a while after that, both of them, without having told us where they were going. When Daddy next came home we hadn't seen them in over six weeks. I checked at their place a few times but the landlady didn't know anything except they were paid up through the next two months.

Then one breezy Saturday morning when Daddy had been back about two weeks and the Spanish moss was fluttering in the oaks and the banana leaves swaying in the courtyard, right after my mother left for the library, Russell showed up.

My mother had said all along that they'd probably gone to Beaumont to look for Jena and maybe do something to the Wilkes fellow. She hoped they wouldn't find either one—which they probably hadn't, she said, and that's why they were taking so long. Daddy'd said maybe they were just off larking somewhere. But my mother was right—Beaumont's where they'd been.

It was the second thing Russell told us after the hugging and backslapping. The first was in answer to Daddy's questions of where the hell was Buck and was he all right.

"He's okay," Russell said, "sorta."

But that was as good as the news got. It's why he'd waited for my mother to leave for the library before he came to the door. He told us the whole thing over a couple of pots of coffee.

They'd arrived in Beaumont late at night and checked into a hotel, but the next morning Buck insisted on going to Wilkes' house alone. He wouldn't even tell Russell the address. He left his car at the hotel and drove off in a Dodge they'd stolen the day before. Russell waited all day, and when Buck still hadn't come back by sundown he had a bad feeling. Then he went down to the dining room for supper and there it all was in the evening edition.

Russell had torn the report out of the newspaper so Daddy and I could read it for ourselves. A local businessman named Roman Wilkes had been assaulted in his home by a suspect who identified himself to police as Ansel Mitchum. The victim was reported to be in a coma and suffering from "severe facial disfigurement." Police had been alerted to the fracas by neighbors who reported screams from the Wilkes residence. On arriving at the scene, police found Wilkes unconscious on the living-room floor. They followed "a trail of blood" out the back door and found the "severely injured" Mitchum crawling across the yard toward a car parked in the alley. Mitchum had been taken to the hospital but refused to give any information other than his name. Police were "not specific about the nature of his injuries." The car, they said, had been reported stolen in Orange the day before.

Neighbors told investigators they'd seen the suspect peeking into Wilkes' windows just prior to entering the house and that "a godawful screaming" ensued shortly after he went inside. According to neighbors, a woman—"a real looker"— had been living with Wilkes for the past several weeks, and police speculated that the assault may have been provoked by a "love triangle." A search was underway for the woman, last seen by neighbors when she ran from the house with a suitcase in hand and drove away in Wilkes' car.

Mitchum had been arraigned in the hospital and stood charged with attempted murder. If Wilkes should die of his injuries, police said, they would amend the charge to murder or manslaughter, depending on the facts brought out in their investigation. Mitchum would remain in the hospital under guard until he was well enough to be transferred to the city jail and there held for trial.

Ansel Mitchum was an alias I hadn't known Buck to use before. Ansel was his middle name and Mitchum was Russell's. Russell's favorite phony name was Caesar Smith—God knows why. Both of them had a slew of names they went by. The idea was never to give the cops a name you already had on a jail record somewhere, even in another state. Most cops couldn't find their ass with both hands, Buck always said, but sometimes they got lucky and came up with a previous-arrest record. You wanted always to be a first-time offender.

The next day Russell had put on a coat and tie and gone to the hospital. He told the uniformed cop guarding Buck's door that he was Luther Sammons of Houston, Texas, a cousin of Ansel Mitchum and his only living relative. They'd lost touch with each other over the past years but had been very close when they were younger. He was in Beaumont on business and had read in the paper about his cousin's awful trouble and that he was badly hurt. He'd brought a basket of fruit and wondered if it would be all right to visit with him for a few minutes. The guard examined every piece of fruit in the basket and then gave Russell a good frisk and said all right, ten minutes.

Russell said Buck's face was orange with iodine and all scabbed up with deep scratches over his eyes and on his cheeks. One hand was manacled to the bed by a yard of narrow chain. A catheter hung down from under the sheet and drained red piss into a plastic bag.

"He got a kick out of me just waltzing in there," Russell said. "I asked him could he go along with me taking down the guard and busting him out, but he said hell no, he was too stove up to even stand."

Buck told him in a whisper how he'd snuck up to Wilkes' house and looked in the windows and saw them together on the sofa. They were in their underwear and laughing at some damn thing on the radio like they didn't have a care in the world. He'd been ready to kick down the door but tried the knob first and found it unlocked. He was practically on top of them before they realized he was there. He got Wilkes on the floor and hit him over and over in the face with a big marble ashtray. Jena was hollering and clawing at his eyes and he snatched her by the hair and slung her across the room. Then he started stomping on Wilkes' head and meant to keep at it for a while except Jena came up from behind and stuck him in the short ribs with a steak knife. He grabbed her by the throat but she swung the knife underhand and stabbed him in the thigh and then swung it up again and got him between the legs.

"He said the pain of it beat all he'd ever known about pain," Russell said. "Said he couldn't holler for the want of breath."

He yanked out the knife but must've fainted because next thing he knew he was on the floor in a mess of his own blood and Jena was gone. Wilkes looked dead. The pain was something to reckon with but he managed to get on his feet and make it out the back door before he fell again and couldn't get up. Then the cops were there. He could remember telling them he was Ansel Mitchum but had no memory of anything else until he woke up in the hospital and got the bad news.

Russell broke off from the story to light a cigarette. He took a deep drag and sighed a long stream of smoke. Then he told us Buck had lost his dick—most of it, anyway.

"He's got about yay much left," he said, holding two fingers an inch apart.

"Oh sweet *Jesus*," Daddy said.

I'd read that some Indian tribes used to cut the dicks off enemies they captured. And heard tales about blackhanders who'd castrated guys in revenge for getting the horns put on them. Such a thing had always seemed so terrible it was almost unreal, like something out of a campfire scare story.

Buck hadn't minded talking about it, Russell said, and even joked about it, although he couldn't keep the bitterness out of his voice when he wisecracked about the greater likelihood of pissing on his shoes from now on. The doctor told him he was lucky they'd been able to save both balls, and lucky he didn't get stabbed in his only kidney. Buck said yeah, he couldn't hardly believe his luck. He agreed with the doctor that it could've been worse—hell, the bitch might've used a spade and took his whole crotch out at the roots.

The doctor insisted he didn't have call to be so pessimistic. The surgery had gone well and would be swift to heal. Buck still had the nerves and blood vessels in place to feel pleasure down there and would still be able to shoot off.

"Buck said that was good news, all right," Russell told us. "Said it'd be easier on his hand too, since now he'd be able to jack off with just his thumb and forefinger."

"Oh man," Daddy said, and sighed and rubbed his face.

After three weeks in the hospital Buck was transferred to the city jail. Despite the efforts of a local attorney Russell had retained for him, he'd been denied bond—he didn't own property and was unemployed and Wilkes was still in a coma, a condition the doctors said would likely be permanent. Without the testimony of either the victim or the woman who'd fled the scene, however, the state would've been hard put to prove attempted murder, so it went with a charge of mayhem. The trial was two weeks later and Russell was right there for it.

Buck's lawyer began by reminding the jury that Texas law so deeply frowned on cuckoldry that it sanctioned a husband's killing of any man he found *in flagrante delicto* with his wife. His client, however, had gone to Wilkes' home unarmed and without malice, solely to try to retrieve the beloved wife stolen from him by that homewrecker of a traveling salesman. Wilkes had met Mitchum at the door and invited him in and then attacked him with a knife, mutilating him in an unspeakable manner and forcing him to defend himself. If anyone was guilty of mayhem, Buck's lawyer told the jurymen, it was Wilkes. He described the wound in detail and offered to have his client lower his trousers so they could see the horror for themselves, but the judge said nothing doing, counselor's description would suffice.

"The jury kinda wormed around in their chairs when he told about Buck's wound," Russell said. "But they did plenty of squirming too when they saw the pictures of Wilkes all laid out like a dead man in a Halloween mask."

The state made hash of the self-defense claim by pointing out that Mitchum couldn't have done the awful damage he did to Wilkes *after* receiving his own incapacitating wound. Furthermore, since Wilkes would've been incapable of inflicting the wound after being beaten so badly, Mitchum must have been wounded by the woman, the only other person on the scene. She'd fled from him to be with Wilkes and then stabbed him in defense of the man she really loved. As for Mitchum's claim that she was his wife and he had a legal right to protect his marriage, where was the proof of their union?—he'd also claimed to have lost his marriage paper in a house fire.

Russell said the jury didn't look all that pleased with themselves for finding him guilty. The judge wasn't entirely unsympathetic to Buck, either. He made a little speech about the difficulty of passing sentence on someone who'd already suffered in a manner to make any man quail just to hear of it. Then again, the defendant *did* put a man in a coma, and there *was* some question as to whether the woman was his legal wife. So the judge gave him three years.

Buck was taken to the state pen in Huntsville for processing, and a few days after that he was transferred to a road prison near Sugarland.

"I just came back to let you all know what happened and how things stand," Russell said. "And to take care of some things—rent and stuff. Visit with Charlie a little. Then I'll be heading back to Texas for a bit."

Why go back there, Daddy wanted to know. What more could he do in Texas? The only thing to do now was hope Buck kept his nose clean and got an early parole.

"Well," Russell said, "I figure to set Buck free of that road camp or know the reason why."

He said it the way somebody might tell you he'd made up his mind to buy a car. I'd been sitting there feeling glum about Buck being in prison and it took a second for Russell's words to sink in— and then my heart jumped up and danced.

Daddy called him a damn fool. He said Russell could end up in prison too. He said they might both get killed. He said it wasn't worth it, not with Buck so likely to get paroled in just a year.

Russell said Buck wasn't likely to think of it as *just* a year. Daddy talked himself blue in the face but couldn't dissuade him. They argued about it until I warned them from the front window that my mother was home for lunch.

She was happy as a pup to see him. Then she noticed Buck's absence and asked where he was. Still at the oil rig in Lake Charles, Russell told her, where they'd been working these past weeks and car-rying home their pay in a wheelbarrow. He apologized for not having sent word but they'd been working double shifts and hadn't had time to do anything else. He was heading back to the rig himself in a few days.

My mother's smile was as phony as a paper cutout. She said she was glad they were doing so well and asked him to stay to supper, but he said he had a date with Charlie. Daddy suggested a short one at the corner speak but Russell said he was already late and had to hurry off. He didn't want to hear any more of Daddy's arguments is what it was.

We didn't see him again before Daddy shipped out a week later on a freighter taking oil-rig parts to Tampico and Veracruz. I don't know what went through Daddy's mind in the three weeks he was gone, but not a day passed by that I didn't wonder if I'd ever see my uncles again.

And then a few days after Daddy's return from Mexico, just as we were finishing supper one night, there came a jaunty little knock at the door and I answered it and there stood Russell—with Buck smiling over his shoulder.

They hugged me so tight I couldn't breathe. We were all laughing and Daddy and Buck wrestled each other around the room as my mother hugged and hugged Russell and then they traded off and kept at it. For my mother's sake, they told a bullshit story about the Lake Charles field going dry and them deciding to come home and see about maybe opening a business of some kind. She said that was wonderful. I think she knew they were lying but didn't care, she was so glad to see they were all right. She made no mention of Jena that night or anytime after, and as far as I would ever know, she never did find out about Buck's maiming or his time in a Texas prison.

To celebrate their homecoming we went out into the summer night and down to the corner café and its crowded backroom speakeasy. Russell telephoned Charlie to come join us. She and my mother and a pretty waitress named Jill took turns dancing with us. The beer kept coming to the table in large foaming pitchers and we cut a rug and laughed it up till almost midnight. Every now and then Buck or Russell would let me take a pull off their beer while my mother wasn't looking. The laughter between them was different from the way they laughed with the rest of us. It was the laughter of men who'd faced danger together. Who would risk their ass for each other.

After my mother left for the library the next morning—the only time she'd ever been late and with the only complaint of hangover I'd ever hear from her—Buck and Russell came by and told us about the break.

Russell had recruited an old pal of theirs to help out, a car mechanic and smalltime thief named Jimmyboy Dolan. They'd driven to Texas and checked into a motor court on the main highway about two miles from the Sugarland prison camp. On Sunday, the visiting day, Russell went to the camp in his guise of cousin Luther Sammons. They sat at an outdoor table and Buck told him all about the guards and the work routine and how to get to the stretch of road where his gang would be clearing ditches the next day. It was a perfect spot, isolated and lightly traveled.

The following morning Russell and Jimmyboy smeared mud on the car's license plates and drove out to the work site. Russell stopped the car next to the transport truck where two of the gun bulls stood in the shade and Jimmyboy asked them for directions to Rosenburg. Next thing the guards knew they had pistols in their faces. The boss bull hollered at the third guard, down near the end of the work line, to throw down his gun too, but the guy just stood there. "Like he was maybe thinking of trying to save the day," Russell said.

Buck came up out of the ditch behind him and knocked the notion out of his head with a shovel.

"Should've seen it," Buck said. "Old boy wobbled around in little circles with his eyes rolled up in his head like he was having a religious experience before he finally thought to fall down."

Some of the cons went hightailing into the woods and some stood there like they wouldn't know what to do until somebody told them. "Sorry bastards," Buck said. "They're exactly where they belong."

While Jimmyboy held a pistol on the guards, Buck collected their guns and tossed them into the car. Russell opened a hood panel on the prison truck and yanked out the coil wire and put it in his pocket. They got back in the car and Russell wheeled it around and Buck said all he saw out the back window as they made their getaway was a yellow cloud of road dust.

He looked over at me and smiled—and I felt my grin get bigger.

The first time I did it was with Solise DuBois, in her family's boathouse, only a few weeks before Buck's escape from the Texas road gang. Over the following months I had the pleasure of lots of other schoolgirls as well and made my first visits to some of the Quarter's best cathouses. With such experience under my belt, so to speak, I naturally thought I knew everything there was to know about sex. But it came as a revelation to me that Buck could still sport with the ladies despite lacking most of his pecker.

I received this enlightenment one evening when I was taking supper with him and Russell in a restaurant. They'd spent most of the afternoon in a speakeasy and were feeling pretty loose. As we watched the waitress sashay off to the kitchen with our order, Buck said he sure wouldn't kick her out of bed. Then he caught my look and laughed.

"I can read your mind, kid," he said. He aped a look of awe and tried to mimic my voice as he said, "Can he still cut the mustard, him?"

Some patrons at a neighboring table turned our way. Buck smiled and winked at them and they gave their attention back to their plates.

He leaned forward and in a lower voice informed me that there were all kinds of pleasures he could still take with women who didn't scare easy at the sight of his stub. He still enjoyed what they could do for him with their mouth and hands, and he could still get off by just rubbing himself on a cooter. If he fit himself just right against it, he could get the woman off too. Between that and the things he could do for them with his own hands and mouth, there was plenty of fun to go around. He said he'd proved it with nearly a dozen women already, and only the first two of them whores.

"Hell, some of them's told me the thing feels better than a whole one," he said. "Say it gets them in the button better."

Russell had known about the whores—the first time Buck tested himself after getting back from Texas was at Miss Quentin's over on St. Ann's, and Russell had gone with him—but the others were news to him and he asked how come Buck hadn't said anything about them before.

"What?" Buck said. "I got to report to you every time I hump a broad? I got to keep a list for you? You practicing to be parole officer?"

"Hey man, *I* don't give a damn who you hump or how you do it," Russell said. "Just don't tell me they like that stump better than they do a whole one."

"I'm telling you what they tell me," Buck said. "Not all of them, but some."

We got more looks from the surrounding tables and I cleared my throat and cut my eyes sideways to let Buck and Russell know it.

Russell made a dismissive gesture, but he lowered his voice. "Look, a whore'll do anybody and say anything, no questions asked except where's my money. But a free woman saying she prefers a stump to a whole one? She's either bullshitting or mighty damn drunk. No offense."

None taken, Buck said. But we'd be surprised at the way a lot of women reacted to his mutilation—which he'd mention to them before they even got anywhere near a bed. He'd tell them he got it in the war.

"It's like it's some kind of challenge or something," he said. "They have to see it. And once they do, they have to see what it feels like."

"Challenge, my ass," Russell said. "Pity freaks, more like it."

"Could be," Buck said. "All I know is I'm getting it more and getting it a lot easier than I used to with a whole one."

Maybe so, Russell said, but if the devil himself came along and promised him all the poontang in the world in exchange for most of his dick, he'd keep what he had, thank you.

"I don't blame you a bit," Buck said. "Those three inches mean a lot to you, I know."

"You dickless shitbird," Russell said.

"You brainless asshole," Buck said.

"I surely do enjoy being privy to these eloquent fraternal conversations," I said.

They turned on me. "You smartmouth jackleg," Russell said.

"You egghead pogue," Buck said.

"Gentlemen," I said, lowering my voice to a whisper and leaning over the table, "have you never before heard that profanity is the linguistic crutch of inarticulate fuckheads?"

Buck grabbed me by the throat and affected to choke me, and Russell hissed, "Snuff that smartass."

"Yes sir," I said in a mock-strangled voice, "eloquent's the word for these little family chats."

Then we were all laughing and trading punches on the arm and drawing stares from all over the dining room. The manager came over to ask frostily if everything was all right.

"Couldn't be better," I told him. "Thank you for asking."

One chill February afternoon in my junior year I came home from school to find my mother on the kitchen floor. A few hours after going into the hospital she had a second stroke and it finished her. My wire got to Daddy while his tanker was loading oil in Texas City. He wired back he'd catch the next train. When I got home the apartment felt way too large. My throat tightened when I leafed through a few of her favorite books, and when I read her margin notes in her copy of Yeats—"So true!" "Yes, exactly!" "I *love* this!"—the tears came. Then I went through her closet and caught the smell on her clothes and wept even harder.

I met Daddy at the station the next day and his eyes too were redly glazed. For more than a week after the funeral he sat around and didn't say much. His aspect was of someone sitting in an empty room. Then suddenly he was all in a rush to be back on a ship, as if the only solace possible to him was out on the open sea. On a cold morning of heavy yellow fog I went with him to the docks and he got a pierhead jump on a rustbucket called the *Yorrike*. It was bound for ports of call all over the Orient and not due to return for nine months. I was old enough to take care of myself and there was enough money in the family account to cover my expenses for several months. He would send more each time he got paid. He'd already asked Buck and Russell to watch out for me. He shook my hand at the foot of the gangplank and told me to study hard. Then went aboard and stood at the rail as the tugs nudged the ship out to the channel and it faded in the downriver mist.

He sent money about every six weeks, each time with a short letter mostly taken up with thumbnail descriptions of the places he'd most recently been—Colombo, Rangoon, Singapore, Manila. He tried hard to sound in good spirits but I could sense his persisting grief. He always closed with an admonishment to keep up my grades and a reminder that my mother would've been disappointed if I didn't.

I shared his letters with Buck and Russell, who read them with glum faces. They never said anything about them except one time when Russell said, "I guess it's rough when you really love them," and Buck nodded and looked out the window.

They kept an eye on me as they'd promised Daddy they would. Except when they were out of town on business, as they always called it, I'd drop in on them about twice a week and we'd usually take supper together. They came to visit me just as often. Sometimes I'd have a girl with me when they stopped by and they'd apologize for the intrusion and take a hasty leave. The next time they'd see me they'd say I'd better not be spending so much time chasing after nooky that I was ignoring my schoolwork. I'd assure them I wasn't and proved it with my monthly grade reports, which they had to sign with Daddy's name for return to the headmaster. I was also on the boxing team again and they never missed a match, not even when it was held at some school in another parish. At the end of my junior year I won the state middleweight title, and afterward they took me out to celebrate.

By that time they'd quit the burglary business for good. They'd never much cared for jobs that required a lot of tools or for sharing the take with fences. They still pulled gambling tricks, but their main livelihood was now armed robbery. Their longtime middleman, Bubber Vicente, was steering them to most of their jobs. They had hit their first bank only a few months before—a small one, way up in Monroe—and I'd never seen them so pleased with themselves as when they told me about it. They said two men were enough for a holdup team but a three-man team was best, so they'd taken on Jimmyboy Dolan to do the driving.

I liked hearing about the holdups they pulled. About the way they'd prepare for them and how the people's mouths came open when they saw the guns and heard them announce the stickup. Their faces got so *alive* when they talked about it. Their eyes looked electric. No question about it, they were naturalborn bandits.

Me too—I just knew it. I'd felt that way since I was a kid, and I'd known it for sure the night they came back from Texas. I didn't know how I knew, but I did, and I would be damned if I'd deny it just because I couldn't explain it. They anyway explained it well enough one night when they were in their cups and talking about the criminal life.

"Everybody knows won money's sweeter than earned money," Buck said, "but stole money—especially *robbed* money—is the sweetest there is. All you need to *win* money is luck. Skill helps but ain't necessary. But to pull a righteous stickup you need luck and skill both—*and* you need balls."

It's why cheating at a table was more exciting than playing it straight. Cheating wasn't gambling, it was robbing, and it raised the stakes as high as they can go.

"Get caught cheating the wrong guys," Buck said, "and it's like to mean blood on the floor."

Russell agreed. "Every time you do a holdup you're risking your ass," he said. "You never know when a guy will resist, when he'll be somebody with a gun of his own and the sand to use it. You never know when you'll have to get down to it with the cops."

That's why more people didn't rob and steal, Buck said. "It ain't because they're so moral like they say. Morality's just a excuse to hide behind. World's full of thieves at heart who don't steal nothing because they're too scared to. They're scared of the law. Scared of being punished."

"They're chickenshits and they know it," Russell said. "Thump on their Bibles to try and cover it up."

No ethics lecture I'd ever heard in school was as plain on the matter as that.

My mother had often remarked that it would be a waste of my intelligence if I didn't go to college, and Daddy agreed, and I had allowed them to think I would. I didn't see the need to disappoint them any sooner than necessary. I figured I'd break the news to them when the time came. But before the time came my mother died, and then ten months later—midway through my senior year, a week before Christmas and two weeks prior to my eighteenth birthday—there came a telegram to inform me that on its way back to New Orleans the *Yorrike* had been caught in a bad storm and foundered somewhere north of the St. Peter and St. Paul Rocks in the South

Atlantic. A rescue ship picked up a lifeboat with the only four survivors and none of them was my father.

The first whiskey drunk of my life lasted for all of a cold and sun-
less week. I sat in the apartment with a bottle at hand and Christmas
carols intoning on the streets. Sometimes, asleep in the chair, I dreamt
of my father on the shadowy ocean floor amid his cadavered ship-
mates, his skin gray as moss, his hair swaying in the current, small fish
feeding in his eyeholes and passing between the bared teeth of his gaping jaws. I'd waken as wet and cold with sweat as if I'd been hauled up
from those very depths.

Buck or Russell came by every day to ensure my store of whiskey.
They didn't want me out drunk on the streets, looking for more. They
didn't say much or stay long, grieving for their brother in their own
way.

Some French writer once said that when a man's father dies his
only true judge is gone. Maybe so. After a week of blurred days and
bad nights I cleaned myself up one morning and packed my two bags
and by noon I had moved into a much smaller and cheaper apartment
on Esplanade. Then I went downstairs and telephoned my uncles and
arranged to meet them for an early supper at Lafitte's.

The place was nearly empty at that hour and we sat at an isolated
table way in the back. I made my pitch over mugs of beer and platters
of oysters on the half shell. I gave them the whole speech without
slowing down long enough to let them say no before I was finished. I
could drive, I told them—I could shoot, I could fight, I wasn't scared,
I knew how they operated, and I knew the rules. I knew that if a thing
went bad it was every man for himself but you never crossed a partner
and if you went down you kept your mouth shut and took the fall and
stayed ready for a chance to break. I had paid attention and I had
learned all that.

I'd half expected them to laugh, to ask what in hell made me think a pair of pros would take on an eighteen-year-old who'd never done a crime in his life.

They didn't even smile. "Well hell, I figured this was coming," Buck said. "I had you pegged for a crook since you were knee high. I always known it's in your blood, me."

"Me too," Russell said. "It's a way about them, a look some kids got, and you always had it. Your momma wasn't the sort to see it, but your daddy was. If he didn't, it was only because he didn't want to."

"The thing is, Sonny," Buck said, "we figured you for going to college, smart cookie like you. It's anyway what your momma wanted."

"That's right," Russell said. "We figured you'd end up doing your thieving with law books or account ledgers. Like that."

I wasn't sure if they were joking. They looked serious as preachers.

"World's full of thieves," Buck said, "but the ones to make the most money is the legal kind."

"And the least likely to get shot or go to jail," Russell said.

"Here you got all this good schooling and you want to be a stickup man," Buck said. He turned to Russell and shrugged. "Could be he ain't as bright as we thought."

Russell turned down the corners of his mouth and shook his head.

I kept looking from one of them to the other. "Law books?" I said. *"Ledgers?"*

"Hell, Sonny," Russell said, "why go the riskier way and for less payoff? What's the sense in that?"

"The sense?" I said. "*You* tell *me*, goddammit! Why aren't you dealing in booze or running a gambling joint? You could be pulling in plenty of dough with a lot less risk than stickups. Why do *you* do it?"

Now they smiled. Buck turned to Russell and said, "See what I mean about he ought be a lawyer?"

Russell nodded. "Still, I guess the man's got a right to make up his own mind. And we *have* been in need of a driver since Jimmyboy's foot."

I didn't know anything about Jimmyboy's foot, but right then I knew they were going to say yes—and my blood sped up.

Buck gave a long sigh. Then smiled. "Oh, what the hell. Who are we to say you can't do like us?"

"May your momma's soul rest in peace, and Lonnie's too," Russell said, "but since there's neither of them here to object . . ."

"And bloodkin's always better for a partner than just some pal," Buck said.

I was grinning with them now.

But there was a catch: I'd have to finish school first. "It's the one thing your daddy trusted us to see to," Buck said. "We mean to keep our word to him."

"Besides," Russell said, "we don't accept no uneducated dumb-shits for partners no more."

They wouldn't listen to a word of argument about it. "You want to leave school and get in the crook life," Buck said, "you go ahead and do it, but it won't be with us."

"But if I finish at Gulliver you'll take me on?"

"*If* you finish with the same good grades as always," Russell said. "No bumming through the little bit you got left."

"*And* if you still want to," Buck said. "Hell kid, you never know. You might decide you'd rather run for Congress and be the biggest kind of thief there is."

$\mathcal{W}$e labored through the winter in blue clouds of our own breath, in daylong clatters of axes and growlings of saws. The calendar finally showed spring but the nights remained chilly into late April. Then a hard rain started coming down—and kept on coming. The river rose and ran fast under daily skies as dark and dirtylooking as old lead. There were reports of overruns along the bottoms, nothing nearly so bad as the monster flood of two years earlier, but portions of the upriver banks had given way and driftwood of all size and sorts was carrying downstream and jamming up in the meanders. Camp M got orders to clear out the prison's northern levee before the accumulating debris extended into the navigation channel.

Every morning before sunrise we hiked out to the levee in the chill morning drizzle, one long heavy flatwagon rumbling ahead of us, the other one trailing behind, each drawn by a brace of mules and jarring over the corduroy road that led through this corner of the misty swamp and out to the river. The guards rode the wagons and watched us front and back. The first time we crested the levee at dawn and looked across the rivermist to the faraway opposite bank with its dark growth of reeds and brush and trees, somebody said, "There it is yonder, boys—the free world." I couldn't get enough of looking at it as we followed the levee road another mile or so to the bend where the biggest clusters of driftwood had built up.

The rain finally ceased but the clouds didn't break and the days continued without color, but at least the mosquitoes were still scant. We pulled flotsam from the river the day long—fence posts and portions of sheds, logs and saplings and entire trees uprooted from upstream. We trimmed the trees on the bank before lugging them up the levee. Every day we'd load the best cuts on the wagons to take back to camp for next winter's firewood. The rest we flung in piles on the other side of the road.

The smaller trees were easy enough to trim and drag up the levee, but we had to section the bigger ones with axes before we could get them up the slope, and even then it sometimes took several of us muscling together to haul up some of the biggest sections. Some portions were still so heavy we had to use the mules to pull them up. To make things even tougher, the slope was slick from all the recent rain, and sometimes a man slipped and went sliding back down to the bank, his load of wood tumbling with him. In the first week two men broke an arm and another an ankle. One guy went all the way off the bank and into the river and got his shirt snagged on a submerged root. We could see his terrified face a half-foot below the surface as we struggled to free him but he drowned before we got him loose.

We'd been at it a week when the rain started falling again. It didn't come down hard enough to raise the river any higher but it fell steadily and cold for most of every day. Debris kept coming downstream and the footing on the slope got even trickier. We ate our noon meals in the rain, lining up at the mess truck for tin plates of beans and rice and then crowding under the big oaks on a stretch of high ground where it wasn't so muddy. But the rain ran through the trees and down into our plates and made cold weak soup of our meal.

One late afternoon a pair of gun bosses named Harlins and Ogg pointed out six of us and said to come with them. We climbed aboard a flatwagon and the teamster trusty hupped the mules into motion. Red Garrison was in our party and asked where we were going but the guards ignored him. Garrison made a mocking face they couldn't see, and a pair of his hardcase buddies named Yates and Witliff grinned at it. The other two cons—old Dupree and a young guy named Chano, a Mexican mute who understood English—paid him no more mind than I did.

We'd gone about half a mile when we began to hear a terrible shrieking up ahead. There was no pause to it, and as we drew closer, Witliff said, "Them's mules." I'd been told Witliff was at Angola for burning down his ex-wife's house while she and her new husband were in it. They'd both survived but the story was they would've been better off if they hadn't.

The teamster, Wakefield, said mules was what it was. He said he and Musial, the other driver, were on their way back from delivering a load of wood to camp and were turning onto the levee road when Musial took his wagon a little too wide and the shoulder gave way. The wagon went over on its side and slid down the levee, dragging the mules with it, then slammed into the muddy bottom of the slope and overturned completely. The mules were tangled up in the harness and screaming with the pain of God knew how many broken legs. Wakefield had gone down and found that Musial was still breathing, but he was unconscious and his legs were pinned under the wagon. There'd been nothing he could do but come get help.

"I don't know if six'll be enough to shove that heavy sonofabitch thing off him," Wakefield said.

When we got to where the wagon had gone off the road, the screaming of the mules was the worst sound I'd ever heard. They were trying to get up, but even if they hadn't been twisted up in the traces, they never could've stood on those legs that were showing broken bone through bloody hide. Musial was on his back with his eyes closed, his legs under the capsized wagon.

"Christ's sake, man," Garrison said. "Put them jugheads out of their misery."

"Shut up, Red," the Harlins guard said. He was already cocking his carbine and taking aim. He shot one of the mules in the head and the animal went into a greater frenzy of lunging and shrieking.

"Shit," Harlins said.

If the guards back at the riverbend heard the gunfire they wouldn't have thought anything of it—the gun bosses were always shooting snakes or crows or at turtles in the river or hawks flying overhead.

Harlins levered another round and shot the mule again and it jerked and bellowed and both of the animals were even more panicked now and thrashing with their broken legs like they were insane.

"Christ's *sake,*" Garrison muttered with heavy disgust.

Then Ogg shot the mule and it fell still.

"About time," Garrison said.

"I told you shut your damn mouth," Harlins said. He shot the other mule and didn't kill it either. The veins stood out on his forehead. Then he and Ogg fired at the same time and the mule slumped dead and the following silence was a relief.

"I guess we know whose bullet did the job," Garrison said.

Harlins jabbed him in the face with the carbine butt and Garrison went backpedaling off the end of the wagon.

"Hey, man!" Yates said, and took a step toward Harlins.

Harlins chambered a round and leveled the carbine at him from the hip. Yates half-raised his hands and the rest of us hustled to the other side of the wagon.

"All right, Connie—all right now," Ogg said to Harlins the way you'd talk to a growling dog. "You shut up that redhead good. Let's see to the teamster now, all right?"

Harlins eased down the hammer of the carbine and said, "Asses off," and we all got down from the wagon. Garrison was back on his feet and trying to stem the blood running from his broken nose. He glared at Harlins, who didn't even look at him.

We scrabbled down the levee and checked Musial. He was still alive and still unconscious. But the wagon was lying at an angle that wouldn't allow for using the mules and ropes to drag it off him from up on the road without crushing him under it. And even if we could get the mules down to the bank without either one breaking a leg, we weren't sure they could make it back up the muddy slope again. There was nothing to do but unhitch the dead animals and try heaving together. But the wagon was so heavy and so fast in the mud that we could barely budge it, never mind lift it enough for Wakefield to pull Musial out from under.

"We could use you up here," Garrison said to Wakefield. His voice had gone deeply nasal and his eyes were bloodshot and already showing dark rings. He licked at the blood still oozing from his swollen nose.

"Do it," Ogg told Wakefield. "I'll grab onto Musial."

Wakefield set himself with the rest of us along the wagonside and Ogg handed his carbine to Harlins and squatted down and took hold of Musial under the arms.

"All right," Garrison said. *"Heave!"*

This time we raised the thing a little but still not enough for Ogg to pull him out. Musial groaned without opening his eyes.

"One more man here and we might can do it," Dupree said, giving Harlins a look.

"Come on, Connie," Ogg said. "Lend a hand."

"This is bullshit," Harlins said. "We need more guys, what we need." But he propped the two carbines against a large piece of driftwood a few yards away and joined us at the wagon.

He was setting himself and trying to find a proper handhold when Garrison bolted for the weapons.

Harlins started after him but Witliff tripped him down on all fours. Ogg jumped up and Yates tried to grab him but he jerked away and backstepped into me and I punched him hard in the kidney and he grunted and went to his knees.

There was a gunshot and a yowl and I spun around and saw Harlins curled on his side, crying and gripping his thigh with both hands, blood running between his fingers.

Garrison chambered another bullet and stepped over to him. Holding the carbine like a pistol, he put the muzzle up close to Harlins' temple and said, "Shut me up now, cocksucker." And shot him. A bright thin cord of blood arced from his head and fell away and that was that.

"Oh Jesus," Ogg said. He was sitting back on his heels and holding his side, starting horrified at Harlins.

Garrison racked the lever and an empty shell flipped out. He smiled at Ogg and said, "You wanna see Jesus, convict? Off you go."

The carbine cracked and Ogg flopped over backward with his legs in an awkward twist.

"*Whooo!*" Witliff said. He'd grabbed up the other carbine and was grinning like he'd hit a jackpot. Yates was all teeth too. But Wakefield looked scared and Dupree looked angry. Chano the Mex was off to the side, cutting his eyes from Garrison to Witliff. It was almost dark now and the rest of the camp would be coming back this way very soon.

"Well boys," Garrison said, "it's nothing but the noose for me now. But if a nigger could run this levee I can too. You all do what you want but I'm gone."

He turned and started off at a trot and Witliff and Yates hastened after him.

Dupree looked from Wakefield to Chano to me. "No sir," he said. "I seen many a one try it, me, and seen they all look like after. No, thank you." He sat down crosslegged and stared off at the river.

I hustled past him, hearing Wakefield and Chano right behind me.

We got a great turn of luck before we'd been on the run an hour—a storm swept in, the kind you don't usually see till later in the year, full of blasting thunder and snake-tongue lightning and a cold wind that shook the trees and slung the rain sideways to sting our faces and chill us to the balls, and it was in no rush to be done with. Not man nor dog could track us in that weather. We figured they wouldn't even start the dogs till the rain quit coming down so hard, and we picked up our pace, trying for the biggest lead we could get before they set out after us.

We bore due south, away from the levee, skirting ponds and leaping ditches and vaulting over cattle fences, tearing through cane fields, slogging through swamp muck and splashing through water to our thighs, going by dead reckoning toward a point where the river curved back around to form the prison's lower border. We ran in single file, Garrison in the lead, Witliff and Yates behind him, then me and Chano, with Wakefield bringing up the rear. Nobody spoke as we went—we couldn't spare the breath. The only sounds were our ragged panting and our feet sucking through the mud. Every once in a while I'd look back and see Wakefield's shadowy form falling farther behind.

Then it got so dark we couldn't see each other anymore except in the intermittent flashes of lightning. When the lightning finally played out and the thunder faded, the only way I could follow Yates was by the sound of him. Wakefield had fallen so far back I couldn't hear him.

Now and then Garrison brought us to a halt to listen for the dogs and check our bearings by feeling the bark of the trees for the moss on the north side. Each time we stoppd, Wakefield would almost catch up to us, but then we'd be off and running again, and again he'd drop behind.

Sometimes Garrison or Whitliff would slip in the mud or trip on a root, and those of us coming behind would run up on him, everybody stumbling and cursing and pushing off each other and then running again, straining through the blackness like blind men, trying to sense the hole underfoot before we stepped into it, the tree branch hanging low before we hit it with our head. Yates was wheezing hard now and had slowed down so much I kept running into him, so I finally just went around him. Chano stayed right behind me.

The rain kept falling and the wind stayed in our favor, strong and at our backs. I ran in a kind of trance, unaware of anything much beyond the feel of the ground under me and a steady burning in my throat. We came onto the levee so unexpectedly I couldn't believe we were there. We sprawled on the slope on our backs and let the rain run down our faces into our mouths. Garrison reckoned we'd been on the run at least eight hours. Witliff said it felt like all his life.

Wakefield was no longer with us. When we'd stopped to check our heading a couple of hours earlier, he hadn't caught up, but we'd heard him splashing in the muck way behind us. Then the last time we'd stopped we hadn't heard him at all.

The rain had slackened to hardly more than a drizzle and the clouds had thinned out and showed the vague gray hue of the coming dawn. The air was thick and smelled of mud. Judging by the lay of the levee, we reckoned we'd come a lot more to southwestward than due south. It was a wonder we hadn't missed the levee altogether and ended up in the heart of the swamp. On the other hand, we figured we were already a good four or five miles below Angola's southern perimeter.

"I tell you, fellers," Garrison said, "I never did believe God loved me, but I guess that blessed storm was His way of letting me know I was wrong. By sunup tomorrow we'll be in Red Stick City and trying to make up our minds which whorehouse to visit first."

I couldn't help chuckling with the others. Then Chano touched my sleeve and I looked at him and he put a finger to his ear.

For a moment I didn't know what he meant. And then I heard it. We all did.

Dogs.

Baying in the distance and heading our way.

We ran and ran along the snaking levee, dark river on our left and black swamp to our right. The dogs were louder but still a good ways behind. You could hear that it was more than one pack. Other camps had likely joined in the hunt. About an hour after we first heard the dogs, there were three or four quick gunshots, and after a moment, a last one. I figured that was it for Wakefield.

The eastern sky was looking like smeared copper when Chano made a high sound to get my attention and I looked back and saw that Yates was down. The way he was spread-eagled facedown in the mud it was obvious he was finished. We ran on. Fifteen or twenty minutes later the hounds' cries went higher and I knew they had him.

We ran and we ran. The sun was above the treetops now and the river was shining the color of rum. We'd gained some distance on the pack when it stopped to deal with Yates, but then the dogs had started coming again and now they sounded no more than a mile behind us.

We went around a long bend in the levee and then Garrison stopped running and leaned over with his carbine across his thighs, huffing like a bellows. Witliff squatted beside him and braced himself on his carbine like he'd run out of sap too.

"Can't keep up," Garrison gasped, and motioned for me and Chano to go on. So we did. A minute later Chano looked back and his face went tight and I turned and saw Garrison and Witliff running off the levee and into the swamp.

I snapped to the trick right off—they meant to use us for dog bait. I'd heard about it from Buck. If a man running from the dogs suddenly cut in a different direction, the pack would usually run past the spot where he turned—sometimes fifty yards or more—before they realized they'd lost the trail and turned back around to find it again. The trick was to start running with some other guys and then cut away from them, let them be the bait to keep leading the dogs on. But there were counters to every trick, Buck said, and he'd taught me one in case anybody ever tried to make me the dog bait.

The pack was louder now but still hadn't come in view around the bend. I beckoned Chano and we ran down the slope and into the trees. It was no trouble to follow their trail over that soft ground, our feet growing large and heavy with mud as we wove through the shadowy pines and cypress, cutting our hands and face on scrub brush and branches, ripping our skunk suits. We hadn't gone fifty yards when we stumbled onto a blackwater creek, and we dropped on our bellies and lapped at it like dogs. There were no footprints on the other bank, which meant that Garrison and Witliff were running in the creek.

We hustled after them, keeping to the bank to leave an easy trail. But my trick wouldn't be worth a damn if they didn't get out of the water pretty soon and start laying down a track of their own. Twenty yards farther on, they did. Where the creek turned off into the deeper swamp, their new tracks angled out and held on a bearing parallel to the levee. We kept after them, right on top of those footprints.

The pack was now so loud I expected to feel teeth in my ass any second. Then I realized the yelping was coming from my left—they had already overshot the spot where we came down the levee. And then the dogs realized it too and their timbre changed and fell away as they started backtracking. Their cries rose again when they recovered the scent, and they came yowling down the slope.

By then we'd caught sight of Garrison and Witliff. They were thirty yards ahead, slapping aside the brush with the barrels of their carbines as they went. They hadn't seen us, and we slowed down and moved deeper into the shadows in case they looked back. Garrison kept glancing in the direction of the levee. He must've been puzzled by the changing direction of the yapping of the dogs. He had expected to hear them catch us on the levee. That would've been the end of any scent for the hounds to follow up there. The hunting party might've searched around a little more after that, but they likely would've reckoned that the two cons still on the loose had headed into the swamp and would die there and good riddance. Once the party turned back, Garrison and Witliff could've cut back up to the levee and pushed on for Baton Rouge.

A neat plan, but I had a neater one—if it worked. The dogs sounded like they were no more than fifty yards behind us. I pointed to a spot up ahead where the ground to our left gave way into the shallow water of a cypress stand. Chano nodded, his eyes enormous. We jumped off the trail and into the shallows and went highstepping and scrabbling into the thick tangles of roots and then hunkered down in the water to our chins. My heart was lunging up into my throat.

They went by not fifteen yards from us—a dark crazed pack of howling beasts. A minute later their cries went even higher and there was a carbine report and then another and a dog was shrieking in pain and then the men's agonized screams were mingling with the dogs' wild snarlings. Then the hunting party went hustling by, a dozen men or more with longarms, huffing and cursing and laughing, saying they had the sumbitches, by God.

As soon as they were past us we were up and splashing through the trees and stumbling over roots and the only screaming we heard now was of the wounded dog. There came several gunshots and then only the high baying of the pack and the whooping of the hunters.

When we reached the edge of the swamp and caught sight of the levee we got down on our bellies in the shadowy muckwater to rest and wait for darkness. We stank so high it was a wonder the dogs didn't smell us from wherever they were—a wonder the men couldn't smell us. It was the first clear day in nearly two weeks and a pretty one, sunlight showing gently through the dense branches overhead, the sky beyond the trees cloudless and pale blue. I told myself to stay alert, be sharp, it wasn't over yet, and then fell asleep, though I didn't know it until I woke to the faint barking of dogs.

Less than a hundred yards north of us the hunting party was back on the levee. The sun was past its meridian. Chano was sleeping on his folded arms, his chin in the water, and I shook him awake and pointed. The dogs were on leashes now, milling and yapping, and the dogboys were loading them onto the wagons. The manhunters carried their rifles slung on their shoulders and were passing bottles around and smoking and their distant laughter rose and fell and then rose again. A pair of convicts in stripes emerged from the trees and started up the slope, carrying a body between them, and then two more cons came behind them with the other one. The bodies looked like they might be naked but I couldn't be sure from that distance, and I couldn't tell which was Garrison and which Witliff. I likely would've had a hard time telling them apart up close.

Even after they all left we stayed put. We took turns sleeping and keeping watch, listening hard for any searchers that might still be prowling the area. We drank from the water we lay in, waiting for dusk. And when at last the sun was down we got moving.

We kept a fast pace, sometimes jogging, mostly fast-walking. The weather helped to keep us stepping lively—the night was cold enough to show our breath, and our ragged skunk suits weren't much help against the chill. But at least there wasn't any wind. Now and then we went down the levee to drink from the river. I'd heard it said that drinking from the Mississippi was like drinking a mix of piss and mud but I didn't see how the river could be any worse than the swampwater we'd been drinking. I was anyway too tired to care. Every time I lay down to drink, it took a greater effort to get back on my feet. Every muscle ached and my joints felt like they'd rusted. The last couple of times we drank, Chano had to help me back up the levee. I had height and weight on the little bastard but not toughness.

The sky was crammed with stars. The moon rose late and cast the landscape in an eerie sepia glow and deep black shadows. Shortly before dawn the swamp began to give way to pastureland and rail fences and we spied a light about a quarter-mile off the levee and decided to see if we could find something to eat there. We went down the slope and into the pines and soon came to a clearing marked by a narrow road that passed through a scattering of ramshackle houses, some of them no more than tarpaper shacks. Several of them were now showing lamplight at their windows and it wouldn't be long before the whole hamlet was awake.

A dog started barking somewhere down the road, and then two others, a little closer by. We stood fast in the darkness under a tree, waiting to see if they'd come for us or if somebody would step outside to see what was nettling them. I wondered if Chano was thinking what I was—if he was remembering the talk at Camp M about how people who lived near the levee prayed every day for the chance to shoot a runaway convict and collect the state reward. But the dogs must've been penned or not very brave and we didn't see anybody come out for a look.

The nearest house looked to be one of the better ones, with a front porch and a tin roof, its side window dimly glowing in the shadow of a live oak, its chimney churning bright white smoke in the moonlight. We caught the aroma of something cooking and I went light in the head. Chano nudged me and I nodded and we snuck up to the window in a crouch and stood to one side of it with our backs to the wall. The windowsill was shoulder-high, the sash raised a few inches and letting out that wonderful smell. I sidled over and looked inside.

The kitchen. An oil lamp stood on a table set with three tin plates and forks and cups. The warmth of the black-iron stove carried to the window—and the aroma of ham frying in a skillet next to a steaming pot of coffee. An uncut loaf of bread was warming beside the stove. Chano peeked around me and turned up his palm in question. I was wondering the same thing: where in hell were they? We looked all around but there was still no sign of anybody out and about. The dogs had quit barking, which meant somebody had shut them up, which meant somebody was awake—but I didn't care, not with the smells of that ham and coffee calling to me. I pushed up gently on the sash and it rose with a tiny creak. I gestured for Chano to give me a boost. He formed a stirrup with his hands and I put my foot in it and he hoisted me. I stepped in through the window and for a long moment stood absolutely still, listening hard but hearing nothing other than the sizzling of the ham.

As I started to tiptoe toward the stove a man stepped into the room with an old single-barrel ten-gauge leveled squarely at my face. An old darkie with thick shoulders and white hair and bloodshot yellow eyes—and no expression on his face except a readiness to kill me if it came to that.

"Move even a little bit I blow off your dumbshit head," he said. The muzzle looked big as a porthole.

I thought, Ah hell, and put my hands up.

He gave a sidelong look to the window and I glanced over and saw Chano with his hands up, facing somebody I couldn't see.

"Any more you?" the old man said.

I shook my head. "No sir."

He ran his eyes over my ragged skunk suit and made a face of disgust. "Don't like convicts come in my house, stink it all up."

"Don't blame you," I said. I wasn't close enough to even try snatching for the gun.

"You run that old levee?" he said.

"Tried to."

"*Try* to? You all don't even know where you at, do you? It's not eight miles to Baton Rouge."

Jesus, I thought, so damn *close*.

A small boy leaned around the door and said, "You gone shoot em, Granddaddy?"

"Hush up, John Adams," the old man said. "Go get two pair my pants, two my shirts. And a pillowcase." The boy scooted away.

"There's tote sacks in that cabinet back you," the old man said to me. "Get you one."

I turned and opened the cabinet door and saw a stack of neatly folded sugar sacks, five-pound size. I took one.

"Put you some ham in it," the old man said. "Don't take it all, we ain't ate breakfast yet."

I stood there, not believing I'd heard him right.

"Go ahead on," he said.

Well hell. I plucked a slice of ham out of the hot pan with two fingers and dropped it in the sack, then snatched out another.

"Cut you some bread there."

I couldn't keep from drooling at the smell of the ham and had to wipe the slobber off my chin. I thought I must look like one of those halfwit bums you see on the streets of New Orleans.

The boy came back with the clothes and pillowcase and the old man said for me to hold out the pillowcase and for the boy to put the clothes in it and we both did as he said.

"Now you get," the old man said. "Don't let me see either you round here no more." He had a wide pale scar around the forward wrist and then I saw he had one on the other wrist too. Manacle scars.

"Listen, Uncle," I said, "I'm grateful to you for—"

"I ain't you uncle and don't be talking stuff. Just get."

He pointed me out the door. Chano was already in front. A large colored boy of maybe sixteen was holding a double-barrel on him.

"See them to the river," the old man said.

The darkness had given way to a gray dawnlight and the sun would soon be in the trees. The boy stayed well behind us as we made our way back through the woods.

When we saw the levee up ahead, we stopped to change clothes.

The old man's khaki pants were stained with blue paint and fit me fairly well around the waist although the leg bottoms didn't cover my ankles, and the shirt, a faded green thing covered with big yellow parrots, was only a little snug through the shoulders. There were two quarters in my skunk pants and I put them in my new pocket. Chano had to roll the bottoms of his black pants and the sleeves of his purple shirt. He looked like a walking bruise.

We put what was left of our prison stripes in the clothes sack and I handed it to the boy. "I know your granddaddy was up the river too," I said. "I seen his chain scars. What'd he do?"

He stared at me hard for a moment. "His family hungry so he stole a chicken. They give him thirty damn years. Take thirty years of a man's life for stealing a chicken. They bigger thieves than anybody."

"He ran this levee, didn't he?" I said. "Long time ago."

He shifted his eyes from one to the other of us. "You all go on and get."

"He's one of them who did it," I said.

You could see he wanted to keep his mouth shut but wanted to brag on it too. There was no hiding the pride in his face. He settled for saying, "You never know."

I couldn't hold back a laugh. "You damn sure don't!"

"Go on now," he said. He backed up into the bushes and then vanished as neatly as a stage trick.

We gobbled down the ham and bread in huge ravenous bites we almost choked on, then scaled back up to the levee crest and got on the move again.

I felt grand to be shed of those convict stripes—like I was somebody real again. I waved at a passing barge and the pilot waved back. I exchanged nods with a colored family fishing for bream from the bank with canepoles. I sang for a while as we went along—"Way

Down Yonder in New Orleans," "Ain't We Got Fun," "Breezin' Along with the Breeze"— mixing in a few oldies for the hell of it: "A Hot Time in the Old Town Tonight" and "The Man That Broke the Bank at Monte Carlo" and "Hello Ma Baby." Chano smiled and bobbed his head in time to the tunes.

The sun was above the trees when we heard the ringings and whistlings and clankings of trains and caught the smells of cinders and lubricating oil. A minute later we came in view of the Baton Rouge rail-yard. We figured to get some sleep in the nearby woods before jumping a freight for New Orleans, but almost as soon as I closed my eyes I was taken with a sharp pain in my gut, and I barely managed to keep from shitting my pants before getting them down and squatting behind a bush.

I had to drop my pants several times over the next two hours. I didn't know what to blame, the water or the food, but Chano didn't have any problem. I'd heard that a Mexican stomach could stand anything and now I believed it. Naturally I didn't get much rest between attacks, and when they finally eased off I was too wrung out to do anything but sleep.

At some point I dreamt I was back in Camp M and hearing the morning bell, and I started awake to the clanging of a train and remembered where I was. I laughed out loud and Chano rolled over and grinned at me. He was probably feeling as goofy as I was to be free. It occurred to me that I didn't know what he had in mind to do.

"Know somebody in New Orleans?" I said.

He shook his head, then jutted his chin at me in question.

"Yeah. It's where I'm headed. Where *you* going?"

He jutted his chin to westward.

"Texas?"

He shrugged.

"Mexico?"

He shrugged again. I didn't blame him. Never tell anybody anything you didn't have to. In his case it was easy to keep from talking too much.

"Good plan," I said, and he smiled.

Right after sundown we cut through the woods and came out by the tracks just past the railyard. I was still feeling a little peaked but at least my gut had settled. We didn't have long to wait before the next southbound started chugging out, slowly gaining speed, and we ran to it and swung up into an empty slat-sided cattle car. I hugged myself against the chill wind as we sat with our legs dangling out and watched the darkening countryside go rolling by.

Not an hour later we saw the lights of New Orleans up ahead and the train began to slow down. About fifty yards before it entered the railyard we jumped off and tumbled down the rocky bed grade and I generally banged up whatever part of me hadn't been sore already.

We brushed ourselves off as the rest of the cars went clacking by. If there was something to be said I was the one who'd have to say it, but I couldn't come up with anything. He flapped a hand at the west side of the railyard and I nodded and hooked my thumb toward town. He looked at the ground around him like somebody checking to see if he'd dropped something.

"Hey," I said. I dug in my pocket and took out the two quarters and held one out to him. "In case you feel like buying yourself a car."

He looked at the two-bit piece a moment, then smiled and took it and put it in his pocket. Then raised a hand in farewell and turned and quickly crossed over the tracks and into the deeper shadows and was gone.

The French Quarter was as loud as usual this Saturday night. Klaxons blatting on the streets, boat horns blaring on the river. People laughing, shouting their conversations. Jazz pulsing from the clubs and all along the streets in a jangling tangle of melodies. I stood on a corner and took it all in, this swell free world I'd been away from for more than nine months.

The sidewalks were packed with carousers, with couples and sailors and here and there some college kids, with tourists and conventioneers. Everybody happy and most of them drunk and trying hard to stay that way, passing their flasks around, Prohibition be damned. Hustlers of every stripe working the streets. Short-conners and whores, monte players, hot-stuff sellers. The rubes getting skinned by pickpockets even as they swayed to the curbside fiddlers and accordionists and popped their fingers along with the tapdancing colored boys.

Women everywhere—sweet Christ, the women. Laughing and

teasing with their beaus. Doing little dance moves as they went down the street, flashing their legs under short flouncy skirts and flapper dresses. Showing off all that skin in numbers with no back to them and necklines down to there. I was already light in the head from the aromas wafting out of the restaurants, and the nearness of so much finelooking stuff after I'd been so long without it made me even dizzier. It didn't help that I was feeling wrung out and a fever was creeping up on me. The evening was pleasantly cool but I was soaked with sweat.

Down the street I spotted some guys I recognized—a pair of second-story men and a fence named Pogo George, who had a store on Canal. They were arguing on the sidewalk in front of the Paris Theatre. I kept my face averted as I went by.

We'd never pulled a job in any part of New Orleans—"You don't shit where you eat" was Buck's eloquent way of explaining it—and naturally we hadn't talked about our business to anybody except those we had to deal with. But the Quarter was a compact world and word got around about everybody in it. The big guys—the Black Hands—left you alone as long as you didn't try cutting in on any of their trade, but the place was full of smalltimers who'd rat you out in a minute if they thought they could gain by it. No telling who might catch sight of me and somehow or other know I was supposed to be in Angola and dash off to make a deal with the cops.

As I passed the Bon Temps restaurant I caught a glimpse of a wild-haired creature in ill-fitting pants and zany shirt and took a few steps more before turning back to have a better look at my reflection in the mirrored doors. The only image I'd seen of myself since Verte Rivage was in shaving mirrors the size of my hand. I regarded a rawboned frame and a dark whiskered face of sharp angles and hot-looking eyes. It was unlikely that anyone would know me without a real careful look. A pair of young girls brushed past in the heavy sidewalk traffic and I saw the pinch of their faces, their swap of horrified looks, their gawping stares back at me, the source of such foul odor.

As much as I wanted to avoid being spotted, what I wanted even more was a cold beer. The nearest speakeasy was in the backroom of the Anchor Café down the street and I made straight for it. I paused inside the door and peered about for familiar faces. When I didn't spot any I went up to the bar and slapped down my quarter. I drank two beers in a row without taking the mug from my mouth each time till I'd drained it. Then let out a sequence of burps that burned my nose and made me wipe my eyes.

"Sometimes it's like a fire we got to put out, ain't it?" the barkeep said. It was hard to tell if he was joking. I got my nickel in change and bummed a cigarette from the guy beside me and went out again.

I headed for the south end of Toulouse, where Buck and Russell shared a two-bedroom apartment in a building called La Maison Dumas. A nice place but not showy. They could easily have afforded something more elegant but they didn't want to live in any way that might raise too many questions about how they made their living.

"On the other hand," Russell had said to me, "there's no need to live in a dump like yours, neither." Actually, I liked my little place on Esplanade precisely because it was a dump. I could abandon it in a heartbeat if I had to and I'd never miss it for a minute. I only hoped Buck or Russell had gone over there and picked up my clothes before the landlord confiscated my stuff and rented the place to somebody else.

I'd been thinking about what I'd say when they answered my knock and saw me standing there. "Got tired of waiting on you boys to bust me out so I took care of the matter myself." Something like that.

But the guy who came to the door was a stranger in undershirt and suspenders. He said he and his wife had been living there for more than two months. I checked with the landlady, who kept the chain on her door as she peeked out and at first didn't recognize me. I smelled gumbo simmering in her kitchen. My uncles had moved away in a hurry, she said. She had no idea where they might have gone. And then I was staring at a shut door.

So. Up Decatur and past the clamor of Jackson Square and the French Market and onto Ursuline. Halfway up the block was an ornate two-story apartment building with a lawn and a spiked wrought-iron fence and a locked front gate that only the residents had a key to. Some of the taller palms in the courtyard showed above the roof, their fronds lit up from below. I scaled the fence in the shadow of an oak and dropped onto the grass on the other side. The simple exertion made everything whirl for a moment and had me sucking for air and pouring sweat.

The courtyard was illuminated by high black-iron lamps and contained a lush garden still several weeks from full flower. A redbrick walkway took me past a large goldfish fountain shadowed by palms and schefflera. I went up the stairs to the second floor. Most of the window shutters were open and as I went along the gallery I caught sight of people at their supper, conversing, listening to radios, reading, staring at nothing. In one place all the mirrors were covered with bedsheets, a common practice in homes where someone had recently died. I stopped at the corner apartment and stared in the window at a dimly lighted, nicely appointed living room with tall shelves of books and framed art works on every wall. A radio on a side table was softly playing. "East of the Moon, West of the Stars."

I was about to rap on the sill when she came out of the bedroom with an empty wineglass in each hand. Barefoot, white terry robe loosely belted. She slung her black hair over her shoulder with a toss of her head and went into the kitchen and a minute later came out again with both glasses showing red wine. She set one glass down on the side table and turned up the volume on the radio. Then closed her eyes and swayed to the music. And then suddenly went still—and quickly turned and saw me. And dropped the other glass to bounce on the carpet and splash wine at her feet.

"Brenda, sugar?" A man's voice from the bedroom. She stared at me, a hand at the open neck of her robe.

I felt the last of my strength draining away and I slumped against the window jamb. I tried to smile at her but couldn't tell if I pulled it off.

"Sonny," she said. And came for me as I went down.

We'd met a year earlier, at an art exhibition sponsored by the mother of one of my schoolmates. I was just a few days graduated from Gulliver Academy and I'd had my fill of everything that smacked of academics, but my buddy said there'd be free champagne and some finelooking women, so I went. I hadn't been there twenty minutes when we were introduced. An hour after that we were in bed at my place on Esplanade.

Brenda Marie Matson. A year older than I, she had been managing the Fontaine Gallery on Dauphine Street since graduating from the Institute of the Magdalene, a ritzy Catholic girls' school over near Loyola. She was smart as a whip and could've breezed through college, but like me she'd had enough of studies. The gallery belonged to a family friend who lived in Paris and let her run it as she saw fit. She certainly didn't need the job—her father was founder of Matson Petroleum. He'd been a wildcatter who brought in one of the biggest gushers in Louisiana. Her mother was a woman of French Creole pedigree whose family never forgave her for marrying the son of ragamuffin Irish, his oil money be damned. Both her parents were four years dead, lost at sea when their chartered yacht sank off the Spanish coast.

She'd won various ballet competitions and could have danced professionally if she'd wanted to. Her toes were gnarled and callused and she didn't like for me to look at them. She told me this one night when we were naked on her bed and I was massaging her feet. I said her toes were the hard proof of her talent and something to be proud of, like a soldier's wounds or a fencing master's scars.

"Oh God," she said, "a romantic."

I lightly bit her big toe and said gruffly, "You better believe it, tootsie"—and she laughed and snared me with her legs and pulled me to her.

She loved books and art and music, but her greatest pleasure was in sex. I knew plenty of girls who enjoyed it but not like Brenda Marie. She had no inhibitions at all in bed, was ready to try anything. I'd never had two girls at the same time until the night she introduced a blonde friend named Candace to our sporting. She called it a special treat for me—and it damn sure was—but they had as much fun as I did, and I suspected it wasn't the first time they'd done such things with each other. I didn't ask her about it, though. And I never asked if she spent time with other men.

That was what she liked best about me, she said—that I wasn't jealous or possessive. "It's because you're not in love with me," she said. "Oh, you love being with me, and I love being with you, and that's just perfect. Only don't fall *in* love with me. Men become bores when they fall in love."

She was preaching to the converted. Most of the love poems and stories I'd read in school, most romantic plays I'd seen and damn near every movie, presented love as either life's greatest happiness or as some kind of thrilling adventure that was worth every minute of it even if it ended in heartache, as it so often did in novels and plays. Both notions had always struck me as a crock. From what I'd seen and heard of love in real life, whatever thrill it provided didn't last all that long, and the aftereffects could be a whole lot worse than just a heartache. Buck was a perfect example. He'd paid a godawful price for falling in love. Brenda Marie didn't have to fret. I wasn't about to fall in love with her or anybody else.

If she had other lovers, they couldn't have been very important. Whenever I telephoned to ask if she wanted to see me, she always said yes, anytime—as long as it was at her place. The one time she'd been to my apartment had been enough for her. As for me, I'd sometimes fool around with some other girl, mainly to remind myself I was free to do it, but most evenings I was with Brenda Marie.

I had told her I was working with my uncles, that they were breaking me in—which was true, only not as a sales representative for a tool company, which was what I told her. I might've picked a better bullshit occupation. She'd looked at me like she was waiting for the punchline of a joke.

I'd known her for two weeks when they took me on my first job, a small bank in Lafayette. The thing went smooth as glass and we pulled down nearly two grand. As I drove us back to Baton Rouge to drop off the stolen Olds and retrieve Buck's Ford, I couldn't stop babbling about how my heart had been in my throat while I waited for them to come out of the bank, how nothing I'd ever done before—not boxing or the midnight car races on the lake shore with my school buddies or shagging girls at high noon under the boardwalk at the lake while people were strolling directly above us, *nothing*—had the kick of what we'd just done. Buck said if I didn't shut up *he'd* give me a kick—he'd kick my ass out of the car. I sang all the way to New Orleans. I was into "I'm Sitting on Top of the World" when Russell put his hands over his ears and said, "Oh Jesus, I surrender. Take me in. *Jail's* better than having to listen to this!" I just laughed and kept on singing.

That evening Brenda Marie said she'd never seen me so "animated," as she put it. I told her it had been a very good day on the job. She said she never would've guessed saleswork could be so stimulating. She was nobody's fool, and I figured she was curious about what I was really doing with Buck and Russell, but she was too cool to press me about it. She smiled at the gusto I took in the dirty rice and étouffée we had for supper, in the high humor I found in everything even mildly funny either of us said. The sex that night was out of this world. She said if she'd known that salesmen were such Valentinos she would've taken up with one long before now.

Three weeks later we hit a loan company all the way over in Mobile. Buck and Russell didn't like to pull more than one heist every six weeks or so—they loved the action, but they also loved to take it easy and enjoy the fruits of their labor. Lately, however, they'd been getting some tips too good to pass up. Mobile was another piece of cake and good for more than a thousand.

I'd asked if this time I could go in on the stickup and one of them do the driving, and they said hell no. "You got lots to learn yet, Sonny," Buck said. "And until you do, you're the driver."

"Of course now, if you don't *want* to do the driving anymore . . ." Russell said with a big smile.

"Hell yeah, I want to," I said. "It's just I'd like to do the stickup sometime, that's all."

"Yeah, well, all in due time," Russell said.

I did like doing the driving—hell, I loved it. The Mobile job left me as exhilarated as the one before, as sharply alive to the taste and feel and smell of things, especially of Brenda. She still didn't question me, but it was obvious she was getting pretty damn curious about what I'd been up to.

She met Buck and Russell only once, when we all took supper together one night at an Italian place on Burgundy. They were at their charming best and she was delighted to discover they were fraternal twins. She said they were so young-looking to be my uncles and she laughed at Buck's obvious pride in being the elder by four minutes. Russell had brought Charlie along and the girls seemed to like each other, though they didn't really have much chance to get well acquainted.

They told her stories about me when I was a boy, including the one about when I was eleven years old and the neighbor woman caught me playing with her daughter's bare behind in the garage.

"The woman brought him home by the ear," Buck said, "and this rascal tells his mother they weren't doing nothing but playing doctor. You be careful, pretty girl, he don't talk you into letting him practice on you for his M.D."

Brenda Marie laughed and said it was too late, I'd already gotten away with that one.

The next day, Charlie told me she thought Brenda was the perfect girl for me. "Not only pretty but so *smart*."

Russell hugged her from behind and said, "You're a smart cookie yourself, girl," and she just beamed. But he agreed that Brenda Marie was a real honey, and Buck did too. Then after Charlie left, Buck went into one of his lectures about how I best be careful not to fall in love if I knew what was good for me. As if I needed to hear it from anybody.

The day before Memorial Day we crossed into Mississippi and hit a bank in Hattiesburg. They were in and out in seven minutes and I casually drove us away with $2,500. It couldn't have been easier if we'd owned the bank.

Buck couldn't believe how simple the last three jobs had gone. Russell said it was having me along that did it. "This Sonny's some kind of charm," he said.

"Kid probably thinks they're always this easy," Buck said. He gave me a tap on the back of the head as I drove us along. "Listen boy, we been real lucky so far, but you never know. You have to be ready for anything, and I mean every time."

"I'm always ready," I said.

"Get a load of this guy," Buck said. "Jesse goddam James."

We got back to the Quarter at sundown and I went to Brenda's without even stopping at my place first. I tossed my Gladstone on her sofa and whirled her around the room like a ballroom dancer, then picked her up and took her to the bedroom.

Afterward I went in the shower. When I came out she was sitting crosslegged on the bed and holding my .44 in her lap like a serious letter she'd just finished reading. The Gladstone was open at the foot of the bed.

"I guess you need this to persuade any customer who won't fall for the standard sales pitch, huh?"

"It's loaded," I said.

"I know it," she said. She raised the revolver in a two-hand shooter's grip and sighted on a ceramic ballet figurine on the dresser. "Daddy taught me to shoot. I'm pretty good. Want to see me murder that toe dancer?" She cocked the piece.

"It'll likely go through that wall and the next one too," I said. "It'll be fun explaining to the cops how you shot the neighbor lady."

She eased down the hammer and rested the piece on her thigh. I'd been about to lay a line of patter on her about needing the gun as protection against hijackers as we drove from town to town on our sales routes, but the way she was looking at me made me forget what I was going to say. The way she was smiling.

"You're no salesman or ever will be," she said. It wasn't an accusation. Her eyes were all over me, like she'd never really seen me before. Her nipples were drawn tight. "You're some kind of goddam *bandit* is what you are."

I smiled back at her.

"*Aren't* you?"

I shrugged. "Ask me no questions, I'll tell you no lies."

"Hell, that's probably a lie right there." But she was still looking at me in that glint-eyed way she did when she was all heated up.

She put the gun aside and lay back and beckoned me with all her fingers.

I dropped my towel and went.

Three weeks later she knew enough not to ask where I was going when I kissed her so long and said I'd be back in a few days.

And I set out with Buck and Russell to take down the bank at Verte Rivage.

The Mexican's file says he is Sebastian Tomas Carrera. Claimed birthplace Brownsville, Texas. Prior convictions—petty theft, Houston; assault and battery, Lafayette. Stabbed a white man dead in a New Iberia poolroom and drew fifty years. Had served nearly four years of his sentence at the time he escaped. Certified mute. Remnant of tongue bears evidence of nonmedical excision, years prior. Eagle tattoo covering large portion of back. Last known address in Houston. No known next of kin.

The record on Lionel Buckman tells of no previous arrests, no official documents on file. The man figures everything in the jacket is bullshit except the photograph and physical details. He's always believed the name was phony but it didn't matter so long as the kid took the fall. Now the bastard is absconded and it matters plenty. He detaches the picture and puts it in his coat pocket. Then tosses both files back on the warden's desk. The warden gawks from the files to the pocket where the man has put the photo. He looks like he's received incorrect change for a twenty. The man's eyes hold on his. The warden clears his throat, then smiles crookedly and resumes his discourse.

A fact's a fact, he says, and for a fact the trail gave out on the levee. The dogs had to turn back around to find it and then chased it into the swamp and brung down two of the sumbitches and we carried out what was left of them. As for the other two, what they obviously did was try to run the swamp, that's what kinda fools they were. No tracking them in that water but so what? Onliest place to track them to woulda been a quicksand pit or a gator hole. Their bones are this minute buried in the muck or been made into gator shit on a bayou bottom. Now sir, everbody understands your interest in the matter even though you done retired, but you can rest easy that the sumbitch who murdered your boy has been made to pay for it, by Jesus. . . .

But the man is already halfway to the door and the warden finally thinks to shut up.

II

*I*n my fevered sleep I heard a deep tolling of bells and had one bad
dream after another, mostly about Camp M. I saw dogs tearing at
convicts like rats fighting over a garbage scrap. Headless men hacking
at cane. A gang of cons with snakes hanging from their faces. Men
hobbling on bare feet twisted by mutilated heelstrings. Sometimes I'd
see Brenda Marie's face over me, but never clearly. I'd hear her voice as
if she were at a distance; I couldn't understand what she was saying.
Sometimes I faintly heard other female voices and high laughter.

And then I was awake. It took me a minute to realize I was in her
bed. The bells were at it again, and now I recognized them as belong-
ing to the Catholic church down the street. Late-afternoon sunlight
slanted through the balcony doorway. Then the bells quit their clangor
and I heard a Brandenburg concerto playing low in the next room.

I was naked under the sheet and smelling slightly sour but not too
bad. My hands and arms were clean, and my whiskered face, and I
knew she'd washed me. The fever had passed, but my mouth was dry,

my throat scratchy. A pitcher and a tumbler stood on the bedside table. I sat up and poured a glass of water and my hand shook slightly as I brought it to my mouth. I'd never tasted anything so sweet. I wasn't in pain but I felt like my bones had been hollowed.

She came into the room carrying a basin of soapy water and an armful of towels and saw me sitting up and she let out a gleeful little yelp and hastened to put the things on the table and almost knocked over the water pitcher, then took my face in her hands and kissed me hard.

"Welcome back to the world, Mr. Van Winkle."

Now that I was awake, she said, she could give me a proper washing. I felt fit enough to bathe myself in a tub but she said to hush and made me lean this way and that while she spread several towels under me so she could go at me with a washcloth while we talked.

She said that at first sight she'd thought I was an Indian at her window, my face was so much darker than when she'd last seen me. The fellow I'd heard in the bedroom had helped her to get me inside and into bed. She told him I was a cousin who'd been working for an oil company in Central America, that a case of malaria I'd picked up last year must have acted up again and got me sent back to New Orleans.

"I doubt he believed a word of it," she said. "I mean, your clothes, for God's sake. But he knows better than to ask me too many questions. Lift up." She tapped my arm and I raised it so she could get at my armpit with a soapy cloth, then rinse it clean with a damp one, then dry it with a towel.

"I have to say, sweetie, the smell of you was enough to chase him off," she said. "He's a violinist in the symphony orchestra—very sensitive type. Truth to tell, I thought of putting you out in the alley for the refuse wagon to pick up." She smiled and pecked me on the lips, then started on the other underarm.

I'd been there two nights and days. She had summoned a doctor yesterday morning, a family acquaintance of reliable discretion. He diagnosed me as a case of fevered exhaustion and gave me an injection of something and told her to give me water every hour. She'd managed a few times to get me to sip from a glass she held to my mouth, and even at some of the chicken broth she spooned for me.

"You'd open your eyes," she said, "but you weren't really seeing me. You had me scared, baby." She washed around my neck and dabbed it dry. What she wanted to know of course was what happened and where the hell I'd been all this time and why I hadn't sent word to her.

The trick to good lying was to tell as much of the truth as you could, only not exactly or entirely, not even to those with no tie to your doings or reason to hurt you—because you never knew who they might pass it on to, deliberately or not. We'd hit a bank in Arkansas, I told her, and the job went bad. Buck and Russell got clear but I was caught and sent up for five years. I didn't write her because I didn't want to think too much about her—it would've made things even rougher if I had. Then I finally escaped and here I was. But Buck and Russell weren't—at least they weren't where they used to live. Did she have any idea where they were?

"That's *it*?" she said. "*Nine* months and that's your story? You went to prison and didn't write me and now you're back. The end?"

"Nothing else to tell," I said. "Take my word for it, honey, there's nothing more boring than prison. What about Buck and Russell?"

She stared at me a moment like she was trying to see behind my eyes, then got up and left the room. She returned with a small envelope and handed it to me. "Sonny" was scrawled on the front. The envelope had been cut open. I looked at her.

"Hey, mister," she said, "I didn't know if you were dead or alive, if I'd ever see you again or what."

The sheet inside read, "Dolan's," and below that, "B."

Jimmyboy Dolan. I had intended to check with him anyway, but they'd wanted to be sure I did. I kept my face blank but my heart was dancing.

"It was under my door one morning," she said. She began laving my chest. "About three months ago, I guess. I thought it meant you'd be showing up soon. But after a couple of months, still no you, so I took a peek. I thought maybe it'd say where you were. It's not the most detailed letter I ever read. I know 'B' is Buck, but what's Dolan's, a speakeasy or what? Or should I say *who*? What's going on?"

"Damned if I know," I said. I slipped the note back in the envelope and put it on the bedside table. "Strange message. Maybe he was drunk when he wrote it."

"You're such a liar," she said. "What?—you think I'm going to blab it all over town? It really vexes me, Sonny, that you don't trust me. You'll probably think I robbed you while you were sleeping. You didn't have but a nickel in your pockets, you know that?"

"Christ's sake, girl, I trust you. I'm *here*, aren't I?"

"*Such* a liar," she said, but I could see her pique was more affected than real. She pushed the sheet down to my hips and began bathing my stomach with slow circular strokes.

She said she'd gotten worried when I still hadn't come back after a week, so she'd gone to my place and slid a note under the door, leaving a tiny corner of it visible. She looked every day and the note was always there. It went like that for more than a month and then one day the apartment was occupied by somebody else. She couldn't check with Buck and Russell because I'd never told her where they lived and there was no listing for them in the directories. She scoured the newspapers every day but saw nothing about anybody who might've been us.

"If you all weren't so damned secretive about everything, I might not've had to fret so much."

"Yeah," I said, "I guess that fiddle player was one way to get your mind off fretting for a while."

She narrowed her eyes at me. "Hey boy, it's not the same thing and you know it. And that fiddler is *my* business—just like I told him *you're* my business."

I raised my hands in a gesture of surrender. "You're right," I said, and I meant it. "It was a lousy crack."

She smiled. "All right then, you're forgiven." Then cut her eyes to my lower belly where she'd been stroking me with the washcloth. "Oh my," she said. "What's this?"

She shoved the sheet off me. "Goodness! Look at this poor rascal trying to raise up on his feet."

"Hey girl, quit it. I'm in no condition for this." That's what I said—but if she'd quit it I might've wept.

"Shush," she said. "Don't scare him. All he needs is a helping hand and a big kiss of encouragement." She bent to it, cooing, "Come here, baby, come to momma."

And it pretty quick did.

I woke the next morning feeling grand. The room was full of soft sunlight. Brenda Marie slept snugly against me, her breath warm on my neck and her black hair draped on my chest, one long leg between mine. She smelled wonderfully of seawater and flowers. I ran my hand over her buttocks and marveled at their trim swells. She came awake without opening her eyes, smiling, pressing herself tighter against me, affecting to purr like a cat. I stroked her flank and she shifted so I could get at her breast. She worked her hand between us and chuckled lewdly on finding me ready as can be. She wriggled herself under me and I slipped in smoothly and her legs closed around me and pulled me deeper. We rocked together and she drew my face down to hers and kissed me and lightly bit my lips and I don't think I lasted thirty seconds before letting go with a groan and col-lapsing on her, gasping like I'd run across town. She laughed softly and thumped me on the back and said to get off her before she smothered, then rolled with me to keep me inside her. And then we slept again.

The next time we woke up it was early afternoon and I was ravenous. We hadn't eaten since the leftover chicken stew she'd warmed up the night before. She had an assistant she trusted to run the gallery in her absence but a collector from Houston was coming late that afternoon to see some of her new acquisitions and she had to be there. We had enough time to have a late lunch before she went.

"Well then, let's get a move on," I said, slapping her on the bottom and getting out of bed. She hadn't seen the scars on my ass until then, and she said, "Oh, those *bastards*." It was the nearest I'd seen her come to crying since the time I'd told her that my father, like hers, had drowned.

I'd always kept a shaving razor and change of clothes in my Gladstone in her closet. As she gave my white suit a cursory pressing she said she'd more than once thought to throw away my stuff but couldn't bring herself to do it—it would've felt like giving up hope of seeing me again. What I couldn't find in the Gladstone was a .38-caliber bulldog I'd left tucked among some undershirts. She saw me digging around in the bag and said, "Here," and went to the bedside table and took the snubnose pistol out of the drawer and handed it to me.

"Made me feel like some kind of desperado to keep it close to hand," she said. I checked the cylinder—five chambers loaded and an empty one under the hammer.

"Every time I'd handle it I'd think of other things of yours I'd handled," she said. "Aren't I just *awful*?"

"You're a shameless wanton and I'll beat purple hell out of anybody who says different."

She laughed deep in her throat and hugged my neck and bit my ear just hard enough to make me wince. "You're *such* a charmer," she said.

She stood in the bathroom door and watched me shave. The tall bath window gave onto a cluster of banana trees mottled with sunlight, their green fronds stirring in a gentle breeze spiced with the aromas of dinner hour. A streetcar bell jangled in the distance. A produce vendor sang his wares. A neighbor's saxophone rendered a slow and rueful version of "Blue Skies." Angola was about 150 miles from where I was standing but seemed farther removed than the moon. I suddenly felt so free my hand shook and I nicked my chin with the straight razor.

The suit pants were a little loose in the butt and I had to cinch my belt two notches higher than before and my shirt collar felt roomier under my finger, but my jacket still hung well on my shoulders. Brenda said she liked my new leanness.

When she went to get dressed I slipped the bulldog under my waistband at my back, then stood out on the balcony and smoked a cigarette. The air rang with the afternoon church bells. Flowers bloomed in large clay pots on every balcony. A formation of yellowhead pelicans sailed over the tiled rooftops and the blarings of shiphorns carried from the river. Schoolgirls in blue-and-white uniforms came clamoring out of St. Cecelia's, set free for the day. They passed in flocks along the lacework iron fence and I recognized their happy chatter as the voices and laughter I'd heard in my fevered sleep.

We ate at a restaurant down the street. I put away a thick steak covered with fried green peppers and onions, a bowl of red beans and rice, a platter of eggs scrambled with chopped sausage. Brenda Marie had softboiled eggs and a buttered croissant and smiled as she watched me gorge myself, at one point touching my arm and giving me a look to keep me from wolfing my food. She asked about my plans for the rest of the afternoon. I said I was going to walk around the Quarter and look at things I hadn't seen since last summer.

Back on the sidewalk she slipped me a ten and gave me her spare keys to the outer courtyard gate and to the apartment. She kissed me full on the mouth and pressed her belly hard against me and said she'd be home around eight and for me not to overexert myself.

"At least not till I get back," she said, licking a fingertip and putting it to my lips. She laughed and waggled her fingers at me and I watched the play of her long trim legs as she strode off down the street.

Jimmyboy Dolan had partnered with Buck and Russell for about a year. But he was a bad gambler and got in arrears for close to a thousand dollars at one of Cockeye Calder's clubs. Cockeye wasn't one for complex negotiations with anybody who owed him money or tried to cheat him. Everyone knew about the Memphis cardsharp who got caught doing tricks at one of Cockeye's tables and paid for his folly with the fingers of one hand. Cockeye told Jimmyboy he had a month to pony up what he owed. He charged him a daily interest that doubled the debt the first week. Jimmyboy could've paid him off with his cut from a job he did with Buck and Russell a few days later but that wasn't his way. He made a partial payment on the debt and spent the rest on good times and gambling at other clubs around town. Who knows what he was thinking. When his month was up he got a visit from a pair of Cockeye's collectors. His tally had inflated to almost five thousand dollars by then but he could only come up with a few hundred. Their disappointment was so great they sawed off his right foot.

When Buck and Russell introduced me to him about three months later, Jimmyboy was working as a car mechanic and living in the back room of the garage and doing his best not to provoke certain kinds of people anymore. He had to give Cockeye Calder all but five dollars of his pay every week and figured to clear his debt in about five years. He wore a cumbersome prosthesis that wasn't much more than a heavy block of wood shaped like a fat dark boot. He walked like he was dragging a ball and chain and the wood foot clumped with every step. Watching him make his way to the men's room, Russell whispered, "I thought *I* had a limp."

I found him all alone in the garage and he seemed pleased to see me. "*Hey*, Sonny boy!" he said. "Ain't seen you in a coon's age, man. Where the hell you been keeping yourself?"

I told him I'd been living with a girl in Atlanta for the past nine months and then recently got a note in the mail from Buck saying he and Russell were moving, but for some damn reason he hadn't told me where. He only said to come see Jimmyboy. So, here I was. Where were they?

He didn't know, but he believed they'd left town, probably left the whole damn state. They'd stopped by the garage about four months ago for just long enough to say so long.

"I figure they were feeling the heat from the Bogalusa job, don't you?"

"What Bogalusa job?"

I didn't know about that? By the time he'd read about it in the newspaper the bank robbery was two days old and Buck and Russell were one day gone. What happened was, a customer tried to be a hero and jumped on one of the two robbers. While the other robber beat the hero on the head with a pistol to get him loose of his partner, the guard retrieved the gun they'd made him drop and opened fire, shooting three times and wounding a woman in the leg but missing both robbers before one of them shot him in the stomach. The bandits ran out and hijacked a car and made a getaway—but without a dime of the bank's money. The guard died a few hours later.

"They came and *told* you about it?"

"No man, I saw it in the paper."

"How'd the paper know it was them?"

"It *didn't*. The cops didn't either. What happened is, the one the hero grabbed lost his hat and sunglasses in the scuffle and a couple of people got a good look at him before he put them back on. The paper had a police sketch in it and wanted to know if anybody recognized him. Well, it wasn't no photograph, but it was a good enough likeness I knew I was looking at Russell."

"And they *hijacked* a car?"

"What the paper said. Sounds like somebody's driver lit a shuck ahead of schedule, you ask me."

"Yeah, it does. Anybody who'd do that is likely to rat out his partners if he gets in a spot. And there's the guys who recognized the newspaper sketch. I can see why they left town."

"Hey, Sonny, never in the *world* would I breathe a word to *anybody*."

"I know," I said. "But you couldn't've been the only one to recognize the sketch. What I don't get is why tell me to come see you if they didn't tell you where they were going."

"Well hell, man, to pick up what they left for you. I thought that's what you come for."

He clumped off into his little back room, its door screeching on its hinges, and returned a minute later with an envelope of the same sort they'd left with Brenda Marie. It was smudged with grease but still sealed.

The note inside said: "Star fill sta next RR depot Houston. See Miller."

It made me proud that they'd thought it was even possible I might break out. And because they knew I'd come looking for them if I did, they'd left this trail for me, despite their own good reasons not to, being on the run themselves. That was them.

Jimmyboy wanted to buy me a drink at a speak down the block but I begged off, saying I had a ladyfriend waiting. I promised to take him up on the offer in a day or two.

I repacked my bag and took fifty dollars from the cash Brenda Marie kept in her desk. Then wrote a note: I had a lead on Buck and Russell and was sorry to go like this but I had to catch the next train. I owed her more than the money and I'd be back as soon as I could and blah blah blah.

I folded the note and propped it against the radio in the living room. Then went out and turned the lock and slipped the key under the door. Then went to the station and bought a ticket and read magazines and drank coffee until my train boarded and then chugged off into the darkness.

The sign for Star's filling station stood atop a high pole and was visible from the front steps of the depot. The late-morning sun was warm and I walked down the street with the Gladstone in hand and my suit jacket slung over my shoulder. The building was fronted by a row of gasoline pumps, its windows dust-coated, its sideboards paint-peeling and warped. A mechanic was bent over the open hood of a Model T at the far end of the lot. Across the street was a small grocery where a man in an apron stood in the door and watched me.

A little bell tinkled over the door when I went in. A husky sandy-haired guy with a toothpick in his mouth sat behind the counter reading an adventure magazine. He looked at me over his reading glasses and then out at the pumps to see if I had a car waiting for gas. He had a drinker's face—puffy bloodshot eyes, his nose and cheeks webbed with red veins.

"If you selling something, boy, save your breath."

"You Mr. Miller?"

"Mr. Faulk."

"There a fella named Miller around here?"

"Sometimes."

"Where can I find him?" I said.

He rolled the toothpick from one side of his mouth to the other. "What you want with him?"

"I got business with him."

"What business is that?"

"Private business. Look mister, just tell me where I can find him."

"You ain't told me *your* name."

"That's none of your concern," I said. "My business is with Miller."

The man sighed and removed his spectacles and massaged the bridge of his nose with two fingers. I told myself to keep cool, there was nothing to be gained by getting blackassed. "All right," I said. "The name's Bill Loomis. Satisfied?"

He seemed to give the name some thought for a moment, then spat away the toothpick. "Sorry," he said. "Can't help you." He put his glasses back on and picked up the magazine.

"Hey man, you wanted my name, you got it."

His expression was utterly blank. I cursed under my breath and started for the door, figuring to ask the mechanic about Miller, ask the grocer across the street. Then I thought, What the hell—you never know. I stopped and turned and said, "LaSalle, goddammit. I'm Sonny LaSalle."

He put the magazine down again and looked like he might be thinking of smiling. "That so?" he said. He glanced out the window again. "Well now tell me, Mr. LaSalle: You ever hear of a fella named Ansel Mitchum?"

I felt like my horse had come in at thirty to one. "I guess I have."

"Didn't old Ansel have him a nickname? I disremember what it was."

"I believe it might be Buck."

He grinned back at me and put out his hand. "Miller Faulk," he said as we shook. "Lived in Narlens most my life and known your uncles since way back when. Sorry for all the caution, Sonny, but it's lots of fellas always looking for lots of other fellas, and a man can't be too careful about who he helps find who, if you know what I mean."

It was an hour's ride to Galveston on an electric railcar over a causeway flanked by gleaming baywater as flat as a tabletop. A humid but pretty afternoon smelling heavily of the sea.

I got my bearings according to the rough pencil map Faulk had drawn for me and made my way along the island's shady residential sidewalks until I came to Avenue H. On a corner two blocks over I found the house number I was looking for. A picket fence ran around the small yard and thick white oleander shrubs lined the porch. The whole place well shaded by a magnolia tree full of jabbering mockingbirds. A bright yellow Pierce-Arrow was parked in the driveway leading to the garage in back.

I stood at the gate, peering past the oleanders and into the dark shadows of the porch. Someone was sitting there, a woman, busy with something in her lap.

"Pardon me, ma'am," I called out. "I'm looking for some kin of mine and I wonder if you can—"

The woman gave a small shriek and a pan clanked on the floor and a scattering of snap beans spilled off the porch. She came scooting down the steps and I saw it was Charlie.

I dropped the Gladstone as she yanked open the gate and flung herself on me. I spun her around and couldn't help laughing as she cried and kissed me all over my face and said, "Sonny, Sonny, Sonny."

"Well, I'll be a monkey's hairy uncle. Hey brother, come see what the tide's washed up."

Russell stood grinning at the top of the porch steps in his undershirt and galluses, hands in his pockets.

Now Buck came out in turned-up shirtsleeves, a newspaper in his hand. "Jesus Christ on a drunken plowhorse. That young scoundrel with his hands on your woman—is that who I think it is?"

"Looks like he's been sunbathing down in Miami, don't it?" Russell said. Beaming would not be too strong a word for the way they were looking at me. I could feel myself beaming right back.

"Can you all *believe* it?" Charlie said. She laughed and clutched me tighter.

"I always hoped you'd find a way out, kid," Buck said, "but I never really . . ." He made a vague gesture.

"I figured if I wanted to see you no-counts again I'd best take measures," I said.

"Listen to him," Buck said. "Take measures. Smartypants is full of himself, ain't he? Same like always."

"Probably wants us to call him Houdini or some such," Russell said. "Escape artist like him."

"You all quit picking on him," Charlie said. She grabbed up the Gladstone and tugged me by the arm, pulling me through the gate and saying to come on, we had a lot of celebrating to do.

And Buck and Russell charged down the porch to hug me hard.

I'd been pleasantly surprised to find Charlie with them but I wasn't sure how freely we could talk in her presence. They must've read the uncertainty on my face. "Everything's jake, kid," Russell said. "She's in."

She was sitting next to him on the sofa and patted his knee. "He gave me ten seconds to decide if I wanted to come along," she said. "I took about seven to make up my mind."

"Had to play hard to get," Russell said.

"Now here I am, a *moll*," she said, affecting to talk tough out of the side of her mouth. Then smiled wryly and said, "My poor momma must be going round and round in her grave."

The bulldog was digging into my hip, so I took it out and set it on the small table beside my chair. Buck and Russell smiled at the sight of it. Charlie didn't.

I was as eager to hear what they'd been up to as they were to ask me questions, and we went through several quarts of homebrew as we caught each other up on things. Sharp Eddie had given them the details about the trouble that put me in Angola. They called me twenty kinds of fool for getting in a tank fight in the first place—especially in defense of some faggot—and in the second for hitting a jailhouse cop, no matter the cop hit me on the head. You couldn't win a fight against a jailhouse cop; you only ended up with more time behind bars. And if you *killed* him, well, kiss your ass goodbye.

"The only thing surprises me," Russell said, "is they didn't hang you. I mean, *John Bones'* kid. Even if it *was* an accident, the only worse trouble you could've made for yourself was if you strangled Huey Long's momma."

"That old sumbitch'll turn Loosiana inside out looking for you," Buck said.

I said I'd heard so much about what a hardcase John Bonham was that finally I didn't believe it. "Maybe he was a rough cob in his younger days, but anymore he's nothing but a gray old man with only one hand, for Christ's sake."

"Old and gray as he is," Buck said, "I wouldn't take him too light, me."

"You ever have dealings with him?"

"No, but we know some who have, and we could tell you stories," Russell said.

"I've heard plenty of stories," I said. "Wouldn't surprise me if he put out most of them himself."

"Can we quit talking about that man?" Charlie said. "You already said he couldn't do a thing to Sonny in Texas even if he knew he was here, so why go on about him?"

"Girl's right," Buck said. "To hell with that coonass."

They wanted to hear all about Angola so I told them. Buck said it had always been one of the roughest prisons in the country and it couldn't have gotten any softer since Long became governor. "I like the Kingfish," he said, "but I wouldn't pick his prison to do my time in."

Charlie said a place like that was proof enough what beasts men really were. Russell affected to growl and gently bite her arm. She playslapped at him and said, "Quit that, or I'll put you back in your cage."

They loved hearing about the escape. When I told about turning the dog-bait trick around on Garrison, Buck laughed and said, "*See? Told* you it'd work!"

They couldn't stop marveling that I'd run the levee. Through the rest of the evening one or the other would every now and again say "How do you *like* this kid?" and punch me in the arm and laugh the way they'd laughed on the night Russell brought Buck home from Texas. And I'd laugh along with them, the way I'd always wanted to.

They told me about their getaway from Verte Rivage, how the truck they'd stolen had busted a wheel in a bad rut and they'd fled into the swamp and were two days slogging through it before coming to another road. They stole a picnicking family's car to get to Plaquemine. Buck won a twenty-dollar bet with Russell when they found the Model A unharmed beside the police station. When they got home they had to wash the mud off the money and spread the bills all over the house to dry. The report that they'd made away with ten grand was bullshit—they got a little over five. And if I'd been wondering what happened to my share, Buck said, it's what they sent to Sharp Eddie to pay for my defense.

"You all ever see the fella gave you the tip on that bank?" I said.

"We did," Buck said. "Claimed he didn't know about the sheriffs' convention. I believed him."

"Me too," said Russell. "It's why all we did was bust his arm."

Charlie stared into her glass of beer. I had a hunch there were aspects to the criminal life she hadn't yet got used to.

After Verte Rivage they kept away from banks for five months. They went back to smalltime stickups, to working the poker and dice tables. Then a couple of weeks before Christmas they got a tip from Bubber Vicente about a Jackson bank. It had never been hit. No guard on the premises. They took on a driver named Buddy Smalls and did the job. It went slick as lard and they came away with over six grand. They figured they were back in bigtime business. Three weeks later, on another tip from Bubber, they hit the bank in Bogalusa. The news report Jimmyboy told me about was true—they didn't get a dime.

"The teller was putting it in a sack when this peckerwood hops on my back like it was some goddam rodeo," Russell said. "You could say our attention was pretty much distracted from the money for the rest of our visit."

"I should've had that dumbshit guard kick the piece to me," Buck said. "I never figured he'd try for it. Man's stupidity got him killed, plain and simple—and added a goodly bit to our troubles."

"Things did get a wee hairy," Russell said. "Bang-bang-bang." He grinned and affected to duck gunfire.

Charlie got up and went to the kitchen, saying we needed more beer. The quart on the table was half full. Russell watched her go, then looked at me and shrugged.

"And here's the kicker," Buck said. "We get outside and Buddy's already flown. Left us high and dry. So I stop this sheba in a little road-ster and say we're taking her car. She says, 'Ah shit,' just like that. Cute little thing. Showed me a lot of leg as she got out. I should've asked her to come with us—you never know."

They'd left their own car in Hammond—the yellow Pierce-Arrow, which they'd bought less than a week before Bogalusa—but when they got there the car was gone. They figured Buddy Smalls had it, so they drove the roadster on into Baton Rouge and stole another car and made for Buddy's place in Metairie. Sure enough, the Arrow was parked around the side of Buddy's house. While Buck knocked loudly at the front door and called out he was the Western Union man, Russell peeked in the back window and then jimmied the kitchen door and tiptoed to the living room and there was Buddy hunched down next to the sofa and holding a gun pointed at the front door.

"I kicked him in the back of the head so hard I near broke my foot," Russell said. He let Buck in and they splashed water on Buddy's face to bring him around. He started crying and saying they always said if a job went bad it was every man for himself. They reminded him that the rule applied only when your partners didn't stand a chance, it didn't mean you ran off and made their chances worse. They took him for a drive way out into the boondocks with Buddy talking the whole way, making every pitch he could to save his ass.

"I felt a little sorry for him," Russell said. "I figured it was partly our fault he run out on us. We should've known he didn't have the sand for a bank job."

Maybe so, Buck said, but if a guy told you he'd be there, he had to be there, and if he wasn't you couldn't let it go. It was one of those lines you had to set, a line a man can't cross without paying a price, otherwise nothing would mean anything.

"Just because it's a world of thieves out there," he said, "don't mean there ain't no rules to it." It wasn't the first time I'd heard him say it.

They figured nobody'd ever find Buddy in those boonies except by accident, and even if they did, they'd never know whose bones they had.

The next morning they'd read about the robbery in the paper and learned that the guard was dead. Then came the afternoon edition with Russell's sketch in it.

"It was only a so-so likeness, *I* thought," Buck said, "but Russell thought it was a little too like for comfort."

They didn't waste any time in removing themselves from Louisiana. They packed their bags and closed their bank account and didn't take the time for anything else except to stop at Charlie's to see if she wanted to go along—and to leave the notes for me at Brenda Marie's and Jimmyboy Dolan's.

They'd come straight to Galveston. They'd been here before and liked it. It struck them in some ways as a smaller version of New Orleans, and not only in the weather.

"It's always been an easygoing town," Buck said. "The cops'll usually give a fella a break in appreciation of a cash contribution to their fight against crime." He looked toward the kitchen, where Charlie was still keeping herself, then said in a lower voice, "When I first heard it's got more cathouses than Narlens, I didn't believe it, but it's true. Most of the cats real young and sweet, too. Two bucks for your regular pussy, three dollars a throw for the best in the house. And every one of them so far real understanding about my, ah, deprived condition."

"There's no shortage of places to get laid, get drunk, or get a bet down," Russell said. "They don't call it the Free State of Galveston for nothing."

"Seems just the place for some sharps I could name," I said, grinning from one to the other of them.

"For relaxing, yeah," Buck said, "but not for working, sad to say." He said that all the big gambling joints and the local booze operations were run by a powerful pair of brothers named Sam and Rose Maceo who didn't look kindly on outsiders trying to profit at their expense. Sharps who tried their trade at the Maceos' tables, bootleggers who tried dealing their wares behind the Maceos' backs—all such interlopers ended up going for a walk in the Gulf of Mexico in a pair of concrete shoes.

"You won't believe how fancy their nightclubs are," Russell said. "In the high-stakes rooms you get free booze while you're playing. We saw the chief of police there one night, drink in one hand and dice in the other. We've had some good times in their places, but all told they've taken more of our money than we have of theirs. I've been tempted to use a trick or two but figured I'd best wait till I grow me some gills."

"We saw them catch a dude playing card tricks at a poker table one night," Buck said. "The strongarms were real polite. Would you come this way, please, sir? Got his coat from the checkroom and helped him on with it. Let him take his drink along. Right this way, sir. Week or so later somebody finds a leg on the beach. Just the bottom part. Still wearing a shoe. Florsheim, like this fella had been wearing. Of course, it could've been some other fella in Florsheims."

"Or could be one kind of shark met another," Russell said.

The same thing went for holdup men and thieves in general. The Maceos would not abide criminals in their midst to make citizens fearful and more demanding of stricter law enforcement. It was in the Maceos' own interest that the locals feel safe enough to enjoy nights on the town. It was an open joke that Sam and Rose did a better job of protecting Galveston than the police department they paid off.

"In other words," I said, "they got a monopoly on the thievery business in this town and mean to keep it that way."

"In other words," Buck said, "yeah."

They'd come away from New Orleans with enough money to tide them over for a while, but between living expenses and gambling losses and Buck's cathouse habit and Russell's good times with Charlie, their stake had dwindled pretty fast. They started going up to Houston, where there were plenty of independent gambling joints. But as strangers they were everywhere suspect from the start and they'd had some close calls. Even where they were able to pocket their winnings without trouble, they were warned not to come back, and pretty soon they ran out of big-money games to sit in on.

So they'd gone back to holdups. Small stuff only—no banks. There'd been so many Houston banks robbed in the year before that the city and county both were now paying a bonus to any cop—and a reward to any private citizen—who shot a holdup man in the act. They paid bounties to manhunters who brought in wanted robbers, dead or alive. It wasn't a policy ever made public, it hadn't been in the newspaper, but the word was on the vine and everybody'd heard it.

"I tell you, kid, it's some gun-crazy sonsofbitches in that damn Houston," Buck said. "We ain't real keen on hitting some bank where everybody in the place is packing a piece and praying for somebody to try a stickup."

"Hell, I break a sweat robbing a *grocery* store anywhere near Houston," Russell said.

Over the past few weeks they'd been taking it easy and talking things over, discussing possibilities, keeping their ears open in the speakeasies and gambling joints. And then last week they'd finally decided what to do. If I'd been a few days later in getting to Galveston they would've had to leave a different message for me with Miller Faulk.

They told me about it over supper at a bayside place overlooking the shrimp docks. We sat at a back corner table and between the four of us ate six dozen raw oysters and two big buckets of smoked shrimp, shucking the peels onto the newspaper the waitress had spread on the tabletop. We talked and talked as we ate, telling each other to keep our voices down, now and then snickering like a bunch of schoolkids.

West Texas was the place. Oil boom country.

"I don't know why we ain't gone out there before now," Buck said. "It's so damn *right*."

East Texas had its share of oil towns, of course—hell, it's where the business got started in this state—but according to Buck the boom-towns around here had mostly tamed down by now. There was still money to be made in them, but not by any Johnnies-come-lately like us. The way the Maceos had a lock on Galveston was how some bunch of big shots or other had a lock in every East Texas oil town—and with the same sort of cozy arrangement with the cops. No independent hustling allowed.

"But the way we hear it, out west it's still wide open," Buck said. "Every man for himself and devil take the hindmost. The cops all as crooked as corkscrews—except for the damn Rangers. But there ain't all that many of them, praise Jesus."

"All those towns full of boomers making money hand over fist," Russell said, "and full of sharpies of every kind parting them from it."

"But what they *ain't* got enough of," Buck said, "is somebody to part the sharpies from it."

"In other words," I said, "you've perceived a shortcoming in the economic system of West Texas. A shortcoming which presents lucrative possibilities to whoever might be bold enough to remedy it."

"Exactly right, Mister smartass," Buck said. "Lucrative possibilities. *Especially* since Bubber Vicente's out there now. Our old job broker. Miller Faulk told us. He used to work for Bubber in Narlens till his wife left him and moved to Houston and he came out to try and get back with her. Anyway, a couple of months ago Bubber came to Houston and—"

"Poor old Miller," Russell broke in. "Back in Narlens, Eula put the horns on him at least twice that I know of. Best thing ever happened to him was when she run off. But then the fool comes chasing after her. Buys that piece-of-shit filling station and tells everybody he's turning a new leaf. I swear, some guys never learn."

"He must love her is what it is," Charlie said.

"I know it," Russell said. "And look what it's got him."

She stuck her tongue out at him.

"If you all don't *mind,*" Buck said, giving Russell and Charlie a look.

He turned back to me. "A couple of months ago Bubber shows up in Houston and tells Miller he had to cut out of Narlens in a hurry after a pair of sonofabitch cops who'd been shaking down everybody in the Quarter were found floating in the river and some other sonofabitches were trying to stick the rap on him. Said he was on his way to West Texas to go partners with a old pal, another job setup man. Wanted Miller to go with him but Miller said no, he was back with Eula again and wanted to stay that way if he could. Bubber said if he changed his mind to get in touch with him at the Bigsby Hotel in Odessa."

"Miller tell him you and Russell were in Galveston?" I said.

"Nope. We'd told him not to tell anybody where we were except you—if you should ever come around—and he took us at our word. He figured he'd tell us about Bubber the next time he saw us, but turned out that wasn't till a couple of weeks ago. So we send Bubber a wire asking how's business and a few days later he wires back it's booming, he's got more jobs than he's got guys to do them, so come on out if we want some of them."

"It'll be just like in Narlens," Russell said. "Bubber'll point them out and we'll do them."

"His leads always been worth every dollar of his cut," Buck said.

"In other words," I said, "West Texas here we come."

"In other words," Buck said, "I can't hardly wait."

"Me neither," Russell said. His grin as big as Buck's and mine.

"Me neither," Charlie said. Her smile small.

The plan was to rent a place to live in as soon as we got out west, a place where Charlie could stay while we were out on a job, a place we could retreat to and where we could pass for straight citizens, a place well removed from Bubber Vicente's base of operations and whatever heat might all of a sudden come down on it. After studying a map of the region, we settled on Fort Stockton. If you drew a circle no more than a hundred miles across to include most of the boomtowns out there, Fort Stockton lay near the south rim of it and Odessa close to the north, some eighty-five miles away.

To beef up the stake we'd need to make the trip and get set up, Buck and Russell decided to sell the Pierce-Arrow—which was anyhow too showy for our line of work. You want a plain Jane of a car that blends right in with most others. They sold the Arrow to Miller Faulk, who'd always admired it and topped all other bids with an offer of five hundred dollars and a fairly new green Model A sedan which he'd had specially fitted with a radio. Miller said we were doing the right thing to swap the sometimes temperamental

Pierce-Arrow for a hardy Model A that could handle that tough West Texas country.

Over the next few days, Buck and Russell settled their accounts and took care of a few other matters—including a special order of business cards with all three of our names listed on them as sales representatives of Matson Oil and Toolworks of Lake Charles, Louisiana.

Meanwhile, Charlie took me shopping for new clothes and showed me the town. We ate lunch in cafés on the Strand or down the street from the docks. We'd always been able to talk frankly with each other back in New Orleans, and we found we still could. We were sipping lemonades in a restaurant across the street from the seawall one afternoon when she told me she'd once asked Russell what he wanted to do with the rest of his life.

"Know what his answer was? He said, 'Hell girl, I'm doing it.' " She shook her head and swayed the dangling gold star she wore on one earlobe. The other was pinned with a pearl stud.

"Well," I said, "that's Russell."

"Yeah it is," she said, "and Buck too. But what I can't figure, Sonny, is why *you're* here. When I heard you got sent to prison I cried. It seemed such a waste. I thought if you ever got out of there any kind of way, the last thing you'd do is go back to robbing. But here you are again. I don't get it. You're so young and so smart and all. You could be anything you want—a doctor, a lawyer, a—"

"An Indian chief," I said, and put a hand to my mouth and went, "Whoo-whoo-whoo."

"Yeah, ha-ha," she said. "Make all jokes you want, but I still don't get you, I just don't."

"There's this story I heard somewhere," I said. "A forest catches on fire and all the animals are swimming across the river to the other side where they'll be safe. Except this rattlesnake can't swim, so he asks a raccoon to let him ride across on his back. The coon says, 'Hell no, if I let you on my back you'll bite me.' The rattler says, 'No I won't. If I did that I'd drown.' Well, that makes sense to the coon, so he lets the rattler get on his back and he starts swimming across the river. Halfway across, the rattler bites him. The coon says, 'You damn fool, why'd you *do* that? Now we'll both die.' And the rattler says, 'I don't know. I guess it's just my nature.' "

She rolled her eyes but I could see she was fighting a smile. "I'll tell you one thing you have in common with your uncles," she said. "You can sure sling the bullshit."

I laughed along with her, and then asked what *she* was doing here. Why did she come along with Russell?

"I wonder sometimes," she said. "I don't know. I guess because he's still the most exciting thing to me. It beats working as a salesgirl or being married to some office manager. I'm not real ready for that."

"Spoken like a true flapper," I said.

"The flapper is *passé,* Sonny," she said. Her smile was rueful. "Don't you read the magazines?"

"Snappy number like you won't ever be *passé.*"

She pursed her lips like she was imparting a kiss. Then smiled and said, "What the hell—maybe it's just my nature."

"Like an old Greek philosopher once said—the unrisked life is not worth living."

"I knew this Greek guy back in Baton Rouge," she said. "Sold life insurance. Biggest liar I ever met."

When I told her about my brief reunion with Brenda Marie she said, "I bet *that* was some memorable whoopee, huh?" and waggled her brows.

"There wasn't near enough of it, truth to tell."

"Well hell, Sonny, whose fault is that? Running off on the poor girl as quick as you did."

"Good thing I did. If I'd stayed longer I might've missed you all. Would've played hell trying to find you in West Texas."

She patted my hand. "That's life, ain't it, honey? Always one tough choice or another."

We took in a movie matinee every afternoon. *Sadie Thompson. Our*

Dancing Daughters. She grinned in the screenlight and elbowed me in the ribs when I whispered during *Wings* that she and Clara Bow could pass for sisters.

One morning we went swimming in the Gulf, then lay on towels on the beach and got sunburns while we told each other what shapes we saw in the clouds. I said she ought to be a zookeeper since she saw nothing but various sorts of animals, and she said I ought to be in jail since I saw nothing but various parts of women's anatomies. I said it was her fault for wearing such a sexy swimsuit—one of those new backless things with an X-halter over her breasts—and said she could quit pretending not to notice all the guys giving her the once-over. She threw sand at me and said all men were sex-crazy. I said I didn't know about *all* men, but *I* sure was, and gave a high wolf howl. She laughed and said to shush up before the dogcatcher came and took me away.

To celebrate our last night in Galveston we all got dressed to the nines and took supper at the Hollywood Dinner Club, the Maceos' fanciest place. It was easy enough to find—all you had to do was head up the beach road toward the source of the big searchlight beacon circling the sky and there you were. They could see that beckoning light miles away on the mainland.

The club's exterior was designed like an old Spanish hacienda, lots of tiles and arches, porticos with torches in the walls. Inside, the ceilings blazed with chandeliers and the furnishings were *très élégant.* We were ushered to one of the dining rooms and agreed among ourselves to order something none of us had eaten before, which left plenty to choose from on the menu. We finally settled on roast partridge stuffed with wild rice and mushrooms and a couple of bottles of French wine.

It was a superb meal, but Buck said that for less than the tip we'd be leaving we could've stuffed ourselves on the best fried chicken in

Texas at a joint he knew of in niggertown—*and* got drunk for three days on bonded bourbon. Charlie told him not to be such a sourpuss. She didn't understand how anybody could not have a good time in such a swell place.

"Hey, goddammit," Buck said, "I *know* how to have a good time. I'm *having* one—*see*?" His grin was so exaggerated Russell said he looked like a lunatic with an electric wire up his ass. Buck rolled his eyes to add to the effect and we all cracked up.

After supper we went into the rooms in back. They were everything I'd heard. There were tables for every kind of game—poker, blackjack, craps, name it. The room was discreetly overseen by the club's handymen, as Buck said they were called. Beefy well-dressed guys with watchful eyes and with bulges under their coats. After an hour of blackjack I was nine dollars to the good, but Buck dropped eighty at stud and Russell was forty dollars poorer after his turns with the dice.

As we made our way through the crowd to get to the speakeasy ballroom Russell whispered, "Goddam, I wish I had my own bones with me. I *know* I could work this place."

Buck cut his eyes at him. "I'd say we ain't getting out of this town any too soon. You'd lose more than a couple of fingers here, buddy-boy."

Buck and I had a drink at the bar while Russell and Charlie took a turn on the dance floor in the company of about two hundred other couples whirling to the band's rendition of "Stardust." The smoky air was laced with perfume. Knockout women everywhere you looked, all of them in the company of highrollers.

"Man, you ever see so much goodlooking stuff under one roof?" Buck said. "What I wouldn't give for a crack at any one of them. But hell, they too rich for my blood."

"Why not try the direct approach?" I said. "Sometimes it does the trick."

"I knew this old boy decided one night to try the direct approach,"

he said. "Picks out this goodlooking thing at the bar and goes up to
her and says, 'Hey, honeybunch, I sure wouldn't mind a little pussy.' Gal
gives him a look and says, 'Me neither, Mac—mine's as big as your
boot.' "

After a while Russell bellied up to the bar and Charlie tugged me
out on the floor as the band started up with "You Do Something to
Me." She was wearing a little black satin number and I felt the play of
her belly and thighs against me as we swirled around in the midst of
the other dancers. And like the times we'd danced so close together
when I was a kid, the same thing happened in my pants.

She smiled wide and said, "Why Sonny, you still know how to pay
a girl the sweetest compliment."

"Sorry," I said. "Can't help it." My ears burned.

"Well of course you can't, sugar. After being so long in that awful
place. You really *did* need more time with that Brenda girl." She
laughed and pinched my cheek. "And you still blush more handsome
than any man I know."

We danced like that for a while and my embarrassing condition
persisted. "Poor baby," she whispered in my ear, her belly tight against
me as we danced to "Amapola."

She glanced at the bar and I looked too and saw Buck and Russell
hunched over the counter in close conversation. She took the lead and
sidestepped us through the dense crowd of dancers to the far side of
the floor and into the darkness behind a partition of potted palms.

"Hey girl," I said, "what the hell are—"

"Hush," she said.

She backed me up against the wall and then slipped her hand off
my shoulder and down between us and her fingers closed around me
through my pants. I couldn't believe it, but I wasn't about to protest. I
was already so worked up that it took her only a few quick squeezes to
set me off. I dug my fingers into her hip and groaned into her hair.

She put her hand back on my shoulder and patted it gently.
"There now. All better, baby?"

All I could think to say was *"Whooo."*

She chuckled softly and pecked me on the cheek. "I'll take that for a yes." Then said: "Good thing we're both wearing black. Stains won't show."

We danced out from behind the palms and into the crowd again and slowly swayed our way across the floor to the rhythms of "In a Little Spanish Town." Buck and Russell were still talking.

She pushed her belly tight against me. "I must say, Mr. LaSalle, you certainly *feel* more relaxed."

I grinned back at her. "No small thanks to you, Miss Hayes, *I* must say."

"And *I* must say, Mr. LaSalle, what's a friend for if not to lend a helping hand?"

Our cackles drew amused looks from the couples nearest to us.

"Listen, honey," she said, "I really think you need to get yourself a girl."

"I really think you may be right," I said.

It was nearly one in the morning when we finally called it a night. The place was even more crowded than before and people were still coming in.

"It don't really get jumping for another hour yet," Russell said. "The highrollers won't get their hats and coats till practically sunup."

The parking lot was jammed and cars were lined on both shoulders of the beach road. The Model A was at the far end of the lot, in the shadows of a thick growth of oleander. Charlie led the way, showing off some slick dance moves as she went. We were almost to the Ford when the car parked next to it pulled out and a white Lincoln wheeled into the vacated spot.

Three good-sized guys in fancy suits got out, laughing like one of them had just told a good joke. One of them said something to Charlie that I didn't catch, and she said, "Oh my, does your momma know you talk like that?" Then the one closest to her grabbed a handful of her ass.

She whirled and took a swipe at him with her purse. "Hands off, Buster!"

I was in front of Buck and Russell and moved in fast. One of them said, "Watch it!" and Buster started to reach in his coat but I caught him with a solid right that put him down. One of the others punched me high on the head but it didn't have any weight behind it and I countered with a hook in the ear, knocking him against the Ford, then drove one into his solar plexus and that was it for him. He slid down the side of the car, trying to suck a breath.

As I stripped the two guys of their pieces—.38 four-inchers, both of them—I heard Russell say, "Do it, tough guy!" and Charlie shrill, "Russell, *don't!*"

He was holding a cocked pistol in the third one's face. The guy looked like he was posing as Napoleon, a hand inside his coat. Buck stepped up and jerked the guy's arm away and relieved him of an army .45 automatic. "Thanks, pal," he said. "I been wanting one of these."

"You assholes got any idea who you're fucken with?" the guy said.

"*Oooooo,*" Buck said in mock fright. "Scary man here."

"We work for Sam and Rose, you stupid shits."

Buck kneed him perfectly in the balls. The guy groaned and sank to his haunches with his hands at his crotch, then fell on his ass, cussing low.

"If I was Sam and Rose," Buck said, "I'd hire me some better help."

We hustled into the Ford and I wheeled us out of the lot and wove through the traffic in front of the club and then we were out of it and breezing along the beach road. The Gulf was shimmering brightly under a silver moon.

"Hot *damn!*" Buck yelled out the window—and Russell and I laughed like he'd said something funny. He held up the .45 for us to see. "Slug from one of these'll knock a man down if it hits him in the little finger, you know that?"

"These are smart little Smith & Wessons too," Russell said, handling the .38s I'd taken off the Maceo men.

In the rearview I saw Charlie looking from one to the other of us. "What am I *doing* with you guys?" she said.

"Why honeybunch, don't you *know*?" Russell said. He snuggled up to her and kissed her neck and ran a hand over her breasts.

"Yeah, I guess," she said, and slapped at his roving hands. "But like you boys are always saying . . . even when you *know,* you never know."

That got another big laugh from all of us.

"What *I* know is, we ain't getting out of this town any too soon," Buck said.

Then he started singing "Bye Bye Blackbird" and we all joined in.

*W*e set out a little before noon under a dark sky full of thunder rolling up from the Gulf. The rain started to fall while we were still on the bridge to the mainland. By the time we got to the outskirts of Houston it was coming down so hard I couldn't see five feet in front of the car and had to pull off the road. Wiping the fog off the glass gave us no better view of the outside world at all. We opened a lee window a little to let out the cigarette smoke and had to turn the radio volume all the way up to hear the music over the rain pounding the roof.

The speaker crackled with every flash of lightning as we sang along. "Ain't Misbehavin'." "Lover Come Back to Me." "It Had to Be You." "Who's Sorry Now." When Charlie started vamping to "Makin' Whoopee," we urged her on with wolf whistles and shouts of "Hubba hubba, red-hot momma!" Russell pretended to be a radio announcer, saying, "Welcome ladies and gents, to the LaSalle Model A Boom-Boom Room, featuring Fifi La Hayes. Yowza, yowza!"

And still the rain came hammering down. After a while Buck and Russell started nipping from their flasks and pouring short ones for Charlie. They let me have a sip but said they didn't want me getting drunk and driving us into a bayou or head-on into another car. I said it didn't look like I'd be driving us anywhere for about forty days and forty nights.

We were there for more than two hours before the storm eased enough to afford a sufficient view of the road to try driving on it. The engine cranked up easily enough—"Love them electric starters," Russell said—but when I tried to get going the tires spun in place and dug themselves in and we got stuck.

"What Ford should've put in these cars is an electric pusher," Buck said. There was nothing to do but let Charlie take the steering wheel while the three of us got out and shoved.

The storm had abated but the rain still fell steadily and we were soaked inside a minute. We cursed at passing cars for the added splashings they gave us as we leaned into the back of the car and struggled for footing and leverage. Charlie revved the engine and the car rocked forward and back in the ruts and the wheels spun and spun and splattered us with mud. We were all shouting at her at once—give it the gas, don't gun it so much, cut the wheel hard, aim the wheels straight. She had turned off the radio but still couldn't hear us very well for the rain on the roof and with the windows up. Her hollers came back muffled—"What? *What?*"

It was a situation to rub tempers a little raw. "Roll down the fucken window, goddammit!" Russell yelled.

She put the window down and stuck her head partway out, shielding herself from the rain with a folded newspaper, and shouted that she did not appreciate him cussing at her like that and would we make up our stupid goddam minds what we wanted her to do.

Just then a large truck went by and raised an enormous splash which could not get any of us any wetter except for Charlie, who was swamped through the open window and hurriedly rolled it up—like she thought she might undo the drenching if only she rolled fast enough. The spectacle had us staggering with laughter.

She glared furiously at us over her shoulder and then the transmission shrieked and the motor raced and the wheels whirled in reverse and found purchase and the car lurched up out of the ruts and came barreling rearward. Russell went sprawling and Buck and I barely managed to scramble out of the way as she roared by. She braked hard and the car slewed to a halt.

"Shitfire," Buck said, gawking at the car and wiping water from his eyes. "Why the hell didn't *you* think to back out of that rut?"

"Why the hell didn't *you* think to suggest it?" I said.

Russell slowly got to his feet, cursing steadily and coated with mud. Charlie was laughing behind the windshield like she was watching a Chaplin movie, her hair plastered to her head.

"You damn crazy cooze!" Russell shouted.

Her grin vanished. She gunned the motor and ground the transmission into low gear. Russell hustled over to join me and Buck in the high weeds off the shoulder.

But she didn't make another try at us. She eased the car forward until she was abreast of us, then reached over and lowered the passenger window a few inches. "Hey there, boys," she called out, smiling with affected sweetness. "Think it'll rain?"

"Crazy cooze," Russell muttered.

"What's that, baby?" Charlie said. Her eyes narrowed and she gunned the engine.

"He said we could sure use some booze," Buck said.

"That's what I thought," she said. "Well, you ain't gonna get it standing out there in the rain, are you?"

She slid over to the passenger side and gave me a smile and wink as I got behind the wheel and Buck and Russell got in the back. Buck cursed low about the mud we were smearing on the seats and floorboards.

I drove slowly through the continuing downpour while they

passed around a flask without saying anything. Then Charlie chuckled and said, "You should've *seen* you all's faces."

"Real damn funny," Russell said. "You might've killed us."

"You're so cute when you're scared shitless, baby. Anybody ever tell you?"

That got me and Buck in on her laughter.

Russell stared in disbelief at Buck and me and shook his head. "She about runs over our asses and you all laugh." Then said to her: "And you ought not to say 'shit.' It ain't ladylike."

And joined in our guffaws.

I turned off into the first motor camp we came to. Russell and Charlie took one room and Buck and I another. We got cleaned up and changed into dry clothes. Charlie had packed a picnic basket in case we got hungry on the day's drive, and it now served for our supper. She brought the basket to our room and had Russell spread a blanket on the floor. He muttered about the foolishness of having a picnic on the floor and she said we could have it outside in the dark and rain if it would make him feel less foolish. She laid out paper plates and we sat down to a meal of ham sandwiches and potato chips, deviled eggs and cold fried chicken. We drank paper cups of lemonade dispensed from a glass jug.

A little later the *Amos 'n' Andy* show came on the radio, and while we laughed at them Buck tended to the nails of his thumbs with a file, keeping them finely serrated for marking cards. Then a music program came on and he and Russell took turns entertaining us with their tricks. Buck needed to shuffle a deck only twice and he'd know any card you picked out of the spread. More impressive was his skill in dealing. Need a ten to fill that inside straight? There it is. An ace or an eight to complete a Hickok full house? Got it. Jack of hearts to make the flush? Here you go. Blackjack was child's play. If he was showing sixteen, he could easily enough give himself the five, but would as often make it a four, to hold down suspicion. Eighteen, and he'd flick himself a deuce or ace, unless the pot was sizable and the other guy was likely holding twenty—then here came the three.

And Russell with his dice. He'd roll with an honest pair a few times, then next thing you knew he was rolling his shaved bones and cleaning you out. Then the straight pair again. I never could spot him making the switch. He said he'd been even better at it when he had all his fingers. He would put down the dice and hold up his hands and all you'd see is empty palms. Then he'd pick up the dice and switch them, and no matter how much Charlie and I asked him to show us how he did it, he wouldn't. Buck knew how he did it, and Charlie begged him to tell.

"Well all right, girl," he said, "if you *must* know . . . he uses magic."

"Goddammit," Russell said, "there you go again, giving away my trade secrets."

"Oh, go to hell," Charlie said. "Both of you."

"Yes ma'am," Russell said, saluting like a soldier. "We're on our way."

Then we finished off the flasks and called it a night.

At dawn the desk clerk told us the weather report was for still more rain. We decided to drive on rather than sit on our hands in that motor court and wait who knew how long for the sky to break. Charlie bought one of the motor court's blankets in case she got chilly on the road. We filled the Ford with gasoline at a nearby station and drove off in a steady windless rain under a sky that looked made of gray mud.

West of Houston the highway was in pretty good shape except that the lowest stretches of it were covered with water and the going was slow. In some places the water came up to the running boards and now and then seeped under the doors. We couldn't get anything but crackling static across the radio dial. Every few miles we'd pass another car stalled by the side of the road, the people in it no more than vague shapes.

Crossing the Brazos bridge we saw the river running over its banks and saw a dead cow whirling in the current. I wondered aloud if it would carry all the way downriver and out into the sea. What if it got snagged by some fisherman trolling in the Gulf at night? What would he think when he reeled it in?

"If it was me," Russell said, "I'd tow it back to the docks and tell everybody what a hell of a fight it put up. I'd claim a world record for the cowfish."

The miles rolled by and the rain kept falling. The clouds looked low enough to poke with a cue stick. The Colorado was booming under its bridge too and close to spilling its banks. About twenty miles farther we came on the Navidad, also running fast but not as high as the rivers behind us.

We pulled in at a café in Schulenburg. The parking lot was full and the place was crowded and smelled of cooking grease and sweat and mud. When we told the waitress we were from Houston she said we'd left there at the right time. She'd heard on the radio that every bayou in town was over its banks and flooding the streets. "You'da waited till tomorrow to get out of there," she said, "you'da needed a dang boat instead of a auty-mobile."

We ate hamburgers and fried potatoes and bought packs of cigarettes and four ham sandwiches in waxed paper to take with us. Buck had a whispered conversation with the fry cook at the kitchen window and I saw him slip the man a dollar.

Russell took over the driving, and as we wheeled out of the parking lot Buck said that according to the cook there was a certain drugstore in a town called Flatonia about fifteen miles down the road where a fella could buy himself a pretty good brand of medicine. We made the stop and fifteen minutes later we were on the road again with both flasks full of hooch and a quart bottle besides.

By late afternoon the rain finally quit and the clouds began to break. The countryside was changed. The Spanish moss had vanished and the pineywoods played out. The oaks shrank. The land opened to grassy ranges and began to gain slow elevation. Pecans and cotton-woods stood thick along the streams.

The towns got farther apart and the radio stations were now fewer and more regional in their programming, less big-hit ballroom and more plunk and twang. Shitkicker music that had us yelling "Yeeeee-haw!" in derision. But a lot of Mexican stuff too, with plenty of accor-dion in it, which we all kind of liked because it reminded us of coonass music. Buck spelled Russell at the wheel and Charlie handed out the sandwiches.

At sunset the sky was almost cloudless. We passed around one of the flasks, doing away with that soldier slow and easy. As the darkness deepened, a few bright stars began to clarify. The waxing moon was high behind us. The night was fully risen when we saw the glow of San Antonio dead ahead.

An hour later we were winding all through the center of town, with me doing the driving again, crossing and recrossing the river, tak-ing in the sights and sounds of a loud and lively Friday night. The whole town smelled of Mexican cooking, reminding us of La Belleza, a Mexican restaurant in New Orleans we all liked, and the spicy aro-mas stirred up our appetites.

We drove through several neighborhoods where everybody was yammering in Spanish and the store signs were all in Spanish and if you didn't know better you'd have thought you were someplace south of the Rio Grande instead of more than a hundred miles this side of it. Then we came to a part of town with plenty of white faces and turned onto a long crowded street of one café after another with names like the Lucky Spur and Rio Rita's and Fat Daddy, all of them loud with string band and boogie-woogie. We figured it for the main goodtime drag. Charlie spied a restaurant called the Texican in the middle of the block and said, "Right *there's* where I want to eat."

There was a ready parking spot near the restaurant but I passed it up in favor of one at the far end of the street. It was something Buck and Russell had taught me—always park on a corner facing an intersection. It allowed for a fast getaway either straight across the street or in a fast right turn, whichever seemed the wiser course at the moment. It was how we parked even when we weren't on a job, a matter of professional habit.

They took their pistols out from under the seat. Buck checked the magazine of his .45. Then pulled back the slide far enough to see that there was a round already snugged in the chamber. He reset the safety and slipped the piece under his coat. Russell unlatched the cylinder of his .38 to check the rounds, then snapped it back in place with a fling of the wrist. It was another rule of theirs—better to have a gun and not need it than to need a gun and not have it, because you never know, especially in a strange town. I didn't see the need for carrying heat just to get a bite in a restaurant. Besides, it was a hot night and I didn't want to wear a jacket. But I knew the rules and so I put on the coat and slid the bulldog in my waistband behind my back. Charlie had already got out of the car and was browsing at a clothing store window.

We walked back to the Texican and went inside and settled ourselves in a window booth. The place was run by an American with red hair and a faceful of freckles but all the waitresses looked Mexican and the radio was tuned to a station putting out a steady stream of the ranchero music we'd gotten to like so well. The waitress came and took our orders. While we waited for the food we drank cold bottles of cola and watched the people going by on the sidewalk.

The food was wonderful. Charlie declared her chicken enchiladas the best she'd ever had, and Buck and Russell said the same about the pork tacos.

"According to a famous old Spanish writer," I said, "hunger makes the tastiest sauce." I was going pretty energetically at a plate of roast kid.

"That's one of those things nobody ever thinks to say till they hear somebody else say it," Russell said. "Then it's 'I know *that*. Why didn't *I* say that and get all famous?' "

"When this guy was in prison," I said, "he'd sometimes go without eating for a day or two, so that on the days he did eat he'd be so hungry even the slop they fed him tasted good. He'd imagine he was dining at a lavish banquet."

"Some imagination," Buck said. "The shit I ate in the joint, I couldn't even imagine it fit for pigs."

"Nice talk for the supper table," Charlie said.

"Say the Spanish guy was in prison?" Russell said. "What for?"

"His biography wasn't specific. For 'financial irregularities,' I think it said."

"I get it," Russell said. "He was a thief."

"Like some others I could mention," Charlie said.

"World's full of them," Russell said, scooping up a mouthful of refried beans with a piece of tortilla. "Always been, always be."

We wiped at our watering eyes and sniffed noisily with the effect of the chile sauces. Buck paused in his eating to blow his nose. "Jesus," he said, "this stuff is great."

While Russell took care of the bill at the register, Buck went to talk with the redhaired owner. Charlie and I went out on the sidewalk and smoked and eyeballed the passing parade of folk. A minute later Russell came out, swirling a toothpick in his mouth. He nudged me and nodded at a pair of cute girls staring out at us from a passing car. Charlie didn't miss it, and gave him a dig of her elbow hard enough to make him wince. "Hey!" he said. "I thought Sonny might get something going with them is all."

She stepped away from him, folding her arms tight over her breasts the way a miffed woman'll do, and he whispered to me, "Jesus, eyes in back of her head."

Buck joined us and said there was a good hotel a few blocks north of where we were. "We can go on over and call it a night," he said. "Or we can have us a drink or two first at a speak at this other hotel down the street from where we parked the car. Place called the Travis. It's got a poker room. Tell you what, if nobody's got any objection to me using the travel money for a stake, I might could make us some jack."

He'd been told about the Travis by the redhaired man. Experience had taught him and Russell to spot smalltimers pretty easily and they'd made the redhead for one the minute they saw him. Buck had introduced himself as John Ansel, a car salesman out of Schulenburg. The redhead said his name was Dickson. Buck told him he was in town visiting his sister, who was expecting her first kid in the next week or two. He said we were his in-laws. He told Dickson he played in a weekly poker game in Schulenburg and always came out pretty good, if he did say so himself, but he'd always hankered to sit in on one of the high-stakes San Antonio games he'd heard about. Now here he was, with wifey at sis' baby shower and the evening to himself. How about it, he asked Dickson, did he know where a fella could get some action? Dickson said he did know of a game close by but was having trouble recollecting exactly where. His memory cleared when Buck ponied up a fin. He went in the back room to make a phone call and a minute later the matter was settled. He told Buck about the Travis and said they were expecting him in room 312. Just say Claude sent him.

"They're all of them businessmen," Buck said, "or so the man says. Not a pro among them. But we best play it safe."

Plan A was this. During the small talk at the table, he would mention to the other players that his wife had been feeling poorly in recent weeks and never would've been able to make this trip to San Antone except she started taking some new kind of goatmilk treatment which seemed to be helping her a good bit. He would also let drop that his nephew was a dishwasher at Dickson's place. That was where I came in. At ten-thirty—after he'd been up there about two hours—I'd go to room 312 with an urgent message for my Uncle John. I'd announce that his wife had collapsed and was in the hospital.

The fiction was intended to get him out of there without any ruckus. Without some sorehead loser insisting too strongly on the chance to win his money back. But if it didn't work? If somebody refused to let his losses leave so soon in Buck's pocket? Or worse, made a nasty accusation about Buck's awfully good luck in his brief two hours at the table?

Then plan B. We'd pull our pieces to give them something to think about while we hustled the hell out of there and down to the car and got ourselves gone.

I didn't have to ask what we'd do if one of them pulled a piece too. Whatever we had to. That was always understood.

Standing there on the sidewalk, I felt like everything had picked up speed—the passing cars and people, the flashings of the neon lights, my heartbeat. I could see Charlie wasn't pleased by this innovation in the evening's activities but she knew to keep her mouth shut. All Russell said was he wished it was a dice game and he was the one going up to room 312.

I took a walk with Russell and Charlie in the cottonwood shadows along the river. We stopped to buy cones in an ice cream shop but Russell and I took only a few licks off ours before pitching them away. Everything was moving fast but the minutes. When Russell wasn't checking his watch I was consulting mine. Charlie tried to make conversation but soon gave it up. With an hour to go, we made our way to the Travis and went into the speakeasy and ordered drinks at the bar. Russell and I barely touched ours but Charlie was soon sipping on her second. We watched the couples on the dance floor but nobody suggested taking a turn.

At twenty after ten Russell slapped my shoulder and said, "See you at the car, bud. Don't you all keep us waiting."

I went out to the elevator. The operator was an old man with a face as gray as his uniform and purple bags under his eyes. "Three," I told him.

"Private floor, Mac," he said. "Unless you got business."

My first impulse was to head for the stairs, wherever they were. But the old guy had likely been through this routine a hundred times before and he knew what I was thinking. "Stairwell door's closed off on three," he said.

For a second I almost spooked, thinking the plan was already in trouble. I had a vision of myself sticking the snubnose in this old guy's ribs. I told him about my stricken aunt and my uncle in the game in 312. Knowing about the game must've been what did the trick. He didn't say okay, didn't nod, nothing—just pulled the folding lattice door closed and worked the lever and we slowly rose in a clank and whine of machinery.

I stepped out at one end of a hallway with a big grimy window under a faded sign saying "Fire Escape." "All the way the other end," the old guy said. He pulled the door to and the elevator groaned and descended.

The hall was musty and dimly lighted, the runner worn along its center. Whatever businesses operated up here weren't the sort to worry much about workplace appearance. The rooms were on my right, beginning with 301. I heard faint music from behind some of the doors as I went by them, the drone of voices behind others. I thought I heard somebody crying in 307. Between 309 and 310 was a door with a sign saying "Exit" over it. Of course I had to try it and of course it was locked.

Just before I got to 312, I did a dozen fast deep-knee bends to help effect a mild breathlessness befitting a bringer of critical news. It'd be no trouble at all to look worried. I adjusted the bulldog at my back, then stepped up to the door and rapped hard.

The door guy was big, in shirtsleeves and apparently unarmed, which I was glad to see. A Japanese screen directly behind him blocked my view of the room but not the heavy waft of cigarette smoke or the drone of voices. I gave him the bit, expecting to see at least a squint of doubt, but he only nodded and let me in.

There were two round tables with a game going at each. A long narrow table against the wall held bottles of bonded whiskey and plates of bread and cold cuts and cheese. I spotted Buck with his back to me and started for him but the door guy put a hand on my shoulder and said softly, "After the hand."

Buck was dealing seven-card stud. Last card going around, face-down. Two other guys still holding. A guy with a goatee bet big and Buck raised him big and the third guy cursed and folded. The goatee raised Buck back and Buck raised him even bigger. The goatee was showing a pair of kings, a ten, a three. Probably had a king down, maybe another ten or trey. I took a sidestep to get a look at Buck's up cards—pair of jacks and one of them a heart, nine of hearts, eight of hearts. Possible straight flush.

"You ain't buying it, buddy," the goatee said with a cocksure grin. "Not from me."

He called. Full house, kings over tens, and the hole ten was a heart—so no straight flush for Buck.

He didn't need it. He turned up all the other eights. The goatee's grin fell off. "Shit!" he said. "You *believe* this?"

As Buck pulled in the fat pot the door guy stepped up and whispered in his ear. Buck turned around and looked so truly surprised I was almost thrown off. "Tommy!" he said. "What you doing here?"

I delivered the bad news. He stared at me a moment, a man taking it in, then said low, "Oh Jesus"—then jumped up so fast he nearly upset his chair and began stuffing his winnings in his pockets.

"Got to go, boys, I got to . . ." He was so "rattled" he dropped some bills and affected not to notice—a perfect touch—and the guy next to him fetched the money up for him.

Buck was the very picture of a shaken man. "Sorry, boys, sorry," he said. "Gotta go."

"Hey now, what the *hell* . . . ?" the goatee said.

"Christ's sake, Parham, it's the man's *wife*," another guy said.

"I'm *really* sorry, fellas," Buck said. He tossed a twenty on the table. "You all have a few on me. Jesus, guys, I wish . . . ah, *hell*. Tommy, get me to that damn hospital. Let's go!"

Then we were out of there and quickstepping down the hall. I could feel the door guy watching us. There was a muffled shriek from one of the rooms along the hall. I heard the door close behind us and let out my breath. We cut our eyes at each other and Buck's grin looked as big as mine felt. He glanced behind us and said, "Dickson was right. Nothing but rubes."

We were passing by 307 when its door flew open and banged the wall and a naked girl came running out.

I had an instant's glimpse of a wide green bloodshot eye and a blackened swollen one, a raised purple cheekbone, a bloody nose—then her arms were tight around my neck and her blond bob was in my mouth and I heard Buck say, "Holy shit!"

I didn't see the burly mustached guy until his fist closed in her hair and yanked her head back, trying to pull her away. But she kept her hold on me and tugged me off balance and I fell on top of her, her breath heaving up in my face with a smell like rotted fruit.

Then Buck and the man were on the floor and grappling beside us. I pried loose of the girl and scrambled to my feet as the guy got his hands on Buck's throat. I gave him a kick in the ear that knocked him against the wall. Then one in the mustache that spattered the wall with blood. He curled up with his arms around his head and said "Okay, *okay!*" like he had a mouthful of marbles. But now Buck was on his feet and kicking him in the head and the guy cried out sharply a couple of times and then slumped still.

A middle-aged guy in shirtsleeves was standing in the doorway of 307 with his mouth open. Behind him was a slackfaced girl in a robe.

He banged the door shut and turned the lock—but not before I got a look at the bright photography lamps set up around a red sofa and a camera on a tripod.

I expected rubberneckers out of every room, but the only door to open was down at 312. The door guy stepped out and looked at us. Buck brought out the .45 and the guy ducked inside and slammed the door. We backed up along the hallway, watching the doors, Buck repeatedly clearing his throat hard and rubbing his neck.

The girl was half-crouched next to the elevator shaft, her knees together and her arms over her breasts. Her eyes were on us but she seemed to be having trouble focusing. Buck gave her the once-over as he stuck the .45 in his pants. The face was a battered fright but the body was something to see. And she was a real blonde. I was still feeling the way she'd flung herself on me. The way she'd held on when the guy tried pulling her back.

"Drunk as a skunk, ain't you, darling?" Buck said.

I didn't think she was. She was looped, all right, but what I'd smelled on her breath wasn't booze.

"They might've called downstairs," Buck said. "Let's skip any surprises."

He raised the fire escape window with a rusty screech. By the hallway's weak light we could make out the bricked wall of a neighboring building not ten feet away.

"Come on," he said, and ducked out under the sash and started clunking down the iron stairs into the greater darkness.

I thought of the camera and told myself she had it coming. For a bare moment her eyes fixed on mine, then slipped out of focus again. I almost said "Good luck" before the stupidity of it struck me. I had one foot out the window when she grabbed me from behind, hugging to me and crying, trembling like a mistreated dog.

I didn't think about it, I just did it. I took off my coat and helped her get her arms in the sleeves and she drew it close around her. The sleeves hung past her fingertips. I went out on the landing and helped her through the window. She hit her head on the sash but hardly seemed aware of it. The alley below us was dark as a grave. Unsteady as she was, I had to hold her close to me as we descended the creaky stairway into a deepening stink. At the second landing the stairs reversed direction and we went down the last flight.

"What the hell's *this*?" Buck's harsh whisper came up from the blackness.

As we came off the stairway she lost her footing and gasped but I caught her before she fell.

"What're you doing, Sonny?"

"We can't leave her up there," I said.

"Goddammit, kid, are you . . . *shit*. Come on."

I followed his vague form in the dark, pulling the girl along by the coat, catching her up each time she stumbled. We went past two alleyway intersections and around the corner of the next one, where Buck drew up so short I bumped into him. We stood still, listening hard, but didn't hear anything except our own heavy breath and the scurrying of rats in the garbage. Nobody coming behind us. No police sirens on the air.

"What's the big idea?" he whispered.

"No big idea," I said. "It's just . . . we don't have to leave her to those guys to beat up some more."

I couldn't see his face in the gloom but I could feel his eyes. "Hey kid, the world's full of punching bags and for all we know that's her husband we kicked the shit out of."

"If he is, I hope we busted his skull," I said.

Like Daddy, I never could abide a womanbeater, and like him I thought guys who hit their wives were the worst of the bunch. The neighbor across the courtyard used to smack his wife around, but one night when he had her crying really loud Daddy went over there and thumped on the door and when the guy opened up Daddy knocked him on his ass. Told him if he hit her again he'd break his neck. They didn't have any children and I figured this time the woman would finally leave him. But when Daddy came back out I saw her sitting on the sofa with the bastard and tending to his busted mouth. I thought she was a fool for staying with him, but my mother said we shouldn't be to hard on her. " 'Love thieves the will to be free,' " she said, quoting some line I'd never heard. That was my mother, always the poetic soul, fond of Byron and Poe and Yeats, all those versifying fools of the heart. "Well, her *love* for that sonofabitch," Daddy said, "is gonna thieve her of her dumb-ass life one of these nights."

Buck struck up a match to illuminate the girl's beatup face. She turned away. "What's your name, Toots?"

She gripped my arm more tightly.

"Rat got your tongue?" Buck said. The match burned out and the dark swallowed us again. "Some breath on her. It ain't hooch, either. She's doped."

"More reason to get her away from those bastards," I said.

"She'll just fall in with some other bastards. It's how these bimbos are."

"Well, we can't leave her *here*." She pulled away from me and we heard her being sick.

"Listen to that," Buck said in disgust. "Christ's sake, Sonny, this business ain't got a lot of room in it for taking pity. It's you and your partners and fuck the rest. Or go sell shoes for a living."

"I *know* that, dammit." And I did. She drew up against me again. I could smell the sick on her breath. "But this isn't business right now and she's already here and we can at least take her someplace else. That's all I'm saying."

"That's all you're saying, my ass. She's built like a brick shithouse and you'd like the chance to climb all over her. Hell, kid, I don't blame you—me too. But goddammit . . ."

That wasn't the whole reason—I didn't *know* the whole reason—but I couldn't deny it was part of it.

He blew out a long breath. Then said, "Goddammit, Sonny, the minute . . . the *minute* she's in the way . . . or even just a pain in the ass—"

"She's gone," I said.

"You goddam right she is."

And that was it. He turned and headed off. I held the girl close to me and followed him to the end of the alley, where it abutted a street that wasn't brightly lighted or heavily trafficked.

"Wait here out of the light," he said. Then left. The girl kept her hold on me and pressed her face into my chest.

Fifteen minutes later the car pulled up in front of the alley. Russell stuck his head out the window and said, "Where you at? What's this surprise you got?"

I steered the girl out of the shadows and over to the car and Russell said, "What the *hell* . . . ?"—smiling kind of crooked, like he thought it might be a joke.

The rear door swung open and Charlie reached out and beckoned impatiently. "Get her *in* here, Sonny."

I helped her duck into the door and Charlie drew her in. "Good Lord, girl," she said, "what happened to *you*?"

I started to get in the back too but Charlie wouldn't have it. She made me sit up front with Buck and Russell so the girl could lie on the seat with her head on Charlie's lap.

"Smells like somebody been using her for a . . . *hey* now," Russell said. I don't think he'd noticed till then that all she had on was the coat.

"You hush up, Russell LaSalle," Charlie said. "And turn around— all of you. It's not a coochie show back here." She unfurled her motor court blanket and spread it over the girl.

Russell got the Ford rolling. Buck drained the last drops of the flask, then got the bottle from under the seat. He uncorked it and took a slug and then handed it to me. I turned it up and swallowed deep and felt the heat of it in my eyes and nose, the flooding warmth in my belly.

Buck said it might be wise to make a beeline out of San Antonio and look for a motor court somewhere down the road. Nobody argued the point.

"You poor thing," Charlie crooned. She was stroking the girl's hair. "You poor . . . Sonny, what's her name?"

"Beats me," I said.

"Belle." Faintly spoken but clear enough.

And then she was asleep.

The Vieux Carré. Three o'clock of a Tuesday morning. Rivermist wafting through the streets and shaping hazy aureoles around the lamplights. Some of the jazz clubs still at it, some of the speaks and sporting houses, others of them calling it a night. Edward Longstreet Charponne emerges from Miss Daniella's front door and makes a final adjustment to his cravat as the proprietress herself smoothes the shoulders of his coat. She kisses his cheek, bids him goodnight and a good long sleep, steps inside and closes the door. He lights a thin cigar, exhales smoke and self-satisfaction, feels vestigial but pleasurable ache in his loins from the evening's ruttish indulgences. He crosses the street to the maroon Packard parked in the shadow of an overhanging balcony, unlocks the door and slides in behind the wheel.

He flinches at the touch of something small and hard against the back of his head as a voice says, Easy does it, counselor. Sharp Eddie is certain that the object at his head is a pistol and he feels a moment's keen urge to urinate. He peers into the rearview but the man's face is obscured by shadows and a white widebrimmed hat.

Have a smoke, the man says. Good for the nerves.

Eddie lights a cigarette and the man leans forward so the glow of the match will clarify his face in the mirror. The gray mustache spreads slightly in what might be a smile as Eddie recognizes him. He shakes out the match, certain that no amount of lawyerly outrage at being confronted in such felonious manner will be of effect with this man. Still, he is quick to recoup his self-confidence and invoke a bravado learned from his years of professional association with the rougher trades.

Wouldn't it be more polite, he says, not to say more productive and less warranting of assault charges, if you'd simply made an appointment to see me in my office?

Who killed Charlton?

Pardon me? His tone affecting a nettled bemusement. Look, deputy, the police have already interrogated me at length about Lionel Buckman's escape, so—

His left ear abruptly afire. His hand flies up to find there the pincers which snap onto the forefinger as well and he hears a small crack of bone. Before he can scream, the pistol barrel is deep in his mouth, scraping palate, grinding tongue on molars, inciting a surge of vomit to burn the nasal passages and cut off breath and spill over his goatee. He thinks he will drown. Then the barrel withdraws sufficiently to permit him to cough and suck a hard breath. The pincers unloose the torn ear and broken finger. Blood cascades hotly on his neck. Tears blur his vision and stream down his face, mucus floods his mustache. He snorts, chokes, gasps around the gun barrel. Tastes oil and steel and his own ferrous blood.

The beslimed muzzle leaves his mouth and presses into his good ear. The man embracing him from behind like a perverse lover, sliding the open pincers down his chest like a caress. Touching them lightly to his crotch.

I won't ask again.

Sharp Eddie gives up the names of Sonny LaSalle and his outlaw uncles—and with hardly a pause offers all he knows of last summer's Verte Rivage bank robbery, volunteers that he recognized the newspaper drawing of the unidentified Bogalusa robber and murder suspect as one of the LaSalle brothers. But he has little else to reveal. The LaSalles have kept him on retainer for nearly two years and occasionally joined him for a drink, but they've always been closemouthed about their business and their associates and never yet required his services in court for themselves.

The man jabs the gun hard into Eddie's ear. I don't give a rat's ass about them. Where's the kid?

Eddie swears he doesn't know. He's heard rumor the brothers fled New Orleans following the botched job in Bogalusa. Maybe the kid's with them. He feels his tender parts constricted small between the ready pincers.

Who else knows them? Other kin? A ladyfriend?

A ladyfriend, yes—a girl!—there was a girl. Eddie tells of an amused reference the brothers once made to a girl their nephew was humping. Last summer. A rich arty girl. Her father was the oil guy who drowned off the coast of Europe a few years back. Matson.

He nearly weeps with relief as the pincers come away from his genitals. Then hears as well as feels the horrifying crunch of them through his throat....

Police investigators speculate that Sharp Eddie's bloodsoaked demise most likely came at the hands of a client with a grievance.

Kind of lowlifes he did business with, I always expected it, me, a detective tells reporters.

The newspaper's pious editorial on the checkered career of Edward Longstreet Charponne closes with the observation that every criminal he set at liberty through the immoral and unethical application of his considerable legal acumen was but one more thief turned loose among the honest, one more seed of peril cast into the law-abiding world. We can hardly be faulted, the editorial opines, for perceiving some small measure of divine retribution in Mr. Charponne's having reaped of the pernicious fruit he sowed.

We pulled into the Guadalupe Motor Camp outside of Kerrville sometime after two in the morning. The hills cast deep shadows under the high oval moon. The air redolent of cedar. The manager wasn't happy about being wakened at that hour but he shuffled to the office door in robe and slippers and let us in. There were two cabins available. Charlie claimed one of them for herself and the girl and told Russell he had another think coming if he thought he was going to share it with them. She helped the girl out of the car and into the cabin and closed the door.

Russell hadn't complained about my "rescue" of the girl, as Buck jokingly insisted on calling it, until he realized he'd have to bunk with the two of us, and he berated me for a meddling fool as we finished off the bottle.

"Next time you get a notion to save some chippy from a fate worse than whatever," he said, "don't do it—not if it's gonna get me kicked out of my fluff's bed."

Even Buck's announcement that the San Antonio take came to $290 did little to soothe Russell's irritation. The cabin had two beds and I didn't think to argue about which one of us was going to sleep on the floor.

We slept till nearly midmorning but still were ready for breakfast before the girls, so we went to wait for them at the camp's café. When they finally came in and headed for our booth, we saw that Charlie had made a heroic effort with her makeup kit, but there was only so much she could do for the girl. The swollen black eye was a squint. Her other cheek looked embedded with a small wedge of plum, and her nose was lightly blue across the bridge. But she'd had a bath and her hair had been washed and brushed and showed a shine. She wore one of Charlie's dresses. It rode high on her legs and was tight across the breasts but otherwise seemed to fit okay. Until now I hadn't realized just how young she was—she didn't look more than sixteen. And I could tell that under the bruises the face was a pretty one.

"Like the blind man said when he passed the shrimp docks," Buck said, "hello, girls."

"For Pete's sake, Buck, *try* to be nice." Charlie said. She slid into the booth next to Russell and patted the seat beside her for the girl to sit there.

"Belle honey," Charlie said, "this here's Buck and that's Russell."

She looked up timidly from under her lashes and her eyes cut from Russell to Buck and her lips made a small twitch in what was probably the best she could do for a smile.

"An ass-kicking hurts even worse the day after, don't it, honeybunch?" Buck said. She lowered her eyes to the table.

Charlie gave Buck a look of reprimand, then touched Belle's arm and said, "And that's Sonny."

She met my eyes across the table for a second and then dropped her gaze again, her ears bright pink.

"My hero," Buck said, grinning at me. I flicked him a two-finger "up yours."

"Wish she'd give somebody a chance to get a word in edgewise," Russell said, smiling at the girl, and her ears got redder.

"She talks plenty," Charlie said, "when she's in company worth talking to."

Russell looked around, checking to see if anybody was within earshot, then said low-voiced, "Ah, exactly how much talking you done with her about us?"

"Enough," Charlie said. "I thought she ought to know what kind of company she was keeping so she could choose not to keep it if she didn't want."

"But here she still is," Buck said. "You got a thing for bad-asses, girl?"

"Buckman, *please*?" Charlie said.

"All right, all right," Buck said. "So now we're all properly intro-duced, can we get something to eat? I'm about starved to death."

He signaled for the waitress. She was an older woman and had probably seen a few things in her time because she never batted an eye at Belle's face.

When Charlie asked Belle what she wanted to eat, she stared at the table and shook her head slightly. She seemed to be trying hard to make herself invisible.

"Tell you what," Charlie said, "I'll get bacon and eggs and you get pancakes and sausage and we'll eat whatever we want off each other's plate, okay?"

But all she did was nibble at a piece of toast and sip her coffee while the rest of us ate like farmhands without much pause for con-versation.

Then we were on the road again, me at the wheel and Buck in the shotgun seat, Russell at a back window, Charlie between him and Belle. I'd take a look at her in the mirror every so often, and every time she was staring steadily out at the passing countryside like an immi-grant entering some strange new world.

Pretty much like us all.

The highway rose and fell and rose again. The towns smaller and fewer and getting farther apart. Hills and cedars and dwarf oaks. The grass turning dull, going sparse, giving way to stony scrub. Mesquites. Low clumps of cactus. The hills shrinking, scattering, the vistas widening, the sky deepening dead ahead.

In the early afternoon we stopped in some burg along the highway to get gasoline. When I shut off the engine the silence was profound. We all sat mute for a moment and all I could hear was the ticking of the hot engine. "Goddam," Buck said. "For minute I thought I'd gone deef." We all got out to stretch and use the restroom. I told the attendant to fill it up.

Russell asked the guy how it felt to live in the middle of nowhere. The guy got the pump going and spat a streak of tobacco juice and said, "It's another four, five hundred miles to anywhere near the middle."

Belle still hadn't said a word other than her name the night before. At one point Russell had casually asked where she was from, but she only gave him a spooked look and then turned her face back to the window. "Nice chatting with you," Russell said. Charlie punched him on the arm and said to leave the girl be. We'd gone along without anyone saying much after that, just listening to the sporadic music we'd pick up on the radio, usually more of the stringband stuff.

While the others were buying the sandwiches and sodas I stood at the side of the highway and stared off into the barrenness ahead, marveling at its vastness. I hadn't known New Orleans could feel so far away.

Buck came up beside me, sipping from a bottle of Dr Pepper and munching a Clark Bar. "We can at least take her somewhere else," he said, trying to mimic my voice. "Well . . . *here's* somewhere else. How about we leave her here?"

I didn't know he was joking and my face must've shown it, judging by the way he laughed. "Hell kid, the more I think on how she looked without a stitch, the more I believe we done the smart thing to bring her." He walked off to the car before I could think of what to say.

Then we were on the road again and pretty soon another station faded off the radio. Buck fiddled with the tuning knob, static rasping along the dial until we picked up a hissing and crackling rendition of "I Can't Give You Anything but Love, Baby." We started singing along—all but Belle, who kept staring out the window for a minute and then put her face in her hands and broke into sobs.

"Honey, *what*?" Charlie said. She took her in her arms.

"That song . . . it was playing when those . . . those men, they were . . . it was so . . . *awful*!"

"Easy, baby," Charlie said, patting her shoulder, rocking her like a child. Russell arched his brow at me in the rearview and I shrugged and turned the radio down. Buck rolled his eyes and shook his head.

And then she told her story. Told it bit by bit as the miles went by. Told it by fits and starts and mostly out of sequence. Told it with pauses to cry some more and to gently blow her tender nose and take a sip of Charlie's strawberry Nehi before resuming.

What it came to was this. She was Kathryn Belle Robinson— Kitty Belle, her daddy'd called her—seventeen years old, born and raised in Corsicana, Texas, and every passing mile was taking her farther from there than she'd ever been before. Her daddy had worked in the oil fields. Her mother came from Tyler, where she'd won some kind of rose festival beauty contest when she was in high school, but she hated oil towns and lamented her foolishness in marrying so young and ruining her dream of becoming a photography model. From the time Belle was a child, her mother advised her not to make the same mistake.

"Don't waste your good looks like a rose in a mudpit" was how her mother put it. Finish school, she told Belle, and then grab the first chance that came along to get away from the stink and grime of oil-town life.

Her daddy himself had been killed in the fields a year ago, gassed to death, him and eight others, by a leak at one of the rigs. They'd brought the bodies into town and laid them all in a row and every man of them had a bright red face and huge eyeballs and their bulging tongues were black. She hated that she still couldn't get that picture of him out of her head. He didn't leave any money so they'd had to move in with his brother Lyle and sickly wife Jean. To help with expenses Belle got a job at a bakery that specialized in fruitcakes. Her mother didn't do much of anything for a couple of months except sleep or sit at the window and stare out at the derricks, and then finally took a job as a waitress at a hotel restaurant.

For a time everything went all right, then her mother started going with a waitress friend to speakeasy parties after work. She sometimes didn't come home till dawn. Uncle Lyle pleaded with her to no effect. She told Belle not to worry, she was only having a little fun. It was like that for weeks and weeks. And then four months ago a policeman showed up at the door late one night. Her mother and some salesman from Waco had kicked up their heels for a while in a couple of speakeasies and then gone speeding off in the man's coupe. A few miles outside of town they'd crashed into a tree and were killed. Belle's mother was at the wheel.

For weeks afterward she felt like she was going around in a kind of trance. School lost the small pleasure it had held for her and she quit going. She stayed with her job because it didn't require much concentration and she could pass the days in the hum and whirr of the batter machines.

The problem was at night, when she'd lie in the dark and feel more alone than she'd ever imagined it was possible to feel. Her boyfriend, Billy Jameson—the only boy she'd ever "been with," as she put it—had got in trouble for breaking into a grocery store and left town without even saying goodbye. And her only two girlfriends had recently moved away with their daddies to some new oil boom in Oklahoma. She got along with her aunt and uncle, but in truth they were little more than strangers to her, and they anyway had their own troubles, what with her aunt now bedridden. The only relief she could find from her loneliness was at the movies. She began going every night. She loved sitting in the dark and getting swept into the stories on the screen, into the daring adventures and grand romances.

And then one night about three weeks ago, as she came out of the moviehouse, she was approached by a pair of well-dressed men who politely introduced themselves as Mr. Benton and Mr. Young. She'd noticed them outside the theater the night before and had felt herself blush when one of them nudged the other and nodded at her. They said they were talent scouts for a Hollywood producer who was sending them to towns all over America in search of fresh new faces. They thought she might be one. Would her parents give permission for her to go to Austin—all expenses paid, of course—to take a screen test?

I saw a look pass between Buck and Russell and knew what they were thinking. We'd heard stories of girls getting conned by guys passing themselves off as bigtime talent scouts. It was fairly easy to do, since singing contests and movie star look-alike competitions were popular entertainments all over the country, and it seemed like every couple of weeks there was another story in the papers of a smalltown girl being discovered and whisked off to New York to sing on the radio or taken to Hollywood by a movie producer who'd been passing through. Charlie had told me that a cousin of hers won twenty-five dollars for finishing third in a Mary Pickford look-alike contest in Baton Rouge.

The offer was so unexpected that Belle couldn't think of what to say except no, thank you. All right, the men said, but in case she should change her mind they gave her a few forms for her parents to sign. They were on their way to Dallas to meet with some other scouts and would then take their talent search into a few more towns in the region before coming back through Corsicana. If she changed her mind, all she had to do was be at the station in exactly two weeks when the Dallas southbound made its daily stop.

She made up her mind before the next sunrise, reminding herself of her mother's urging to get out of Corsicana at the first chance. She was scared, of course—she didn't know these men from Cain and Abel—but who knew when, if ever again, she'd have another chance to make her getaway? Over the next thirteen days and nights she bit her nails raw, afraid the men might not come back.

But they did. She met them at the station, suitcase in one hand, forged papers in the other. They had another pretty girl with them, Gladys Somebody from Waxahachie. She and Belle hit it off and talked about how swell it'd feel to be a movie star someday.

They changed trains three times before finally arriving in Austin, but they didn't get off there, after all. Instead they were joined by yet another girl—Lucy Somebody. Change of plan, the men told Belle and Gladys. The producer had decided to hold the screen tests in San Antonio. If either Belle or Gladys wanted to return home rather than go to San Antone with them, just say so and they'd be on the next train back. Neither Belle nor Gladys wanted that. How about calling home to tell the folks about the change in plan? Neither Belle nor Gladys felt the need to do that either.

"They knew you wouldn't," Russell said. "They'd already checked to see if either of you had any family that might be a problem. Asking did you want to call home about going to San Antonio was the last check to be sure." Buck stared out the window and nodded.

When the train got to San Antonio, Benton and Young took them to supper at a nice restaurant and then checked them into a hotel—the Travis. She and Gladys shared a room, and they figured Lucy must've been given a room of her own. She never did see Lucy again.

After breakfast the next morning they went to a room on the third floor that had been made into a sort of studio, with a camera set up in the living room to take what they called portfolio stills, and a movie camera in the other room for the screen tests. The windows were kept draped so the lighting would be consistent in all the pictures. There was a closet full of clothes of all kinds and sizes, and Young took a series of pictures of her and Gladys in turn wearing different outfits. He said they were naturals, the camera loved them. It was fun and she was enjoying herself. Then Benton brought lunch up to the room, sandwiches and a pitcher of ice-cold fruit juice.

"It's hard to remember things real clear after that," she said. And started crying again.

"The old Mickey Finn," Buck said. "In the Quarter one time a guy I knew was having trouble getting past first base with this girl. One night I run into them as they're coming out of a speak and the girl's smiling and all shitfaced and the guy's grinning like tonight's the night. She'd always said no to more than one drink, see, but I thought he'd finally figured some way to get her soused. Then she gives me a sloppy kiss hello and her breath didn't smell of booze, it smelled like this girl's did last night. Few days later the guy tells me she only had the one drink but he'd slipped a mickey in it. Worked like a damn charm, he said. A sweet drink'll hide the taste at the time but you sure breathe it out afterward."

Belle accepted Charlie's hankie to wipe her tears and swab her nose, then went on with her tale. She said it was like knowing you're having a dream but you can't wake up. She was vaguely aware of time going by but she had no idea how much of it passed before she realized she didn't have any clothes on and that somebody was "doing it" to her. A young curlyhaired blond guy. She was terrified and wanted to tell him to stop, to let her out of there, but it was like she'd forgotten how to talk. She felt so puny—it was all she could do to raise her hands to his chest, never mind push him away.

She heard music and voices and a low steady whirring. She saw Gladys sprawled in an easy chair by the wall, naked under an open robe and looking like she was drunk. The music was coming from a radio on a little table beside the chair—"I Can't Give You Anything but Love, Baby." The whirring came from a movie camera. Young was operating it. Benton was at his side. By now her head was clearing and she felt some of her strength returning, but she still couldn't push the guy off. He cursed her and pinned her arms over her head.

She heard Young say, "She needs another dose." He sounded farther away than he looked. Benton said, "In a minute." He was giving the blond kid directions, telling him to change positions on her, to touch her here, there, do this to her, do that. Finally the blond guy scooted up so that he was kneeling next to her face, pinning one of her arms with his knee and the other with one hand, trying to make her—

She broke off and started crying again. Charlie reached for her but the girl held her off. "No," she said, "I'm going to tell it, I *am*. He tried to . . . he was trying to put his . . . you know, his *thing* . . . to put it in my mouth. So I . . . I *bit* him. I did!"

Her face dropped into her hands again and her shoulders shook.

Buck turned around to look at her. In the mirror, Charlie was openmouthed and staring at her too.

"You mean," Russell said, "you bit the guy's *johnson*?"

She kept her face in her hands and nodded. *"Hard,"* she said, the word muffled.

"Not for long, I bet it wasn't," Russell said—and we all busted out laughing. Belle looked up and gaped around at us like we were crazy.

"Oh *honey*," Charlie said, and hugged her close.

"I'd say you evened the score pretty good," Russell said. He put his knees together and made a face of pain.

"You're damn lucky he didn't kill you," Buck said.

"It wasn't for lack of trying," she said—and for the first time seemed truly angry. "Next thing I knew I was seeing stars. That son of . . . that man started—"

"Sonofabitch," I said. "Say it. It's what he was."

She looked at me in the mirror. "That son of a bitch started hitting me with his fists. Benton was hollering for him not to mess me up and trying to get him off me and when he finally did, I up and ran."

"Right out into the hall," Buck said, "wearing nothing but that shiner, as I recall."

She blushed under the bruises and cut her eyes away. Charlie shook her head at Buck.

"Benton the mustache guy we laid out in the hall?" Buck said.

Belle nodded. "Thank you for . . . getting him away."

"I only gave him the finishing touches," Buck said. "Sonny here took the ambition out of him."

She fixed her green eyes on me in the mirror. "Thank you," she said.

The countryside expanded to an immensity of craggy rockland and thorny scrub under a cloudless sky beyond measure. We'd seen this West Texas country in photographs and in movieshows without having known its colors. Low blue mountains in the distance, long red mesas, conical purple buttes with peppercorn hides. Pale orange dust devils rising off the flats and swirling for miles before vanishing into the emptiness. Hawks sailing high, arcing over the scrub. Charlie had persuaded Russell to buy her a good pair of binoculars, and they turned out to be so much fun we all wanted a pair of our own. But no other place we stopped at sold them, and so Charlie let us take turns with hers.

All through the day, roadrunners would suddenly appear along the shoulder of the road, scooting with their long bills and tail feathers low to the ground, then veering away into the scrub. In midafternoon we spied a small herd of white-assed antelopes not a quarter-mile from the road and a pair of them butting heads. We pulled off the highway to watch them with the field glasses, and when I cut off the engine you could hear the faint smacking of their tall curved horns. We wished the bucks were distinctly different colors so we could lay bets, but it was impossible to tell them apart at that range.

We were still a couple of hours from Fort Stockton when the engine started to overheat. Luckily we came on a filling station within the next few miles, just beyond the Pecos River. I wheeled into the place with steam billowing from under the hood panels. We'd hoped the problem was nothing more than a ruptured hose but discovered it was a leak in the radiator. The station man said it would have to be soldered but he didn't have the iron for the job. He did, however, keep a few eggs handy for such emergencies as this and he went inside and got one.

We'd uncapped the radiator to let it steam off and Buck refilled it with water. With the motor idling, the station man broke open the egg and dropped it in the radiator and put the cap back on. As the hot water circulated through the engine it cooked the egg and plugged up the leak. It was an old trick we were all familiar with, one which sometimes worked and sometimes didn't. The station man said the makeshift repair should hold us till we got to the Sundowner Motor Camp and Diner about twenty miles down the highway. The place had a garage and a mechanic who lived on the premises.

We bought cold drinks and bags of potato chips. Charlie asked the station man the names of the more common plants around us. He pointed out broad-daggered yucca and skeletal ocotillo and long-stemmed lechugilla, scraggly creosote shrubs, the red tuna of the prickly pear. The tuna had spines so fine you couldn't see them, and as Russell found out when he touched one, you can't get those spines out even with tweezers. He'd feel their sting in his finger for days until his body finally absorbed them.

We drove on, everyone wearing dark glasses against the glare of the sun. The heat rose off the road in shimmering waves. Where the highway met the horizon behind us, a constant mirage gleamed like a pool of quicksilver.

The sun was a blinding incandescence at the ridge of the distant mountains when we spotted the Sundowner Motor Camp a mile or so ahead. A little ways beyond it stood a butte shaped exactly like a woman's breast with an erect nipple.

"You believe *that?*" Buck said. The likeness was so true we thought it might've been sculpted by some half-crazed artist who had devoted years or maybe his whole life to the project.

I parked in front of the camp's small garage and the mechanic came out and looked things over and said he could easy enough solder the radiator but it would have to wait till first thing in the morning. That was fine with us. Better to rest up tonight and get to Stockton feeling fresh tomorrow. We asked about the butte and he said it was a natural formation locally known as Squaw Tit Peak.

"Only one who can lay claim to that work of art is the Lord Almighty," he said, "and He didn't use no tools but wind and sand."

We took our bags out of the car and went over to the office to check in. The place was run by a married couple, the wife taking care of the desk, the husband doing the cooking in the café. The camp had a dozen cabins and ten of them were available. We took three—one for me and Buck, one for Russell and Charlie, one for Belle. We put the bags in the cabins and then went for supper in the café.

When the waitress saw Belle's face she glowered at us like she was trying to figure which one had done it to her—and looked ready to bite whoever it was. Belle read her expression and said, "These fellas are real nice. They fixed the one who . . ." She gestured at her bruises.

"That so?" the waitress said. "Well, I hope you all fixed the sumbitch good."

We had big bowls of chili beans that stung our mouths, huge hamburgers with all the trimmings, baskets of thick french fries slathered with ketchup. Tall glasses of lemonade with mint and lots of crushed ice. After nothing but a nibble of breakfast and a couple of bites of a cheese sandwich for lunch, Belle finally showed an appetite. Russell nudged me and nodded at her. She was bent over her plate and wolfing the burger, the juices running out of the bun and down her wrists. Charlie and Buck were watching her too. She stopped chewing and looked up at us.

"Welcome back among the living," Russell said.

She blushed through her bulging smile, her cheeks full of burger. Charlie reached over with a napkin and wiped a smear of mustard off her lip.

For dessert we had slabs of peach pie thick with fresh peach chunks and rich grainy sugar. Then Buck went to have a chat with the manager. In a little while he came back with the irksome news that there was no hooch to be had at this place. But an oil camp about twelve miles north was said to have its own still, and the crew was said to sometimes be of a mind to sell a little something to a fella in need.

We finished our coffee and went outside and stopped short. The whole world was steeped in a dying daylight so deeply red and darkly yellow it seemed unreal.

The manager stood in the door behind us and said, "Does it every time. I come out here from Ohio near to twenty-five years ago and still can't believe it. It's like the light's made of blood and gold."

I smiled and said, "You're a poet, mister."

"Not me, son," he said. "I'm just glad to see it with my own eyes and hope to do it again tomorrow." He flicked away his cigarette and went inside.

Buck drove off in the Model A and the rest of us went to the cabins. After a long shower and a change of clothes I went outside into the gathered darkness. The air smelled of dust and cooling stone. At the foot of a nearby rise I found a low flat boulder that made a good bench. A narrow streak of violet still showed above the western mountains, but the rest of the sky had gone black and glimmered with early stars. The first fireflies were out and flashing softly. The moon was up in the east, nearly full, the color of a new penny.

Highway traffic was sparse. You could see the lights of an approaching vehicle from a long way off before it finally went whirring by. A series of high yowls rose somewhere to the distant south, and it took me a minute to realize they must be coyotes.

"I heard them before." I started at the sound of her voice in the darkness slightly behind me—then made out her vague silhouette about ten feet away. "Sorry," she said. "Didn't mean to spook you."

"How long you been there?" I said.

"Only a little bit."

"I didn't see you come out."

"Huh?"

"Out of your room," I said. "I didn't see you come out."

"*Oh,* you mean you didn't see me from out *here.* Well, no, you couldn't've seen me come out from out here. I already was."

"What?"

"I already *was* out here."

"You were already out here when *I* came out?"

"It's what I just said. Is there something wrong with how I'm talking?"

"I *know* what you said. I mean, why didn't you say something?"

"What do you mean? Jeepers, I *did* say something. I said I'd heard—"

"No, before."

"Before *when?*"

"When I first came out here, goddammit. Why didn't you say something right away instead of lurking in the dark? Jesus Christ, what a conversation."

"You don't have to swear at me," she said. "And I wasn't *lurking.* And I could say the same, you know—about this conversation."

I blew a long breath, surprised at my own agitation. "Yeah," I said. "I suppose you could."

"All right, then," she said.

There was a faraway keening of a train whistle. The highway lay dark in either direction.

"I didn't say anything before," she said, "because . . . well, you don't talk as much as the others. I thought maybe you don't care to. That answer your question?"

I nodded and said, "Utterly."

She only half succeeded in suppressing a snicker. "I don't guess this chat's going to do a whole lot to change your attitude about not talking much."

It was the first time I'd heard her try to be even a little bit funny, and coming when it did it struck me as so funny I busted out laughing—and she did too, laughing hard, from deep in the belly, like she hadn't done it in a hell of a while.

I moved over on the boulder and patted it for her to have a seat beside me. She accepted an Old Gold from the pack I offered. She smelled freshly clean, and when I struck a match to light the cigarettes, I saw that her hair hung damp and straight. She took a small puff and coughed. She was no practiced smoker.

"You never even smoked a cigarette before?"

"In secret a couple of times with this girl back home. We didn't have all that much chance to get good at it."

"What about that boyfriend you had? You didn't smoke with him?"

"He didn't smoke, he chewed. I wasn't *about* to try that."

"I guess love has its limits, huh?"

"Maybe," she said. "It anyway wasn't love, I don't believe, not really. I think I was only . . . I don't know."

In the ensuing silence I sensed she was embarrassed at having told too much, so I said in a tough-guy rasp, "Well, stick with me, kid, and you can practice at smoking all you want. I'll show you all the fastest ways to hell."

"Look who's calling anybody kid," she said. "How old are you—eighteen, nineteen?"

"Right the second time," I said.

The high cries of the coyotes rose again and seemed keener in the greater darkness. She said she used to hear them all the time at her grandparents' farm in Comanche County when she was a child.

"They sound different ways if you listen really careful," she said. "Sometimes it's like they're having a high old time, and sometimes like they're trying to tell you something you'll never in the world understand." There came a long solitary howl and then another right behind it from another coyote and of different timbre. "And sometimes it's like that—like the loneliest talk there is."

We sat and smoked in the dark, our cigarette tips glowing red among the pale green sparks of the fireflies, our smoky exhalations mingling in the light of the rising moon. We stayed like that for a long time without speaking. Russell and Charlie had remained in their room and I figured he was making up for what he'd missed the night before. The thought of them going at it made me keenly conscious of Belle's nearness. I thought I could feel her body heat on my bare arm. I lit another cigarette and she asked if she could have one too.

I struck a match and she touched my hand as she leaned forward to accept the light. She looked up at me from under her lashes, her good eye wide and bright and a little scared. Then blew out the flame and took away her hand.

And then here came headlights down the road, brightening as they approached—and sweeping over us when the car turned into the parking lot. The Model A halted in front of the cabins and the engine shut off and the door opened and then banged shut. Buck called out, "You all come on down here and see what I got us."

When we got to the room, he had already set out drinks for us in a pair of tumblers. He'd sweet-talked the oil crew into selling him three bottles. He'd tapped into one of them on the drive back and it showed in the high shine of his eyes. The bottle was already down by a third. He tossed off his drink and smacked his lips, smiled at us and served himself another. I took a sip of mine and had to admit it seemed like pretty good hooch.

Belle hadn't picked up her glass. Buck gestured at it and said, "It's aged plenty enough, honey. Down the hatch."

"I don't guess I want any," she said, rising from her chair. "I'm really awful tired. Think I'll go on to bed." She said goodnight to Buck and waggled her fingers at me and left.

He got up and went to the window and pushed the curtain aside to watch her go to her cabin.

"She's probably still hungover from the mickey," I said.

"Yeah," he said. "If it *was* a mickey."

"What do you mean if it *was*?"

He turned and arched his brow at me. "Just because she says she was Shanghaied into it don't make it so. Most of them who do those movies do it because it pays good and because they like it."

"What are you saying? She was doped, man. You smelled it on her breath, you said—like on that girl in New Orleans."

"Yeah—and what I didn't say was I'd smelled it even before that. In a Chink dope den in New York. Me and another doughboy went in to see what it was like and got looped just breathing the air in there. You can mix that stuff all kinds of ways. Makes a swell mickey in a drink, but they mostly smoke it in pipes with a little hose. They do it for the dreams, but a right dose'll let you stay awake and keep you smiling at nothing all night. The stag movie guys like to have the girls take a puff to loosen them up, put a dreamy look on their face for the camera, but some like it *too* much—sucking the devil's dick, they call it. Get too dopey to do anything but lay there like the dead."

I watched him pour another, then light a cigarette and blow three perfect smoke rings. "You think her story's bullshit?" I said.

"Who knows?" he said. "Maybe not. Or maybe everything she's said is bullshit—all that stuff about her momma and daddy, everything. Maybe she was willing enough to fuck in front of a camera for the right price or a little encouragement from the pipe, or both. I wouldn't hold my breath waiting for her to admit it, though. Only thing we know for sure is she got somebody damn mad at her."

"Russell believes her," I said.

"Hell he does. He's like me—he just doesn't give a shit if she's lying. What difference does it make if she's a good girl on the stray or some bullshitting little tramp? Who *cares*? Those tits are as nice either way, and those tits are why she's here, right? You've had plenty of schoolgirl tail, Sonny, but this one's a different breed, so don't be a sap and think that she's—"

There came a hard rapping on the door and then it swung open and Russell and Charlie came charging in with wide smiles, their faces flushed with their recent sporting.

"There it is!" Russell said, making a beeline for the booze. "Can we count on this man to come through or can we count on him to come through?" He poured drinks for him and Charlie.

Charlie was sorry to hear Belle had called it a night but said she didn't blame her, all she'd been through the last couple of days. Russell toasted our arrival in this strange new world. He said he loved the dryness of the heat, so different from New Orleans, where you could drown in the humidity. Charlie said she felt smaller out here. "It's that big old sky and hardly any trees," she said. "I can't get used to hardly any trees."

We finished the bottle and started on another. Russell told a joke he'd heard from a filling station guy. Fella goes to the doctor for a checkup and the doctor tells him it's bad news, he doesn't have long to live. Fella says, "Oh my God, that's terrible! How long do I have?"

Doctor says, "Ten." Fella says, "Ten *what*? Months? Weeks?" Doctor says, "Nine . . . eight . . . seven . . ."

Buck told one he'd heard from the oil rig guys. The queen of England was riding in her carriage with her guest the king of Belgium when one of the carriage horses lets go with a tremendous fart. The queen turns all red and says to the king, "Oh dear, I must apologize for that." The king says, "Quite all right, your highness—actually, I had thought it was the horse."

The bottle was down to its last couple of inches and Russell took it with him when he and Charlie said goodnight—a little hair of the dog for the morning, he said. Buck and I stood at the door and watched them go. Belle's cabin window was dark.

We went back inside and Buck uncorked the last bottle and filled a tumbler to the brim. "That ought to hold you," he said. Then gave me a wink. "Don't bother to wait up." He took the rest of the bottle and went out and shut the door behind him.

I sat on the bed and took off my shoes and stared at the floor for a time. I couldn't clarify what I was feeling. I picked up the tumbler and took a swallow. And then another. Then got up and went to the curtain and pushed it aside. Her window curtain was dimly yellow. I stared at it till my eyes burned. Then the window went dark.

Of course she wouldn't admit it if she'd done it willingly. So what? He was right. Who gave a rat's ass if she lied or even what she lied about? What difference did it make to any of us? Those tits were terrific either way and that's why we'd brought her along. Goddam right.

Then I pictured myself standing there and felt like a damned fool. I dropped the curtain and took another big gulp from the tumbler, striped to my underwear, turned off the light and got into bed. And the booze carried me right off.

It was still dark when I woke with a parched tongue and a throbbing head. I felt my way along the wall to the bathroom and switched on the light. With my mouth to the spigot I drank till my belly was bloated. I was about to snap off the light when I saw somebody on the floor by the door and for a moment thought Buck had come back and passed out before he could make it to his bed. And then I saw it was her.

She was sitting up and watching me, hugging her knees to her breasts, the skirt of her dress tucked between her legs. The way the shadows fell across her face her bad eye looked like a black patch.

"The light woke me," she said. "For a minute I didn't remember where I was and I couldn't see it was you in there and I thought I was having a bad dream."

"When'd you come in?"

"I don't know. A while ago."

"Buck?"

"The other cabin." She sniffed and wiped at her nose. "I didn't mean to come in without asking, but I didn't want to wake you. I tried to sleep in the car but it's got so cold out and I didn't have a blanket or anything and . . . I'm sorry."

"Why you on the floor? Why didn't you get in the other bed?"

"I didn't want to be using his bed if he came over here."

I helped her up and sat her on the edge of my bed. I lit two cigarettes and handed her one. "So what happened?" I said.

She'd been awakened by his knocking on the door. He said to open up, it was cold out there. She thought we were getting ready to leave right away for some reason. She turned on the light and quickly got dressed, then unlocked the door. He came in and locked it again. When she saw his eyes she knew he was very drunk and knew what it was he wanted. She'd seen a lot of drunk men back in Corsicana and had learned to fear them all. She asked him please to go, but he said there wasn't any need to play the innocent, not with him.

She was afraid to do anything but stand there while he ran his hands over her and up under her dress. He told her to take her clothes off and get on the bed. Then he switched off the light and took off his shoes and pants and got in bed with her. At first she thought he had his hand down there and was pushing on her with the tip of his thumb—and then was astonished to realize that what was rubbing on her was his "thing." What there was of it. He rubbed and rubbed himself on her and then it was over and he rolled off her and turned his face to the wall. She thought he might've been crying. She hadn't known she'd been crying too until she got up and went into the bathroom to clean herself and saw her face in the mirror.

When she came out he had the cover pulled over him and was snoring. She had no idea how long she stood there before finally putting on her dress and shoes and going out to the car and lying down on the seat. But she couldn't sleep for the cold and she kept listening for her cabin door to open. Finally she came to my door and tried it and found it unlocked and came in real quiet and curled up next to the wall. She didn't think she'd be able to sleep but she must've because next thing she knew she saw the light in the bathroom.

"He threaten to hurt you if you didn't do like he said?"

"No, he never."

"Then why do it if you didn't want to?"

"I thought I had to. I thought you were right outside."

"Come again? You thought *I* was right outside? Outside your *cabin*? Then why didn't you run out?"

"I thought . . . I thought you were waiting to be next."

And then she was crying into her hands again.

Well hell. After a minute I put an arm around her and she leaned into me with her face on my chest. Her crying became a case of hiccups, and when I chuckled at the mix of hics and sobs, she hit me lightly on the shoulder with her fist and said, "It's not—*hic*—funny"—and we both laughed.

"Let's try and get some sleep," I said. "Sun'll be up soon. You can have this bed."

She lay down and I covered her with the blanket and tucked it around her. Then got in Buck's bed and under the blanket.

I don't know how much time passed before she said, "Sonny?" She said it so softly I wasn't sure I'd heard it. "You awake?"

"What?"

"Charlie told me the trouble you had in Loosiana."

"She did, huh?"

"Was it terrible in prison?"

"What do you think?"

"It must've been terrible."

"Go to sleep."

"I'm glad you got away."

"Not as glad as I am. Now go to sleep."

Another minute went by.

"Sonny?"

"Christ's sake, what?"

"I'm glad you weren't waiting to be next."

"Do I have to go knock you on the head to shut you up?"

She chuckled. "You wouldn't neither. You're too nice."

❧

I came awake up with my head still hurting and discovered her lying beside me. No telling how long she'd been there. She was rolled in her blanket like an Indian, her back to me, her ass against my hip. I had an urgent erection, and my first inclination was to use it on her. Then I remembered how pathetic she'd looked last night, and how she'd thought I'd been waiting to take a turn. I'd never been prone to confusion about myself or about women, but if somebody had put a gun to my head at that moment and demanded to know exactly what I was feeling, I couldn't have given a straight answer.

She stirred and started to come awake. I rolled on my side away from her and feigned to be still sleeping. She lay still for a minute, then eased out of bed. I waited till I heard the bathroom door click shut and then got up and put my clothes on.

When she came out and saw me she blushed. Then looked down at herself and said, "Will you *look* at this dress? You'd think somebody'd been sleeping in it, for Pete's sake." I smiled at that and then she smiled too. Then we went over to the café.

The others weren't there yet but we went ahead and ordered. Several mugs of coffee and some fried eggs and sausage and hashbrowns and biscuits dripping with butter all helped put a cushion on my hangover. Belle ordered the same thing but only picked at it. She was nervous and kept cutting her eyes to the front door. I was feeling a little squirmy myself. She probably sensed it and didn't even try to make small talk.

I was done eating when Buck showed up. I'd figured he'd get there ahead of Russell and Charlie, who were prone to a morning hump and were usually the last ones to the table. He slid into the seat opposite us in the booth and gave a lopsided grin. His eyes were badly bloodshot. "Feel like I been run over by a damn booze truck," he said. The waitress came with a mug of coffee for him and took his order and went away again.

He lit a cigarette and smiled at Belle. She was looking at her plate and pushing her food around with her fork. "When I woke up by my lonesome," he said, "I figured you'd gone to see if young Romeo here could use some company too." He winked at me. "She's a darling, ain't she?"

I wasn't smiling, and he finally seemed to tune in to our mood.

"What?" he said.

"She didn't like what you did last night," I said. I hadn't intended to be so blunt, but there it was.

"Say what?" He looked at me like I'd spoken in a foreign language.

"You scared her, man," I said. "She'd rather you don't do that again."

He laughed. "She'd *rather,* would she?" He looked at Belle. "Is this rascal telling me true, missy? I *scared* you?"

She kept her gaze on her plate and nodded. I was pulled between pity and the urge to slap her on the head for being so damned sheepish.

"And so?" Buck said. "You don't want me to come creeping into your tent no more?"

She looked all set to start crying again. It really irked me. "It's what she said, Buck."

"Not to me, she didn't—and she can speak for herself."

She laid her fork alongside her plate and for the first time looked at him directly. "I don't want you to do that again."

He stared at her without any expression at all.

"Please," she said.

Which got a smile from him. "Well hell, honey. All you had to do was say so. I never in my life forced myself on a woman and I ain't starting now. This how you want it, this is how you got it. Good enough?"

She nodded.

"Still friends?"

She looked like she'd never heard such a question. Then made a small smile and nodded again.

"Well, all right then," he said.

The waitress arrived with his food and the coffeepot and refilled our mugs. Buck cut into his pork chop and said it was done just right. Belle started nibbling the sausage links off her plate with her fingers. The matter of last night had been so swiftly settled it felt like I'd missed something, but she seemed well satisfied with the way it went.

Buck said he'd already checked on the car—radiator all patched up and ready to go. Then Russell and Charlie showed up and ordered big well-done steaks with scrambled eggs and hashbrown potatoes and biscuits and gravy and tall glasses of milk.

Charlie was happy to see how much the swelling had gone down in Belle's cheekbone. She lightly traced the bruises with a forefinger and said, "Look here where the purple part's already turning blue. This spot here'll be green by tomorrow, and here's some yellow starting to show. Declare, girl, right now you got about the most colorful face in Texas."

Russell leaned over for a closer look at the swellings. "You're lucky the bastard wasn't wearing some kind of mean ring," he said. "You won't have no scar at all."

A half hour later we'd retrieved our bags from the cabins and loaded them in the car. The girls got in the back seat with Russell. Our old road map was practically in tatters so I went in the office to buy a new one. Buck had settled the bill for the car repair and the rooms and was standing outside the office, counting what was left of our stake money. He was still there when I came out.

"Here's the lucky stud gets her all to himself," he said, punching me lightly on the arm.

He was smiling but there was something in his tone. I smiled back and shrugged. "I guess," I said.

"I want you to know," he said, "if she said I forced her it's a lie."

"She didn't say that. Only that she asked you to go."

"I don't recall that she did."

"We were all pretty soused," I said. "Except for her."

He spat and looked off at the distant mountains. "I wasn't so soused I ain't sure she didn't say no." He turned to me again. "I ain't no rape fiend, kid. I can't abide a rape fiend."

"Hell, Buck, I know that."

"Like as not she couldn't deal with Mr. Stub," he said, using the name he'd given his mutilated pecker. "It's some who can't."

I made a wry smile and shrugged. "Maybe. She's pretty much the fraidy-cat type as it is."

"I thought I had her figured," he said, "but now I ain't so certain."

"Cries at the drop of a damn hat," I said.

He smiled. "Yeah she does." He looked over at the car, where she and Charlie were laughing at something Russell was saying. "But Lordy, don't that body beat all?"

"You said a mouthful."

"Couple of nice mouthfuls is what she got. Well, hell, enjoy it while it lasts, kid." He narrowed his eyes at me. "Just one thing. You sappy for her?"

"*Sappy?*" I said. I peered at the car and lowered my voice. "Hell no, man, it's not like *that*." And told myself I meant it.

He studied my face. "Good," he said.

"I mean it."

"All right." He smiled. "Let's go."

On our way to the car he said in a low voice, "You know, even if I *had* tried to force her—and I sure as shit didn't, but even if I *had*—it couldn't've been but *attempted* rape nohow. Can't be nothing *but* attempted with a damn one-inch pecker, right?"

We were laughing when we got to the car, and Charlie asked what was so funny.

"This damn Sonny," Buck said. "Listen here to the dumbass joke he just told me."

As I drove out of the parking lot and started down the highway with the sun directly behind us, he told the one about the woman who goes to the doctor and tells him she just all of a sudden went deaf in one ear. The doctor takes a look and says, "Well, I see your problem—you've got a suppository in there." And the woman says, "Oh for Pete's sake . . . *now* I know what happened to my hearing aid."

Indigo night of drizzling rain. Water dripping from eaves and clattering on banana fronds, running off gutters and spattering on cobblestones. Sporadic and trembling heat lightning. Hoarse bellows of ships' horns out on the river.

He works the pick gently. Feels the lock yield to his expert application. Eases the door ajar and listens intently. Opens it further and slips inside and closes it softly behind. Stands immobile and studies the geography of the place by the intermittent flares of lightning at the windows. There the kitchen. There the bath. There the bedroom door. Light and dark, light and dark. Mapping in his head the furniture's array. And then a quavering illumination finds him gone from the front door, transported as by the darkness itself to the bedroom threshold.

The bed stands empty and neatly made. He cannot know if she will return this selfsame evening, whether she will be alone or in company. The lightning quits. He positions himself in a chair in the bedroom and listens in the darkness for sound at the front door. And remains thus for hours. The rain ceases. The windows turn pink with the rising of the morn. When the place is sufficiently daylit he begins to search. And comes to find an envelope in the bedside drawer. The word Sonny inscribed upon it. Two items within. A sheet of paper with the single word Dolan's and the initial B. And a note.

> *Chérie—Sorry to leave this way, but got word of B & R! Have to catch a train in 15 min. Took $50. I owe you more than $. Be back soon. You're an angel—an incomparably lovely vixen—the classiest dame in the Quarter—the most erotic of dreams made flesh—the cat's veriest whiskers. In other words, you ain't bad, kiddo. Think of me, S.*

She will never know of her inestimable good fortune in choosing to go to St. Louis at this time to appraise an oil collection for possible exhibit in the Fontaine. So deft was his search she will also never suspect that someone was prowling her home in her absence and prying into the recesses of her life. Some days after her return she will hear a neighbor play Blue Skies on the saxophone and her lingering resentment toward Sonny for his rude departure will quite suddenly give way to missing him terribly. She will go to the bedside drawer for his goodbye note and read it yet again for reassurance of his intention to come back. And will again get nothing from it but the sinking feeling that she has seen him for the last time.

Though well outside his bailiwick, the Quarter is not unfamiliar to him. He has made occasional visits to its ranker pockets, has had dealing with various of its meaner denizens, is not without notion of where to begin his search. And thus, on an early-darkening evening of impending rain, after two days of discreet inquisitions he stands informed of the Dolan who worked for a time with the brothers LaSalle. . . .

At his small table in the back room of the garage Jimmyboy sups on a small pot of tomato soup and listens to the radio. He has the volume turned up loud against the rain's drumming on the roof, but the reception is poor and crackles with static. Rudy Vallee opens the show with his customary greeting of Heigh-ho, everybody! and the band swings into a rendition of I'm Just a Vagabond Lover.

So badly rusted are the hinges of the door at Jimmyboy's back that the radio's loudness does not mute their screech. He turns with a sardonic intention of telling the intruder to learn to read so he can understand window signs that say Closed, then sees a tall lean man with gray face and mustache, a broad-brimmed hat dripping rainwater, a chrome contraption where his hand should be. A man not here with complaint of car trouble. A man—and Jimmyboy knows this with instant and iron certainty—of grave intolerance for bullshit.

He turns down the radio and pushes his chair back and points at his prosthetic foot. I got a part missing too, mister, he says, and it done give me all the pain I care to know in this life. I ain't no tough guy even a tiny bit. You tell me what you want and if I can give it to you I will, believe you me.

John Bones holds up Sonny LaSalle's prison photograph. Name? he says. Seeking to see how truthful this gimp is.

Jimmyboy names Sonny without hesitation. He tells everything he knows about the LaSalles, even producing the sketch of Russell attached to the newspaper report of the Bogalusa bank robbery, and concluding with what he learned by steaming open the envelope the brothers had left for Sonny and reading its contents before sealing it up again. He tells of the note's instruction to go to a filling station that he's sorry he can't remember the name of but he remembers it's right next to the Houston train depot and it said talk to a guy named Miller.

I'd say that's where he's gone, sure enough, Jimmyboy says.

The man's eyes never blink.

You see, mister, Jimmyboy says. You see how I'm cooperating? Not a need in the world to get rough, not with me, no sir. You only got to ask is all.

Jimmie Rodgers starts yodeling on the crackling radio.

The man smiles. I like that, he says. Turn it up some.

Sure thing, Jimmyboy says. He turns around and raises the volume—and all in an instant there is a large-caliber pistolblast and his forehead bursts in a spray of blood and brain and his ruined head thumps the table.

The radio yodels on as John Bones goes out of the room and through the garage and into a dark and sodden night beshrouding the deserted streets in this empty neighborhood of padlocked warehouses and shuttered shops.

The police will record Jimmyboy Dolan's death as an unsolved homicide—hardly rare fate among smalltime New Orleans crooks. No one will attend his pauper's burial, but at least one of his familiars will feel something akin to grief on learning of his demise. Cockeye Calder will be near to tears when he sorrowfully laments, That sonofabitch still owed me four grand!

*U*nder a midmorning sun and high blue sky we rolled into Fort Stockton, seat of Pecos County. The place had its share of oil fields and oil money, but we would try for none of it. This town would be our refuge, where we'd return after pulling jobs in other places. We wanted no trouble with the local citizens or police. As far as they were concerned, we were sales reps for Matson Oil and Toolworks, assigned to the West Texas circuit.

We went to a real estate office and told the lady there what we were looking for. She said we were in luck, a local oil rigger had put his house up for rent just two days ago. He'd been offered a job in some panhandle boomtown too good to turn down. He'd taken his family with him and expected to be gone a year. The place was at the south edge of town and she led us over there in her car and showed it to us. Three bedrooms and fully furnished, styled sort of like a double-barreled version of the shotgun houses you saw in Louisiana. All the bedrooms were along one side and a narrow hallway separated them from the parlor, bathroom and kitchen. The bathroom had an old clawfoot tub that had been rigged with a showerbath pipe and nozzle. The kitchen was equipped with a spanking new Frigidaire and a good gas stove. Both the parlor and the kitchen had doors that opened onto an L-shaped porch running the length of the house and around the back of it. The sideporch had a long picnic table and afforded a grand view of the mountain sunsets. The rent was steep and we'd have to put up a large damage deposit, but when Buck looked at me and Russell we both nodded.

"We'll take it," he told the woman.

Buck claimed the front bedroom for himself, and Charlie took the middle one for her and Russell because she liked the mesquite tree that stood against the window. "That leaves you two with the private one in back," she said, winking at Belle and getting a blushing smile out of her.

After we unpacked we went shopping and bought groceries and cigarettes, cookware and towels. Buck made inquiries and learned that if a man wanted really good beer and top-grade moonshine he should go to a certain green house at the end of Callaghan Street and tell whoever came to the door that Grover sent him. So we did—and bought a dozen quarts of excellent beer and three quarts of pretty fair corn liquor.

According to the real estate lady the town had sprung up next to an army fort back around 1860 and then became a main station on the stage line. What made the location so desirable was that it had water—Comanche Springs, where the Indians had been refreshing themselves for God knew how long before the white man showed up. She'd said the spring was now the site of a pretty park about fifty yards up the road from our house. When we got back from town we walked over to have a look at it.

There was a swimming hole with grassy banks, shade trees, barbecue pits, picnic tables and benches. "A veritable oasis," I said, and got
one of Buck's "Ain't you smart?" looks.

Nobody was happier about this geographical marvel than Charlie.
"I hadn't wanted to say anything and be a spoilsport," she said, "but
the farther we've come into this damn desert the more I've been wondering how I can live in such a godforsaken place. This little patch of
trees and water is exactly what I need to keep from losing my mind."

It was a roasting afternoon and the swimming hole too tempting
to resist. Buck and Russell and I stripped down to our trousers and
dove in. That was all the encouragement the girls needed to kick off
their shoes and take the plunge in their dresses. The water was chilly
and dark green and smelled wonderfully fresh. We splashed and
dunked each other and took turns on the rope somebody had tied to a
high tree branch overhanging the pool. You'd swing way out over the
deep part and let go of the rope and stay suspended in the air for one
marvelous instant before dropping into the water.

An old couple sat at a table and seemed to enjoy our frolic. Every
time Charlie or Belle swung out on the rope and dropped off, their
skirts flapped up around their hips, affording us a good look at their
legs all the way up to their underwear—and every time, the old man
would yell "Ya-*hooo!*" along with me and Buck and Russell. When the
girls came out of the water to take another swing, we'd grin and grin
at the way their thin sopping dresses clung to them.

"You bunch of oversexed galoots," Charlie said.

"And they always will be, honey," the old woman said, giving the
old guy a reproving look. He shrugged with his palms turned up in the
universal gesture of "Who, *me?*"

Russell dunked Charlie every chance he got, heedless of her
repeated cries of "Quit it, Russell!" Then she got even. He was standing in belly-deep water and admiring Belle's legs as she swung out on
the rope when he suddenly went under like the pool bottom had
given way. Charlie burst up from the water, laughing and crowing that

she'd pulled his feet from under him. He came up thrashing and coughing and she grabbed him from behind by the head and pulled him under again and scooted out of his reach. He flailed wildly at the surface as he struggled to get his footing but kept slipping and couldn't get up for a breath. I was about to jump over there and haul him up when his head broke water and he finally managed to stand, choking and wild-eyed. Charlie shook a finger at him from the other side of the pool and said, "When I say no more I mean no more, dammit!"

The old woman at the table applauded and called out, "That's telling him, girl!"

"You crazy cooze," Russell managed to say through a coughing fit. "You about drowned me."

"Take it for a warning, Buster," she said. But she was careful to keep her distance from him until he cooled off.

"Rough as they play, it's a wonder they ain't *all* got black eyes," the old man said to nobody in particular, but staring at Belle's bruises.

After a while we climbed up on the bank and stretched out in the grass and let the sun beat down on us. The old couple called goodbye and we waved so long. When we were about half dry we put our shoes on and went back to the house.

We ate supper at the long table on the sideporch—fried beefsteaks and baked potatoes and buttered rolls, big glasses of iced tea with lemon so tart you could taste it in your nose and sugar so coarse you felt the grains against your teeth. Then Buck and I opened a couple of the quarts of beer and poured a glass for everybody and the cigarettes got passed around and we all sat there sipping and smoking and watching the sun set in a welter of reds and golds and purples.

Belle took a sip of her beer and made a face, then went to the Frigidaire and came back with a bottle of Coke. She was sitting beside me, and as the darkness began to rise around us I felt her leg press against mine. I put my hand on her thigh and looked at her but couldn't make out her expression in the closing gloom. "Go for a walk?" I said.

"Sure," she said. I took one of the packs of smokes and said we'd be back in a while.

The moon was risen low, hugely full and saffron yellow, and a cool breeze had kicked up. She took my hand and we strolled up the road to the park. The trees rustled in the easy wind and cast long undulant shadows.

The pool held the moon's glimmering image. We sat on a shadowed bench and smoked without talking. After a while I put my arm around her and she put her head on my shoulder, and a while after that she turned her face up to me and I kissed her. She moved up and sat on my lap and I stroked her flank and bottom while we kissed some more. I slipped my hands inside her shirt and felt her breast and fingered its tightened nipple. She put her hand over mine and pressed it harder to her. We were using our tongues now and breathing heavily.

"Let's go to the room," she said.

On the way back we stopped every few yards and kissed and ran our hands over each other and then started walking again, moving a little faster against the encroaching chill and in our eagerness to get to our bed, laughing and groping at each other as we went. When we came in view of the house we saw the parlor and kitchen windows brightly yellow.

"Looks nice, doesn't it?" she said. "Like some safe little place way out here in a big nowhere."

We went in by the front door and headed for our room at the end of the lighted hallway. As we passed the kitchen door, Buck looked at us from the table, where he was cleaning his pistols. Belle waved at him but he only stared blankly and then gave his attention back to the guns. The porch door was open behind him and we heard Russell and Charlie laughing out there.

"What's with him?" she whispered. I shrugged, not really paying much mind to anything at the moment except her. I steered her into the room with a hand on her ass and she laughed and was already unbuttoning her shirt as I closed the door behind us.

For somebody who claimed to have no experience at it except with a thieving boyfriend in Corsicana and with the sonofabitch who did her when she was drugged, she was pretty adept—and as avid as any woman I'd been with, including Brenda Marie. I'd pulled the bed away from the wall to avoid thumping, but I guess we were pretty loud anyway with our gasping and moaning and rocking so hard the bed's feet scraped the floor.

When we paused to catch our breath she whispered, "You think they can hear us in the next room?"

"Don't know," I said. "Don't care."

"Me neither," she said, and pulled me to her.

No telling how long we were at it before finally going to sleep with me spooned against her from behind, but it didn't seem very long before I woke to a window full of sunlight and the smells of coffee and bacon seeping into the room. The faint strains of a string band came from the radio Charlie had bought for the kitchen.

"Hungry?" Belle murmured, nuzzling my neck. Her hand moved up my thigh and found me rigid. "Merciful heavens, boy, don't you ever get enough?"

"As if you do," I said, caressing the smooth swells of her buttocks.

She giggled and kissed my ear and slid a leg over me and mounted up.

After a time we got out of bed and put on our clothes and went into the kitchen. Russell and Charlie were sharing the newspaper.

Buck had a road map spread in front of him. Charlie looked up and smiled brightly.

"Well now," Russell said, "here the slugabeds are—and walking a little bowlegged it appears to me." He smiled lewdly and tapped his open palm several times with the top of his fist. I gave him the finger.

Belle was blushing. "Morning, you all," she said and got a pair of mugs from the cabinet and filled them from the coffeepot on the stove. She added cream and sugar to one and handed it to me. Charlie got up and gave her a brief hug around the shoulders and told us to sit down, she'd fix us some bacon and eggs.

Buck's expression was of put-upon patience. He lit a cigarette and sighed a long stream of smoke. "Like I already told these two," he said to me, "it's enough of fun and games. We're set up now and it's time to get to work."

We spent the next two days getting ready, checking maps, tending to the car. We changed the oil, lubricated the joints, replaced the radiator rather than taking a chance on the soldered spot coming open again. On the day we were leaving, Buck said to come in his room for a minute, he had something for me. He dug in his travel bag and took out a Smith & Wesson .38 with a six-inch barrel.

"I got another of these plus the .45," he said, releasing the cylinder to check the loads, then snapping it back in place. "You can have this one. Bulldog's okay for indoors, but if we get into an outside scrap you'll need something more accurate."

He said it as casually as a fisherman might explain the advantage of one type of reel over another, but the remark reminded me of the mean possibilities in this business and I felt my skin tighten. He handed me the piece and smiled. "Still feel like last summer?"

"Better," I said. "Probably because I spent nine months thinking I might not ever get to feel it again."

"Sure you wouldn't rather get your ass in college and learn how to steal all nice and legal? Lot more profitable."

"Could be it is," I said, "but I'll bet anything it ain't near as much fun."

"That's my guess too," he said, grinning back at me.

We packed a change of clothes and put our small bags in the car, then sat down with the girls to a lunch of grilled cheese sandwiches and iced tea. Charlie and Belle put on a show of good spirits, joking about what a relief it would be to have the house to themselves for a while, to be free of our rude male smells and loudness. We didn't know how long we'd be gone, a few days, maybe longer, depending on what Bubber Vicente might have for us. Now and then—for an instant before she'd snatch up the smile again—I'd catch Belle looking at me the way my mother used to look at my father on the nights before he'd ship out. Like she was trying to memorize his face.

Out at the car the girls gave us each a hug and kiss and we smacked them on the bottom for luck and told them to hold the fort.

The road to Odessa cut through the heart of West Texas oil country—the landscape mostly flat and wholly bleak, the sky hazy with dust and oil fumes, the air acrid with the smells of gas. We drove through more and more oil fields, great black forests of derricks and bobbing pumpjacks. Sometimes we had to shout to hear each other above the pounding drills. The road thickened with the traffic in and out of the fields and from neighboring towns, most of it moving in a big dusty hurry. And then we'd be out in the open country again and the traffic would thin out once more and the main sounds were of the motor's puttering and the wind flapping through the windows.

We passed through Grandfalls, loud and overcrowded and the dirtiest town any of us had ever seen—until we got to Crane, about thirty miles from Odessa. The streets of Crane were so clogged with cars and transport trucks and mule-drawn wagons we could have crossed the town faster on foot. The clamor made you wince—klaxons blatting, motors racing, transport trucks unloading pipe and heavy equipment with great iron crashings, men communicating in shouts and hollers, music blaring from radios at full volume. Swarms of dreamers chasing after their share of oil money in another town too small to shelter them all. We'd seen a few tent camps on the outskirts of Grandfalls—ragtowns, the boomers called them—but Crane looked like a vast republic of ragtowns and shantyvilles raised from every kind of scrap. Men with pockets crammed with money were living in their trucks, their cars, whole families were residing in packing crates, men bedding in sections of pipe. Privies everywhere, their effluvia thickening the general stench.

"I don't know what's worse," I yelled, "the noise or the stink!"

"I know it!" Buck hollered. Then took a deep breath and added, "But you catch that one sweet smell mixed in there with all them stinks?"

"*What* sweet smell?" I said, making a show of fanning my nose with my hand.

"You don't detect that aroma?" Russell said. He inhaled more deeply of the foul air. "Money, son. Money."

The main street was chockablock with stores selling everything from tools to tents to workclothes, with groceries and drugstores and cafés, hotels and boardinghouses and fleabag flops, moviehouses, barbershops, bathhouses, pool halls and dime-a-dance joints. Every place had a sign proclaiming it was open twenty-four hours a day. A line of people stood at a truck that was selling water at a dollar a gallon.

"Whoo!" Buck said. "Ain't this something? I bet you there's a dozen high-stakes games going on this minute all over this town."

"They say this Crane is nice as a church compared to some of the other boomtowns out here," Russell said. "But godawmighty, looks like mostly clip joints to me."

"Remember that dime-a-dance place we went to in East Texas a coupla months back?" Buck said. "Talk about clip joints."

"Was it ever," Russell said. "Some dances didn't last even a minute before the band switched to a different number and you had to give the girl another ticket or get off the floor. You could go through a dollar's worth of dance tickets in less than ten minutes."

"Bunch of damn thieves," Buck said.

"They had a preacher on about every corner," Russell said, "hustling for handouts and threatening you with hellfire if you didn't pony up—like that one there!"

He pointed to a man in black standing on a wooden crate and shaking a Bible above his head as he harangued passersby, few of whom even glanced at him. There was a large bucket at his feet, and painted on it was "$ for Jesus."

"Dollars for himself, more like it," Buck said. "I wouldn't reckon Jesus needs anybody to hustle money for him."

Cars were parked two deep along the street. We saw an unattended car being pushed out of the way so the car it was blocking against the curb could get out—and then the pushed car was abandoned in the street, one more obstacle for the tangle of traffic to negotiate.

Crane was only a few blocks long but it took us almost an hour to get through it. Finally we were clear of the town and out past the traffic of its northern oil fields and breezing through the open country toward Odessa.

"Well, like the monkey said when he got his tail caught in the lawn mower," Buck said, "it won't be long now."

Bubber had left word with the desk man of the Bigsby that he'd be at Earl's Café on 1st Street if anybody came looking for him, so that's where we went. The café was large and jammed with oil workers, every booth and table full, every counter stool occupied. Raucous with loud conversation and laughter, the clash of dishware, music from a radio turned up high. Bubber wasn't in sight, so Buck asked one of the harried waitresses if she knew him and where he might be. The waitress narrowed her eyes and wanted to know who was asking. Buck told her and she said to hold on a minute, then disappeared through a hallway door flanking the entrance to the kitchen. She came back shortly and said to go all the way down the hall and tell the fella sitting by a door there who we were.

We did—and the man let us into a speakeasy with tables and chairs, a bar running the length of the back wall. Even at this early-afternoon hour the place was loud and nearly packed. The dance floor full of couples swaying to "The Birth of the Blues" coming out of a radio behind the bar.

"Well, godawmighty damn, lookee who's here!" A dark-bearded man heaved his large bulk off a bar stool and came toward us with a wide smile and arms outstretched. He gave Buck and Russell in turn a big hug and they all cursed each other amiably and smacked each other's backs.

Buck introduced me and Bubber Vicente said, "Your *nephew*? Be goddam! What say, young fella?" He nearly crushed my hand as he shook it in his big paw. His right cheek bore an old oval scar that had pretty obviously been made by somebody's teeth.

The man he'd been sitting with was his partner, Earl Cue, a good name for him, so skinny he looked like a pool stick with a pompadour. He had the most badly pitted face I'd ever seen. "It's like his face caught fire and somebody put it out with an ice pick" is how Russell later described it. But he was friendly enough and set us up with drinks at a corner table against the back wall.

They caught each other up a little on their doings since they'd last been together in New Orleans. We were eager to hear about the jobs Bubber had for us, but he'd got onto the subject of Mona Holiday, whom he'd met a few weeks ago and who at first sight had become the love of his life. She was beautiful, she was smart, she had a great sense of humor, she had tits round and sweet as cantaloupes. Plus, she had a sharp head for business and ran one of the most profitable whorehouses in West Texas.

"Trouble is," Bubber said, "her cathouse is in Blackpatch, about sixty-five miles southways. If it wasn't for going to see her once or twice a week, I wouldn't be caught dead in that place. Wait'll you get a load of it—one of the jobs I got you boys is in Blackpatch. It's way the hell in nowhere. But that's why Mona's house does so good, see? Them boys in Blackpatch don't have much choice about where to get laid."

But she also did so well, he said, because the Wildcat Dance Club—a tidy two-story smack in the center of town—was one of the cleanest houses in Texas. She had her girls examined once a week by a doctor who kept an office in an upstairs room of the place. If a girl didn't pass muster, out she went. "Not a dirtyleg in the house," Bubber said, his voice proud. "Man who gets laid at Mona's can rest assured he won't pick up a nail."

Despite Mona's prosperity in Blackpatch, he had been trying to talk her into moving her business to Odessa. It wasn't only that he wanted her living closer to him, but that he believed Blackpatch was just too damn dangerous a place to live. It had been called Copper Hill way back when there was a mine there, though the hill it was named for wasn't but forty feet high. The mine had pretty soon played out, however, and it wasn't till about five years ago that a wildcatter tried his luck there and struck it rich. Then three years ago—before Mona got there and when the place still had fewer than a dozen buildings and but a single street—one of the gas wells blew up and the whole town caught on fire. When it was all over, fifty-one of the 135 souls who'd lived there were dead and dozens of the survivors had been badly burned. There hadn't been anything left of the town of Copper Hill but a bare black patch of sand. But there was still a hell of a lot of oil under that hill, and not a month after the fire they struck a new gusher. A new town sprang up on the sludgy ashes of the old one and they called it Blackpatch.

"Every oil town stinks," Bubber said, "but Blackpatch stinks the worst of them. They say it's because it's not only got all the usual stinks of an oil patch, it's got the stink of all them people who got burnt into the ground. Now they got even more wells on the hill *and* a fifty-thousand-barrel holding tank up there. Looks like a giant soup can. *I* sure's hell wouldn't want to live down there under it. Mona says the only reason I'm worried is because I'm from Loosiana and naturally scared of hills. Now I ask you boys, how do you argue with a remark like that? I offered to pay whatever it'd cost her to set up in Odessa and she finally said maybe, she'd have to think it over. She likes her independence, she says. Doesn't want to be beholden, she says. *Christ*. I love the woman, boys, no lie, but damn if she don't about make me *in*sane sometimes."

"Sounds like love, all right," Buck said, and Russell said he'd drink to that, and everybody laughed.

Then we got down to business.

The first job Bubber had for us was in Wink, some sixty miles away in the neighboring county. We checked out of the Bigsby early the next morning and had breakfast at the Rancho Restaurant across the street. The orange sun was clearing the rooftops behind us as we drove past the city limit sign and onto the Pecos highway. The setting moon looked like a bruised pearl.

We hadn't been on the road an hour, rolling through the flat and barren scrubland, when a low cloud of strange brown haze began rising directly ahead of us.

"What in the hell's that?" Russell said.

"Beats me," Buck said. "Smoke?"

"Maybe," Russell said.

I said I didn't think so. I'd never seen smoke that color or in a cloud that shape.

"Well, whatever it is," Russell said, "it's coming this way."

We watched it swelling as we bore toward it. Then Buck said, "Oh, shit."

Russell said "Sand" at the same time I said "Dust" and we were both right.

We'd been told about such storms and what to do if we got caught in one out on the open road. There was no traffic ahead of us, only a solitary truck far behind. I slowed the car and pulled off the highway, then wheeled into a U-turn across the road and onto the opposite shoulder. I switched off the engine and set the brake and we rolled the windows up tight.

The idea was to have the rear of the car turned toward the wind to protect the radiator and engine from the driving sand, the windshield from flying debris. We looked through the back window at the growing dust cloud, the road disappearing under its advance.

The car lurched with the thump of the wind's impact and the world around us abruptly dimmed and went obscure. Each gust rocked the Ford on its creaking springs like a railcar riding uneven tracks. The doorjambs whistled. Tumbleweeds caromed off the rear window like headlong drunks. Sand and grit drilled into the glass, hissed against the back of the car, rasped over the roof and fenders. The floorboards quivered under our feet and a fine dust came up through the pedal openings. We couldn't see at all behind us or even to the other side of the road, could see only a few yards ahead of the car.

"Bubber told me some men who been caught out in a storm like this ended up blind in one or both eyes," Buck said. "Said he's heard of some fellas with the bad luck to be passed out drunk on the ground when a sandstorm hit and covered them up and smothered them— buried them alive. Some weren't found till days or weeks afterward and some were never found at all. He said one guy got caught in one and couldn't think of what to do except sit down with his back to the wind and hug tight to his knees. By the time it was all over, the only parts of him still showing was the tops of his knees and his head and shoulders. Lost some of the hair off the back of his head, and his ears and the back of his neck were bloody raw. Guy's still got the scars of it, Bubber says."

Russell coughed against the rising dust in the car. "Damn me for a liar if I wouldn't rather go through a hurricane than this," he said. "Any day."

A half hour later the worst was over. A dusty wind still held and the sky was still hazed, but the strongest gusts were done with and you could see for a distance down the road. The rear window had been scoured to a pale translucence. We got out and saw that the back end of the car was now of fainter green and rougher finish than before. This region was full of motor vehicles patchworked with portions of bare metal—a phenomenon locally referred to as a West Texas paint job.

We got back in the Ford and I turned it around again and we pressed on.

"All that dust," Buck said, "reminds me of the fella who goes to the doctor and the doc tells him he ain't got but a few weeks to live. Fella says, 'Goddamn, ain't there nothing you can suggest?' Doc says, 'Well, you could go to one of them spas, take you a mud bath every day.' Fella says, 'Will that help my condition?' Doc says, 'No, but it'll help you get used to the feel of dirt.' "

For the last two hours before getting into Wink we had to poke along behind a long muletrain of bunkhouses being hauled to an oil company camp at the edge of town. Overall, the town wasn't much different from the other oil towns we'd seen—as loud and crowded and smelly and dusty, as overrun with ragtowns. Workers coming and going with every change in shift, the cafés and stores doing business round the clock. But Wink had the rare advantage of its own ice plant, and it had a scad of moviehouses. Russell counted six of them as we went down the central street.

We made our way over to E Street and found the house we were looking for and studied it as we drove by. A fading yellow bungalow on the corner of a neighborhood as crowded and noisy as every other.

Most boomtown homeowners were raking in cash by renting rooms in their house—or in some cases simply the cots in a room, renting each cot to a different man on every shift. But this house showed none of the frenetic activity of so many of the others. "Looks just like the man told us," Buck said.

Despite the delays of the sandstorm and the muletrain, we still had plenty of time to kill, so we went to a café and ordered hamburgers and coffee. The place was so jammed we couldn't converse without shouting. Then we took a walk through the teeming streets.

At the corner of an intersection, we heard a surge of cheering and high laughter from a large crowd gathered in an open lot down the street, so we went to see what was going on. Spectators were bunched on two sides of the lot and hollering exhortations at a dozen men staggering like drunks. Then we drew closer and saw that the men weren't only drunk but crippled. Every man's feet twisted in some awkward attitude and his legs in twitching rebellion, some with a leg dragging like a dead weight, all of them trying to navigate toward a rope stretched across the far end of the lot. They listed and stumbled and fell, struggled to their feet and tried to bear toward the rope and went veering off at a tangent and fell again, the crowd roaring at their antics, shouting encouragements. Some careened into the spectators and were shoved back toward the center of the lot and urged to keep trying to reach the rope. There were steady outcries of betting.

"Jakeleg race," Buck said.

Bubber had told us all about the jakeleg, a disorder of the nervous system brought on by drinking a bad batch of ginger jake—a fiery booze made with Jamaican ginger—and most batches of it were bad. He'd shown us a half-full bottle of the stuff, a meanlooking dark brown, and when he pulled the cork we caught a smell like rotten peppers.

"Christ!" Buck had said. "People *drink* that?"

"And some ask for more," Bubber said. "There's every manner of wicked hooch in the world, boys, and West Texas has a goodly portion of it. You all be careful of what you toast your health with or you might could ruin your health real quick."

From one of the men beside us we learned that every contestant had been given a few free slugs of ginger jake prior to the start of the race. "To get them good and primed," the man said with a laugh.

"The winner get a prize or anything?" Russell asked.

"Why, hell yes," another man said. "Winner gets a pint of jake. It's about the only prize they'll race for."

We watched awhile longer, then Russell checked his watch and arched his brow at Buck. It was one o'clock.

"Yeah," Buck said. "Let's go."

As usual with Bubber's jobs, he'd gotten his information on this one from an inside man—somebody'd who'd come to him and was in a position to know how much the job would reap, where and when it could be done, the kind of resistance likely to be encountered, and whatever other key details might be pertinent. If Bubber liked the setup, he'd pass the job on to a holdup team for thirty-five percent of the haul, which included the inside man's cut.

This one was a White Star Oil payroll, coming from Fort Worth. Seventy-five hundred in cash, according to the inside man. Three guys bringing it in—a courier named Sewell, a guard named Hatten, a driver named Lane—all three armed with pistols and they had a shotgun in the car, a blue '27 Dodge sedan with Oklahoma plates. Unless they had trouble on the road, they were due to reach the company field office around four o'clock that afternoon. Once the money got to the field office, forget it—there'd be more than a hundred workers already there, lined up and waiting to be paid, and anybody who tried sticking up the place would be killed on the spot, no matter how well armed. And you couldn't simply lay for the carriers a few miles outside of town and hijack them when they came along—there was way too much traffic for that.

But the inside man had provided one other important detail, the one that decided Bubber on doing the job. The courier, Sewell, had a sweetheart in Wink, the wife of a White Star tool pusher who worked the afternoon shift. Whenever he delivered a payroll to Wink, Sewell always arrived in town about an hour or two before the money was due at the field office, giving himself enough time to pop into the pusher's house on E Street for a roll in the hay with the wayward wife. They felt pretty safe about it because they knew hubby would be out at the field, waiting for his pay.

We spied a couple of Dodges on E Street but neither of them blue or showing an Okie license. We circled the block twice before somebody pulled away from the curb ahead of us and opened a parking space, and I wheeled into it. We were a half-block from the yellow house and had a clear view of the place.

By three o'clock the courier still hadn't shown. We started to worry that maybe he'd had car trouble, that he and the woman had called it quits, that the company had sent somebody else to deliver the money this time.

And then a blue Dodge came from behind us, and even in the rearview I could tell the Okie tag. The car passed us by and stopped in front of the yellow house and a man carrying a briefcase and fitting the description we'd been given of Sewell got out and said something to the driver. Then headed for the front door of the house, where the screen door had already opened to reveal a woman standing there in a long pink robe.

"She sure don't mind taking chances, does she?" I said. "A neighbor might see her."

"Maybe the bitch wants it that way," Buck said. "Maybe she wants hubby to hear a few rumors and eat his guts out wondering if they're true."

"Could be," Russell said. "But even a sap has his limits. She and loverboy might could find theirselves looking up into his pistol one of these days."

"I'd wager she's planning to take a powder before he gets to that point," Buck said.

"Toot, Toot, Tootsie, goodbye," Russell sang.

The Dodge was still idling in the street. We figured the driver was waiting for a parking place to open up, so we gave him one. Buck and Russell got out of the car and waved so long to me and I pulled out. As I drove off, I watched the Dodge in the rearview mirror as it backed up to take the spot I'd vacated.

I went around the block, and when I got back to where the Dodge was, Buck and Russell were in the back seat of it. They smiled at me as I pulled up alongside. The two guys in the front seat were staring straight ahead and looking unhappy. Russell was grinning big. He raised a pump-action shotgun high enough for me to see it and then lowered it out of sight again.

Buck got out of the Dodge and leaned into the Ford's passenger-side window. "I guess it would've been *too* easy if these assholes had it," he said. "The Sewell guy took it in the house with him. It's in the briefcase. I'll just run on over and get it." A car behind me squalled its klaxon and Buck glared and waved for him to go around us.

"Keep driving around till I get back," Buck told me. "Russell's got these guys." Then he walked off toward the house.

Even though the traffic was so heavy I was moving hardly faster than a walking pace, I circled the block twice before Buck reappeared at the Dodge again. He was standing by the driver's door and holding the courier's briefcase. He was all smiles when I pulled up. "All right," he said into the Dodge.

The guy sitting on the passenger side, the guard named Hatten, got out and came around the Dodge and got in beside me. He looked abject. Buck sat in the back, directly behind him. Russell sat behind the driver of the Dodge, the Lane guy.

"We're off, kid," Buck said. "Head for the Pecos highway."

We made our slow way through the street traffic, the Dodge trailing close. I looked at Buck in the mirror and said, "So?"

"Seventy-five hundred on the nose," Buck said. "I counted it."

"I mean, how'd it go?" I wanted details, a picture of the job.

"Oh, well," Buck said, "I slipped the hook off the door with my pocketknife and snuck on down to the bedroom and there they were, going at it like a couple of happy rabbits. I eased over to the chair where he'd put his clothes and gun and stood there watching them until the gal spots me over his shoulder and it's like she was struck paralyzed. Sweet piece of calico. The fella keeps on hunching for a bit and then it must've dawned on him he's doing all the work, so he rears up and sees she's looking past him and he turns around and sees me holding the .45 on him and his eyes got *this* big. I told him to go ahead and finish, don't mind me, but he didn't have it in him to keep it up, I guess."

"You were in there a while," I said.

"Took a while to truss them up," he said. "On the bed and belly to belly. Hands behind them."

"Still bare-assed?" I asked.

"Goddam right. You reckon they'll manage another hump before hubby gets home? I'd like to be a fly on that wall when he does, wouldn't you?"

The Hatten guy shook his head. "It's shitty, man. Her husband's an ox. He's liable to kill him. Her too. Bust them up bad at the least."

Buck laughed. "You reckon?"

"Shit," Hatten said.

I cold see how much Buck was enjoying himself. Hatten's face was shiny with sweat. He had to be wondering if we were going to kill him.

About a quarter-mile north of the Pecos highway, Buck had me turn off onto a rough ranch road that curved around a scrubby rise. As soon as we were out of sight of the passing traffic he said to stop the car. The Dodge pulled up behind us and we all got out, the dust settling over us. Russell was holding the shotgun he'd taken from them, a Remington twelve-gauge. He had their revolvers—.44s—stuck in his pants.

Buck told Hatten and Lane to sit on the ground. They had the aspects of condemned men. I hadn't thought he would shoot them but now I wasn't so sure.

He told them the word was already going around Wink that they had been in on the payroll theft. "I told Sewell you guys were the inside men for the job," Buck said, "and it looked to me like he believed it. Hell's bells, far as I know, one of you or both you *was* the inside man. Don't matter true or false. Them boys at White Star are going to be awful mad their pay got stole and you'll play hell trying to get them to believe you wasn't in it with us. If I was you I wouldn't even try to explain it, no sir, not at the risk of getting lynched on a derrick. I was you, I'd get in my car and get out of West Texas as fast as I could and I wouldn't never come back, me."

He gestured for me to get behind the wheel of the Ford again. He got in the front with me, and Russell sat in the back.

"Keys are in the car, boys," Buck called out. "Good luck!" They were still on the ground, looking like they couldn't believe their reprieve.

I wheeled around and gunned the engine and waved at them as we went by and they vanished behind us in the raise of dust.

Back on the highway and barreling south, I hollered *"Whoo-eeee!"* for no reason except I thought I'd bust if I didn't. I looked over at Buck, my grin feeling almost too big for my mouth, then laughed at Russell in the mirror.

"Cheer up, kid," Buck said, looking at me with a wry smile.

"This damn Sonny," Russell said, joining in my laughter and clapping me on the shoulder from behind. "I never did know of such a good luck charm, I swear."

When we pulled up in front of the house, the sun was starting to dip behind the western range under a sky in riot with all the colors of fire. I cut off the motor and we got out and I breathed deeply of the warm dry wind coming gently from the south. The screen door screeched open and Belle and Charlie came running out, shrilling like schoolgirls, coming to greet us like we'd been gone for weeks instead of only two days.

Belle flung herself on me, hugging me by the neck and locking her legs around my waist. "I thought you'd *never* get back!" she said, and kissed my ears and the top of my head.

Her ass felt wonderful in my hands and I laughed and spun us around. I was amazed at how much her bruises had improved in the brief time we'd been away. Only a smudge of yellow remained on her cheekbone, and although the flesh around her eye was still blue, it was no longer swollen. She was even prettier than I'd thought.

Charlie made the same sort of fuss over Russell and then let go of him and ran over to me as Belle turned loose and went to Russell and there was more hugging and kissing. Then Charlie looked over her shoulder at Buck, who was headed for the door with the Wink briefcase in one hand and his travel valise in the other. She gave me one more peck on the forehead and set out after him, calling, "Hey you." Buck turned as she threw herself on him and jarred him off balance and they went down in a heap.

Belle hesitated, then went over and stood smiling down on them as Charlie straddled Buck's stomach and mussed his hair and planted kisses on his face and babbled at him in babytalk. He cussed mildly and made like he was trying to ward her off, but you could see how much he was enjoying it, how gently he got her off him. She kept petting him as he got to his feet muttering that a man could get his back broken being greeted by such a crazy woman. Belle playslapped him on the shoulder and said, "Oh, you love it and you know it"—then gave him a sidelong hug and said, "Welcome home."

It wasn't often you'd see him look as surprised as he did then, but she released him before he could hug her in return. Then Charlie had her arms around him from behind and lightly nipped his ear and he let out an exaggerated yelp and squirmed free of her and said, "Christ's sake! Didn't you nutty broads get enough to eat while we were gone?"

We took the bags out of the car and wrapped the shotgun in a coat before carrying it to the house—in case some curious neighbor who'd been watching the welcome-home show was still looking on. Not knowing we were going to show up, Charlie and Belle had planned to make sandwiches for their supper, but now they started getting out the pots and pans to cook us a proper meal. Buck told them to forget it, we'd go out to eat. We washed up and put on clean shirts while the girls changed into nicer dresses. Charlie had taken Belle shopping for clothes and she put on a blue sleeveless one I liked a lot.

We went to a barbecue place on Main Street and gorged on pork ribs and French fries and coleslaw, joking and laughing the whole while, and the patrons sitting around us smiled at our boisterous spirits. Afterward we went home by way of the house on Callaghan Street, where we stopped and bought six bottles of moonshine and a dozen quarts of beer.

Neither of the girls had asked about the job. From the beginning of her acquaintance with Russell, Charlie had known what he did for a living, but he'd made it clear that she shouldn't question him about his business. He might now and then deign to share something of it with her but she was never to pry. And she never did. I'd always had a hunch she was glad to have it that way, that she preferred not to know any of the specifics about the risks he took. All through supper, though, I'd caught Belle looking at me with an eagerness that went beyond her pleasure in my return. She was dying to know about the past two days, I could see it in her eyes.

Not till we were on the way back to the house did Russell tell Charlie that we were heading back out tomorrow. "We got a matter to tend to tomorrow night and then another one a couple of nights after that," he said. "That puts us back here in four days, if my arithmetic's correct."

"And if nothing goes wrong," Charlie said softly.

"Right," Russell said. "Like the sun'll come up tomorrow if nothing goes wrong. Like I'll wake up in the morning if nothing goes wrong. Like we'll be leaving after lunch if nothing goes wrong."

Whenever he thought she was being smart-mouth with him he would come back at her even more so. He rarely did it, though, because she rarely gave him cause.

It was too dark in the car to make out Charlie's expression in the rearview mirror. She sat very still for the span of another block and then turned and snuggled up close to him and said, "Well then, I think we ought to get to bed early, don't you?"

I hadn't said anything to Belle, either, about our leaving on another job tomorrow. She was sitting in front between me and Buck and I felt her hand on my leg as she leaned close and said low, "I think she's got the right idea."

Buck stared out at the darkness and said nothing.

Later that night, after a round of humping that left us gleaming with sweat on the moonlit bed, I told her all about it while our cigarettes flared and dimmed and a soft breeze lifted the gauzy window curtain. I told her about Bubber Vicente, the sandstorm, about Crane and Odessa and Wink, about the payroll team and how we'd taken them down, how Buck left the courier and his married honey bound together naked for the hubby to find, how the other two had looked as we drove them out of town, thinking we were going to kill them, and then the way they'd looked when they realized we weren't.

She stroked my chest and listened without interruption. When I was done with the telling I was rigid again and she had her hand around me. I rolled up over her and she took me in.

And when we were once again spent, she whispered in my ear, "It all sounds . . . so *fun*."

"It's more than that," I said. "There's nothing like it."

"*Nothing?*" She rubbed her blonde sex against my belly and made a low growl.

"Almost nothing," I said, and laughed with her.

On the following evening we were in Blackpatch. The place was as isolated as Bubber had said—and smelled even worse, like an open grave soaked in oil and giving off gas. The nearest town was Rankin, thirteen miles away as the crow flies, but the country directly between them was too rugged and too cut up with gullies and draws to lay any kind of road, and so to get to Rankin from Blackpatch you had to drive eighteen winding miles west on a dusty junction road to the Iraan highway and then go north another eleven miles.

Bubber had said there was one other route into and out of

Blackpatch, if you didn't mind taking a chance on busting a wheel or snapping an axle. An old mule trace the copper mine had used for packing ore out to the railroad. It twisted and turned for almost twenty miles from Blackpatch out to the rail tracks flanking the Big Lake highway, emerging at a spot about thirteen miles east of Rankin with a rusted water tower and a dilapidated loading platform. Hardly anybody ever used that trail anymore, Bubber said. He'd taken it once and it was the roughest drive he'd ever made. He'd braved it in broad daylight and it took him two hours to cover the twenty miles—not counting the time it took to fix the two flats he had on the way. "I'd have to be more damn desperate than I can imagine to drive on that sonofabitch again," Bubber said.

We'd arrived at sundown. Derricks everywhere. Pumpjacks steadily dipping like monstrous primeval birds at their feed. The old copper-mine hill stood a hundred yards or so to the east of town and the holding tank on top of it was cast in the dying red light of day. It really did look like an enormous soup can. Jagged gullies ran like black scars down the hill and right to the edge of town. The town itself was composed of four short blocks to north and south, three longer ones to east and west, and included a sizable shantyville of tents on its west side. Every building was either a store, a place of entertainment, an eatery, a hotel or a boardinghouse. Most men lived in the ragtown or in their vehicles. There wasn't a private house in Blackpatch. Mona's girls lived in the rooms where they worked, and Mona herself kept a room at the Wellhead Hotel.

The junction road passed through the tent colony and ran directly onto the main street. We crawled along in the heavy traffic, the cafés and juke joints and pool halls all roaring with music. According to Bubber, about six hundred people lived here now—all of them men except for a couple of dozen wives, even fewer daughters, and Mona's girls—and it sounded like they were all yelling at once to make themselves heard above the music and the incessant pounding of the drills. Drunks staggered in the streets and sidewalks, doing the hurricane walk, as we called it in New Orleans. Bubber said the local police force was paid for by the oil company. It consisted of a sheriff and two deputies and they pretty much let the workers take their fun as they pleased—mostly drinking and gambling and fighting each other, and sporting at Mona's place. The cops intervened only in matters of flagrant robbery, deadly violence, or undue property damage.

We saw a pair of men grappling in an alley, each with a headlock on the other and stumbling around like jakeleg dancers, a small crowd looking on and laughing, most pedestrians simply passing by without paying the combatants much notice. We drove around and around until we finally found an alleyway niche to park the car in.

Buck kept the briefcase with the Wink money on his lap while we ate a supper of fried chicken in still one more clamorous café, and then we went over to the Wildcat Dance Club and introduced ourselves to Mona Holiday. She wasn't exactly as Bubber had painted her. For one thing, she looked older than I'd expected—a few years older than Bubber, I would've guessed. Not that she wasn't pretty, because she was, in a rough-edged, bottle-blonde sort of way. But she had some hard wear on her and it showed around her eyes and in the corners of her mouth, in the slack skin of her neck. But a man in love is blind to such minor flaws, of course, so none of us was all that surprised to find she was a shade less breathtaking in the actual flesh than Bubber's description.

But she was every bit as pleasant and gracious as he'd said. She'd heard about Buck and Russell from Bubber, and she seemed truly pleased to make our acquaintance. She ushered us into her nicely appointed downstairs office and poured us all a drink—Jamaican rum, the real stuff, smuggled in by way of Mexico. We all touched glasses and she said, "Here's yours."

When Buck told her about the jakeleg race we'd seen in Wink, she made a disapproving face and said, "Isn't it terrible, the spectacles some people find amusing?" She said we didn't have to worry about being poisoned by the hooch in Blackpatch, it was some of the best moonshine to be had in West Texas. She was personal friends with Gus

Scroggins—the bootlegger who brought Blackpatch its hooch from a sizable distillery in El Paso—and she would vouch for the excellence of the stuff, though she generally stayed with the factory-bottled product herself.

Bubber had told us she wouldn't ask us our business and she didn't. It was one more reason she fared so well—men knew she kept to her business and wouldn't pry into theirs. She had a reputation for asking no questions and telling no tales. But neither did she ever grant a man a hump on the house or even on the cuff. It was strictly pay before play in her place. Special friends of Bubber, however, she would give a cut rate—two dollars, rather than the standard four. Were any of us, she asked with a smile, inclined to go upstairs and take advantage of this bargain?

Buck checked his watch, arched his brow, looked at Russell and me in turn, and we grinned back at him.

An hour later we were in her backroom speakeasy, ensconced at a nice corner table with a good view of the rest of the room, sipping at our labeled rum and telling each other of the girls we'd had.

Buck said the redhead he'd chosen had looked a little shocked when he dropped his pants and she got her first look at Mr. Stub.

"I say, 'What's wrong, honey?' and look down at myself like I got no idea. 'Oh *that*,' I say. 'Well, see, I borrowed some money from the bank the other day and they insisted on the most valuable thing I owned for collateral.' That's all it took to set her at ease. Had us so much fun it ought to be illegal."

He wanted to hear about the pretty girl I'd picked out—brown hair and green eyes, tits shaped like pears. He'd almost selected her for himself before deciding on the redhead. When I said she'd been a lot of fun—which was true—he said he wished we had more time, he'd go back in there and have a go with her himself.

Russell said he'd enjoyed the little half-Mexican girl he'd picked.

"A man's got to have himself some variety, it's only natural. But I'll tell you what—truth be told, I ain't found another woman yet as much fun as Charlie when she drops her underpants."

I kept it to myself but I was glad to hear him say that, because in the middle of sporting with the pear-tits girl, I'd had the fleeting thought I'd rather be doing it with Belle. I'd enjoyed myself with the girl, but thinking of Belle while I was at it had left me feeling a little edgy for some reason I couldn't put my finger on. Russell's remark clarified things and set me at ease. He preferred putting it to Charlie but that didn't interfere with his enjoyment of others—and why should it? Damn right.

"Of course Charlie's more fun," Buck said. "She don't charge you two dollars a throw."

Russell laughed. "By Jesus, that must be it." He looked at me and winked. "Man's got a point, huh, kid?"

I laughed too. "Damn sure does," I said. And told myself he did.

We'd been nursing our rum like it was the last to be had in Texas. One drink apiece was all we were allowing ourselves till the job was done. And now, at a little before nine, it was time to get to it.

We were out to rob Gus Scroggins, the El Paso bootlegger Mona Holiday had mentioned. He was making a delivery tonight to his Blackpatch buyer, a local whiskey dealer named Lester Wills, who would have five thousand dollars to pay for the load of white lightning. Scroggins transported his moonshine in barrels loaded on trucks that looked like every other oil truck in the region. He had two deliveries to make en route from El Paso and would be carrying the proceeds from those deals—ten thousand dollars, according to Bubber's inside man—when he met with Wills. We were looking at a take of fifteen grand in greenbacks and a load of hooch worth another five.

The transaction was to take place in an abandoned oil camp about a mile north of the Blackpatch junction road. The only way to get there was over a narrow trail laid out by an oil company that had drilled all over the region before striking it rich in Copper Hill. We'd been out there earlier in the day to have a look at the place and lay out a plan. The trail meandered around sandhills and gullies strewn with scrawny tumbleweeds, around rocky outcrops and thick patches of scrub brush. Before you'd gone a hundred yards you were out of sight of the road. At a couple of points along the trail, the oil crews had cut clearings wide enough for truck turnarounds. The camp itself had occupied a circular clearing roughly fifty yards in diameter and almost entirely enclosed by a thickly shrubbed, stony rise that had served to protect the place from windstorms. A ramshackle wooden derrick stood over a litter of oil drums and castoff machine parts. Gus Scroggins liked to make his deliveries on moonbright nights in case the Texas Rangers somehow got wind of the deal and figured to charge in and make a pinch. A lookout on the derrick could spot them coming in time to give ample warning. The bootleg party could scatter on foot into the darkness beyond the rise and the Rangers wouldn't be able to give chase in their cars over that rugged terrain.

For the last two hundred yards before reaching the clearing, the trail assumed a slight upward grade and was flanked on both sides by high dense brush. But about forty yards from the entrance, we'd found a small open spot in the scrub. We could pull in there and turn the car around to point back toward the trail, hidden behind a pile of tumbleweeds and loose brush and ready for a fast getaway.

By ten o'clock that's where we were, sitting in the scrub shadows and watching the trail. A bright gibbous moon was midway up the eastern sky and illuminating the countryside with a ghostly blue light. The air smelled of creosote and warm dust. The Ford was well camouflaged, its license plate freshly transplanted from a car parked in the alley behind a Blackpatch pool hall. Buck and I carried a pair of pistols each—he'd given me one of the two .44 revolvers they'd taken off the payroll guys. Besides his pistol, Russell had the Remington pump.

A few minutes before eleven we heard the distant growl of a car motor from the direction of the junction road. We peered over the scrub and spied it, small and dark against the moonlit landscape, coming slowly and without lights, raising only the barest trace of dust as it wound its way toward us, now and then going out of view as it went into a dip or behind a rise. We knew it was the advance men, checking for anything out of place, for signs of a trap by Rangers or rival bootleggers or hijackers like us.

Buck had the army automatic in his hand, and I drew the .44 from my front waistband. The longbarrel .38 was snugged against the small of my back. As the car got closer we hunched back down in the scrub and sat still and quiet as stones. Pretty soon it came easing by with its engine rumbling and tires crunching over the stony trail. A black Oldsmobile sedan. Through a gap in the scrub I saw the silhouettes of two men in the car.

The Olds passed out of sight into the clearing behind the rise. We heard the engine slow to an idle and a door squeak open and bang shut—one of the guys getting out to check things on foot. The engine rumbled as the car took a slow turn around the clearing. Then its dark shape was again at the trailhead and the headlights flashed on and off, twice, in swift succession. Exactly the signal Bubber said his inside man had described. The Olds then backed up into the clearing and its motor shut off. A door opened and shut. Faint unintelligible voices. Low laughter.

Russell grunted and pointed south. Another unlighted car was coming our way. Lester Wills and his five grand. Him and his driver.

Buck patted me on the shoulder to let me know he and Russell were heading off. They pulled their dark bandannas up over their mouth and nose and tugged down their hats and vanished quietly into the brush. The camp shithouse had been placed outside the camp, at the bottom of the slope, and a path to it had been worn over the scrubby rise. Buck and Russell could quietly follow the path up through the scrub and come down behind the advance men.

I stayed put and watched the approaching car. If it had done any-thing other than keep coming I would've hurried to inform Buck and Russell. But the car steadily advanced. When it closed to within a hundred yards, I pulled up my bandanna mask and hustled away to the clearing.

The moon was higher now but the derrick's shadow still reached across the west side of the clearing and angled halfway up the slope. The Oldsmobile was parked in front of the derrick, one of the men slouching against a front fender, his hands in his pants pockets. I couldn't see his face under his hatbrim but his head turned to follow me as I jogged across the clearing and over to a row of barrels in the derrick's long shadow. It looked like everything was going according to plan—Buck and Russell had taken them by surprise and disarmed them, then put one guy in the Olds' trunk and told the other to perch on that fender and keep his mouth shut. I couldn't see them but I knew Buck was in the shadows of a clump of yuccas near the entrance to the clearing and Russell somewhere behind the low outcrop to my right.

I was surprised to feel my pulse thumping so hard in my throat, to find my mouth nearly spitless. *We'll play it any way we have to*—that was Buck's instruction. It seemed to be taking too long for the car to get here. I thought maybe it had turned back, maybe I'd been spotted as I made for the clearing and they had retreated in alarm.

And then there the car was, a shiny Plymouth coupe, rolling slowly into the clearing. I cocked the .44.

The Plymouth made a half-turn and stopped parallel to the Olds, next to the man on the fender. The passenger door opened and Lester Wills got out. We'd had a look at him earlier that evening at a speakeasy a block over from Mona's place, and even in this light there was no mistaking the pompadour he took such pride in he would not cover it with a hat. The driver stayed put and kept the motor running.

"What the hell you doing?" Wills said to the man. "You suppose to be in the car."

A detail we hadn't known.

Now Wills was looking up at the derrick and saying, "Yo, Walsh! You see them? *Walsh?* Hey, what the hell . . . ?"

The man on the fender said something too low for me to make out. Buck yelled, "Stand fast, mister!"—but Wills was already spinning around and diving back into the coupe, hollering, *"Go!"*

Buck's pistol started popping and showing bright yellow muzzle flashes as the car's back wheels ripped through the sand and the Plymouth slewed toward the barrels I was hunkered behind. I jumped aside as the car made a tight turn and the open passenger door hit some of the barrels and sent them clangoring end over end.

I scrambled to my feet and Russell cut loose with the shotgun and buckshot raked the Plymouth as it angled toward the clearing exit. I fired and fired and there were loud gunfire sparks from the car and from the yuccas where Buck was and bullets were thunking the car and whanging against oil drums and there was another orange boom from Russell's shotgun and the car veered sharply and went bounding up the rocky incline for about a dozen yards with its klaxon blaring before the motor stalled. The car slid back down on the loose rock, its rear wheels locked, and jarred to a stop at the foot of the slope and the horn quit. Steam was hissing loudly from various holes in the radiator. I couldn't see the men inside but could hear one of them moaning.

There was a slide of stones behind me and I turned in time to see the man who'd been on the fender go scurrying into the brush at the top of the rise. I started after him but Russell called, "Forget it. He can't warn nobody from over there."

Buck went up to the Plymouth in a crouch and warily raised his head at the driver's window—and just did manage to fling himself aside as a gunshot lit up the interior and a bullet caromed off some part of the window frame.

Russell yelled, *"Down!"* and threw the shotgun to his shoulder and fired and glass shattered and flew and he smoothly pumped and fired three more flaring loads of buckshot into the car before lowering the gun again.

The ensuing silence was enormous. Acrid gunsmoke rose off the clearing in a blue haze and slowly drifted over the rise.

Holding his .45 ready, Buck jerked open the coupe's left door and the driver seemed to just drain out. I didn't have to ask if he was dead. Buck picked up the man's pistol. I wondered if one of my shots had hit him, had maybe been the fatal one—and then reminded myself how close he'd come to running over me with the car. My chest was so tight it was an effort to breathe. My hands felt charged with electricity. I was afraid Buck or Russell might see them trembling and think I was scared. The truth was, I'd never felt more alive.

Buck and I went around to the other side of the car and pointed our pistols at the door and Buck nodded to let Russell know we were set and Russell pulled open the door. Wills was slumped on the seat. Russell poked him twice with the shotgun muzzle and then yanked on him by the coat collar and Wills tumbled from the car. We stood over him and tugged down our bandannas. His breathing was ragged and wet and his eyes were closed. He was shivering like he was cold. His shirtfront and one coatsleeve and the right side of his face were dark with blood, his pompadour was skewed. Buck knelt beside him and went through his pockets. I retrieved his gun from the car floor—a .380 automatic—and stuck it in my waistband. The money was in an envelope in his pants pocket. Buck chuckled and stood up and put the envelope in his coat.

Wills suddenly arched up like he'd been stabbed in the spine, his eyes wide. His mouth moved as if he were trying to say something, but if he was he never got it out. He fell slack and gave a rasping sigh. And even in the moonlight you could tell that his open eyes weren't seeing a damn thing anymore.

"Dumb bastard," Buck said. "If he'd done like I told him he could've got drunk tonight, he could've got laid. He could've been around tomorrow to complain about being robbed."

"He called the play, all right," Russell said. "But I have to say, we've done smoother jobs."

"Yeah well," Buck said. "We got the money, ain't we?" He

checked his watch. "Let's get set for Scroggins. He'll be looking for the lights in about twenty minutes. Get the car, Sonny."

I got in the Olds and cranked it up and started to bring it around to the mouth of the clearing. As Wills had done, Scroggins would wait somewhere down on the trail until he got an all-clear headlight signal before coming the rest of the way.

Buck and Russell were already at the clearing entrance and scanning the moonlit country to the south. Then Buck grabbed Russell's arm and pointed. He whirled around and beckoned me wildly, yelling, *"Come on!"*

I goosed the Olds up to them and Russell yanked the door open and jumped in beside me and Buck hopped up on the running board and hollered, "Go! *Go!*"

I hit the gas and the tires spun on the loose trailrock and found purchase and the Olds leapt forward.

"They're wise to us!" Russell yelled. "Kick this thing, kid!" And now I saw the cloud of dust far down the trail. And the truck that was making it. Heading away from us and back toward the junction road.

As we closed on the spot where we'd hidden the Ford, Buck hollered through the window, "Keep after him, I'm right behind you!" He jumped off and went rolling into the brush.

I stomped on the accelerator and the Olds bounced and yawed along the snaking trail, flinging up stones and raising dust, leaning one way and then the other.

"Bastards must've got here early," Russell said. "Must've heard the shooting, that damn klaxon, something, everything. *Shit!*"

The truck was more than half a mile ahead of us and moving in and out of sight as it went over and around rises and outcrops. In the rearview mirror the lights of the Model A showed far behind us.

"Which way will he go when he hits the junction road?" I said.

"Not to Blackpatch," Russell said. "Too small. Only one way in and out. He'll head for the highway."

"Then to Rankin?"

"Yeah. Mix in with all them other trucks. Lots of roads out of town. It's what I'd do. He beats us there, we'll lose him sure."

I didn't intend to let that happen. With my foot to the floor we went over a rise at a speed that took all four wheels off the ground. The Olds lit hard and bounced on its springs and went slewing off the trail in an explosion of dust and brush and rocks hammering the floorboards. I thought I heard a scream behind me. I kept the pedal to the floor and managed to wrench the car back onto the trail, wrestling with the wheel as we swerved all over the place, and then we were straightened out and barreling on.

"Helllllp! Christ *Jeeesus*! Let me *out*! *Let me ouuuuuuut*!"

The muted hollers came from directly back of me. I glanced in the rearview but saw only Buck's headlights, even farther behind than they'd been before. Russell half-turned in his seat and shouted, "Shut the hell up, you pitiful pussy!"

The guy they'd stuck in the trunk. Walsh, Wills had called him. He had to be taking a pounding back there.

The trail rose and dipped and curved, the Olds slid, lost traction, tore through brush and banged against rocks with the undercarriage, regained the trail, powered ahead. If we didn't blow a tire or rupture the oil pan or break an axle, I figured we could catch them. We slid through a tight turn that tilted the car so far over I was sure we were going to roll but we didn't.

"God *dammmn*, boy!" Russell said. He was clutching to the dashboard and grinning crazily. "I'd say we're going to run down the sumbitch, we don't crash and die first."

We went around another rise and the junction road came in view. Scroggins' truck was making a right turn onto it, heading west toward the Rankin road.

"Yessir, yessir!" Russell whooped. "We got them. That ten grand is good as ours!"

Steam started blowing back from under the Olds' hood panels but the motor was still going strong and I kept my foot down hard. The junction road was almost empty of other traffic at this hour, but an oil truck was coming from off to our right, heading for Blackpatch, and I could see that we'd reach the road before he passed by.

"We gonna cut it close with that sumbitch," Russell said, watching the coming truck. "Don't the fool see our dust?"

I made the turn onto the road with the tires shrieking. Walsh wailed in the trunk as the Olds carried all the way across the road and the left wheels went off onto the shoulder and flung up dust and the rear end fought for traction and here came the truck with its blinding headlights bearing straight at us and then the Olds' wheels grabbed again and I cut to the right an instant before the truck went by in a whooshing blur, its horn wailing. All I could see in the rearview was a mass of dust.

I floored the accelerator once more and the Olds sped up. The steam streaking from under the hood was thicker now but on this smoother surface we were fast gaining ground. Russell was shoving shells into the shotgun.

We closed to within fifty yards of Scroggins' truck. Thirty. Fifteen. A pair of headlights showed way behind us. I hoped they were Buck's. Now the Olds' engine was knocking. We'd probably torn a hole in the oil pan and were about to throw a rod.

Russell pumped a shell into the chamber and got in position at the window. "Closer!" he yelled.

I brought the Olds to within ten yards of the truck. There was no traffic in sight ahead of us, so I pulled out to the middle of the road to give Russell a better angle. He leaned out the window and took aim on the left rear wheel. The truck's driver must've seen what we were up to—he cut sharply to the left as Russell fired and missed the tire and the buckshot caromed up against the truck's underside and ricocheted every which way and some of it slung back and busted our headlamp and rang off the fender and Russell yelped.

He swore and shook his left arm, then pumped the slide and the empty shell case flew off into the dark and he set himself again. The engine was knocking louder now and I could smell it beginning to burn. Any minute now it would lose power and seize up and that would be it, we'd lose them. The driver was rocking the truck from one side of the road to the other to try to throw off our aim, but Russell took his time and gauged the truck's movements just right and the next boom of the shotgun blew the tire apart.

The truck sagged and started fishtailing and the ruined tire flew off the rim and came back and hit the Olds' windshield, shattering the right side and spraying us with shards and spiderwebbing the glass in front of me. I flinched and hit the brakes instinctively and too hard and the car started to skid sideways but I steered into the slide and managed to stay on the road.

The truck veered away, pitching and bouncing over the rough ground, and then swung into a tight turn and its left wheels left the ground and kept on rising and the truck capsized in a great crashing cloud of dust and skidded to a halt upside down.

And *BOOM!*—it exploded into an enormous, quivering sphere of orange fire.

I pulled over on the shoulder, the engine clattering like skeletons wrestling in a tin tub, black smoke streaming from the tailpipe. I switched off the ignition and we got out of the car but there was nothing we could do except watch the truck burn. The fire looked like molten gold, it was so thick and richly fueled. It lit up the countryside for a good hundred yards all around. We were thirty yards away but a light wind pressed the heat hard on our faces. Rivulets of flaming whiskey snaked from the truck in all directions over the stony ground. There were no screams, no cry at all except for Walsh's muffled cries for help from the Oldsmobile trunk. Russell picked up a large rock and flung it against the back of the car and the trunk fell quiet.

Buck arrived and parked the Model A behind the Olds. He left the motor running and got out and came to stand beside us and stare at the fireball wreckage. He looked grieved. So did Russell. Probably so did I. It was ten thousand in cash money plus a valuable load of hooch going up in flames.

Another truck was approaching from the west, slowing down as it drew closer. The driver leaned out the window and we turned back toward the fire to hide our faces from him. "Hey!" he called out. "What the hell happened?" But none of us turned around or answered him, and if he'd been thinking about stopping he changed his mind. His gearbox clashed and the engine wound up and he rolled on by.

And then on top of the odors of burning gasoline and oil and alcohol came a sickening smell unlike any I'd ever known, one I couldn't begin to describe for the lack of anything to compare it with.

"Jesus," Buck said. "Been a while since I had a whiff of that."

"Since France," Russell said. "Since them flamethrowers." He'd rolled up his left sleeve and was examining two small bloody spots on his arm where he'd been hit by ricocheting buckshot.

More headlights came in view a long way down the road.

"Well hell, we best get a move on," Buck said, and we headed back to the Ford.

"What about him?" Russell said, nodding at the Olds.

Buck shrugged. "He don't know who we are or even what we look like. If you owned that load of hooch, wouldn't you wonder why he's the only one still alive? Maybe wonder if he was some kind of inside man? Let him try and talk his way out of it."

"What if he *is* the inside man?" I said.

"Tough luck for him," Buck said. "You drive."

I went around to the other side of the Model A and slid in behind the wheel. Buck sat in the shotgun seat and Russell got in back. I wheeled the car onto the road and got rolling.

"I got to tell you, kid," Buck said, "that was some piece of driving. It was all I could do to keep you in sight."

I smiled my pleasure at the compliment.

He looked back at Russell. "What say, little brother? This boy shake you up some with that hairy ride?"

"Naw," Russell said. "Not so bad a change of pants and a few drinks won't fix me right up."

*W*ell, sir, I've been the grease monkey here for six months, and I can tell you for a fact he'd had his suspicions for a while. Couldn't hardly blame him—you ever seen Eula? Real piece of calico, I'm telling you, and she damn well knows it. Likes to strut it, know what I mean? My daddy always said the worst trouble a man could have was to be married to a goodlooking woman. It's about the only trouble I ain't had in this life—just don't tell my wife I said so.

Like I say, it wasn't nothing that took him by real big surprise, but still. Happened just last week. He says to me, Weldon, watch the place for me, and off he goes to home in the middle of the morning. Snuck into the house and sure enough there she was—riding the baloney pony with this old boy turned out to be a shipworker. Miller had him a ball bat and from what I hear he really laid it to the bastard. They say it'll be a while before he gets out of traction and he'll probably need a wheelchair when he does. Hard price to pay, but that's the chance you take when you go thieving from another man's quim, ain't it? He can thank his lucky stars he ain't dead. Miller coulda shot him and been within *his legal rights except he ain't a naturally mean sort. As for her, hell, he only punched her up some, knocked out a tooth. Mighta done worse except she took off running while he was still whaling on the shipworker and he had to chase her down the block. He'd only just started in on her when this neighbor runs over and tries to get him to stop. So Miller starts in on him. When the cops got there he had the fella down in the middle of the street and letting him have it with both fists and Eula screaming bloody murder. They said she wasn't wearing nothing but this little T-shirt—what I wouldn't've give to seen that! But like I say, they were lucky Miller only kicked their asses ruther than give them a load of buckshot. The neighbor's the only reason he's in jail. The judge figured he had good reason for what he did to Eula and the shipworker but said beating up on the neighbor was uncalled for. Gave him thirty days in the cooler and promised him sixty more if he didn't behave while he was in there. I took him some smokes yesterday and he said, Well, buddy, four down and twenty-six to go. I'd say he's keeping his spirits up real good.*

The lean gray mustached man holds his coat draped over one arm and thanks him for his time and information and again apologizes for not having realized Miller was not Mr. Faulk's last name, having been told only that a man named Miller owned this station and might be willing to sell it.

Well, Mr. Cheval, I expect he'll be real glad to know your company's interested in owning this place. I got a feeling he's about had his fill of Houston anyhow. Said he was thinking about heading back to Loosiana.

He departs in an agitation and a rare inclination to profanity. Visiting Faulk in jail is out of the question. There is no choice but to wait until he is released. Twenty-five days to go. Twenty-five crawling days. Yet he well knows the unreliability of jail sentences and so, upon checking into a hotel near the Buffalo Bayou, he telephones an acquaintance on the Houston police force. The detective owes him a favor for his assistance some years ago in extraditing to Texas a fugitive apprehended in a Terrebonne Parish and wanted by three other states. The fugitive's conviction in a Houston courtroom did much to elevate the

detective's career. Even so, the detective is not his friend—nor is any man—and does not seem pleased to hear from him until he understands the simplicity of the requital that will clear his debt, and he agrees to it. Every day thence the detective will telephone him at his hotel and—without ever asking to know why, or caring—will read to him a list of the names of all the men released that day from the Harris County Jail.

He will spend a portion of every day watching the ships come and go along the channel with no curiosity of where they have been or where they are bound. He will sometimes sip from a flask, sometimes puff his pipe. He will lie abed for portions of the day and stare at the ceiling. He will not turn on the radio at his bedside, never open a newspaper, enter no moviehouse. He will speak only to order from menus. One morning he will drive to Galveston and sit on a seawall bench and stare out at the Gulf the day long. One late night when he is walking the Houston streets he will be accosted by a large Negro wielding a lead pipe and demanding money. He will seize the thief's pipe hand in the pincers and leave him maimed and moaning on his knees. And that night sleep better than in many nights previous.

Thus will he pass the days until Miller Faulk's release.

*B*ubber Vicente was as blackassed as we were by the loss of Scroggins' money and the truckload of moonshine.

"We wouldn't've lost a nickel or a drop of hooch if we'd had better information," Buck said, "but *nobody* told us the advance men were supposed to be in certain places when Wills showed up. That's why the job went to hell."

"Well, don't look at *me*," Bubber said from behind his desk. "Ain't my fault you didn't now it. *I* didn't know it either, goddammit. And neither did the inside man or he'd've told me."

"Well, an inside man worth his salt *should've* known it," Buck said.

"Yeah, well, I can't argue with you there," Bubber said. He scratched his beard and looked both angry and sad.

"Whatever his cut's supposed to be," Buck said, "I'd reconsider it if I was you."

"I been doing that very thing while we been sitting here discussing things," Bubber said. "His cut's come way down, I'll tell you.

And I don't believe he'll complain about it a whole lot, neither, not once he understands how his information wasn't all it should've been." He lit a cigarette and exhaled a long stream of smoke. "But don't you boys go shining me on about the risk you run. Robbery's *supposed* to be risky. Otherwise everybody'd be doing it."

Buck looked away for a moment and then broke into a wide smile. Bubber laughed and shook his finger at him. He knew he had a point.

"It's why I got out of you all's end of the business," he said. We knew he'd been an armed robber before he started fencing and then finally became a setup man. "The riskiness got to me. You never know how a job'll go, and it ain't in my nature to take a lot of chances. Then again, that's exactly what some men *like* about the robber life." He smiled around at the three of us. "Or so I been told."

We all grinned back at him.

Buck had given Bubber his portion of the takes from Wink and Wills—$4,375. The remaining money cut three ways would give each of us a little over $2,700. Buck had put all our money in his valise. On the ride back from Wink I'd asked him and Russell what was to keep somebody from holding out on Bubber, how he could know for sure how much his men really got from a job.

"Well now, think about it, Sonny," Russell said. "The inside man's done told him what the job'll bring and Bubber's figured his cut of it. You can't hand him any less than he's expecting unless you and the inside man give him the same explanation for the difference. To get away with it, you'd have to know who the inside man is and be able to bring him into the cross. But even if you could do that, you'd be robbing Peter to pay Paul. Where's the percentage?"

"What's more," Buck said, "you and Paul would have it on each other that you cheated Peter, and you'd both always be worried that the other might let it slip. No sir, any way you figure it, it's bad business to cross a partner. You make a deal, kid, you're best off sticking to it."

"In other words," I said, "just because it's a world of thieves out there . . ."

" . . . don't mean there ain't no rules to it," he said. "Smartass."

Now Bubber pushed back in his chair and looked around at us. "You boys still on for Midland tomorrow? I can get somebody else for it if you ain't." Midland was only about twenty miles up the road and was where he'd set up our next job.

"Goddam right we are," Buck said. "Why wouldn't we be?"

"Well, I mean, after a scrape like you all had last night, some guys might not be too eager to do another job right away."

"Up yours, Bubber," Buck said. "We been in closer scrapes than last night. We're doing Midland."

Bubber raised his palms defensively. "Okay, okay, good enough. Now how about we let our hair down some? Drinks are on me."

We went out of the office and into the smoky speakeasy and settled at Bubber's private table in the back corner. We drank and talked and heard the latest jokes going around Odessa. There was a good band playing up on a small stage and all of us now and then got up to dance with some of the women in the place.

Bubber's partner, Earl Cue, hadn't been around all evening, and when Buck asked after him, Bubber said he'd been in the hospital since yesterday and probably wouldn't get out till tomorrow.

"He caught him a case of the runs from a bad batch of stew he ate over at Stella's Café," Bubber said. "It wasn't the runs that put him in the hospital, though—except I guess in a way it was. Earl lives in a boardinghouse, see, and has to share a bathroom with about seven other fellas. Bathroom's occupied as often as not, and sometimes when somebody gets a call of nature he's got to go out back and use the two-holer. It's what happened to Earl yesterday morning. A big old tool-pusher named Harvey Neumann was out there on one of the holes, taking his ease with a cigar and the newspaper, and he said old Earl came charging in with his belt undone and his pants already unbuttoned and he just did manage to slap his ass over the other hole before cutting loose with his load. Even in the stink of that jake it smelled like he was shitting dead cats, according to Harvey. Earl didn't set there but a few seconds, though, before he lets a hell of a holler and jumps to his feet with the shit still coming out of him and splattering all over everything, including Harvey's pants and shoes. Well, that naturally riled Harvey something terrible and he jumped up too and socked Earl a good one in the jaw and laid him out cold. Said he did it without thinking, which ain't hard to believe, considering the situation. Then he saw how Earl's balls were all swole up like apples and he right away knew Earl had been bit by a spider. Ain't the first time it's happened to some poor fella who didn't rattle a stick around the hole before setting down on it. Can't really fault Earl for not taking the time for such precaution, I guess, but that's what can happen when you don't. A man can't be too careful, even when he's caught short. Anyway, that's how he come to be in the hospital with swole-up balls and a broke jaw. I'll be sure and tell him you asked after him. He'll appreciate it."

"Lord Jesus," Russell said. "I guess the only good thing you could say about an experience like that is you ain't likely to have too many worse ones."

"I know it," Bubber said. "Spiderbite in the balls—can you *imagine* what that feels like?"

"I believe maybe I can," Buck said.

Bubber was eager to know what we thought of Mona. We said she was every bit as beautiful and smart and gracious as he'd said she was. He asked if we'd sampled the wares in her house and we said they were first-rate. He was beaming with pride. He said he'd thought he'd been in love before but he didn't know what real love was until he met Mona. Jesus, he had it bad. It was all we could do to keep a straight face, listening to him go on and on about her.

We laughed out loud, though, when he told of a time when they were going at it hot and heavy and she called out the name "Natty" in the middle of things. She didn't even know she'd said it until afterward, when she noticed Bubber had sulled up a little and she asked what was wrong.

"Who the fuck's Natty?" he said.

Turned out to be an old boyfriend, a leg-breaker she'd lived with for a time in Tucson. She swore she hadn't thought of him in years and assured Bubber she'd gotten over him long ago. Maybe so, Bubber told her, but hearing her call out another man's name at a moment like that had a way of taking the edge off his pleasure.

"Well," she'd said, "would you rather I was doing it with him and saying your name, or doing it with you and saying his?"

"Now I ask you, boys," he said, "how's a man supposed to answer a question like that?"

"Don't allow for nothing but hard choice," Russell said.

"They never do," Buck said.

"What you think, Sonny?" Bubber said.

"I'd tell her I'd rather she did it with me *and* called out my name," I said—and smiled real big.

Bubber stared at me without expression for a moment, then turned to Buck and Russell and all three of them busted out laughing.

"He's real young, ain't he?" Bubber said.

It was close to eleven o'clock as we made our way through Midland's residential streets, the trees along the sidewalks casting long shadows in the light of a yellow-horned moon low in the western sky. A rich aroma came off the paper sacks of Mexican food on the front seat between me and Buck, but the last thing on our minds at the moment was eating. Buck took a pillowcase from under the seat and put it in his coat pocket.

We came into a well-kept neighborhood of spacious lawns and white paling fences. Most of the homes already dark and asleep, but a big two-story house in the middle of the block was showing faint yellow light behind drawn curtains, a shadowy porch with a pair of wooden armchairs. There were three cars in the driveway and three more out in front, all of them brandnew. I parked the Model A at the head of the row of cars by the fence and cut off the lights but left the motor running. We stayed put for a minute, but nobody came to the door or moved a window curtain to have a look outside. Russell racked a shell into the chamber of the Remington pump.

"All right, boys," Buck said. "In and out, slick as a dick."

He and Russell got out of the car and I handed Buck the sacks of food one at a time and then got out too. They went through the front gate and left it open wide while I used my clasp knife to puncture a tire on each of the three cars by the fence, catching the smell of stale air with each hissing deflation. I went to the driveway and did the same thing to the cars there, then I put the knife away and hustled up to the porch. Buck and Russell already had their bandannas on and I pulled mine up too.

The house belonged to a man named Allford, a onetime wildcatter who'd struck it big up around the Red River before coming out to drill in West Texas. With him tonight were the president of the biggest construction company in the county, a rancher from up around Lubbock, two other local oilmen, and a bootlegger from Hobbs. According to Bubber, these six well-heeled buddies came together at Allford's house once a month to play high-stakes poker. The game ran from six in the evening till six in the morning and the rules required that every man buy $2,500 worth of chips and stay in the game till the end of it or he went bust, whichever came first. In any case, we knew there'd be at least fifteen grand at the table.

Thanks to Bubber's inside man we also knew that it was their poker-night custom to make a late-night telephone call to Concha's Café in town and order some food and have it delivered to the house. Tonight they had called for one sack of chicken tacos, one of enchiladas, one of sugar-and-cinnamon doughnuts. As we stood on the porch, ready to make our move, the deliveryman from Concha's was lying bound and gagged in the back seat of his car in an alley five bocks away.

"Set?" Buck said. Russell and I nodded and pressed ourselves back against the wall so we couldn't be seen from the little window in the front door. I had the .380 in hand. Buck sucked a deep breath and then gave the door a hard rapping. He wore a baseball cap, the better to look like a deliveryman, and held the three sacks in front of him, one on top of the other, to hide the masked lower part of his face. He rapped again, and the curtain must've pulled away from the little window—a small cast of light illuminated the food sacks and Buck's hands holding them, his cap. A man's gruff voice said, "Concha's?"

"Yeah," Buck said.

The lock turned and the door swung inward and a brighter wash of light fell over Buck as he passed the sacks in to somebody—and then pulled the .45 and raised it and said, "Not a word, Mac—just back up real easy." He went into the house and Russell and I followed.

A beefy half-bald guy in shirtsleeves and carrying a .38 in a shoulder holster was holding the sacks of food and gawking at us like we were a magic trick. He was the bootlegger's bodyguard and his face had the baggy look of somebody who'd been dozing. He was probably wondering how he was going to explain this to his boss.

Buck snatched the guy's gun from the holster and stuck it in his own pants. He pointed at the sofa and the man sat down on it. The bottoms of the food sacks were dark with grease and he held them off his lap to keep from staining his white trousers. Russell had the shotgun leveled at the guy from the hip. I stood back by the door where I could cover the whole room.

The house was laid out exactly as we'd been told. The parlor was spacious and expensively furnished, the adjoining dining room as well. A door at the rear of the dining room opened to the kitchen, and a staircase at the near end of the hall led up to the family bedrooms and the maid's room. A telephone was mounted on the wall at the foot of the stairs and Buck yanked out the cord. As he started toward the kitchen a woman's voice called out, "Was that the food, Warren?" and she came out into the dining room, drying her hands on a dish towel. She saw us and stopped short.

Buck raised his pistol at her and put a finger to his masked mouth. The woman stood silent. He beckoned her into the parlor and she came. She looked scared but not so much as I'd expected. She was tall and middle-aged and had the weathered face of somebody who'd spent much of her life out of doors, a country woman's face. Hands rough and big-knuckled.

At the far end of the hallway and to the left, next to the back door, was an arched passageway to the kitchen. There were three doors on the right side of the hall—the first to a den, the next to a bathroom, the last to a billiards room. That last one was the one we wanted.

"Take the sacks," Buck said softly to the woman, and the Warren guy handed them up to her, making a face when a drop of grease spotted his pants leg. Russell took the woman by the elbow and steered her into the hallway to where she couldn't see the sofa—or the swat Buck gave the guy across the nose with the barrel of the .45. She heard it, though, and the groan he let out, and she tried to look around Russell to see what it was, but he gently pushed her back and shook his head.

It was a wonder the Warren guy stayed conscious. He had his hands over his nose but the blood ran out between his fingers and down into his sleeves and dripped on his white shirt and pants. His eyes were streaming and he was gasping against the pain and moaning low. You bust somebody's nose like that, it hurts so bad he goes nearly mute—and lets go of any notion he might've had to try to jump you.

Buck gave me a wink, then whispered into the woman's ear and steered her down the hall ahead of him. He and Russell stood to either side of the farthest door and Buck nodded at her and she carefully balanced the sacks on one arm and opened the door with her free hand. Somebody in the room said, "Hey now—about time that chili-belly chow got here!"

Buck shoved her into the room and he and Russell ran in and Buck shouted, "Hands on the table—on the table—now, now, *now*!"

Somebody started swearing and there was a smack and a yelp and the same voice said, "Ah *goddam,* ah *shit*!" the way you do when you hit your thumb with a hammer.

I knew Russell was holding them under the shotgun and I heard Buck tell them to empty their pockets, to pull them inside out. He told somebody to clear the table, put it all in the bag, faster, goddammit, *faster.*

I stood by the front door, pointing the .380 down the hall, ready to shoot whoever I had to. The Warren guy was trying to stem the blood from his broken nose, but each time he put his head back he'd start choking and have to sit up again and add to the mess on his clothes. The woman came out of the room and stopped short when she saw me. I gestured with the pistol for her to get the hell out of there and she hurried through the rear passageway into the kitchen.

They weren't in there two minutes before coming out again, Buck first, gun in one hand, the pillowcase with the money in the other, two revolvers in the front of his waistband. Then Russell backed out of the room, saying, "First man out gets splattered." He shut the door and came sidling down the hall, watching behind him.

"Go," Buck said. I slung open the front door and went out fast, taking the porch steps two at a time, running up the walkway and hearing Buck coming behind me and laughing low.

I went through the gate and started for the Ford—and then there was a loud blast and somebody cried out.

I turned and saw Buck at the gate, looking back at Russell down on all fours on the walkway. The woman was at the door with a smoking single-barrel shotgun, breaking it open to reload again. She darted behind the wall as Buck brought up the .45 and fired three fast rounds, two smacking the wall, the third caroming off the doorjamb and smashing something of glass in the living room.

Russell up now, using the Remington like a cane and striding awkwardly. Buck hustling to him, putting an arm around him from

the side, starting back toward the gate. The woman leaned around the
door and fired in the same instant I did. My bullet by pure chance hit
some part of the shotgun and it seemed to wrest itself from her hands.
She yipped and ducked out of sight.

But Buck and Russell were down. As I ran to them Buck rose to
one knee, still holding the moneybag and his pistol. Russell was cursing low, struggling to get up on hands and knees. I stuck my gun in my
pants and bent down to take hold of him and lugged him upright and
felt the warm dampness of his back.

"Jeeesus!" he said.

"Go on!" Buck said.

I half-dragged Russell out the gate and to the Ford, glancing back
to see Buck up on his feet and backing toward the gate. At the idling
car I opened a rear door and pushed Russell onto the seat but he
slipped to the floorboard, swearing, his legs still outside the car.

Gunfire sounded behind us—Buck's .45, other pistols.

I shoved Russell's legs up onto the seat and shut the door. Then
looked back for Buck but didn't see him.

And then did. Sprawled on the walkway and not moving at all.

Dead. The word in my mind like a whisper.

A bullet whined off the car roof not a foot from my head and
another punched into the front door at my hip. I crouched and ran
around to the other side of the car and scrambled in behind the
wheel—gunshots cracking, men shouting and swearing, slugs clanging through the hood panel and ringing off the engine, thunking the
sides of the car, popping through the window glass.

I yanked the gearshift into low and gunned the Ford out into the
street and went wheeling around the first corner at a wide lean, skid-
ding a little and nearly hitting a car parked at the curb. I took rights
and lefts at random, glad as hell for the emptiness of the streets at this
hour but not sure now which way the highway was. Then we were at
the edge of town and I got my bearings and knew the main road was
to my right and I cut over in that direction. But then the motor started

missing and began to lug. I pumped and pumped the accelerator to no avail. Maybe a bullet hit the gas line or the fuel pump, something. Before we'd gone another block the engine quit altogether and I coasted into a grocery store parking lot.

Except for the moon, the only illumination on the street was from a small naked bulb burning over the entrance to the grocery. I sat in the silenced car with my hands locked on the steering wheel. Russell groaned in the back. I couldn't form a clear thought. Then I saw a sales lot just across the street, with a dozen or so cars on it.

A truck was coming down the street and I waited for it to go by and saw its headlights wash over some bum curled up on a bench at the corner. Then the truck was past and I told Russell I'd be right back, but I wasn't sure he even heard me. I jogged over to the lot and slipped into a little Model A roadster with its top up and ducked my head under the dashboard. It didn't take but a minute to snip and strip the ignition wires with my clasp knife and twist them together. I hit the starter and the motor cranked right up.

I drove across the street and pulled up beside the sedan, looked all around to make sure the coast was clear, then got out and opened Russell's door and told him we had to change cars. I helped him out of the Ford, saying sorry, man, sorry, as he flinched and moaned and cursed me for the pain I was causing him. He wanted to know where his shotgun was and I said probably back in the yard where he dropped it and he cursed me for that too.

"*Love* that shotgun," he said.

I got him into the roadster, his coat sopping now, my hands slick with his blood. I shut his door and went around and got behind the wheel. He was slumped in the seat, grunting with almost every breath. I got us rolling.

"Buck?" he said.

I shook a cigarette out of my pack and leaned forward to light it, steering with my forearms, then held it out to him but he turned away from it.

"Where's he?" he said.

"He went down," I said.

"Went down got caught or . . . went down got killed?"

"Killed." The word brought up a surge of bile behind it and for a moment I thought I'd throw up. I swallowed and cleared my throat hard. My eyes burned. I said it again to prove I could. "They killed him is what I mean."

I turned onto the Odessa highway and gave the roadster the gas. The road had been badly washboarded by heavy truck traffic and the shock absorbers took a beating as we jarred along. Russell moaned low.

"For sure?" he said.

"Sure looked it."

"*Looked* it?"

"That's right, man. *Shit*."

I could feel him staring at me. I swerved around a sizable pothole only to run right over another with such impact it was a wonder the tire didn't blow. Russell sucked a deep breath against the pain, then let it out in a long sigh.

By sunrise he was stitched and bandaged and full of drugs against pain and infection, asleep in the isolated house of a tall silver-haired surgeon named Gustafson. Many of the doctor's patients were associates of Bubber Vicente, gunshot men in need of surgical repair who could not risk going to a hospital and piquing official curiosity about their wounds. Such emergencies usually came to Gustafson in the wee hours, as we had tonight.

According to Bubber, Gustafson had once had a prosperous practice in Dallas. But he'd gotten a socially prominent young woman in the family way, and because neither of them wanted to get married, he felt obliged to help her get shed of the problem. He attended to her in his office, but complications came up and he had to rush her to a hospital in order to save her life. "And like they say after a lynching," Bubber said, "the jig was up." Only the family's wish to keep the scandal out of the newspapers saved him from prison, but he still lost his license. Ever since then he'd had to practice underground. In addition to the office he maintained in his Odessa house, he had one in Blackpatch—in Mona Holiday's dance club—where he kept a well-trained nurse on daily duty and himself went three days a week. "He hates Blackpatch as much as everybody else," Bubber said, "but it's the last place in the world where anybody's ever gonna ask to see his license, and he makes a steady dollar down there." In addition to treating injured oil workers, he tended to the medical welfare of Mona's girls, helping them stay free of venereal disease and pregnancy, and relieving them of either problem when preventive measures failed.

He had extracted six buckshot pellets from the area around Russell's left shoulder blade and another six from the hamstring muscle of the same leg that got shot up in the war. Red-eyed and haggard by the time he was finished, Gustafson told me Russell would have to stay off the leg for a month and then need crutches for another couple of months before he could start getting by with a cane—which, he was sorry to say, he would probably need for the rest of his life. He said we could let Russell sleep for a little while longer but then we'd have to get him out of there. He couldn't risk having fugitives in his house for very long. He gave me a bottle of pills to give Russell for the pain and then went back to bed.

While the doc had been attending to Russell, Bubber made a telephone call to an associate in Midland and asked him to get whatever information he could about the card game robbery. The associate called back sometime after sunrise, while I was drinking my umpteenth cup of coffee. He reported that a man named Loomis Mitchum, no record of previous arrests, was in the county jail under charges of armed robbery and assault in regard to a card game holdup. He'd first been taken to the hospital with a head wound—which proved to be nothing more than a bullet graze on the skull. He'd also had a couple of shotgun pellets in his shoulder. Neither wound serious enough to keep the cops from taking him to jail as soon as he'd been patched up. He'd probably go in front of a judge inside the next two weeks. The robbery was pretty much open-and-shut, but the money had been recovered at the scene. And an able lawyer could likely wiggle him out of the assault rap, especially since the only two persons Mitchum had injured were both known crooks and neither one was eager to press the matter in court. Warren Taos, who'd had his nose broken, was an ex-convict who'd done time for manslaughter, and Leo "Bad Dog" Richardson, who'd suffered a broken arm, was a bootlegger several times arrested but never yet convicted. All in all, the chances were good that Loomis Mitchum would get no more than eighteen months at the state road prison at Santa Rita—in Reagan County, about seventy miles from Fort Stockton—and draw parole in six.

"I'll get him a lawyer who makes sure that's how it goes," Bubber told me.

I hadn't realized the tightness of the grip I'd been keeping on myself until we got the news Buck was alive. Bubber must've read the relief on my face. He smiled and punched me on the arm and said, "Hell kid, we ought to know they can't never hurt that uncle of yours by shooting him in his hard head."

I tried to smile but could feel the bad job I did of it.

"I didn't want to say nothing about it before," Bubber said, "but it's too bad he was the one holding the loot."

Yes it was. And then I remembered the Wink money. It had been in Buck's valise. And the valise had been under the front seat of the Model A.

Bubber winced when I told him.

Forty minutes later I was back in Midland, driving Bubber's Chrysler up and down the streets, searching for the grocery store where I'd left the Ford, the town even more unfamiliar in all this daylight and heavy traffic. *Fool,* I kept thinking, *fool.* And then there the store was—and the Model A, right where I'd left it, only now there were other cars in the lot too. I'd been afraid it would be gone by now, towed away by the cops, that somebody would've called them to report a car with a bunch of bullet holes in it. Then again, the holes weren't readily noticeable except up close, and people generally weren't very observant, anyway. I turned into the lot and drew up next to the Model A, remembering now that I'd left the back passenger door wide open, telling myself somebody probably closed it as a favor, but feeling a hollowness in my gut.

The valise wasn't there. Not under the seat stained dark with Russell's blood, not in the trunk, not anywhere in the car. I went in the grocery and studied the bored-looking woman at the register, the freckled kid stocking the shelves, the chubby manager being harried by some woman about the poor quality of his produce. None of them had found the money—you could tell by looking at them. I went back out and stood on the glaring sidewalk and regarded the passing traffic.

Maybe somebody had seen us switch cars and then looked through the Model A the minute we were gone. Maybe that bum on the bench across the street hadn't been asleep, or maybe some other tramp had come along. Maybe a cop had happened on the car and found the dough and was now making plans on how to spend it.

I got back in the Chrysler and drove across the street and around the block and parked at a corner that gave me a good view of the Ford in the lot. I was hoping whoever had taken the valise had made off in a haste, before he'd searched the rest of the car, before he knew what the valise held. Once he knew, he might start wondering if there was more money still in the Model A and maybe come back for another look. It was a stupidly desperate hope and I knew it, but I sat there till noon before conceding that the money was gone for good.

When I got back to Gustafson's, Russell was dressed and waiting for me on the doctor's backporch couch, lying on his side to keep his weight off the wounds. The doc was still sleeping and Bubber had gone back to the hotel to get some rest too. Earl Cue had brought Russell a fresh change of clothes and helped him to get dressed and then kept him company while they waited for me to return. Russell was smiling, so I knew Bubber had given him the news about Buck.

"He *looked* dead, huh?" he said to me. He was dopey yet from the drugs. His smile was lopsided and his speech was heavy and slow. "Better get some specs, kid."

"I've never been happier to be wrong," I said. My voice nearly cracked on the words but both of them had the good grace not to smile about it. I started to tell Russell about the Wink money but he said Earl had already informed him.

"I feel like such a goddam fool," I said. "About Buck. About the money. Christ."

"You thought he's dead," Russell said thickly. "The only reason you left, I know. And don't worry about the money. Can always get money."

"At's rye, hell widdit," Earl Cue said, nodding sagely. "Kin awheeze ged munny."

Sipping juice through a straw, Earl looked even more skeletal than the last time I'd seen him. He'd been released from the hospital the day before but was still in tender shape from his outhouse misadventure. His left cheek was swollen and purple and he couldn't speak very clearly for the wires clamping his jaws. He had to wear baggy pants and walk bowlegged in order to accommodate his balls, which he said weren't as swollen anymore but were still sore as hell.

"Bubber's getting Buck a lawyer," Russell said. "Pay him back after our next job." He squinted against a stab of pain.

"Bess geddum home," Earl said to me. "Leddum ress."

"You sound like a damn rummy," Russell said.

"Ook ooze talken."

I helped Russell out to the roadster. Earl tried to help, but he had enough pain of his own to contend with, grunting and grimacing as much as Russell as we made our slow limping way to the car. The passenger side of the seat was darkly stained with dried blood. I got Russell settled into the seat and Earl shook our hands and said, "Gome, gessum ress, eel up."

He slept for most of the drive to Fort Stockton, now and then groaning, shifting on the seat to try to ease his pain. As we went through McCamey the boomtown clamor woke him.

He stared around at the heavy traffic, the air hazed and acrid with gas and oil fumes. Then scrutinized the interior of the roadster. "Oughta got one with a damn radio," he said. And went back to sleep.

A few miles farther along he woke again and looked at me like he'd just been told something very important and had to share it immediately.

"Busted him out one time, I'll do it again," he said. "*We'll* do it, Sonny."

And closed his eyes once more.

IV

The girls must've been in the kitchen and not heard us until my car door banged shut. They came running out with wide smiles that collapsed into fearful looks when they saw me helping Russell out of the roadster.

"Oh my God," Charlie said. Russell had one arm over my shoulders and she put his other over hers. "Where's Buck?"

"Hell, he's all right," Russell said. "He's a guest of the state at the moment but not for long, believe you me."

Belle put a hand on my arm. "You okay?"

I winked at her and she showed a quick weak smile.

As we made our way toward the porch, Charlie said, "How bad is it, baby?" Her eyes were brimming.

"If you gonna cry," Russell said, gritting his teeth with every step, "you can go somewhere else to do it."

"And you can go to hell," she said. But it was all the admonition she needed to soldier up.

We had to take the porch steps slowly. Belle ran ahead of us into the house, moving chairs out of our way, opening their bedroom door, pulling down the bedcovers. I braced him up while Charlie took off his shirt. She bit her lip when she saw the bandage around his chest and the red stains at his back where the wounds had been seeping. She undid his belt and started tugging down his pants and he flinched and sucked a breath and said, "*Easy*, goddammit." She gently lowered the trousers past the bandage on his thigh. I eased him to a sitting position on the edge of the bed and she removed his shoes and socks and then took off his pants.

Belle fetched a glass of water and I gave Russell a pill to wash down with it. We helped him to squirm further up onto the bed and accommodate himself on his side. He was asleep almost immediately but pouring sweat from heat and pain. We went out of the room and left the door open a crack so we could easily hear him if he should wake and call out.

In the kitchen I drank a full glass of iced tea without taking it from my mouth until it was drained, then asked Belle for a refill. Charlie wanted to use the car to go buy an electric fan to keep Russell cool during the day. I went out to the roadster with her and showed her how to connect the ignition wires.

"Nice new car and no key for it," she said. "That's a good one." She gave me a look I couldn't read and drove off.

Belle and I sat in the kitchen for a while, smoking cigarettes and sipping iced tea, not saying much. She offered to fix me something to eat but I was too tired. I'd been two days without sleep, and now that we were back at the house I felt exhausted. I snubbed the cigarette and finished off the tea, got up and went to the bedroom, stripping off my shirt. She came in behind me and watched me finish undressing and get into bed. She sat down beside me and brushed the hair out of my eyes and I was asleep before she took her hand away.

I woke in the dark, spooned up against her from behind, my face in her hair. The open window was moonless and the curtains hung lank, the air cool despite the lack of breeze. I fingered her nipples and she came awake and made a small sound of pleasure. She rubbed her bottom against me and felt my readiness and I squirmed down for a better angle and easily slipped into her slickness. She was breathing through her teeth.

When we were done, she turned her face to kiss me, to whisper, "I'm so glad it wasn't you."

For most of the following week Russell was asleep as often as not. Charlie fed him a pain pill every couple of hours. "It keeps him from hurting too much and it helps him sleep," she said. "He needs all the sleep he can get."

Because she wanted him to rest as comfortably as possible she let him have the bed to himself and she slept on a foldout army cot she'd bought somewhere. The electric fan stood on the dresser, humming and oscillating, keeping the heat off him. She was hardly ever out of his hailing distance, never further away than the kitchen. She spent much of every day in a chair at his bedside, leafing through magazines and listening to radio music at low volume. There was always a pot of warm broth on the stove, and whenever he woke she spooned some into him.

The first time he was awake when I looked in on him, he smiled weakly and said, "Hey kid, how you doing?"

"Better than you, I'd say."

"Not for long," he said. And was asleep again in a minute.

He was awake again that evening when I looked in. "Next time," he said, "*I'll* lead the way out and you or Buck can bring up the rear."

"Anyway you want it, Uncle," I said, grinning back at him. The way he said it, you'd have thought Buck was in the next room rather than in a Midland jail cell.

Whenever I checked to see how he was coming along over the next few days, Charlie would often as not be ministering to him—feeding him, bathing him, shaving him, changing the bandage around his upper torso and shoulder or the one on his leg. He had dark circles around his eyes and was uncommonly pale, but he said he was doing fine. "Be right as the rain in no time," he said.

"Yeah, sure," Charlie said. "Only it hardly ever rains around here, so don't let's get too far ahead of ourselves."

We'd been back twelve days when the telegram came from Bubber: GOOD LAWYER BUT HARD JUDGE STOP TWO YEARS SANTA RITA STOP LM WELL STOP TRANSFERS TOMORROW STOP BV.

Charlie didn't want me to wake him up just to read him the telegram but I did anyway. He listened to it and rubbed his face and scowled. "Two years. Bastards."

"That's not so bad, is it?" Charlie said. "He can get parole in, what, seven or eight months, right?"

Russell looked at her like she was trying to sell him something—then turned to me and said, "If only I was in better shape we could've sprung him when they were transferring him to the farm. That would've been the ticket."

"What are you *talking* about?" Charlie said.

He ignored the question. "Send a telegram," he said to me. "Tell Bubber we need everything he can give us on this Santa Rita joint. Once we have that we can figure how to—"

He had a sudden coughing fit. There'd been a hard wind for the past two days and the air was full of dust. He said it didn't hurt his back wounds when he coughed but it looked to me like he was flinching despite his best effort not to. He tried to resume what he'd been saying but got caught up in coughing once again, this time the pain of it starkly evident on his face. He slumped back on the pillows, gasping.

"All right, that's enough visiting now," Charlie said sharply. "Come on, Sonny, let the man get his rest." I let her steer me to the door.

"Send it now, Sonny," Russell said in a tight rasp, then fell to coughing again. I said I was on my way. Then Charlie closed the door on me.

She'd been testy ever since our return, and I was pretty sure it had to do with our business. She'd never much cared for Russell's being in the robbery trade, and now she seemed to get upset by any talk of it at all. I had the feeling they'd been arguing about it, but if that was the case, they were keeping it between themselves. We'd always shared confidences, Charlie and I, but just the day before, when I asked her what was wrong, she'd said, "Nothing" in a way that made clear she wasn't going to bring me into it.

Belle didn't know what was troubling Charlie, either. She'd gotten to know her at least as well as I did, maybe better, and she'd tried to feel her out a couple of times, but Charlie wasn't confiding in anybody.

"I think she's real scared he might get hurt worse," Belle said. "But she's just as scared to say anything to him about it. You know how he is when she complains about you all's work."

"I don't get it," I said. "She's always known what he does. She's always known it's a risky business."

"Yeah, well. Being told something's risky is a lot different from seeing what can happen."

I figured she was probably right—Charlie was just scared. Russell's blood was her first look at what can happen when the job goes bad. And I realized how different Belle was in that respect. She'd seen plenty of cases of risk gone bad. She'd seen what men looked like after falling off derricks, after getting their heads smashed by falling drill pipe. She'd seen men who'd been burned up so bad in field fires they looked, as she put it, like big charred dolls and gave off a smell you'd never forget. In the case of her own daddy, she'd seen what they looked like after being gassed to death. I doubted that Charlie had ever seen any such things or their like.

By the time we got the word about Buck, we had another problem—we were nearly broke. After the latest visit to the grocer's and then to the Callaghan Street house to get some beer and hooch, I had less than ten dollars. I searched Buck's room in case he might've stashed some money in there but all I found was sixty-three cents in a dresser drawer. Belle had about two dollars left of the grocery money I'd given her before I went to Odessa. Maybe Russell had enough money to cover our rent and groceries and booze and so forth until he was ready to work again, but I had a feeling he didn't. He'd always let Buck take care of the money and only carried enough himself to pay for incidentals or to take Charlie out for a night on the town. Forget borrowing money from Bubber. I'd heard Buck say that Bubber never lent money to his holdup men—not because he didn't trust them, but because the risk was too great that something would happen to them before they could repay him. Nobody faulted him for his caution.

That night in bed I explained our financial problem to Belle and told her if Russell was as flat as I was I'd have to go out on a job pretty soon.

At first she didn't say anything, but although it was too dark to see her face, I could feel her eyes on me. Finally she said, "Who'd do it with you?"

"Nobody," I said. "It won't be that big a one."

"It's always better if somebody stays with the car and has it ready for the getaway."

"Do tell," I said. "What do you know about it?"

"I've heard you all talk, you know."

I'd had no idea she'd listened so closely to any of our shop talk.

"Let me go with you, Sonny. I can drive for you, you know I can."

Until a little over a week ago I hadn't known she could drive a car at all, never mind drive as well as she did. For lack of anything else to do one afternoon, we'd gone for a long drive way out into the desert.

We put the top up on the roadster to keep the dust off us and I sped us over an old truck trail that went winding every which way around outcrops and arroyos and came to an end at an abandoned oil camp. She loved it, yahooing along with me as the roadster went leaning through the turns, raising high rooster tails of dust behind us. I told her about the rough trails we'd had to drive on in doing the Blackpatch hijack, and she said she'd learned to drive on some pretty rough roads around Corsicana.

"I was fourteen when Daddy started teaching me in his Dodge," she said. "He loved to speed around like you, and he'd always let me drive fast too. I don't mean to brag on myself, but he said I was a regular Barney Oldfield. He taught me lots of stuff—how to fish, how to use tools. I was an only child, so he didn't have anybody else to teach."

"Want to show me what a hotshot driver you are?" I said.

"Think I'm lying, don't you?"

We traded seats and she got us going, smoothly working the gearshift and clutch. At first she took it easy, rolling along at moderate speed, taking the turns slowly. But I could tell she was only getting the feel of the car. Then she began to accelerate. As we headed for the next curve she gave me a sidelong glance and said, "Hold on to your hat."

She smoothly shifted down into second gear and gunned the motor and I fell against my door as she wheeled through a tight left turn. She took the next two curves just as nicely, and I whooped along with her.

But she got a little too cocky and took the next one too fast. We skidded off the trial and onto the softer sand and the car slogged to a stop and stalled before she could shove in the clutch. She started it up again and put it in low but the back wheels spun in the sand.

"Dammit!" she said. Her face was redly angry. "I'm sorry, Sonny."

"Nice ride," I said. "But now I'm going to have to sweat my ass off getting us unstuck."

"No, you're not."

She got out of the car and ducked down out of sight for a minute by one of the rear wheels and then went around and squatted by the other one and then got back in the car. She put the car in gear and eased out the clutch and we slowly rolled forward and back onto the trail.

"What'd you do?" I said.

"Let a bunch of air out the back tires so they get a better grip in the sand. It's an old trick Daddy taught me. We got to take it kind of easy getting back, though. Till we can fill them back up again." She was smiling as we plodded along.

I said, "Stop the car a minute."

She did, and looked at me in question. I leaned over and kissed her a good one.

"Whoo," she said. "What's *that* for?"

"Call it a yen. Any objections?"

"Oh no sir," she said with a big grin. "Matter of fact I'm getting some yens of my own. Why don't we hustle on back home and I'll show you them?"

"Let's do that," I said.

Her driving wasn't the only surprise of the week. The next day we were out on another truck trail and she was barreling through the curves with even more skill and confidence than the day before—and then she unexpectedly hit the brakes in the middle of a long straight stretch. The sudden stop threw me hard against the dash and I bonked my head on the windshield. A cloud of raised dust rolled over us.

"Oh baby, I'm sorry—you all right?" She was all big-eyed. "But jeezo, did you see the *size* of it?"

"Of *what*?" I said, rubbing my forehead.

"Rattlesnake. In the road ahead. He's probably gone now."

We strained to see through the settling dust. "I don't see it no more," she said.

"There," I said, and pointed.

It was a good-sized rattler, all right, about fifteen yards away and alongside the trail, coiled in front of a creosote shrub. It was nearly the same color as the sand and hard to spot. Except for the darker bush behind it I might not have seen it.

I took the Smith & Wesson six-inch out from under the seat and eased the door open and stepped out. I held the revolver in a two-hand grip and braced my arms on top of the windshield frame, then cocked the piece and took a bead and squeezed off the shot.

The bang was swallowed almost instantly in all that open space and the sand kicked up a little to the right and slightly behind the snake. It drew into a tighter coil.

"Almost," Belle said.

"Almost only counts in horseshoes," I said.

I hit it with the next one—knocking the rattler into a writhing tangle. I walked up to within a few feet of it and shot it twice more and it stopped moving. Belle came up beside me as I straightened it out some with my foot. It was close to five feet long, even bigger than I'd thought.

"Wow," she said. "*Look* at it."

"It's one less hardcase in the world," I said, and headed back to the car. I released the revolver's cylinder and put my thumb over the two live rounds still in it and shook out the empty shells. I had a box of .38 cartridges under the driver's seat and I got it out and reloaded.

She lingered over the snake a moment before coming back to the car.

"Nice shooting, huh?" I was a little surprised to realize I'd been showing off, that I wanted to impress her.

"Yeah," she said. "Nice." There was something else on her mind.

"What?" I said.

"Sonny," she said. It was the voice she used when she didn't quite know how to broach a subject. She looked over at a bunch of prickly pear, then off at the mountains, then finally back at me. "Teach me?"

"What? You mean shoot?"

"Yeah."

"You never fired a gun?"

"Daddy was always going to show me but never did get the chance."

I took the bullets out of the .38 and passed it to her so she could get the feel of its heft and its fit in her grip. I showed her how to stand sidelong to the target to shoot with one hand and how to face it when you shoot with two and how to use the front sight. I showed her how to squeeze the trigger rather than jerk it. How to cock the hammer and uncock it again without firing. How to unlock the cylinder and how the ejector rod worked and how to load the chambers.

"I love the sounds of it," she said. She spun the cylinder to hear its soft whirr. She cocked the hammer with its softly ratcheting double click and snapped it on an empty chamber. "It sounds so . . . I don't know. Efficient."

"That's the word for it," I said.

I gathered a few stones about the size of my fist and set them in a row on top of a waist-high mound of sand, then backed up about a dozen yards and reloaded the piece and handed it to her. I told her to shoot into the mound first, to get used to the report and the recoil.

She stood facing forward with a two-hand grip. *Pop!* She flinched hardly at all. She turned and looked at me and silently formed the word, "Wow!" Then stood sideways and fired two one-hand shots.

"Oh man!" she said. "I can do this. Watch the rock on the right."

She took careful aim. *Pop!* Sand spurted an inch to the side of the rock.

"Hey girl, *almost.*" I was impressed.

"Almost is for horseshoes," she said without looking at me, taking aim again, the tip of her tongue in the corner of her mouth. Missing again, this time by a slightly wider margin.

"Dammit!"

She drew another bead and held it. Then lowered the revolver to her waist and regarded the rock like she was seeing it in some different way. Then brought the gun up smoothly and fired and the rock went flying.

"*Whooo!*" I applauded. "Give em hell, Kitty Belle!"

She whirled around to me, wide-eyed. "Know how I did it? I didn't think about it or even *aim* so much, I just sort of up and *pointed* at it, like with my finger. It felt, I don't know, so *natural*."

"I'll be damn," I said. "Fired six rounds in her life and already she's giving lessons how to shoot." I was smiling when I said it, but I was also flat amazed.

She opened the cylinder and shoved out the empty shells with the ejector rod. "More bullets, please," she said.

I let her shoot up the whole box. She missed about as much as she hit but she always came close. It was damn good shooting, any way you looked at it. And you could see she loved it. It was in the brightness of her eyes, in the way she set herself to fire, in her eagerness to reload. By the time she'd used up the last of the cartridges she was as easy with a gun as she was behind the wheel of a car. It comes that naturally to some.

"Not bad, girl," I said when she was done. "If you want, I'll bring the .380 tomorrow and show you how to shoot that."

She leaped into my arms, locking her legs around my waist and giving me an unintentional conk on the back of the head with the revolver in her hand.

"Oh I'm sorry, I'm sorry," she said, and kissed my head—and then we were both laughing as I swung her around.

We stopped at the swimming hole to cool off before going home. There were a few kids there, swinging on the rope and splashing around, but they left pretty soon after we arrived, and we had the place to ourselves. We dogpaddled over to a shady spot under a dense overhang of tree branches where we could stand with the water up to our necks. We ran our hands all over each other under the water and she undid my pants and took hold of me and I slipped my hand up under her dress and underwear and we hugged close and gasped against each other's neck as we used our hands on each other and a minute later both of us groaned with our climax. Then hugged and kissed and got into another laughing fit.

"You really think I'm good?" she said. "At shooting, I mean. You *really?*" She looked radiant. Her face had fully healed and every passing day I'd marveled even more at how truly lovely she was.

"Your daddy didn't know the half of it," I said. "You're a regular Barney Oldfield *and* a regular Annie Oakley."

And so, a week later, when I told her what I had in mind and she said she wanted to do the job with me, I said, "Well now, I don't know about that. Let me think about it."

The truth was, I'd been thinking about it for days.

The day after the arrival of Bubber's telegram, we heard Russell and Charlie arguing in their room. He'd had her go into town that morning and buy a crutch—"To have ready for when I'm able," he'd said. But when she got back with it he wanted to use it immediately. He said he needed to get up and walk around some before he went crazy from being on his ass day and night.

"I knew it!" she said. "What a dope I am! The doctor said to stay off that leg a month and you know it."

"What the hell do doctors know? I'm turning into a goddam vegetable lying here all day."

"If you put weight on the leg before it's ready you might hurt it worse. It needs to mend more."

"That's what a crutch is for, to keep weight off it. Now quit arguing and hand it over here."

"*No.* Quit acting like such a child!"

"Quit acting like my goddam mother!"

She stormed out of the room and slammed the door behind her and stomped into the kitchen to snatch up her cigarettes without a glance at me and Belle and headed out the back door, letting it bang shut on its spring. Belle gave me a look and then went after her.

I went to Russell's door and opened it. He was sitting up on the edge of the bed looking gloomy.

"Jesus," he said. "Bad enough without having to put up with her shit too."

He gestured for the crutch leaning in the corner and I got it for him.

"Easy does it," I said, helping him up and slipping the crutch under his arm.

"Beep beep," he said to get me out of his way. He stepped off a few awkward paces, repositioned the crutch for a more comfortable fit, then slowly gimped out of the room and into the parlor and all around it and came back down the hall and into the kitchen. Bracing himself on his good leg, he eased down into a chair and let out a hard breath.

"Christ damn," he said. "Feel like I run a mile." His face shone with sweat.

I checked the bandages. The one on his back was still spotless, but there were a couple of rosy stains showing on the back of the one around his leg.

"Best keep off it yet for a while longer," I said.

"Goddammit," he muttered.

I offered to get him a cold soda pop but he said the hell with that, give him a beer. I got one for each of us and sat across from him and we clinked bottles in a silent toast and drank. Then I told him about our tight money situation and asked how much he had.

"Had about twenty bucks on me in Midland," he said. "Charlie's probably spent most of it by now."

"Well," I said, "there's only one thing for it."

"Hell kid, I'll be ready to go in a few days. First we deliver Buck and then we get back to working Bubber's jobs."

"Bullshit, Russell. You're still leaking, man. Be a couple of weeks, at least, before you can even get around on that crutch worth a damn."

"Coupla weeks, my ass," he said. He looked miserable.

He shook a Chesterfield out of an open pack on the table and I struck a match and lit it for him. He drew deep on it and exhaled slowly. We didn't say anything for a minute as he thought things over.

"One score might be enough," I said. "Might need two. Filling station, grocery. Enough to see us through till you're okay."

He took another deep drag, exhaled a long stream of smoke and nodded. "Yeah, I guess. But you can't hit anyplace around here. Got to be out of the county, at least, and the further the better. If you do more than one, spread them way out."

"I know it," I said.

"And no lone wolfing," he said. "Even with nickel-and-dime jobs, you can run into a world of trouble. You'll need a guy at the wheel and ready for backup. I'll give Bubber a call, see if he can get you—"

"I already got somebody in mind," I said.

"Who's that?"

"Belle."

He looked at me like he thought I was pulling his leg.

I told him all about how well she could drive, how naturally she'd taken to handling a handgun. He listened with a smile.

"Well, that girl's full of surprises, ain't she?" he said. "All the same—"

"And," I said, "a woman partner would be perfect. She can put her hair up under her hat, see, and wear a jacket to hide her tits. Unless somebody gets right up close to her, everybody'll think she's a man. Once we drive off, she ditches the hat and jacket and we're a married couple on a car trip and the cops are looking for two guys."

"Real clever," he said. "But just because she was good at shooting rocks didn't mean she'd be good at shooting at a real person, if it came to that—especially if the real person had a gun too and was shooting at her.

"It's a whole different thing, Sonny, and you damn well know it.

And speeding around in the desert ain't like making a getaway through streets full of cars and people and with the cops maybe right on your tail. I don't have to tell you this stuff."

"No you don't," I said. "I've talked it over with her and told her how it can be. She thinks she can handle whatever comes up."

"Oh she *thinks* so? What if she can't and you get taken down because of it? Goddammit, I need you to help me with Buck." He leaned back and let out a long breath. "I'd ruther we asked Bubber to get you somebody experienced."

"Then we'd have to give them a piece of the take," I said, "and the take'll be awful small as it is. I wouldn't think Bubber'd care to have anything to do with such smalltime jobs anyway. Look, man, she can do it. It's only the driving."

"Well hell, it's your job, kid," he said. "You got my advice for what it's worth, take it or leave it." But I could tell how mad he was by the way he gave his attention to the bandage on his leg and then to lighting a fresh cigarette, to anything that kept him from having to look me in the eye.

"I guess I'll give her a try," I said.

*M*iller Faulk made no trouble in the county lockup, not whenever any guard was in earshot. His fellows in the tank were mostly drunks and petty thieves and it had not proved difficult to make his point to them that he wished to be let alone. He passed his days in his rude bunk, brooding on the perfidy of women, the absurdity of love, the cruel nature of existence. A week into his sentence he received a visit from Weldon, who brought him cigarettes and tidings that Eula had departed for places unknown. This news came as no surprise to Faulk and saddened him but little until Weldon added that she'd departed in his yellow Pierce-Arrow—whereupon Faulk had with the fervor of a true believer supplicated the Lord Almighty to afflict her with cancer of the cunt. That, he told Weldon, would pretty much cover her from head to toe. Still and all, he comported himself as a model prisoner, and after twenty-one days behind bars he was granted a good-time release into the supposed free world.

And only a few hours later John Bones hears Faulk's name, the sixth one of the thirteen names on the list of that day's jail releases. But he says nothing *until the man on the telephone has read them all. Then says, Thank you, detective, and hangs up.*

The Closed sign faces out through the glass but the door is unlocked. He steps from the outer dark into the weak yellow light of the station's office and a small bell jingles over the door. He slides the bolt lock home. The door to the garage is to his left and stands open. He goes to it and sees them within, staring at him, each man with a quart bottle of beer in hand, standing next to a new DeSoto with its engine exposed under the open hood. The garage bay doors are shut.

Sorry, mister, the bigger one says, his eyes narrowing. We already closed. There's a filling station a few blocks down still open at this hour.

No, man, the Weldon one says, that's the fella I was telling you wants to buy the place. Howdy, Mr. Cheval.

He nods at Weldon, sees that Faulk is not so obtuse as the mechanic, that the man has jailbird eyes and knows a policeman on sight.

That right, Mr. Cheval? Faulk says. You looking to buy this gold mine from me? He sets down his beer bottle and picks up a heavy crescent wrench.

He steps into the garage and shuts the office door behind him, draws a short-barreled .44 revolver from under his coat, withdraws the pincer contraption from his coat pocket to reveal the two sets of handcuffs dangling from it.

It requires artistry to mete pain in sufficient degree to make its recipient desire nothing on earth so much as its cessation, yet not to such extent as to grant him even the briefest respite of swoon. In this regard John Bones is an artist. He has known a few true hardcases in his time and Miller Faulk proves one of the most admirable of his experience—outdone only by a grizzled Cajun of years ago who withstood John Bones' interrogation for more than two heroic hours before his heart abruptly failed, thus distinguishing himself as the

only one ever to deny him the information he desired. Faulk lasts roughly half
that long, yet is only the second to endure beyond an hour before finally—when
John Bones again loosens his gag to permit him to speak—whispering in a
nasal rasp: Bubber Vicente. Bigsby . . . Hotel . . . Odessa. That's where . . . I
swear.

That's where, you swear, John Bones echoes with a smile. You're a poet, sir.

Crouching beside Faulk, he studies the man's remaining eye and reads the
verity therein, knows that unlike previous names and places Faulk has cried
out in the course of their fragmented colloquy, these are the truth. Knows too
that Faulk's surrender is to the only hope left to him—a sooner rather than later
demise. Supine on a concrete floor amid smears of grease and oil and blood,
hands over his head and cuffed to the DeSoto bumper, legs at awkward attitude
for their hammer-shattered knees effected to keep him from kicking, pants down
to his thighs and his manly parts in ruin, a few toes rawly absent from the bared
feet . . . what can he hope for except a quick end to it all?

And Weldon? Lying close by. Facedown, hands cuffed behind him. Intact
but for his pincered Adam's apple and his drained blood gelling in a dark mat
under his head. He would have done better to keep other company this evening.

John Bones takes up the ball peen hammer once again.

You did good, he tells Faulk. Nothing to be ashamed of.

The hammer describes a blurred arc and in the instant of bonecrack Faulk
is forevermore delivered from pain.

He stands and unrolls his sleeves, so deft with the pincers he can rebutton a
cuff as facilely as he undid it. Puts on his jacket, his hat. Sets the brim at his
preferred angle. Goes out of the garage and out of the office and over to the
Model T sedan parked in the shadows. He sets the throttle and ignition and
goes to the front of the car and positions the handcrank and whirls it hard and
the well-tuned motor rumbles into throaty combustion. He gets into the driver's
seat and readjusts the fuel flow and spark settings and his feet adeptly operate
the planetary transmission pedals and he sets out for the westward highway.
Bearing into the darker remnant of the night.

*I*t was close to midnight when we pulled into a little filling station a mile south of Pecos. I chose it because the traffic at this hour wasn't very heavy and there were no other cars at the pumps and only one parked alongside the building. A lamp on a high post glowed over the two pumps but we had the car top up and she had her hair bunched under her hat and wore a baggy windbreaker zipped up to her neck. A big bulge of chewing gum in her cheek the better to distort her face. It wasn't likely anyone would take her for a woman even if they passed close to the car. She had the four-inch .38 beside her on the seat and covered with a fold of her skirt. I was wearing a hat too, and a paste-on mustache.

"Set?" I said.

She nodded, and revved the motor with a little goose of the gas pedal.

"Remember, if somebody pulls in—"

"I'll tell them the guy'll be right out and I'll honk the klaxon. I'm okay, Sonny."

I got out of the car as the attendant swung open the screen door and said, "Gas, mister?"

"A road map's all," I said, and followed him back inside.

There was another guy in there, sitting at a small table with a checkerboard on it and a game in progress. I drew the .380 from under my belt and let them see it, then held it in the side pocket of my coat and told the attendant to sit in the other chair at the table and for both of them to put their hands under their ass. I went around behind the counter and yanked out the telephone cord. I found a Colt six-inch in the shelf under the counter. I looked at the attendant and he said, "The owner's." I put it in my other coat pocket, then opened the register and took out all the bills and stuffed them in the same pocket with the Colt. I told them I'd shoot the first man to stick his head out the door. Then I slipped the .380 back in my pants and walked out to the roadster and got in and Belle drove us off, smoothly shifting through the gears and accelerating steadily. I watched out the back window but didn't see either guy come to the door before we were out of sight. The whole thing didn't take three minutes.

After we swung east at the highway intersection at Pecos, I quickly counted the take by the light of the lampposts—$375. More than it had looked like in the till, but awful puny compared to the hauls I was used to with Buck and Russell.

Belle was singing, "Ain't We Got Fun?"

We checked into a motor camp more than twenty miles away, outside of a place called Pyote. The camp was well off the main highway, set back in a grove of scraggly mesquites and flanked by a high sand hill. I parked the car behind the cabin and we went inside and locked the door and laughed at each other in our comic rush to get our clothes off. I started to take off the mustache too but she stopped me and kissed me and said she'd never kissed anybody with a mustache before. It made me look like Douglas Fairbanks, she said. She stared down between us and said, "You even got a pirate sword and everything."

She shrilled happily as I swept her up in my arms and said, "Prepare to be ravished, woman!" and slung her onto the bed and leaped in after her. She hurriedly guided me into her, already panting the way she did when she was close, and before we'd been at it a half-minute she was digging her fingers into my back and tightening her legs around me and letting out her long low cry of climax. I'd never known her to get there so fast.

After a while we sat up and lit cigarettes. I took off the mustache and she said, "Well hey there, Sonny LaSalle! Where you been? I just now had the best time with Douglas Fairbanks, you wouldn't believe!"

I got out the pint of mash I'd brought along and took a long pull and then offered her the bottle. She took a small sip off it and arched her brows and smiled and took another.

Once she got started talking about the heist, she couldn't stop. "In one way it was like you were taking so long in there I couldn't stand it. But at the same time it was like I didn't want it to be over with. Does that make *any* sense?"

I smiled at her.

She said she could hardly imagine how it must feel to rob a bank. The way she was carrying on made me laugh and remember my own happy babblings to Buck and Russell the first few times I went on jobs with them.

"I was scared," she said, "but I felt so . . . I don't know . . . so *real*. Does it ever make you feel like that too?"

"Only every time," I said.

"Wow," she said.

And then we were at it again.

We didn't check out of the cabin until midmorning and we stopped at the first café we came to. We sat in a booth in back and ate like we hadn't seen food in days, each of us putting away a platter of fried eggs, pork chops, and potatoes, with a side of open-face biscuits covered with sausage gravy. We lingered awhile over coffee and cigarettes and then hit the road again.

As we passed through various oil patches and the towns around them, she said it all reminded her of Corsicana. The landscape out here was different, but the derricks and pumps and storage tanks and trucks, the mule wagons and the crowded stores and cafés, the dirty streets teeming with oil workers, the constant racket and hazy air and awful stinks were the same as they'd been back home.

"It's the same in every oil town I've seen," I said, "and I've seen a few lately."

We were in no rush, taking it slow and easy, stopping alongside the road once so I could help an old man change a flat tire on his truck, pulling up another time to watch a herd of pronghorns bounding over the grassy flats in the distance.

The sun was almost down when we arrived in Crane. As rough as Corsicana was she didn't think it was as rough as this little town, or as loud. Pulling a job in such a place was unthinkable—you'd never get away through all the traffic. We finally emerged at the east end of town into the gathering twilight and the traffic began to thin. A mile farther on we passed an isolated grocery store where several men were loading large cardboard boxes onto the beds of a couple of red pickup trucks parked in front. A supply run for an oil camp kitchen, probably.

Neither of us spoke for the next minute or so as the road rolled under us. Then she looked at me and said, "That was a big bunch of groceries them boys bought."

"Yes it was," I said.

"They must've run up some bill," she said. "I wonder has business been that good all day?"

"Turn it around," I said.

As we drove back to the store I steered the car with my left hand for a moment while she put her hair up in her hat and zipped up the baggy windbreaker. The red pickups went past us in the other direction. We pulled into the lot and parked near the front door. It wasn't a particularly large place, but through the front windows it looked jammed with goods. I figured it for a main supplier to a lot of the camps around there, and it must've recently received deliveries of new stock. There were a couple of other trucks in the lot, and one car, so there were at least three customers in there and who knew how many employees. Too many for one man to watch. It was a two-man job, but I didn't want Belle out of the car. I was about to say forget it and tell her to get going again, but then a couple of guys came out, each with a boxful of groceries. As they were putting their goods in one of the trucks, another man came out with two big sacks and got in the car. A minute later both car and truck were gone.

I decided to wait a little longer. I took the paste-on mustache from my pocket and put it on, turned to Belle and said, "Okay?" She smiled and winked. She had a big wad of gum going in her mouth. I checked the .380 and put it back into my waistband against my side.

Five minutes later two more guys came out with groceries and got into the other truck and left. Ours was the only vehicle in the lot. I had her pull the car up directly in front of the entrance with the passenger side toward the door. Then I got out and went in, the screen door jingling a little bell hung atop the frame.

There were several aisles of shelves and a pair of men were replenishing them with canned goods from various open cartons. The younger guy was big, beefy, with a red face and curly hair, the other was grayhaired, shorter and leaner, but I could see a family resemblance. The younger one looked at me and I nodded a greeting. The elder said, "Help you, sir?"

"Need some cigarettes," I said.

The elder motioned to the younger and went back to his shelving. The younger left off what he was doing and went around behind the front counter where the register was. "What kind you want?" he said.

"Old Golds," I said. "Two packs." I stood sideways so I could watch his father too.

He set the smokes on the counter and I brought out the automatic. "Don't even think about going for a gun," I said.

For a second he looked at me like he wasn't sure he'd heard me right—and then like I was some longtime enemy he recognized.

The old man stood up and said, "We ain't got a gun here, mister. A shotgun in the house out back is all, I swear."

"Give me every greenback in the till," I said to the younger.

"Hell I will," he said.

In all the jobs I'd done with Buck and Russell, in all the jobs they'd done without me, nobody, so far as I knew, had ever said no when they were under the gun.

"Want to get shot, asshole?"

"I ain't scared of you."

Well goddam, I thought.

"Justin," the elder said. He had his hands half raised. "Take it easy, mister. The boy don't mean it. You can have what we got."

"Do so mean it," the Justin one said.

The roadster's klaxon sounded. Somebody was pulling in.

I kept the gun on the younger but spoke to the elder. "Listen, mister, *somebody* better open that register right goddam *now* and put all the bills in a sack. I don't mean maybe."

"Yessir," the grayhead said. He hustled around the counter and pushed Justin aside and chinged open the drawer and started grabbing up handfuls of bills and sticking them in a paper bag. He shoved the bag across the counter at me and I snatched it up.

As I started backing toward the door the little bell tinkled and I lowered the gun to my waist to hide it. I turned to see a burly guy in oil-stained workclothes come walking in. The guy smiled and nodded at me and then looked past me and his eyes widened and his mouth fell open and I was already dropping to my haunches as I spun around to see the old man raising a shotgun.

The blast was loud as a cannon in those close quarters. My hat shifted on my head and I heard a crashing behind me and the oil guy started screaming.

It was a single-barrel breechloader so that was his only shot. I stood up slowly, my heart ramming against my ribs and my ears ringing. The old man was holding the smoking weapon like it was something he'd been caught stealing. The Justin one stood there with his mouth open.

"You son of a bitch," I said to the elder. I put the .380 in his face and cocked it.

He said, "Oh, *God*"—and then the door banged open and I whirled and came within a hair of shooting Belle.

She held the six-inch straight out in front of her with both hands and her aspect was all readiness in spite of her bulging cheek.

"Okay?" she said in a muffled voice. The oil guy was still hollering on the floor, rolling from side to side and clutching his bloody shoulder.

"Yeah," I said. I reached over the counter and took the shotgun from the elder. "Let's go!"

I ran out behind her. She'd left the passenger door open and she dove in and slid up behind the wheel as smoothly as if she'd been doing it all her life. I tossed in the shotgun and was only partway in the car when it leaped forward and I almost fell out but caught hold of the doorjamb and pulled myself inside.

"Holy shit, girl!"

She made a tight left turn in the lot, slinging my door wide open as she wheeled us onto the highway, then floored the accelerator and the door swung back and slammed shut and we barreled off into the darkness.

Twenty minutes later we were on some truck road deep in a forest of derricks illuminated by field lights and flaring gas heads. She pulled over to the shoulder and stopped. The road lay empty in both directions, and there was no sign of anyone at any of the nearest derricks. There was only the steady pounding of the drills and the hiss of the flaring blue gas heads. I pitched the shotgun into a scrub patch.

Neither of us had said a word since tearing away from the store, and I thought maybe she was going to be sick. The roadster's cab was dimly lit by the field lights and she was turned toward me, but I couldn't see her face in the shadow of her hat brim. I hadn't been aware of how much my hands were shaking until I lit a cigarette. I passed it to her and she spat her gum out the window and took a couple of deep drags and handed the cigarette back and I took one more pull and flicked it away. She took off her hat and let her hair fall to her nape and I saw the glitter of her eyes. She pressed against me and kissed me like she was trying to breathe me into herself. Then her hands were at my belt buckle and I raised my hips so she could tug my pants down to my thighs. She pulled up her skirt and straddled me on the seat, tugged aside the hem of her panties and mounted me. I bucked and bucked into her and we were kissing each other's mouth and eyes and ears and I squeezed her breasts and she bit my neck and then both of us yelled and clutched each other harder. . . .

When we got back on a main road I pulled into a diner parking lot and made fast work of swapping the roadster's plates with those on a Plymouth. We then sped on to Rankin and checked into the Dustdevil Motor Inn. Not until after I'd counted the take—$650, a tidy sum for a grocery heist—did I discover the pellet holes in the crown of my hat.

I sat on the bed and wiggled a couple of fingers through the holes.

"Look here how close I came to getting my stupid head blown off," I said.

She came and stood beside me, wearing only a towel around her hips after her showerbath. Her hair was still wet and her skin gleamed. She put her fingers in the holes.

"I felt it," I said. "I didn't realize what it was."

"Feel this," she said, and held my hand to her breast. Her heart was racing.

"It ain't slowed down even a little," she said. Nor had the brightness in her eyes reduced.

She let the towel slide from her hips.

We had more than enough now to cover our Fort Stockton expenses for a good while, but she thought we deserved to treat ourselves to a good time in some town of greater size than Fort Stockton.

"You know what I mean," she said. "Someplace with a real nice dance club. I've always wanted to go to a fancy dance club. And with a nice dress shop where I can buy myself something fine and pretty to wear there."

Midland was fifty miles up the road, but we weren't about to visit there in a car I'd stolen from that town barely more than two weeks earlier. So we headed east, puttering along with the top down under a sky less hazy than usual, and three hours later we were in San Angelo.

Under the names of Mr. and Mrs. Mitch Russell we checked into the brandnew Riverside Hotel, which a streetcorner cop had advised us was the best in town. I asked the bellboy if there was someplace nearby where a man might get a bottle of labeled spirits, and he said, "Name your preference, pal." I said bourbon would be vastly appreciated, and a couple of limes if he could manage it. Twenty minutes later he was back with a paper-sacked fifth of bourbon and a roller tray holding a bucket of ice, the limes, two seltzer bottles and two tumblers. I gave him a lavish tip.

Belle loved everything about the hotel. She said she'd never been in any place so fine. She went around the room, touching the flowers in the dresser vase, the furniture, the bedcovers, the towels and soaps and shampoos in the bath, as if making sure everything was real. I said if she thought this place was fancy she ought to see the hotels in New Orleans.

"Will you show me New Orleans one of these days?" she said.

"Sure," I said. "I think you'd like it."

She came into my arms and tucked her head under my chin. "I think I'd love it," she said.

We went out and found a dress shop, but each dress she tried on she liked better than the one before, and after nearly two hours she still couldn't decide between three of them. She and the salesgirl kept blabbing on and on about yokes and bratelles and peplums, hems and flounces and God-knows-what. I settled the matter by buying all three dresses for her. She gave me a kiss full on the mouth and smiled at the salesgirl and said, "Aren't I the lucky one?"

The girl was goodlooking, with a deep Texas accent and thick honey hair, and she grinned and said, "He's a regular sugar daddy, only lots younger and better-looking than most, if you don't mind me saying so."

Belle winked at her and said she didn't mind at all. I would've been lying if I'd said I wasn't enjoying myself.

From there we went to a Mexican restaurant for a lunch of guacamole and strips of roast kid in a red chile sauce, with flour tortillas so freshly hot they powdered and almost burned our fingers. Across the street was a lush green park with the Conchos River running through it, and when we were done eating we went for a long walk in the shade of the cottonwoods along the bank. Then back to the hotel and I fixed us each a glass of bourbon and Coke full of crushed ice and a touch of lime juice, something I'd learned from Russell. She took a careful sip and grinned and said she loved it. We filled the tub with bubble lotion and got in it together and sipped the drinks slowly. After a long soak we soaped each other up and then rinsed off and dried each other with thick towels and went to bed and made love and then napped until dark.

We took supper in a good steakhouse across the street—filets as thick as my wrist and heaped with finely sliced fried onion rings—then went back to the hotel and descended the wide staircase to the ballroom. Belle was wearing one of her new dresses, a little black number that hugged her hips and had a short fringed hem and a sort of halter top cut way low in the back. She was a knockout.

The dancefloor was crowded this Friday night and the big band up on the stand was damned good, finishing up an excellent rendition of "Stardust." Then it started in on "Am I Blue?" and we took to the floor.

We'd just finished kicking up our heels to "Baby Face" and were applauding along with the other dancers when the brass section swung into the opening bars of "I Can't Give You Anything but Love."

"Let's sit this one out," I said. "We can go outside for a minute if you want."

She shook her head. "There's no need. That song doesn't bother me anymore, really it doesn't."

"Sure?"

"You know," she said, "it's funny, but everything from before feels . . . I don't know . . . *made up*. Like it all happened to somebody else, somebody I hardly know anymore and I'm glad of it."

She gave me a peck on the lips and a smile and asked if I'd be a real sweetie and get her a cold Coke while she went to powder her nose. "Meet you at the refreshment bar," she said. "Then we'll get back to showing these suckers how to dance."

The lounges were on the other side of the room and down a

hallway, and she drew a good bit of attention as she made her way around the edge of the dancefloor. I went to the bar and ordered two Cokes. There was a scattering of small tables along the walls to either side of the bar, all of them occupied, but then a couple got up to return to the floor and I was quick to take over their spot.

I was nearly done with my Coke when I caught sight of her emerging from the crowd. Her face was tight with excitement, a look I'd come to know well. She didn't see me at the bar and scanned around and I waved to catch her attention. She spotted me and came over and sat down.

"What?" I said.

Her eyes had that peculiar light they took on when she was really wound up. She sucked a deep draft of her Coke through the straw, took a look back toward the dancing crowd, then leaned close to me. "Listen to this. When I came out of the ladies' room just now? These two fellas come out of the gents' and start talking to me. They'd been doing some drinking, you could tell, and I took them for just a couple of funny drunks. Then one of them says to me, 'Look here,' and steps over by this big potted plant and stands sort of half-turned so nobody but me and his buddy can see, and he takes a roll of bills out of his coat pocket and I mean to tell you, Sonny, it was *this* thick." She held her thumb and forefinger three inches apart. "Looked bigger than a Coke bottle except fat at both ends. The top bill was a hundred, I swear. And the other one says real low in my ear, 'Name your price, honey. One time around the world for each of us.' "

I stood up. "Come point them out."

"Sonny, sit *down*. Please. Just listen a minute Okay?"

I sat. "I'll kick their ass." It was an effort to keep my voice down.

"I told them I had to make a phone call but I'd be right back. They're waiting for me in the lounge hallway."

I started to get up again but she flapped her hand at me to sit back down.

"*Listen* to me," she said. "You want to get them? Let's *really* get them. I had this idea—I mean it just *bang* came to me when that galoot said what they wanted."

"What the hell are you—"

"What if you went up to the room right now and then I took *them* up there?"

Her expression was pure readiness, her green eyes sparking. She slid her hand across the table and gripped mine.

"What do you say?" she said.

Twenty minutes later I was in the bathroom, the door slightly ajar, the room in darkness, when I heard her key rattling in the lock and then their laughter as they came in.

There was the click of a lamp switch—but the bathroom was situated in such a way that all I could see through the cracked door was a narrow portion of the back wall and part of the window.

The room door shut. The guys laughed louder. Sloppy kissing sounds, murmurings, chucklings. One of them said something I didn't catch except for "Molly, honey." I felt my pulse in my eardrums.

"Whoa now, boys, hold your horses!" Belle said loudly, her laughter sort of tinny. "Lookee there the good bourbon I got. Why don't we pour us a . . . now, *behave* yourself, you rascal, we got all night! Why don't we all have us a little drink and—"

I didn't catch the rest of it for the sudden blaring of a big band playing "Always." One of them had turned on the radio on the bedside table.

We hadn't counted on that. The signal we'd arranged was "Here's to wicked times," which she'd say when she had them standing together by the chest of drawers, where the bourbon was. I'd come out and get the drop on them and she'd snatch up her own gun from under the pillow. But with the radio up so loud I couldn't make out what anybody was saying, only the guys' harsh laughter.

Damn the signal. I was about to pull the door open when it swung in hard and hit me in the forehead and knocked me back against the sink and my feet went out from under me. A large man was in the doorway with his hand at his fly—and quick as a cat he was all over me before I could raise the gun. He gripped my gun wrist with one hand and started punching with the other, cussing a blue streak. He must've had thirty pounds on me and was damn strong. I tried to cover up with my free arm but still caught some on the face and neck and then I tucked my chin down and took the next ones on top of the head. They hurt like hell but then he yowled and I knew he'd busted his hand. I grabbed him by the hair and lunged sideways and rammed his head hard against the rim of the bathtub. He groaned and lost his hold on me and I got better leverage and banged his head again and this one knocked him cold.

I got untangled from him and scrambled to my feet and rushed into the other room and there was Belle—standing beside the bed and holding the cocked Colt in the other guys' face. One of her straps was broken and her top hung down and exposed a breast. The guy sat on the edge of the bed looking terrified, hands way up. "Always" was still blasting.

"Belle!" I said.

She didn't even look at me. She jabbed the guy in the forehead with the muzzle of the gun and he fell on his back and said, "Jesus, lady . . . *please!*"

She held the gun to his eye. "Want to tear my dress some more, highroller? Want another grab up under my skirt?"

"No, I'm sorry, I'm *sorry!*" He shut his eyes and gritted his teeth.

She tapped his teeth with the muzzle and said, "Open up." Then slid a good portion of the barrel into his mouth—and now his eyes couldn't get any bigger.

The telephone rang. She looked at it and then at me, her face blank. It rang again. I went over and turned down the radio and picked up the receiver.

The front desk. They'd received a complaint from the room next door about the loud music. Could we please be more considerate? I saw myself in the mirror, my nose bleeding, a dark swelling over one eye and on one cheek. The knots on my scalp hurt but didn't show. "Certainly," I said. "My apologies."

I hung up. Belle still had the pistol barrel in the guy's mouth.

"The desk clerk wonders if you'd be kind enough not to shoot that asshole," I said. "They're afraid the noise might disturb some of the guests."

She held the blank look on me a moment longer—and then grinned wide and beautifully.

We bound their hands behind them with their own belts and gagged them with towels. It wouldn't take much effort to get free of the belts, but that's how I wanted it. The guy on the bathroom floor had a concussion for sure, maybe a skull fracture, and the sooner he made it to a hospital the better. At least he was breathing and it looked to me like he'd stay that way. He'd been the one to flash the roll of money at Belle—$3,500, by my hasty count before I stuck the wad in my coat. The other guy was carrying a little more than a grand, and that roll went into my coat too. They'd told Belle they were drilling contractors just back from setting up a new field in Mexico and about to start a job outside San Angelo.

Belle hurriedly changed dresses, and because I didn't want to raise any curiosity about my bruises, I sent her down to the desk to check us out while I finished putting our stuff in the valises. I told the guy on the bed he ought to be more careful about the women he took up. He nodded like he meant it. When she telephoned me from the lobby to say we were set to go, I pulled my hat low and grabbed our bags and took the elevator down.

I went out the front door and a moment later she pulled up in the roadster. She slid over to the passenger side and I got behind the wheel.

Before we'd gone two blocks she was hugging my neck and kissing me, running her hand inside my shirt. It was all I could do to steer.

"Jesus, girl—you're gonna make us wreck!"

"Did you see how scared he was, baby? Did you *see*? I had him *crying*. I could've made that bullying bastard do *anything*, he was so scared of me."

"A gun in the mouth can do that, all right."

Then we were past the city limit sign and she placed my right hand up under her dress and panties so I could feel how wet she was. She fondled me through my trousers. I was suddenly aware of being so hard it hurt. She unbuttoned me and hunched down and took me in her mouth. She'd never done that before. In bed one time I'd made it obvious I wanted that, but she'd pulled away and said no, that her Corsicana boyfriend had practically forced her to do it once, and once was enough. So I'd let the matter drop. Now here she was, doing it to me in the car as we barreled along the dark highway. I had to pull over to the shoulder to avoid a collision. I sat there gripping the wheel while she kept at me below the sweep of passing headlights. When I shot off—rocking back and forth and banging my fist on the wheel— some of my fellow motorists must've thought I was having a fit.

We checked into a motor camp outside of Big Lake and frolicked into the wee hours. We did it every which way—sideways, dog style, standing, sitting, name it. Having seen the lunatic delight I'd taken from her special treat in the car, she was avid to pleasure me that way. And even though she'd previously been as shy of receiving my mouth on her as of putting hers to me, this time she didn't resist as I kissed my way down her belly. When I used my tongue on her she dug her fingers into the back of my head and arched herself against my mouth and climaxed with such a shriek I hoped the neighboring cabin was unoccupied or somebody might call the cops to report a murder taking place.

For a minute afterward, she lay open-mouthed, breathing deeply, an arm over her eyes. Then let out a long sigh and said, "My *God*. I'd heard things, but I never imagined it could be *soooooo* fine." She lowered her arm and looked at me. "Who taught you to do that, the *devil?*"

Actually, Brenda Marie Matson had given me the best instruction I ever received on oral sexual technique, but I didn't think Belle would want to hear about her, so I simply grinned and waggled my eyebrows. I told her that at Gulliver we used to refer to the clitoris as the "little man in the boat," and we'd spend hours discussing the best ways to get him up on tiptoes. She laughed so hard she got the hiccups.

I'd brought along the remaining bourbon and we sat up in bed and had a drink and a cigarette, but both of us were so tired we didn't even finish the smokes before snuffing them out and spooning up, her ass snug against me.

I was almost asleep when her voice came to me from what seemed very far away. . . . "What's it feel like to shoot somebody?"

I wanted to say, "Not sure I ever did," but only managed a low mumble.

I thought I heard her say, "Must be something," but I wasn't certain. And then I was asleep.

We got back in the middle of the afternoon. Russell met us at the front door, leaning on his crutch, returning Belle's hug with his free arm.

"Perfect timing with them reinforcements," he said, nodding at the sackful of booze and beer I was carrying. I'd made a stop at the Callaghan Street house as soon as we rolled into town. "I'm about down to my last swallow," he said. His breath smelled of drink and his eyes were red.

"You run out of pills?" I said as we headed for the kitchen.

"That's all right," he said. "Don't need them."

"Not if you're using Dr. Barleycorn's prescription, I guess."

"You mind your health, kid, I'll mind mine," he said. "Tell me how-all you did."

I'd expected to see Charlie in the kitchen but she wasn't there. Belle stepped across the hall to peek into their bedroom, then started for the sideporch door.

"She's down the park," Russell said, grimacing slightly as he gingerly accommodated himself in a chair at the table, positioning his leg out in front of him. There was a nearly empty bottle and a tumbler on the table, together with some kind of map and what looked like a letter. "She's been spending lots of time down there." He waved his hand in indication that the matter was something he didn't fully understand or care to discuss. Things between them didn't look to have improved much while we'd been away.

He looked from Belle to me and then at her again. "I'm sure she'll be glad to know you're back."

Belle got the hint. "I'll just go and see how she's doing," she said. She fluttered her fingers at me and went out the back door.

He poured the last of his bottle into the tumbler. I got another glass down from the cabinet and opened one of the new bottles and built up his drink and poured myself one. We touched glasses and took a sip.

"So?" he said.

I opened my valise and reached in and took out two big handfuls of currency and dropped them on the table. Russell smiled and picked up a few bills and spread them in his hand like oversized playing cards.

"That new money won't never feel as real as these," he said. The federal government was replacing all paper money with bills only about half the present size, and lots of people felt about it the way he did—the smaller money didn't look or feel as real. "Don't tell me you hit a bank," he said.

He put the money back in the valise and I gave him a quick rundown on the jobs, focusing on the lucrative San Angelo caper.

"She made him *suck* the piece?" he said.

"Guy thought his days were done. I think he pissed his pants."

"And it was her idea to take them down?"

"Forty-five-hundred-dollar idea," I said.

"Ain't no end to her surprises," he said. "Here's to her." We clinked glasses.

"It's more than enough here to pay off Bubber for the lawyer and Gustafson too," I said. "I'd say we're sitting pretty."

"Pretty much," Russell said. "Only we owe Bubber for something else too." He gestured at the map and note in front of him.

I pulled my chair around beside his. It was an oil map of Reagan County, showing various oil field sites, each with a lot of numbers and hieroglyphics around it, and the truck trails that connected them to the main roads. The only town shown was Big Lake, where the east-west and north-south highways intersected. A few other county roads were on the map too. Under a penciled arrow pointing west from Big Lake was written "Rankin, 30 mi." A large penciled X indicated as being five miles east of the western county line and twenty miles north of the highway to Rankin was labeled "S.R.R.C." There was a smaller X below and southeast of the larger one and "6 mi" scribbled alongside the arrow between them. A squiggly pencil line ran west from the small X to the north-south highway, and the distance between them was noted as half a mile.

"What's all this?" I said.

"From Bubber," he said. "He didn't waste any time after he got your telegram."

The map and the letter had arrived yesterday morning, hand-delivered by a guy who'd shown up at the door and told Charlie he'd been instructed to give the material to no one but Russell or me. Russell heard her arguing with him and came out on his crutch. The guy gladly accepted his offer of a glass of beer before heading off. Russell didn't say whether Charlie had joined them in the beer, but my guess was she hadn't.

The letter was actually a long note, addressing no one in particular and unsigned. It was written in pencil in an awkward hand—by some inside man, Russell figured, maybe a Santa Rita inmate but more likely by a hack. It described the prison's daily routine and recent work assignments, including Loomis Mitchum's. Every day the prison sent out a half-dozen work crews to various kinds of jobs. Mitchum was assigned to a crew of eleven other cons overseen by three guards, including the driver, every guard armed with a pump shotgun. The big X showed the location of the Santa Rita camp, and the little one below it was where Mitchum's crew had been working at clearing a new drilling site for an oil company. The squiggly line was a truck trail joining the site to the north-south Big Lake highway. Although Mitchum's crew was scheduled to work at this site for another few weeks, the note said, labor assignments were subject to change at any time, so there was no certainty of how much longer Mitchum would actually be at that site. Wherever they were assigned, however, each crew always went out on the same truck, and each truck carried an identifying number on the doors. Mitchum's crew was transported on truck 526.

"It's practically the same setup as when I busted him out of Sugarland," Russell said.

"Except like this guy says, no telling when they'll put Buck on some other job. Maybe he'll still be on this job when your leg's all better, maybe he won't. We'll have to see how—"

"That's why we'll do it tomorrow," Russell said. "They could take him off the road anytime. They could transfer him to some other joint, a tighter one. You never know. All I know is it ain't likely to get no easier than Santa Rita. So we get him tomorrow."

I saw that he was absolutely serious. "Russell," I said, "we haven't even had a look at the place. And we need a third man. And you can hardly *walk,* for Christ's sake."

"I ain't *got* to walk. I can cover you and the girl from the car. Truth to tell, I think we can do it just us two if we have to, but if she's as cool as you say, she'll be good for third man."

It took me a moment to understand he was talking about Belle.

"You should see your face, kid," he said. "What? Were you bull-shitting me about how good she is?"

I was seized by some misgiving I couldn't name. "No, man, she did fine," I said. "It's only that, well, this is a whole different thing...."

"It ain't *that* different. If she could handle herself on the road like you said, she can handle this." He gave me a narrow look. "Ah shit, Sonny, don't tell me you've gone goofy for the broad. Is that it? She your main lookout now, and the hell with your partners? Hell with old Uncle Buck?"

"Hell no, man," I said. And thought, *Hell* no.

"I hope not, kid. Last thing we need's a partner with his head up his ass over some chippy."

The crack stung but I took it. If he saw it made me sore he'd think he'd hit a nerve, that he was right that I'd gone sappy—and he wasn't right, goddammit. He wasn't.

"It's just that she might not want to be in on something like this," I said. It sounded lame even to me.

"Well, I know one way to find out real fast," he said. "We'll ask her."

What could I say? "Okay by me."

"But listen, kid, yea or nay, with or without her, you and me go get him tomorrow. Right?"

"Hell yeah, man."

He grinned. He knew as well as I did what she was going to say.

We'd do it like he and Jimmyboy had done it at Sugarland. Russell was sure he could cover at least two of the guards from the roadster's rumble seat, but in any case he could cover at least one of them. I'd be the one to get out and disarm the hacks and disable the prison truck. If we needed a backup outside the car, Belle would do it.

We had just finished roughing out the plan when the girls came in. Charlie had obviously been crying. She went to the cabinet over the sink and got a fresh pack of cigarettes and busied herself opening it. Belle got a bottle of Coke from the Frigidaire and pried off the cap with the opener attached to the end of the counter and then went and sat on a stool by the stove. Charlie lit a smoke and took a few deep drags and stared at Russell, who stared right back.

"So?" she said. "You make up your mind?"

"There was nothing to make up about it," he said.

"You're going to do it, then?"

"What's it look like?" he said.

"Goddammit, Russell, can't you for once give me a straight answer? *Are* you going to do it?"

"What's it look like?"

She ran her eyes over the papers and maps, her face a mix of anger and despair. I glanced at Belle but she was staring down at her soda pop.

"I can't do this anymore," Charlie said. "I can't always be waiting around to see if you've been . . . to see if you come back in one piece."

Russell sighed and looked bored. A man who'd heard all this too many times.

"You make me feel like one of those fools in the romance magazines," she said. "But you don't give a damn, do you? It doesn't matter one bit that I love you, does it? Well, I'll tell you something, Russell, you're going to . . . ah, the *hell* with it." She stubbed the cigarette in an ashtray and left it crumpled and smoldering.

"Only be a minute," she said to Belle, and went to the bedroom.

"There's a bus coming through in a half hour," Belle said softly. "Stops at the hotel on Main, she already checked. I said I'd drive her over. It'll take her to San Antone and she can catch a train to New Orleans from there."

Russell reached into the valise and took out a handful of bills and swiftly counted out about a thousand. He handed Belle the money. "Give it to her when she's getting on the bus. Don't let her give it back. If you can sneak it in her bag, do it that way."

Belle nodded and put the money in her pocket.

Russell poured me another drink and one for himself. We sat there, not saying anything, hearing her working the drawers in the bedroom, hearing her footsteps on the wooden floor as she went into the bathroom, hearing them come out again. A minute later she set her bag down at the kitchen door and came over to me and I got up and we hugged and she gave me a peck on the cheek.

"Take care of yourself, Sonny," she said low in my ear. "Her too."

She stepped over to Russell and bent down and kissed him on the mouth. "Bye, baby."

"Bon voyage, girl," he said, looking her in the eye.

She went out and Belle followed and we heard the front door open and close. Then the car doors. Then the roadster motor fire up. Then the car driving away.

A sweltering summer afternoon no different from most in West Texas but for the low reef of dark clouds on the eastern horizon. People on the streets joke about the vague possibility of rain, of an actual storm perhaps, which would be an even more uncommon turn of weather.

The Bigsby desk clerk directs him to Earl's Café. He goes to the café in shirtsleeves, the pincers hidden under his draped jacket. A waitress guides him to Earl Cue in the rear-room speakeasy. Earl still wearing the jaw wires but much improved in his enunciation for all his practice. When he insists on knowing the lean gray man's business with Bubber, the man says it's a business proposition which he is not at liberty to discuss with anyone else.

Well sir, Earl tells him, I happen to be Mr. Vicente's business partner, so any business deal you have for him is gonna have me in it too.

Very well then, the gray man says, why don't we go see Mr. Vicente and the three of us discuss it?

No can do, Earl says. Mr. Vicente is out of town right now and no telling when he'll be back. Could be another week, maybe two, no telling.

I see, the gray man says. And where might Mr. Vicente be, then?

He might be someplace that's none of your business, grandpa, Earl Cue says, nettled by this old goat's obvious supposition that Bubber's the main man of the partners.

The gray man smiles and says, Yes, of course. Tell you what, Mr. Cue, why don't I explain my proposition to you? After all, if it doesn't interest you, what chance do I have of winning over Mr. Vicente?

Well now, Earl Cue thinks, that is way more like it. He makes a show of checking his watch. I guess I got the time to hear it.

Actually, the gray man says, it'll be better if you see it. He tells Earl of two hundred cases of prime Scotch whisky he has stored in an old warehouse outside of town. He has to move the stuff immediately, he says, and whispers a price that is half the going rate. Would Mr. Cue care to see the goods for himself, maybe taste a sample to assure himself of their authenticity?

Well hell, Mr. Cue says, why not?

It takes much longer to drive out to the isolated warehouse than it does to gain the information he desires. No witnesses but jackrabbits in the brush and horned lizards in the rocks, a pair of buzzards wheeling in the white sky—and no auditors but them to the screams that shortly ensue.

Fifteen minutes after entering the dilapidated building, John Bones emerges from its dim confines, brushing dust and smears of cobweb from his hat and coat sleeves. Earl Cue will not come out again for another five weeks, when his remains are removed by authorities after being discovered by a pair of roving boys in search of a day's adventure.

"It's them," Russell said, squinting into the high-power binoculars against the glare of the sun. "Truck number 526." He moved the glasses in a slow pan and then held on something. "*Yowsa—* there's old Buckaroo. Looking over here, all sneaky like. Ten to one he knows it's us." His voice was tight, the way it got when he was up for it. I remembered when he'd bought the binoculars for Charlie at some roadside café in the middle of nowhere. It seemed a long time ago.

We were on the crest of a sand hill, the roadster idling on the narrow trail of crushed rock. I was behind the wheel, Belle next to me, Russell in the rumble seat. The surrounding country was shaped of rolling sand mounds and rocky outcrops, cactus and scrub brush. We had the top down and Belle's bare shoulders in her sundress were pink with sunburn. Russell and I were in rolled shirtsleeves. We all wore sunglasses and hats. The sky was clear except behind us, where a darkly purple bank of thunderheads had risen high in the east and was slowly heading our way. We'd yet to see rain in West Texas.

The site was about 250 yards away. To the naked eye the truck was a dark shape on the far side of the site, the men of the work party only speck figures. Then Russell passed the glasses up to me, and I spotted two of the guards by their uniforms. One was on this side of the site, the other way over on the other, standing at the truck with one foot up on the running board like he was talking to somebody in the cab, probably the third guard. Both of the guards in view carried shotguns. The convicts wore prison whites and were scattered around the area, which had already been cleared of brush. They were busting up the rocky outcrops with sledgehammers and picks and clearing away the broken stone, laboring in a dusty yellow haze, lifting and toting the larger chunks, scooping the smaller ones into wheelbarrows, dumping all of it outside the perimeter of the site. But even with the field glasses, at this distance it was hard for me to tell one convict from another. It didn't surprise me that Russell could—his hawkeye was why they'd made him a sniper in the war.

"See him?" Russell said. I could hear the smile in his voice.

"No."

"Look at the two cons closest to the near guard."

I sighted in on the guard, then the convicts a few yards from him. They were loading rocks by hand into a wheelbarrow. Now one of them started away with a barrowload and the other looked our way and for a minute I wasn't sure, and then I was.

"Got him," I said.

"Like he *knew* we were coming today," Russell said.

"The guard's looking over," I said.

"Wondering who the hell we are," Russell said. "Let's get on down there. Off with the hat, girl."

Belle took off her hat and shook her hair out, and I put the roadster in gear and got us moving again. When we got down there she would turn on the smile. We figured the sight of a woman in our bunch would ease their wariness. Except for that advantage, Russell figured to do it just like he had at Sugarland. He would call out to the guard that we were looking for the Burchard Oil drill site but had obviously taken a wrong turn, and could he give us directions. When the guard got close to the car he'd put a gun in his face and I'd jump out and relieve him of the shotgun and put it to his head and he'd tell the other two guards to come on over to us with their hands up and empty. Russell would cover them from the car and Buck would grab up their weapons while I disabled the truck and Belle got in the rumble seat with Russell. Then Buck and I would hop in the car and I'd wheel it around and barrel us out of there.

The night before, after Russell had gone over the plan with us, Belle had whispered to me in bed, "Will it really be that simple, one-two-three?" I said the plan had worked well for them once before and left it at that. I could feel her wanting to say something else but she didn't. For a minute I felt like some kind of liar for not admitting my doubts to her—then told myself there was no reason to think the thing wouldn't go as well this time.

But of course you never know. Even from the crest of the sand hill, parts of the trail between us and the work site had been hidden from view behind other mounds. We were within forty yards of the site when we came around a rise and saw a pair of large rocks that had been placed in the trail to block it. They were too big for the car to clear, and if we tried driving around them we'd get stuck in the sand for sure. And the trail was too narrow to turn the car around on it.

"Fuck a duck," Russell said. "The inside guy didn't say anything about *this*." His right hand was down out of sight and I knew he had the revolver in it.

The near guard came out to the trail and started toward us, the butt of his shotgun braced on his hip. The other guard was coming at a brisk stride from the far side of the site. Prisoners were looking our way even as they went on wielding their tools.

"What do we do?" Belle said.

Buck decided it. He grabbed a big rock and scurried up behind the guard, his arm cocked to brain him. The guy must've heard him coming—he spun around and halfway ducked and took the blow on the shoulder. They started grappling for the shotgun.

"Help him out!" Russell shouted, bringing up the long-barreled .38 and bracing his shooting arm on the front seat. I jumped out and ran toward them, slipping the .380 out of my pants.

The other guard was coming on the run. I heard men shouting in the distance and the pop . . . pop . . . pop . . . pop of Russell's .38 behind me and the running guard went down and his hat rolled off. He rose to all fours and Russell's revolver popped twice more and the guard's head jerked and he fell over.

I was almost to them when Buck wrested the shotgun from the guard and hooked him on the side of the head with the stock, staggering him backward. Belle's pistol popped behind me and the guard grabbed at his side. Then Buck shot him from a span of six feet and he lofted rearward, arms and legs flung wide and portions of his midsection spraying red.

Buck whirled toward me and hollered, "Let's go get a beer, kid!" He was grinning like a lunatic and I was astonished to hear myself laugh.

Belle was between us and the car, the .38 up and ready. We ran toward her and Buck yelled, "*Move* that pretty ass!"

She turned and ran, with me on her heels and Buck right behind me.

Then a rifleshot sounded—and Russell hollered, *"Nooo!"*

I turned and saw Buck sprawled facedown . . . the back of his head bright red . . . the ground before him smeared with what must've been his brains.

The rifle cracked again and Belle cried out.

She was sitting, clutching her bloody arm, her pistol in the dirt.

"*Buck!*" Russell shouted. "Get *Buck,* goddammit!"

I stuck the .380 in my pants and ran to her and scooped her up and lumbered to the car, hearing another rifleshot and the tick of a sudden hole in the windshield.

"*Damn* you, God *damn* you!" Russell hollered. He was trying to get out of the rumble seat, hampered by his bad leg. I heaved Belle into the car and slammed the door and ran around to the driver's side, shouting for Russell to get down—just as the rifle fired again and he jerked and grunted and fell back in the seat.

I rammed the gearshift into reverse and twisted around to see behind me and floored the accelerator. The roadster went tearing backward over the narrow trail, fishtailing and raising a plume of rock dust, the motor whining so high I couldn't hear anything else. I drove in reverse all the way back to the highway and then wheeled out onto it backward and barely missed getting clobbered by an oil carrier that swerved past with a long angry blare of its horn.

I ground the gears with every shift and sped about a mile down the highway and then pulled over onto the shoulder and stopped.

The sun was low and deeply orange and the dust we'd raised was red. I was pouring sweat. My tongue kept sticking to the roof of my mouth.

Belle was hunkered against the door, holding to her wound, her eyes huge on me. Russell groaned. I hadn't known if he was dead or alive. I put the gearshift in neutral and squirmed around up on my knees to see how he was doing.

He was slumped down low and looking at me and holding the .38 at his hip, cocked and pointed at my face. The right side of his shirt was sopped with blood.

"You left him," he said. His voice was wet.

"He was dead," I said.

"As dead as last time? He's your *partner,* Sonny, you bastard! He's your *blood*!"

"Point that somewhere else, man."

Belle sat up and said, "He *is* dead, I *saw* him. His head was all—"

"Nobody's asking you, you—"

In the instant he shifted his eyes to her I grabbed his gun and pushed it away, the hammer snapping on an empty chamber, and arched up and drilled him with a straight right that took his eyes out of focus. Then gave him another shot, right under the ear, and this one put his lights out.

Another oil truck coming. I opened a road map and spread it over his chest to hide the blood and pulled his hatbrim over his eyes, then slid down behind the wheel and put his pistol under the seat. The truck went clattering by.

I got out the flask and took a pull, then offered it to Belle, but she shook her head. "How bad are you?" I said.

"Not too, I don't think. It hurts." She cut a look toward the rumble seat. "*Jesus,* Sonny. Is he gone *crazy*?"

"Let's see," I said, leaning for a better look at her wound.

She took her hand away. The bullet had cut through the flesh of her inner arm just above the elbow. She was lucky it hadn't hit bone.

"Just hold tight to it," I said, and then knelt up on the seat again to tend to Russell. I ripped his shirt open to examine the wound and was relieved to see the blood was oozing, not pumping. I got his coat off the rumble seat floor and formed it into a thick pad, packed it against the wound and tied it firmly in place with his shirttails. His jaw was swelling up bad. I'd probably busted it.

No traffic in sight in either direction.

I rinsed her wound with booze and bandaged it with my handkerchief. She flinched and sucked hard breaths between her teeth but didn't cry out.

"That'll have to do for now," I said.

"He was gonna *shoot* you, Sonny!"

I blew out a long breath.

"He was," she said.

"That's his *brother* dead back there, for Christ's sake!"

"I know that," she said softly. "It's no reason."

I stared out at the empty road ahead. I thought of saying, Of course it is—except I wasn't sure what that meant. How could I explain to her what I couldn't explain to myself? It couldn't be explained. You knew it or you didn't.

I forced myself to think clearly. Odessa was at least seventy-five miles away. And we'd have to go through Midland to get there—which would slow us down even more. But Bubber said Gustafson had an office in Blackpatch. A nurse there even when Gustafson wasn't around. And there was that shortcut he'd mentioned—running from an old water tower on the Rankin highway. Fifteen rough miles, he'd said, but it was a hell of a lot closer than Odessa.

I put the roadster in gear and got us going, heading for the Rankin road.

"He gonna live?" Belle said.

"If I get him to a doctor fast enough, maybe."

"Think he's gonna feel any different if he does?"

I didn't know how to even try to answer that. And I wasn't aware of my tears until she reached over and wiped at them.

The sun was almost out of sight behind the distant mountains when I finally spotted the water tower and then found the junction of the old wagon trace on the other side of the rail tracks. The route was as rough as Bubber had said. We'd gone about seven miles and were into the last of the twilight when the right rear tire blew.

By the time I finished putting on the spare, the sky had clouded over and swallowed the crescent moon and stars and we were in full darkness. Russell's coat bandage had darkened with blood. I couldn't make out his face but I could hear his ragged breathing. I would've preferred to have him in the cab but the handling necessary to move him would only have worsened his bleeding. Belle got in the rumble seat with him and held him close to cushion him against the jarring of the car and keep the bandage pressed tight against the wound.

"You never been shot, have you?" she said.

"Not yet," I said. Sometimes I had no idea at all of what was going on in her head.

We pushed on. The wind picked up and a low rumble of thunder came out of the east. A few miles farther on the left rear tire blew. There was nothing to do but keep riding on it, the roadster at a sag. I could've jogged almost as fast as we were moving now, but we had to take it easy or risk losing a wheel or breaking an axle.

Russell now and then muttered unintelligibly but never really came awake. It wasn't the sock on the jaw holding him down now, it was pain and loss of blood. When we finally spied the lights of Blackpatch up ahead we'd blown the left front tire too and the car was listing like a foundering boat. The storm was closing in behind us, the rolling thunder growing louder—and the only thing we knew for sure about Russell's condition was that he was still alive.

The nearest spot to the Wildcat Dance Club I could find to park the car was in an alley a block away. The first rush of raindrops spattered on the ragtop. Lightning was showing in the east, thunderclaps following a few seconds behind every flash. I put my coat on and slid the .380 under my belt. Belle was still holding Russell's bandage in place but the wound had been seeping steadily and the coat was sopped with blood. I told her I'd be right back and went down the alley and across the street and up to the back door of the Wildcat.

I was hoping the door wasn't locked and it wasn't, but when I stepped inside I nearly bumped into a big galoot sitting on a stool and leafing through a movie magazine in the weak hallway light. He stood up like he meant to throw me out and I put my hand to the .380—and then we recognized each other from the time I'd been to the club before. He was one of Mona's bouncers, a Swede named Max. I said I had to see Mona right away and he said she'd gone into her office with Bubber and they probably didn't want to be disturbed. I said I'd take the chance and he shrugged and said, "Your funeral."

Mona's office was near the end of the hallway, which formed a

corner junction with a shorter hall to the left that contained the stairway and, a few feet further on, opened onto the main parlor. Muted
music and laughter came from around the corner, the faint smell of
cigarette smoke and booze and perfume. I tried the door but it was
locked, so I banged on it with the heel of my fist. I looked back at Max
and saw him shake his head—and heard Bubber say from behind the
door, "This place better be on fire!"

The lock clacked and the door swung open. "What the *hell* you
think—" Bubber said, his face hard as a fist, and then he recognized
me and his aspect eased. He was in his undershirt and holding up his
unbelted and unbuttoned pants. "Sonny! What the hell . . . ?" Behind
him Mona Holiday was sitting on the edge of a bed, looking at me and
hugging her removed blouse to her breasts.

He ushered me into the room and did up his pants while I gave
him a fast rundown of the break attempt. Mona stood up and turned
her back and put her blouse on. Rain was clattering against the panes
of the curtained window. When I told them Buck was dead, Bubber's
face creased up and he muttered, "Ah, shit," and slumped against the
dresser and rubbed his face like he was suddenly exhausted. Mona
came over and put an arm around him. But they got a move on when
I told about Belle and Russell. Mona ran off to alert Doc Gustafson,
and Bubber put his shirt on and followed me down the hall.

He said we were lucky the doc was still in town. "He come to give
the girls their checkups," he said, "but there's a rumor been going
around the Rangers are about to make a raid. Gus figured maybe he
oughta get back to Odessa ruther than risk any of that. Then we seen
this storm brewing and, hell, ain't gonna be no raid on a night like this.
He's up there with a girl."

He told Max to come with us and we went out into a hard rain
blowing sideways. Max was the only one wearing a hat and he lost it to
the wind as we ran across the street. A bright branch of lightning was
followed two seconds later by a prolonged crackle of thunder.

In the rumble seat of the tilted roadster Russell and Belle looked like castaways. Russell was still unconscious. I helped Belle down from the rumble seat and then swung up into it and lugged Russell upright and eased him down to Bubber and Max. They carried him to the Wildcat through the blowing rain with Belle and me right behind them. We followed them through the back door and down the hall, but as they took Russell around to the stairway I steered her into Mona's office. I inspected the handkerchief bandage on her arm and saw that it was holding all right, then told her to stay put and hurried out to the stairs.

The second-floor landing was at the end of a long hall lined with rooms to either side. Bubber and Max were coming out of a room at the far end, followed by Mona and another woman. The woman carried a small black bag and shut the door behind her. Some of the girls were peeking out of their rooms and Mona ordered them to mind their own business and get back to work. There was some muttered cursing and laughter but as Mona came down the hall they all ducked back inside with a staccato of door slams.

Bubber said Gustafson was doing all he could for Russell and didn't want anybody in there and getting in his way. He introduced the woman with the bag as Nurse Rose. She was longfaced and bony and sharp-eyed, and she came downstairs with us to tend to Belle.

*He drives into Blackpatch on the junction road, the Model T lurching
with every gust of wind, the tires sucking through mud, the windshield
wiper sweeping vainly against the hard crosswind rain. In the shimmering casts
of lightning the surrounding derricks look like a spectral forest. He passes
through a dense collection of tent residences, some of them broken free of portions
of their moorings and flapping wildly in the wind, their drenched inhabitants
flailing and tumbling about in their efforts to catch the loose flaps, to prevent still
more of their possessions from sailing away into the night.*

    *Now the junction road becomes the town's main street and the bright lights
are a wavering glare on the watery windshield. He has to strain to read the signs
on the slowly passing establishments—the Miscue Pool Emporium, the
Monkeyboard Game Palace, the Pipeline Café, the Yellow Rose Ballroom . . .
one after another.*

    *Despite the wind and the closed car windows, the stink and tumult of the
town carry into the Model T. He breathes the pestilential exhalations, hears
muted shrieks and bellows from within each place he passes, raucous laughter, a*

squalling welter of music. He has looked upon many oil towns and despises them all as dens of rank iniquity. He abhors the worthless sorts who inhabit them—drifters and grifters, whores and gamblers and cons, thieves of every persuasion. It seems fitting to him that the brute he hunts after should find his way here, down to this foul pit.

And then—in the next smeary swipe of the wiper, as another crack of thunder tremors the car and a snake-tongue of lightning illuminates the entire street in an eerie violet light almost bright as day—he sees the sign he seeks. The Wildcat Dance Club. . . .

*S*he was skilled at her calling, Nurse Rose. In fifteen minutes she had Belle's wound cleaned out and bandaged, and she gave her some pills to take against the pain. The flashes of lightning had increased in frequency, the window curtain brightening with every flare, the sash rattling with every thunderclap. Max had gone back to his post in the hallway. Mona poured drinks for us all, but Nurse Rose politely declined. She closed up her bag and headed for the door, saying she should get back upstairs to assist the doctor.

Bubber said it would likely be a while before Gustafson could tell us anything about Russell's condition, and what I ought to do in the meantime was get our bags out of the roadster before somebody else did.

"In case you ain't never heard," he said with a tired smile, "the world's full of damn thieves. A man can't be too careful."

We did need dry clothes, and I wanted to retrieve Russell's revolver from under the car seat. And I had three hundred dollars in

my valise. Back at the house, Russell had put the rest of the money in
an envelope and taped it behind the water tank over the toilet. Belle
asked if it wouldn't be safer in a bank and Russell said, "You kidding?
With so many damn bank robbers on the loose?" It was an argument
Buck had always used against putting money in a bank.

Bubber took a key ring from his pocket and detached two keys
and handed them to me. "The skinny one's an extry to my Chrysler,"
he said. "It's down the street a couple of blocks, over by ragtown, front
of a pool joint. I let a buddy borrow it to carry some of Mona's hooch
over there. You can use it to fetch your goods to the Hightower without getting them all wet. The other key's to the room. You all can sleep
there tonight."

He kept a permanent room at the Hightower Hotel, with a private parking spot in back. He and Mona usually stayed there when he
was in town because it was farther removed from the oil field and not
as noisy as the Wellhead, where she lived.

Mona thought we should wait till the storm passed. "You'll be
soaked to the skin before you take two steps out there."

Belle laughed and said she didn't think she could get any wetter
than she already was. And I thought Bubber was right—no telling
how long the storm would keep up, and the sooner we got our bags
out of the stolen roadster the better.

"I'll ring you at the hotel soon as we know about Russell," he said.

Belle gave me a look. I hadn't told Bubber about Russell calling
me a bastard and holding a gun on me. About punching him out.
About having no idea what his inclination toward me would be if he
pulled through.

The car was parked in front of the Miscue Pool Emporium, right
where the junction road came into town. We were sodden by the time
we reached it and got in out of the slinging sheets of rain.

"Whooo!" Belle said, laughing, swiping water off her face with her hand.

An explosion of thunder made us both flinch—and we busted out laughing. She leaned into me and put her hand to my face and kissed me.

Then came the brightest flashes yet, three or four in rapid sequence and accompanied by a barrage of thunderclaps that shook the Chrysler. I looked out the rear window just as a jagged lightning fork hit the holding tank on the hilltop.

For an arrested moment the entire tank was encased in an incandescent blue light and shedding sparks like a welding torch—and then its roof burst into fire.

Belle turned to look, and her mouth came open.

A tower of orange flames rose from the tank roof and swirled in the gusting wind, casting the street in a quavering light. The handful of people out in the storm began hollering and running to the nearest doors to give warning.

The lightning strike had also undone some of the tank's welds—streams of burning oil were running down the tank sides. Running into the gullies. Riding the flow of rainwater down the hill and toward the town.

Belle grabbed my arm. "My *God,* Sonny . . . let's *go!*"

Her expression was as resolute as fearful. I followed her gaze out to the road in front of us. It ran past the ragtown and lay clear of traffic, thanks to the storm. Straight ahead and we'd be free as birds. Just a quick swing through Fort Stockton to get the money from the house.

In that moment, looking out at the road, I envisioned us at our ease at an iron lacework table in a courtyard of stone fountains and deep green shade, sipping bourbon sprigged with mint, myself suited like a dandy, she in a sleek black dress cut low, wearing pearls, her hair grown long and woven in a braid, our conversation soft and teasing as we discussed how best to take our pleasure in the evening ahead, the days to come, the years.

Men were scrambling out of bloated wind-whipped tents, clutching their hats to their heads, gaping in the glowing orange rain at the flaming tank behind us. I cranked up the engine and put the car in gear, everything in me saying *Go.*

The clamor of alarm was swelling as people swarmed into the street. The rearview mirror shone with firelight. I looked back at the burning oil snaking down the gullies to the foot of the hill and spreading into a widening tide of fire coming steadily on. Cars slewing into the street. People running. Abandoning everything but what they carried with them.

I put the gearshift into neutral and got out of the car.

She slid across the seat and grabbed my coatsleeve as I shut the door. "Sonny, no!"

"Meet you at the house tomorrow," I said. "Go on."

"Sonny, *please*—you'll burn up!" Her grip twisted in my sleeve.

"Go on, I said!"

"He's probably dead. He'll kill you if he's not. He's *crazy.*"

I pulled free of her and backed away from the car. I half expected her to refuse to go, was already telling myself I didn't have time to argue about it. Her face at the window was golden.

Men came racing past us, yelling, cursing, wearing lunatic looks of panic, of jubilation. The first of the getaway cars swung around the Chrysler with engines racing and klaxons blaring. Another minute and the junction road would be jammed.

Maybe she was crying, maybe it was only the rain. I couldn't hear what she said for the surrounding pandemonium, but her lips were easy to read.

I love you too, Sonny.

And she drove off in the firelit rain.

$\mathcal{I}$ ran down the muddy street, dodging vehicles, shouldering through the throng rushing in the other direction. Men clambering into the beds of passing trucks, hopping onto running boards and bumpers, the stronger shoving aside the weaker. The advancing flow of fire had arrived at the far end of the street and several buildings were already in flame. And still the rain fell and lightning blazed and thunder kept crashing.

There was a tangle of cars in front of the Wildcat, some with a star on their doors. A transport truck with a star too. Men in big hats and gunbelts. Rangers. The rumored raid come true. The lawmen hustling now to rescue those they'd come to arrest. A crush of people at the Wildcat's front door.

I ran down the alley to the rear of the building and went in by the back way, thinking to get Max's help in getting Russell downstairs.

He wasn't at his post. The hallway was dark and hot, smelling of smoke. From the parlor side of the wall came frightened female cries and rough male voices shouting things I couldn't make out.

The door to Mona's office was open and I rushed to it, hoping Bubber was still there.

He was. On his back in the middle of the room. On a carpet of blood from his ripped throat. Max beside him, an ear to the floor, a small stained hole in the back of his jacket over the spot where his heart would be.

The room seemed suddenly to lack air.

Mona sat in a corner, knees up to her breasts, hand to her mouth, terrified eyes on Bubber. Then another shuddering crash of thunder and she put her face in her hands and wailed.

Whatever happened here, Russell was upstairs.

I bolted from the room and around to the stairway just as Nurse Rose came swooping down to the landing, face wrenched in terror—and she ran headlong into a beefy Ranger coming from the parlor.

"Whoa, Nellie!" he said, catching her by the shoulders, but she twisted from his grasp and fled around the corner.

As he turned toward me I drew the .380 and swung it backhand and caught him with the barrel just over the ear. His head slung sideways and his big hat tumbled from his redhaired head and he did a couple of shaky sidesteps and his knees buckled and he went down in a heap.

I took the steps two at a time to the landing and ran down the hall to the last door on the right. The heat much greater now, the smell of smoke stronger.

I yanked open the door and it banged against the wall—and all in an instant saw a man whirl around from looming over Russell, saw the cords standing on Russell's neck and his mouth open wide in rasping screams almost inaudible in the din from outside, saw that the man's hand at Russell's bloody crotch was no hand at all but a bright metal contraption. Saw John Bones grinning fiercely . . . and the yellow spark of his pistol.

I caromed off the doorjamb and staggered breathless along the wall and heard another gunshot and the room tilted and the floor hit me in the face.

Pain boiling in my gut, wrenching at my knee. The .380 four feet away. Gustafson prone and glass-eyed at the foot of the bed.

Hard gruntings. John Bones arching backward, his neck clenched in Russell's forearm, his gunhand in Russell's grip, the pincers somehow wedged behind him.

Crawling to the .380, feeling my belly smearing. The air hazed pink, the floor steaming.

John Bones' revolver thunks the floor at his booted feet.

Russell screaming—the pincers seized on his forearm, broken bones jutting.

John Bones wresting himself around, clamping the pincers to Russell's throat. Blood jumps and Russell spasms and falls still.

The .380 in my hand. Cocking.

John Bones crouching, hand closing on his gun.

The .380 kicks and he flings back against the wall and sits hard, legs splaying, gun arm dropping limp under a bloody shoulder, pistol unhanded. His eyes bright on me, pincers on his lap, opening and closing.

Boots stomping hard to the door.

My pistol on John Bones' great white grin.

Somebody shrieking, "Drop it or die!"

I shoot.

*S*he finds the back door jimmied, every drawer emptied on the floor, every closet rummaged, every mattress upended. The place ransacked by someone practiced. The envelope gone from behind the toilet tank. The best hiding place for it, they'd said, but what some thieves know, so do others. She takes lunch in a local diner where all the talk is of Blackpatch. The fire reported to be still burning on this following noon. Sixty-three dead and counting. Not a building left standing. Gonna have to call it *Blacker*patch, some wiseguy snickers, and gets more hard looks than laughs. She waits three days before admitting to herself what she has known from the moment he got out of the car. Then fuels the Chrysler and heads east, in the direction of New Orleans. She has a total of two dollars and forty cents, which meager stake might have been worrisome but for her discovery of a fully loaded .44 under the car seat. It is all she will need, she knows, to make her way in this world.

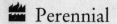 Perennial

Books by James C. Blake:

In the Rogue Blood
ISBN 0-380-79241-9 (paperback)

The offspring of a whore mother and a homicidal father, Edward and John Little are driven from their home in the Florida swamplands by a shameful, horrific act that will haunt their dreams for the rest of their days. Then, in the lawless "Dixie City" of New Orleans, the brothers are separated and dispatched by destiny to opposing sides of a fierce and desperate territorial struggle between Mexico and the United States.

"Powerful . . . impressive . . . [an] epic of the 1840s frontier." —*Dallas Morning News*

Red Grass River: *A Legend*
ISBN 0-380-79242-7 (paperback)

The legend of two men: one a criminal, a fold hero, a man of intense passions and his family's brightest star; the other a lawman born of lawmen, a husband and father, a symbol of a community thriving. As youths, they were close companions. As men, they were most bitter adversaries.

"A striking noir historical western and an inventive addition to Blake's work."
—*Publishers Weekly*

Wildwood Boys: *A Novel*
ISBN 0-380-80593-6 (paperback)

From the raw clay of historical fact, Blake has sculpted a powerful novel revealing the heroic and unsettling saga of "Bloody Bill" Anderson, a fearsome guerrilla captain of a band of Kansas "redlegs."

"Blake's prose is a coarse, gritty, and seamless poetry that fistfights and breaks the law and takes no prisoners." —*Milwaukee Journal Sentinel*

A World of Thieves
ISBN 0-06-051247-4 (paperback)

Set in 1928 New Orleans, 18-year-old Sonny LaSalle is a top prep student and champion amateur boxer. But with the sudden death of his parents, he is drawn into his uncle's profession of crime and treachery. Hurtling toward a thunderous climax, this is the story of a young man's reckoning with the truth of his own soul.

"Classic Blake, mixing violence with passion, the hardnose with the sensitive. . . . No one out there does this better." —*Denver Post*

New in Hardcover, February, 2003: *Under The Skin*
ISBN 0-380-97751-6

Available wherever books are sold, or call 1-800-331-3761 to order.